PENGUIN BOOKS

PETROPOLIS

Anya Ulinich was seventeen when her family left Moscow and emigrated to the United States. She attended the Art Institute of Chicago and received an MFA in painting from the University of California, Davis. Ulinich was awarded the National Book Foundation's "5 Under 35"—a recognition that her fiction writing is among the best of her generation. She lives in Brooklyn, New York.

Praise for *Petropolis* by Anya Ulinich

"Not many novels take us to ugly but exotic Siberian towns, or even to ugly, exotic Arizona sprawl, let alone to millionaires' Chicago fantasias. [Ulinich's] young heroine has sharp vision and a pragmatic view of life's difficulties. . . . Anya Ulinich will be back."
—*The Washington Post Book World*

"Ulinich has a knack for the tragicomic. . . . *Petropolis* is engaging, funny and genuinely moving in all the right places. It is a sparkling debut. . . . A unique comic novel."
—*Los Angeles Times*

"Audacious, clever and lively . . . Nervy social satire in the spirit of . . . Tom Wolfe, Aleksander Hemon, Gish Jen, Gary Shteyngart."
—*Chicago Tribune*

"When a coming-of-age novel is truly different, it [sends] shock waves through unsuspecting readers. This brave blend of satire, farce, and heart-wrenching realism delivers the necessary voltage to do just that. . . . Ulinich plays this absurdist immigrant's journey for all its black-comedic potential, but she never loses sight of Sasha's bedrock humanity. Her triumphs are attenuated at every turn by lingering levels of despair, but her ability to find a pulse of life in even the most outrageous turns of fortune lifts the novel as far beyond parody as it is beyond convention."
—Bill Ott, *Booklist* (starred review)

"Ulinich has a great eye and ear for the weird details of Soviet scarcity and American plenty."   —*The Boston Globe*

"Add Ulinich to the roster of talented contemporary writers of Russian background, such as Gary Shteyngart, David Bezmozgis and Lara Vapynar. Skilled at satire but not limited by it, they deftly perform that delicate maneuver by which humor can break your heart."   —*The Hartfort Courant*

"First-time novelist Ulinich, who emigrated to the United States at seventeen . . . received an MFA in painting, and boy, does it show. Her USSR and USA are awash in colors and images prismed through an alien sensibility, then focused by literary art. . . . That Ulinich, a native Russian speaker, wrote the novel in such assured, glasslike English, however, makes it somewhat annoying: Where does she get off, anyway? You'd think she was a member of the intelligentsia or something."
                                               —*The San Diego Union-Tribune*

"Becoming a citizen of the world is no simple matter in this impressive first novel, which examines the immigrant experience in a fresh and winsome way. . . . *Petropolis* is rich with black humor, acerbic wit and a charm entirely free from preciousness."   —*The Moscow Times*

"Like much of Russian literature, *Petropolis* is stuffed with a cast of colorful characters who swirl around Sasha as she works her way painfully toward both self-knowledge and a better life. This novel, as do most good ones, leaves readers feeling they've accompanied the protagonist on a rewarding journey, while still wondering what lies ahead for her."
                                                            —*BookPage*

"*Petropolis* bursts with artful details of an immigrant's peripatetic youth and quest for home—the grappling for the strong woman inside a lost girl."
                                                                 —*Ms.*

"How did she do it? Anya Ulinich has written—and in a second language, no less—a smashing debut, at once a deeply moving coming-of-age odyssey and a globe-spanning satire of societies gone desperately and hilariously awry. I loved *Petropolis* for its bone-dry humor, eye-popping authenticity, and vividly realized characters. Most of all, I loved Sasha Goldberg. Through its darkest and most comic moments, this book made me very, very happy."   —Katherine Shonk, author of *The Red Passport*

"*Petropolis* is a real feast of sharp wit, quirky characters and amazing situations."   —Lara Vapnyar, author of *Memoirs of a Muse* and *There Are Jews in My House*

"Anya Ulinich's *Petropolis* did all of the things you hope a novel will do: It moved me, it made me laugh, it kept me constantly entertained. *Petropolis* was a constant joy to read—and almost unbearable to put down. Ulinich has a classically sardonic, Eastern European tone. Comparisons do it no justice. Read it for yourself—you will not be disappointed."
                      —Pauls Toutonghi, author of *Red Weather*

"A beautiful, far-ranging voice equally at home on both sides of the Atlantic. . . . Anya Ulinich's satiric romp gives new meaning to the word 'bittersweet.'"   —Gary Shteyngart, author of *The Russian Debutante's Handbook* and *Absurdistan*

"An irresistible comedy with an authentic Russian voice."
                —Martin Cruz Smith, author of *Gorky Park* and *Stalin's Ghost*

PETROPOLIS

ANYA ULINICH

Penguin Books

PENGUIN BOOKS

Published by the Penguin Group

Penguin Group (USA) Inc., 375 Hudson Street, New York, New York 10014, U.S.A.

Penguin Group (Canada), 90 Eglinton Avenue East, Suite 700, Toronto,
Ontario, Canada M4P 2Y3 (a division of Pearson Penguin Canada Inc.)

Penguin Books Ltd, 80 Strand, London WC2R 0RL, England

Penguin Ireland, 25 St Stephen's Green, Dublin 2, Ireland (a division of Penguin Books Ltd)

Penguin Group (Australia), 250 Camberwell Road, Camberwell,
Victoria 3124, Australia (a division of Pearson Australia Group Pty Ltd)

Penguin Books India Pvt Ltd, 11 Community Centre, Panchsheel Park, New Delhi – 110 017, India

Penguin Group (NZ), 67 Apollo Drive, Rosedale, North Shore 0632,
New Zealand (a division of Pearson New Zealand Ltd)

Penguin Books (South Africa) (Pty) Ltd, 24 Sturdee Avenue,
Rosebank, Johannesburg 2196, South Africa

Penguin Books Ltd, Registered Offices:
80 Strand, London WC2R 0RL, England

First published in the United States of America by Viking Penguin,
a member of Penguin Group (USA) Inc. 2007
Published in Penguin Books 2008

10 9 8 7 6 5 4 3 2 1

PUBLISHER'S NOTE
This is a work of fiction. Names, characters, places, and incidents are either the product
of the author's imagination or are used fictitiously, and any resemblance to actual persons,
living or dead, business establishments, events, or locales is entirely coincidental.

ISBN 978-0-670-03819-0 (hc.)
ISBN 978-0-14-311301-0 (pbk.)
CIP data available

Printed in the United States of America
Set in Vendetta with Equipoize
Designed by Daniel Lagin

To Sofia and Rebecca

Part One

свалка

ТАБАК

№3

лс

Третий до конечной. За киоском - направо.
Через дырку в заборе и сразу налево.
Держись слева от свалки. №1 увидишь с
дороги. Мы в №2.

1

An Unspoiled Quality

A CORRUGATED FENCE RAN THE ENTIRE LENGTH OF A STREET with no name, until it crossed another street with no name. At the end of the fence, there were six evenly spaced brick apartment buildings and a grocery. Just under the buildings' cornices, meter-high red letters spelled: GLORY TO THE, SOVIET ARMY, BRUSH TEETH, AFTER EATIN, WELCOME TO, AS-BESTOS 2, and MODEL TOWN! Whoever painted the slogans had been less concerned with their meaning than with the finite number of bricks in each facade.

In the fall of 1992, Lubov Alexandrovna Goldberg decided to find an extra-curricular activity for her fourteen-year-old daughter.

"Children of the intelligentsia don't just come home in the afternoon and engage in idiocy," declared Mrs. Goldberg.

She would've loved it if Sasha played the piano, but the Goldbergs didn't have a piano, and there wasn't even space for a hypothetical piano in the two crowded rooms where Sasha and her mother lived.

Mrs. Goldberg's second choice was the violin. She liked to imagine a three-quarter view of Sasha in black and white, minus the frizzy bangs. *This is Sasha practicing her violin. As you can see, there is a place for the arts in the increasing austerity of our lives*, she wrote in her imaginary letter to Mr. Goldberg, whose address she didn't know. But after the money was spent and the violin purchased, three consecutive violin instructors declared Sasha profoundly tone deaf and musically uneducable.

"A bear stepped on her ear," Mrs. Goldberg complained to the neighbors, and Sasha thought about the weight of the bear and whether in stepping on her ear the animal would also destroy her head, cracking it like a walnut.

"Sit up, Sasha," said Mrs. Goldberg, "and chew with your mouth closed."

Then came auditions for ballet and figure-skating classes, which even Mrs. Goldberg knew were a long shot for Sasha. On the way home from the last skating audition, where the instructor delicately described her daughter as overweight and uncoordinated, Lubov Alexandrovna walked two steps ahead of Sasha in a tense and loaded silence. Trudging through the snow behind her mother, Sasha contemplated the street lamps. She tried to determine the direction of the wind by the trajectories of snowflakes in the circles of light, but the snow seemed to be flying every which way. Sasha was staring straight up when her foot hit the curb and she landed flat on her face in a snowbank. This was more than Mrs. Goldberg could take.

"I told you to stop taking such wide steps. You want to see what you look like walking? Here!" Mrs. Goldberg swung her arms wildly and took a giant step. "See? This is why you fall all the time! You trip over your own feet!"

Sasha got up and dusted herself off. Her right coat sleeve was packed with snow all the way up to her elbow, and the anticipation of it melting made her shiver.

"I have some advice for you!" shrieked Mrs. Goldberg. "Watch your step! You should see yourself in the mirror, the way you move!"

Sasha woke up and stared at the water stain on the ceiling. For a while, her eyes were empty. She allowed the horror of life to seep into them gradually, replacing the traces of forgotten dreams. It was the first day of winter recess. *The Fruit Day.*

Mrs. Goldberg had a new diet for Sasha: each week, six days of regular food, one day of fruit only. Fruit meant a shriveled Moroccan orange from the bottom of the fridge and a mother's promise of more, since oranges were the only fruit found, if one was lucky, in midwinter Siberia. Mrs. Goldberg was already at work or orange-hunting somewhere, her bed neat as a furniture display.

Sasha got up and went to the kitchen. Feeling faintly revolutionary, she boiled water in a calcified communal teapot and pulled a chair up to the cupboard. In the corner of the top shelf was her mother's can of Indian instant coffee. Sasha put four spoons of coffee granules and four spoons of sugar in her cup and added water. The next stop was the fridge. Her mother had hidden all the food that belonged to the Goldbergs, but the other tenants still had theirs.

Sasha found half a bologna butt wrapped in brown paper, an egg, a brick of black bread, and half a can of sweetened condensed milk. She ate a bologna omelet and washed it down with burning coffee. For dessert she had the bread with condensed milk. Some of the milk seeped through the pores in the bread and made a mess. "Fruit!" cursed Sasha, licking the drips off her fingers. When her hands were clean, she made another cup of coffee and returned to the fridge.

Sasha Goldberg was determined to enjoy her vacation. Winter recess would be over in six days, and her fellow inmates would be waiting for her by the gates of the Asbestos 2 Secondary School Number 13, ready to knock her bag out of her hands and send her flying backward down the iced-over staircase. *Hello, Ugly! Wanna die now or later?* She would pluck her books and her indoor shoes out of the deep snow like birthday candles out of frosting and hurry to class.

Sasha excavated the Stepanovs' enamel pot from the back of the fridge and lifted the lid. Inside, bits of boiled chicken floated in the greenish broth. Drinking the broth straight out of the pot, Sasha briefly imagined telling her mother what went on at Number 13. Of course, she would never do that. That her daughter was an oaf sticking an icicle into her bleeding nostril before going to algebra didn't belong in Lubov Goldberg's reality. Mrs. Goldberg would try, by sheer force of will, to dehumiliate Sasha on the spot. There would be questions—"Why are they doing it to you?"—and suggestions—"Perhaps you need to be friendlier. I notice you don't have any girlfriends." A multitude of diets could emerge from the stack of old *Burda* magazines; the spiked rubber mat for flatfoot exercises might return from the utility closet. Sasha knew that every measure would fail, and in the end, she would glimpse the true magnitude of her mother's contempt.

She poured another cup of coffee. Now she had no dessert, except for an old honey jar filled with cough drops. For as long as Sasha could remember, those cough drops had been in the fridge. She tried the lid, but it had crystallized onto the jar. Shaking from too much coffee, Sasha slammed the jar against the sink, washed the shards of glass down the drain, and sucked the mass of congealed menthol until it turned into a translucent green disc.

After her third cup of coffee, Sasha ran out of sugar. It was almost lunchtime. The neighbors who worked at the asbestos mill were about to come home to eat. Sasha dumped the dishes in the sink, took her orange out of the fridge, discarded a diamond-shaped Morocco sticker, and returned to bed. In bed, she disassembled the orange, tossed the peel behind the headboard, and, sucking on the sour sections, read Jules Verne until dark.

At six o'clock she heard her mother's footsteps in the corridor and, seconds later, a shouting match in the kitchen. It wasn't really a match, because the neighbors were the only ones shouting. Mrs. Goldberg never raised her voice; she wouldn't stoop to it. Sasha knew that her mother just stood there, pale and stoic, like St. Sebastian tied to a tree.

"Don't you ever feed that child?" yelled Mrs. Stepanova.

Mrs. Goldberg shut the door in Mrs. Stepanova's face and crossed her arms. "Explain, Alexandra."

This was a purely symbolic offer. Sasha shrugged.

"Take off your pants," said Mrs. Goldberg.

Sasha got out of bed, hiked up her flannel nightgown, and pulled off her bloomers.

After beating Sasha with a dainty patent leather belt, Mrs. Goldberg dragged a chair over to Baba Zhenia's Romanian plywood armoire and took down a roll of Sasha's drawings and watercolors. Sasha looked away, preparing for the shredding. It was important to show that she didn't care. Oblivious to the suspense she had created, Mrs. Goldberg set the drawings on the desk and flipped through them slowly, sucking her lower lip with the tiniest whistle.

"I've set up an interview at the District 7 Art Studio tomorrow," she said in a faintly conciliatory voice. "If you're admitted, you'll be going three days a week, after school."

"District 7 is all the way up the devil's horns," replied Sasha, trying hard to hide her relief. "Are you sure the place is fit for the intelligentsia?"

"Don't sneer, *detka*," sighed Mrs. Goldberg. "You don't need another tic."

They got off the streetcar and walked along the fence, pulling a granny cart with rolled-up drawings over icy acne on the sidewalk; Mrs. Goldberg, slim and graceful, in camel spike heels she wore for the occasion, and Sasha, a brown lump in her babyish synthetic fur coat. A not quite-right, counterfeit Mickey Mouse smiled his toothy, savage smile from the coat's back.

Soon they saw a row of apartment buildings, and Mrs. Goldberg stopped to pull a scrap of paper with directions out of her glove. Sasha was careful to keep her face frozen in a mask of aloof defiance, but inside she was more apprehensive. According to the directions, the District 7 Evening Art Studio for Children was located in the basement of the AFTER EATIN building, and Sasha considered that to be a good omen.

That morning, Mrs. Goldberg had offered Sasha some of her precious coffee in exchange for the promise that during the interview Sasha would not:

> *stare at the wall with her mouth open like a carp*
> *twirl her hair*
> *bite her nails*

and that she would:

> *keep her knees closed*
> *keep her tongue in her mouth*
> *smile*

"Please, bunny, I want you to try," Mrs. Goldberg had said sweetly, putting her manicured fingers on Sasha's hand.

They walked past GLORY TO THE, SOVIET ARMY, and BRUSH TEETH and turned left. Sasha pushed open the heavy steel door, stepped down, and felt moisture seeping through the zipper of her boot. Looking down, she saw that the front of the basement was flooded. A plank led to a second door.

With the outside door shut, Sasha and Mrs. Goldberg walked the plank in airless darkness, balancing the granny cart between them like a couple of suddenly dexterous sleepwalkers.

"What a nightmare," mouthed Mrs. Goldberg, sliding her fingers along the dripping wall for support. Sasha sneered.

Someone opened the second door, and Sasha smelled plaster dust. She pushed past a thick curtain, and when her eyes adjusted to the light, she realized that she'd just stepped into her own dream. In the messy entryway, plaster busts were haphazardly scattered among easels and space heaters. In the next room, Sasha saw a claw-foot tub filled with wet clay, a stuffed fox, and a basket of wax fruit. It was as if everything old, ornate, and intricate, every shred of Western Civilization ever found in the vicinity of Asbestos 2 were stored in the basement of AFTER EATIN. Sasha would keep her knees closed, keep her tongue in her mouth, not bite her nails, and, if necessary, also lick boots, eat rocks, cry, and beg to be allowed to stay in this place.

A dour ponytailed man helped Mrs. Goldberg unroll Sasha's drawings on an antique tabletop. Sasha noticed a concrete torso in the corner. The torso must have belonged to Lenin, because it wore a suit and held a rolled-up cap in one of its fisted hands. Someone had stuck a bent aluminum fork into the other. Two ancient anatomy textbooks rested on top, where the head should have been.

The ponytailed man gave Sasha a pencil, a sheet of paper, and four rusted pushpins. She was to draw a still life, he explained, leading her down a narrow hallway into the classroom.

The five kids in the room looked up in anticipation as the man took an eraser out of his pants pocket and started making the rounds, erasing parts of their drawings. Halfway through the room, his eraser gummed up and Sasha watched him make greasy graphite smudges over drawings that seemed perfect to her.

"You can start now, Goldberg. See you in two hours." The man patted Sasha on the shoulder and disappeared, leaving behind a waft of tobacco smell.

Sasha pinned up her paper and stared at the still life. It consisted of an egg, a butter knife, and a white enameled bowl, three minutes' worth of work. Why did the man give her two hours? Maybe she misunderstood the assignment.

"Okay, let's see the damage," said one of the boys.

"Oh, fucking Bedbug with his petrified eraser. Who wants to take up a collection for a new eraser for Bedbug? Hey, what's your name?" A small long-haired boy was leaning over the top of Sasha's easel. "Donate money to get Bedbug a nice soft eraser?"

Sasha mutely pointed to the corner of her paper, where her name was written.

"I'm Katia Kotelnikova," said a tall girl with a braid. She unpinned her drawing and folded it in half. "Sasha, did you bring any extra paper? I have to start this over."

"No," said Sasha, staring at the girl's unusual costume. Katia wore felt boots with rubber galoshes and a vintage Soviet school uniform: a brown wool dress with a black apron. Sasha wondered if she was so poor that she had to wear it, or whether she was trying for a certain look.

"Why aren't you starting?" Katia asked. "You haven't got all day."

Sasha Goldberg looked around the room. The kids were still carrying on about the eraser, and she sensed that in this particular group even the beautiful ones didn't mean her any harm. It was a pleasant surprise, this feeling.

"I don't know what he expects from me. I've never done this before," she muttered, putting her pencil down.

"A comrade in trouble should never be afraid to ask for help," the long-haired boy said with a smirk. "In this basement, it's from each according to his abilities, to each according to his incompetence."

Sasha allowed herself a thin smile. These people were clearly harmless. Only the harmless and the old still made jokes about communism.

Apparently happy about the distraction, the kids nudged Sasha aside and took over her drawing. From a corner of the room, she watched them do her work. First, the boy with long hair constructed the geometric skeleton of the composition. He took into account the deep shadow of the bowl, shifting the whole setup to the right to make space for it. A fat girl with a bureaucrat's haircut drew the contours of the egg and the bowl, and then it was Katia's turn to work on the shading.

For a while the room was quiet. Katia perched upright on the edge of Sasha's stool, deftly filling the still life's contours with swatches of crosshatching. Biting her nails, Sasha watched with fascination as the egg in the drawing acquired illusory volume, growing out of the paper's surface like an exceptionally healthy mushroom.

"It seems that Evgeny Mikhailovich has been bitten by a white-on-white bug," explained Katia. "Last week we spent six hours on a plaster cube and a dish rag, and the week before it was this big, dry"—she laughed a short, sneezelike laugh—"bone. By the time I got here, all the good spots were taken, and I had to draw the damn bone end-on. There was no way it was going to look like anything."

"It looked like a giant belly button," the boy disagreed.

"Shut up!" Katia laughed, squinting at the drawing. Both the egg and the bowl now looked three-dimensional, firmly planted on the horizontal plane of the tabletop, with the dark table edge decisively in front. "Sasha, finish it. It needs your personal touch."

Back at her easel, Sasha lamely dragged her pencil along the contour of the bowl and the edge of the butter knife. Every line she made, no matter how light, looked entirely out of place and threatened to disturb the illusion, to flatten out the little pocket of space. Sasha was relieved to see that she was almost out of time. She chewed the cool aluminum tube at the end of her pencil and waited for Bedbug to return. Instead, an old man with a wooden leg hobbled into the classroom. The end of his nose twitched nervously and whatever was left of his hair flew around his head like a pair of poorly designed wings. There was a war hero medal on the lapel of his greasy suit.

"Goldberg?" the old man said. "Let's see."

Sasha felt every one of her muscles ball up into rocks and blood rush up to her face.

The old man stood behind her back for a small eternity. He smelled like acetone. Sasha could feel his every twitch reverberating in the rotten floorboards and her rickety stool.

"Aha," he said finally, and then, thunderously, "You are all expelled! Out! And never come back! You are all a bunch of ungrateful pigs . . ." He paused, surveying the room. "Cows!"

The old man seemed to be at a loss for words. He turned around sharply and left, the clicks and scrapes of his wooden leg receding down the hall.

Sasha was mortified. Without taking her eyes off the floor, she got up and followed the man out of the classroom.

"Moo," Katia said behind her back. "Welcome to the collective farm!"

The classroom exploded with laughter.

Idiots, thought Sasha Goldberg, blinking away tears.

She didn't see her mother right away, only her boots, propped up on top of a cracked glass coffee table next to a bottle of cognac and a plate of thin-sliced lemons. She followed the direction of the boots and found Mrs. Goldberg sprawled out on a dirty little sofa behind a drape.

Sasha never suspected that her mother was capable of being sprawled out. This was the same mother who, Sasha was convinced, was born wearing a starched shirt and a string of pearls. Sasha suspected that the world would have to turn ninety degrees to force Lubov Goldberg to put her feet up on a coffee table. She stood, grim and disbelieving, and watched Bedbug refill her mother's glass.

Mrs. Goldberg was laughing. Her cheeks glowed red, and her one gold canine caught the light, making her look like a vampire. Was this all it took, two glasses of cognac? Sasha waited for the one-legged man to tell her mother what had happened in the classroom, but he seemed to have forgotten all about it.

"Will you allow me the pleasure of painting your portrait someday?" he asked Mrs. Goldberg.

"We'll have to see about that, Evgeny Mikhailovich," she warbled, noticing Sasha.

Sasha struggled into her coat, and Bedbug helped Mrs. Goldberg into hers. The air outside was cold and clear. At four o'clock it was completely dark. The nearest streetlight was down by GLORY TO THE, and Sasha was able to see the moon and some stars. She stared hard, and when she looked ahead into the dark street, she saw an afterimage of black pinholes.

She looked sideways at her mother, waiting for the first hiss, but Mrs. Goldberg didn't say anything. In the absence of an assault, Sasha was left face-to-face with her own despair. Walking alongside Mrs. Goldberg, she felt self-pity so pure it bordered on ecstasy. If somebody said, "Sasha Goldberg, give up five years of your life to be admitted to the District 7 Evening Art Studio for Children," she would. She wished she hadn't cheated. If she had done her own work, her effort might have counted for something.

"Hope the streetcar will be here soon," Mrs. Goldberg said when they got to the tram stop. "I'm tired. Are you cold?"

Sasha was surprised by her peaceful tone. "Aren't you mad at me?" she asked flatly.

"What for?"

The tram came clanging around the corner, carrying a promise of warmth in its old-fashioned streamlined shape and incandescent yellow light. The light was deceptive; it was as cold inside the streetcar as outside. Mrs. Goldberg stuck the tickets into the hole puncher and sat down on a torn vinyl seat.

"You've been accepted. You start next week."

Sasha stared.

"Are you happy?"

"But I thought I . . ."

"They liked your drawings. Evgeny Mikhailovich said they had an unspoiled quality." Mrs. Goldberg laughed, a melodic, relaxed laugh.

Speechless, Sasha caught her mother's small golden head in a fake fur embrace.

Mrs. Goldberg liberated herself and adjusted her hair.

"Pay attention to the route, now. I won't be taking you every day." She put her leather glove on Sasha's sleeve and laughed again. "You know what else Evgeny Mikhailovich told me? He said that you look like me, only diluted with something stronger."

"Something stronger" was her father, and Sasha thought her mother must still be drunk because normally she never mentioned him, even obliquely. Sasha knew she didn't look anything like her mother, who was an archetypal Russian beauty. Thanks to "something stronger," Sasha Goldberg had yellow freckled skin, frizzy auburn hair, and eyes like chocolate eggs.

"You can't *dilute* with something stronger," she said.

"That's the smartest thing that's ever come out of your mouth, *detka*," agreed Mrs. Goldberg.

2

The Friendship of Peoples

THE YEAR SASHA STARTED FIRST GRADE AT ASBESTOS 2 SEC-ondary School Number 13, her teacher approached Victor Goldberg after the November parents' meeting. She needed to discuss the upcoming Winter Pageant. The first-grade girls, the teacher explained, would play Snowflake Fairies, but Sasha, along with Inna the amputee, would be involved elsewhere. Surely Victor could understand. Victor Goldberg smiled at the teacher's apologetic tone. Of course he understood. He'd never insist that Sasha be allowed to disturb the uniform backdrop of twirling tutus, flying blond braids, and flushed pink faces, against which Grandpa Frost and Snegurochka were to display their benevolence. Besides, a grade school pageant ranked so high on Victor's scale of silliness that he couldn't imagine why it would possibly matter to Sasha.

A week later, Victor had entirely forgotten about the parents' meeting. He was making sauerkraut when Sasha walked into the kitchen with a look on her face that he'd seen twice before: the first time when the yard cat died in childbirth and the second time when Baba Zhenia returned from her last hospital stay tied to a wooden chair, paralyzed after a stroke.

"Why can't I be a Snowflake Fairy?" she asked.

"Go look at yourself in the mirror!" Victor laughed, setting down the bucket of sauerkraut.

He didn't intend to be cruel. He was only teasing a little. Not sufficiently older than his daughter, Victor Goldberg lacked the distance that compelled adults to protect, lie, and gloss over. He was surprised to find Sasha by the mirror. She had undone her pigtails and was squishing the auburn sponge of her hair with a brush.

"Your problem, *lapochka*, stems from the Friendship of Peoples. The world's peoples got overly friendly with each other, and now Grandpa Frost doesn't want you as his little helper."

Sasha gave him a glum stare. Victor could tell that she was trying to classify his remark, to decide if it was an upsetting truth or just another of his *Voice of America jokes*, which was Sasha's name for his cryptic, halfhearted *antisovietchina*.

"Keep your tongue behind your teeth, Vitya!" Baba Zhenia yelled from her deathbed.

"Seriously," Sasha asked, "why *can't* I be a Snowflake Fairy?"

Victor Goldberg sat on the bed, pulled his daughter onto his lap, and addressed her in a slow and patient voice that he only employed when he thought he was speaking the obvious.

"Because," he said, "you don't look like a Snowflake Fairy. What color hair do Snowflake Fairies have?"

"Blond," sighed Sasha. She sounded as if she'd finally guessed where this was going. But Victor Goldberg was getting into it, wanting to flaunt his relative wisdom.

"They have to be white all over, Sasha," he said. "White dresses, white hair, blue eyes. They're *snowflakes*. They're from the north," he added.

"So am I," said Sasha. "This *is* the north."

"Well, no. . . ." Victor Goldberg was starting to flounder. Was he supposed to tell the truth? He cringed, imagining her questions once she knew that her *real* grandpa hailed from Africa, a cartoon continent. She would ask about giraffes and coconuts, grass skirts, and the possibility of a pet monkey. Suddenly Victor felt the correct answer coming to him, blossoming out of some paternal instinct he didn't know he possessed.

"I mean, yes, you were *born* here," he said. "But our family isn't from the north. We're all from the south. We're from Moscow."

It worked. Sasha seemed impressed.

"And you, too? You've been to Moscow?"

"Sure," said Victor Goldberg. "I was born there, and I went to school there, and—"

"Have you seen the Red Square?"

"A million times."

"And Lenin?"

"Sure."

"Is he dead? Is he scary?"

"No," said Victor Goldberg, "he's a mummy. He can't move, and even if he could, he can't get out. They keep him behind glass."

Victor Goldberg was relieved. His origins seemed to elevate him in his daughter's eyes. He was enjoying Sasha's admiring stare, the silent awe of her upturned face as she was reconsidering him, perhaps imagining him as a character in one of her picture books whose stories always took place in Moscow, never in Asbestos 2. The north of children's literature was all igloos, dog sleds, and seal-bone harpoons, printed in chilly Soviet blues and earth tones on pulpy paper. Victor Goldberg laughed, imagining an illustration: a communal apartment's kitchen; a black man in a holey undershirt, squishing a bucket of sauerkraut with a *Complete Biography of Gogol* wrapped in cellophane. The sauerkraut was fermenting nicely, little bubbles coming up to the surface. The book was just the right weight.

In the play, Sasha was a tree. She shared the back of the stage with scrappy boys who couldn't be trusted with speaking parts. In the auditorium below, Victor Goldberg felt Lubov shift impatiently in her seat. She always suffered humiliation more acutely than he did. Victor almost enjoyed the show. He liked watching Sasha sway back and forth, indistinguishable from the others under the layers of frayed green felt. Only when, following an invisible cue, the trees tossed back their costumes and Sasha emerged into the limelight, sweaty and rumpled, for a bow, did Victor realize something that had never occurred to him before.

Ever since the first time he'd laid eyes on his daughter, a tightly swaddled bundle with a face the color of wood stain, he knew Sasha would be punished the same way he'd been punished. In this town of towheaded drunks, she would bear the weight of her difference, doled out in murmurs, taunts, and shoves. But now it occurred to Victor that she would suffer more than he ever had because, unlike him, she had been loved, and her punishment would come as a surprise.

He remembered Sasha at two years old, playing on the kitchen floor. Baba Zhenia stirred borscht on the stove. "Who is the smartest little girl?" the old lady cooed while Victor trained his Smena camera on Sasha's face. He didn't own a flash, and taking pictures indoors involved much preparation: he had to bring in extra lights and cajole Sasha to sit still for the long exposure. Later, Victor developed the film in the darkness of the communal bathroom while the neighbors beat the door, *not about to go shit in the snow.*

Victor Goldberg easily admitted to himself that he often preferred the child's photos to the real Sasha, with her tears and troubles, fairy problems, and all the other painful discoveries of the obvious that were yet to come. Someday, Victor thought wearily, Sasha's comrades would catch on to the meaning of her last name and nickname her a *zhid.* This was a simple, predictable milestone, but the thought of Sasha approaching it exhausted Victor.

In the front of the auditorium, the music teacher folded her long body over the piano bench and struck a chord. The children, now lined up along the outer edge of the stage, began to sing:

> *A pine was born in the forest*
> *And in the forest she grew.*
> *In winter and summer*
> *She stood graceful and green.*

Victor Goldberg closed his eyes and let his head droop to his chest. His tie was choking him but he felt too tired to adjust it. An enormous fatigue flattened him in his chair, tied his forearms to the scratched wooden armrests.

"Vitya?"

With his wife's elbow between his ribs, Victor Goldberg had no choice but to look up. The Winter Pageant was over. Holding hands in pairs, the children descended the stairs on either side of the stage. Some parents got up and began to applaud, but the Goldbergs remained seated.

Afterward, they walked home in the gentle snowfall: Lubov and Victor on either side, Sasha in the middle. An inflexible lozenge of woolen layers, with a mohair scarf crossed on her chest, the child walked slowly, setting her feet gingerly in the snow.

"What's the matter, Sasha? Hurry up, Babushka will worry," said Lubov, yanking her by the sleeve.

Victor guessed that Sasha took special pleasure in her new shoes, which, with each step, stamped CHILDRENS FOOTWARE FACTORY SUNRISE into the white powder on the pavement. Perhaps she would be able to arm herself with her seven years of happy childhood. Maybe that was how it worked.

When they got home, Baba Zhenia was already asleep. Lubov went to check on her—the old woman usually stayed up to wait for them, no matter how late they came home. After her last stroke, the stories of their day had become her main amusement. Victor stayed in the corridor to help Sasha undress. He was untying Sasha's shoes when Lubov came back from her grandmother's room with her hands over her mouth. Baba Zhenia had stopped breathing in her sleep.

They didn't tell Sasha, who was half asleep anyway. Victor tucked her into her bed and followed Lubov into Baba Zhenia's room, wondering about the funeral. He'd been expecting Baba Zhenia to die ever since he first laid eyes on her eight years ago. Yet it took three strokes to finish her off. Victor both admired and despised Baba Zhenia, who seemed to understand him better than Lubov ever had, and who never stopped treating him as an imposter, an inconvenient houseguest.

"Luba, what should we do about the funeral?" he asked, trying not to look at the body. It was hard to believe that the child-sized lump under the blanket had only recently been a wide-bottomed, flat-footed bully.

Lubov sat down on the edge of Baba Zhenia's bed and waved Victor off. He noticed that she was crying and took a step back, hurriedly screwing his face into an expression of sympathy. Lubov rarely cried, and her distorted face made Victor panic.

"We are all alone now, Vitya," Lubov whispered. "Who will take care of us?"

Victor cracked his knuckles. He felt as if his wife were appealing to him in a foreign language, and no matter what he replied, he'd give the wrong answer.

"I will take care of everything," he mumbled.

Lubov wiped her tears and looked up at him.

"Get out, Vitya," she said firmly.

"What can I do?"

"Go to bed."

Happy to obey, Victor tiptoed out of Baba Zhenia's room and closed the door. In his room, he undressed quickly and, feeling the draft on his back, hurried to get under the blanket. He would insulate the windows tomorrow. He thought with pleasure about stuffing lumps of cotton between the window frames, cutting strips of paper to cover them, making the glue paste. He'd keep out of the way and let Lubov deal with the funeral.

Every time someone died in their building, the family of the *pokoinik* left the coffin lid outside their apartment, leaning against the wall of the stairwell. Children discovered the frilly satin-covered lids and spread the news of the deaths in the yard. Victor had always assumed that the lids were exhibited for that very reason, to serve as announcements of deaths. Now, looking around the room, he realized that people simply didn't have enough space in their apartments, and the lids had to be stored in the stairwell while the dead waited to be buried. What a nice word, *pokoinik*: "a calm one," "a resting one." Victor yawned, wondering if the building's children would gather by his door the next day, daring each other to touch the coffin's silky ruche trim.

Sasha snored and kicked the wall with the heel of her foot. Victor never minded her snoring, but Lubov insisted on taking the girl to an otolaryngologist in Prostuda. Lubov was always the one taking care of things. Why did she sound so helpless now? "Who will take care of us?" she repeated, over and over, until the phrase began to sound circular, like one of Sasha's tongue twisters. Victor pulled the blanket over his head to block out the noise. Baba Zhenia had raised Lubov from childhood. Did Lubov feel that her grandmother had been protecting her all this time, looking out for her, even after the old woman had become bedridden and demanding, a practical burden? The floorboards creaked in the corridor. A neighbor paused on the way from the bathroom and stood by Baba Zhenia's door, listening. *"Who will take care of us?"* Was this how it felt to lose a mother?

Shivering, Victor kicked back the blanket and groped under the bed for a pair of wool socks. He always felt incompetent and insufficient around his wife, but now the feeling was magnified. Incompetent, insufficient, semi-human. He realized that he envied Lubov's grief.

Victor Goldberg had lost two mothers. The first one abandoned him, when he was a day old, at the Moscow Birthing House Number 8. Victor was one of three infants left at the Birthing House that week. They were all Festival Babies, the mixed-raced children of Moscow girls and the guests of the Sixth International Youth Festival.

"We picked you because you were the lightest, kitten," Raya Goldberg, Victor's second mother, had explained.

Victor guessed that Raya would have preferred to keep the adoption under wraps, the way normal families did. But he looked so different from both of his parents that the conversation was unavoidable.

Raya called Victor's birth mother *idiotka,* but tended to forgive the young fool the "internationalist impulse" that led to Victor's conception. "It was a special time. Most of us had never seen a foreigner before, let alone talked to one! No wonder *idiotka* got seduced," she said, showing Victor a daisy-shaped festival pin. The brass daisy had a pleasant weight. Futuristic script spelled *FOR PEACE AND FRIENDSHIP* inside a blue enamel globe at its center.

The Youth Festival had been Khrushchev's government's effort to open the country to the world after years of Stalinist freeze. In the summer of 1957, thousands of guests from over a hundred countries descended on Moscow. Kremlin opened to the public, Gorky Park of Culture and Recreation stopped charging for admission, love poems in first person singular appeared in print, and, in an unprecedented move, the government allowed direct contact between festival guests and ordinary Muscovites. According to Raya, the guests from Friendly Africa were especially popular with the girls.

"Where do you think my real father was from?" Victor had asked Raya.

"I don't know." She shrugged. "Liberia? Ghana? Ethiopia? *Idiotka* should've thought nine months ahead, imagine bringing a Negro baby home to her parents! It's difficult to raise such children in this country. But you know, kitten, Semyon and I are modern people without prejudice."

Victor had always called his parents by their first names: Semyon and Raya. The Goldbergs were both engineers. They were handsome, cosmopolitan, and, like many members of the Soviet *nomenklatura* in the 1960s, easily nonconformist among their intimate friends. Although Raya had briefly lost her job during Stalin's anti-Semitic campaign, Semyon came through more or less untouched and went on to have a spectacular career. Shortly before they adopted Victor, the Goldbergs received a sprawling three-room apartment in a prestigious complex on the Garden Ring.

Victor liked to picture his parents bent over the hospital tray of babies, picking. He imagined Raya in her mink-collared coat and Semyon in a herringbone suit, the luxurious fabric matching his salt-and-pepper hair. While happy to indulge his infertile wife's strange feminine need for a child, Semyon probably felt nervous that the nurses might think *he had a problem.* Victor guessed it was Raya who finally made the choice. He pictured Semyon nodding distractedly, then shifting his attention back to some pretty young nurse's white-coated ass.

Victor's earliest memories were of his live-in nanny, a sixteen-year-old village girl named Marusia. He loved Marusia's small, callused hands and the way she ate sugar cubes, like candy, with her tea. Marusia used to spit on ribwort leaves and apply them to Victor's scraped knees. Raya deemed the practice an unsanitary superstition, but Victor was sure the cool leaves made the pain tolerable. More than once, while Victor was supposed to be napping, he spied Marusia playing with his toys: the tin windup bear, the miniature train set, the striped rubber ball. The girl's behavior didn't surprise Victor. He knew he had the best toys in the building—Raya made sure of that.

When Victor turned four, he had his first real birthday party. The living room filled with his parents' friends, and he clung to Marusia, shy around strangers. When Raya tried to pick him up, he screamed and arched his back until his mother gave him back to the nanny. Victor spent the rest of the party on Marusia's lap in a corner armchair, while the adults talked and clinked glasses around the oval dining table. After the party, Victor sat on a windowsill and watched Marusia clean. She was sweeping the paper confetti off a high wall shelf when she dropped and broke one of Semyon's Bach records. Semyon merely glared, but it proved enough to make Marusia cry. Victor remembered stroking the girl's soft bobbed hair and kissing her pink, tear-streaked face until she laughed.

He didn't have many physical memories of his parents. A black Volga picked Raya and Semyon up at seven in the morning and drove them to work. In the evenings, Raya, a senior scientific colleague at the Institute of Steel and Its Alloys, returned home by bus. The car and the chauffeur belonged to Semyon, who usually came home after Victor was already asleep. Because of this, Victor mostly remembered his father's things: his crystal ashtray, silver cigarette holder, a pair of amber cuff links, and a pin with the Aviation Institute's insignia. He remembered playing with Semyon's gold-tipped fountain pen and spraying ink all over his *Sputnik* paperweight. He didn't worry about punishment. Even then, Victor knew that his father was too busy to get upset about ink stains. Semyon Goldberg had just received the Lenin Prize for his investigations into building dependable navigation systems. Shortly after, he became a department head at the Aviation Institute.

Among the members of the Academy of Sciences, Semyon Goldberg was a media star. He was always featured in newspapers and on TV talking about his and others' research. For a while, he even hosted a weekly TV show entitled *The Science Hour*. Even though Victor enjoyed the short animation of a tipping beaker in the beginning of the show, he realized that *The Science Hour* would be as boring as *The Agriculture Hour*, if it weren't for his father's angular movie-star face and tooth-baring smile. Victor liked to imagine that Semyon was sending him secret messages, encoded in the incomprehensible science talk. If his father came home for dinner on the day of *The Science Hour*, Victor hid in his room, protecting their imaginary conversations from the flesh-and-blood Semyon's preoccupied, dismissive presence.

In addition to his demanding schedule, Semyon Goldberg had an insatiable appetite for junior scientific colleagues, and his affairs often kept him away from home for days at a time. Victor remembered Raya complaining to someone on the phone that Semyon was stretched across two households. At the time, Victor imagined it literally. His father's legs became thin as noodles as he did a split across the roofs of many apartment blocks. *One leg here, another there*, Raya had said. Perhaps because of this image, Victor always thought of Semyon as a giant. In his earliest memories, he was of comparable size to his mother and Marusia, but never any taller than his father's knee.

When Victor turned ten, the Goldbergs decided that he no longer needed a nanny.

The night Marusia left, Victor lay down on her empty bed and picked a random book from a small bookshelf above the headboard. The book was Semyon's treasured first edition of Mandelstam's *Tristia*. Normally, Victor disliked poetry. A poem always started out boring as a locked door, then yawned like a trap, sucking him into a vertiginous understanding he hadn't asked for. That night, he welcomed the unsafe space behind the words. These were old poems, and Victor preferred the poet's worn-out laments to the terrifying absence in the room. He read for a long time, stroking the velvety, crumbling edge of the paper cover.

There was a hesitant knock on the door, and a second later Victor saw Raya, in her nightgown, carrying a plate of sliced green apples. He guessed that she came to tell him to mind his bedtime, but she just smiled, as if unsure of the words she should use. Victor thanked her for the apples, and she retreated toward the door, saying nothing. *Vitya,* Victor remembered telling himself in his best Marusia voice, *it's midnight! What are you doing up?* Something scary was tangled in the sheets. Stifling a scream, the boy groped at its dry exoskeleton, swatted it away. It landed on the parquet and stayed there. A white paper rectangle, the dumb book.

Over the next four years, Victor Goldberg lived like a guest in his parents' airy apartment. The mornings were his own. Often, he stayed up late and slept through school the next day. In the afternoons, he watched TV until his French tutor rang the doorbell. After French, Victor opened the fridge and stared at the contents for a few minutes, though he always ate the same things: cottage cheese with raspberry jam, followed by caviar on white bread.

Victor was fourteen when a cement truck swerved in the rain and hit the Goldbergs' Volga, killing his parents. He wasn't alarmed when Raya and Semyon didn't come home at night; he'd assumed they simply forgot to inform him of their plans. The following afternoon he came from school and found the apartment filled with adults. For a good half hour, nobody paid attention to him. He wandered around, listening. It was instant, he learned. *When the ambulance got to the scene, Semyon's cigarette still clung to his lips. There was a half-finished crossword puzzle in the back seat.* None of the adults, except for Semyon's two ex-wives, were family, and none had any idea what to do with

Victor. A week after his parents' funeral, a social worker came to take him to Moscow Children's House Number 1.

Victor Goldberg remembered looking at the yellow stucco building where he grew up through the back window of a government van. The crumbling statues around the perimeter of the building's roof stood wrapped in nets. Their outstretched arms protruded from the wrappings, and Victor pretended they were waving goodbye.

Most residents of the Children's House were retarded, sick, or deformed. The kind of children people didn't keep. Victor saw harelips, flat Down's faces, faceted ears of fetal alcoholics. There was Half-a-Boy, a shriveled body with a huge, mute, perpetually grinning head, that the nurses carried in a sack fashioned out of bedsheets.

When Victor wasn't at school, he lay on his bed by the wall, trying to ignore the moans and head-banging of those who never left their cribs.

He didn't miss his parents. He missed his privacy, his room, the creaky bookshelf, volumes of Tolstoy, Hugo, and Thackeray that smelled of old glue, the view of the Moscow River out the window. Shortly before she died, Raya had taken the fuse out of the TV set to stop Victor from watching too much. He'd bought a new fuse at a radio store and popped it in when his parents were at work. In the evenings, he used to slip the fuse under the papier-mâché tiger mask on the wall. It had occurred to Victor that the fuse could still be there, under the tiger mask in a sealed, vacant apartment, and he cried silently into his flat Children's House pillow. That was as close as he'd ever come to grief, he realized now. Lubov wept for Baba Zhenia. He cried for the TV fuse.

When Victor turned eighteen, he was drafted into the army. His life at a remote base in Siberia resembled his life in the orphanage: shaved heads, a room shared with thirty men in horrible, viscous idleness. The "granddads" roughed him up in the shower twice, yelled, "Get the Jew!" and "Your mama fucked a monkey," but barely drew blood, perhaps sensing that as a ward of the state, Victor was used to maltreatment and numb to hazing.

What Victor couldn't stand were the conversations, strangers whispering to each other in the night. Floating in the dark sea of muttering and snores, with no place to hide, he strained to remember what silence sounded like. All he wanted then was to be alone, to free his mind from the parasitic community of strangers' voices.

Victor Goldberg couldn't say why, on one particular day, he decided he'd had enough. He remembered waiting for everyone to fall asleep and then cutting his wrists in the barrack's latrine. He had expected it to take some effort, but the knife readily went through his skin, and right away there was so much blood. It must have been the smell of blood that made him pass out.

He met Lubov in the Asbestos 2 hospital, where the army had sent him to recover. She'd bribed the hospital psychiatrist to get him out of both the hospital and the army.

Victor Goldberg turned toward the wall and pressed his face against the cold, pulpy wallpaper. This apartment was his first noninstitutional dwelling since his parents died, and when he'd entered it eight years ago, its arrangement of mismatched furniture worked better than a spoken welcome. The lace curtains, the sewing machine, the skis in the corner, the picture of Akhmatova tacked to the wall above the desk had made Victor want to close his eyes and sleep off his orphanage years like a hangover.

The door creaked, and Lubov tiptoed into the room. Victor lay still, pretending to be asleep. He listened to her careful steps as she undressed and put on her nightgown. He heard the whine of the armoire's door and the clink of glass. Lubov was getting a drink of vodka from Baba Zhenia's crystal carafe. The carafe was there for emergencies: when Sasha had a cold, Lubov made her throat compresses out of plastic bags and vodka-soaked cotton wool. Victor briefly considered putting his arms around his wife when she got into bed. But his hands were cold, and he was convinced that Lubov would move away from his touch. During the years they'd spent together, Lubov had taught him the complex tricks of empathy, then turned around and began to call him on his act.

On his first night here, after Lubov had brought him from the hospital, he woke up to find her sitting on his bed in her pale blue housedress. Her hair was plain, tucked behind her ears. She reminded Victor of a nurse at the Children's House who used to sit by the door of his room when he first arrived, except the nurse rarely looked up from her knitting, and Lubov clearly expected something of him. Victor remembered feeling cornered, suffocated under the weight of her stare, frantically thinking of the things a grown man might say to a woman sitting on his bed.

Eight years later, he still wasn't sure what she wanted from him in exchange for the rescue. All he knew was that he hadn't given it to her, and that he never would.

3
Wallpaper

"GOLDBERG! HAVE YOU ANY BRAIN? LEAVE YOUR SHOES BY the door!"

Sasha took off her muddy boots and walked down the corridor to the classroom.

"*Uzhas,* this mud," Bedbug muttered behind her. "GOLDBERG!"

"What?"

"Perspective, Goldberg. Today we're drawing the shadow of two cones and a sphere. It would help if you arrived on time. Because we have no more paper."

"Sorry. What do you want me to do, then?"

"I don't care what you do!" squawked Bedbug. "Go draw on your forehead!"

Sasha waited. After two weeks at AFTER EATIN she was aware that Bedbug's high-volume teaching technique had a benign underbelly.

"Check in the corner closet," grumbled Bedbug.

The District 7 Evening Art Studio for Children was the only art school in Asbestos 2, a ghost of the Soviet times. It cost eight rubles a year to attend; its teaching philosophy was unrepentant academic sadism. The staff consisted of Evgeny Mikhailovich, Bedbug, and an art history lecturer who visited once a week from the Prostuda House of Culture with her cracked slide projector. The three of them shared an odd number of legs, a handful of teeth, and a belief in the redemptive nature of art. Only Evgeny Mikhailovich received a salary. Bedbug and the art history teacher went unpaid except for an occasional package of humanitarian aid buckwheat that they were entitled to as education workers. On national holidays, the parents thanked the teachers with vodka and brought them boxes of chocolates that were too moldy or damaged to give to doctors and plumbers. For the week that followed a holiday, Evgeny Mikhailovich and Bedbug remained falling-down drunk and everybody ate candy. The insides of box lids made perfect sketch paper.

It was such an unlikely institution that every time Sasha Goldberg pushed open the steel door and stepped down, she wondered if the place would still be there. She worried about the extension cords suspended over puddles, and whether Evgeny Mikhailovich would finally keel over during one of his angry tirades. She worried about the beam that supported the sagging ceiling and the rusty vibrating pipe in the corner. But AFTER EATIN remained. The pipe shook and groaned, and Evgeny Mikhailovich stormed in and out of the classrooms on his wooden leg roaring, "You are all expelled!" in his scariest voice.

At first, Sasha winced at that roar.

"It's shell shock," Katia said with a smirk. "Blame the Germans. According to Mikhailovich, he personally stormed the Reichstag."

"Single-handedly," piped in the others, as if on cue.

Sasha felt that she was being initiated into their union, swaddled in a soft blanket of their clawless sarcasm. This was a painless initiation. They were crediting her with their friendship. Would she have to pay the price and, if so, what kind?

"You want to see them?" Katia asked, running her finger along the classroom's doorframe.

"Who?"

"The Germans. Cut here."

Sasha pierced the wall with her razor blade. The blade went in easily: layers of paper had bubbled up under the paint. She pried the paper with the tip of the blade. "Today the Motherland Forces . . ." read the WWII headline. In a photograph of a factory floor, workers hunched over a conveyor belt. It was a textbook image, but finding it on the wall made the people in the photo real. They could still be alive. Sasha thought about the last of them dying, hunched over and gaunt, with a bald shiny skull where the youthful flap of 1940s hair had been. She imagined the man's elderly niece clearing out his closet, leaving extra-wide pleated pants, moth-bitten along the folds, on top of a trash heap.

Katia found a profile of Stalin next to the newspaper's masthead and passed it around. In the first years of Perestroika, journalists from Moscow and Leningrad had descended on Asbestos 2. They had photographed the gulag artifacts: clumps of barbed wire in the fields, lengths of old fences, ashtrays made of human skulls. They had written of atrocities. Now the country was done regurgitating, finished being horrified by its own past. History was back in the classroom, once again a tedious succession of czars and battles, beards and wigs. Sasha felt as if she were stabbing history with her razor blade, stirring it up, breathing it in with the dust.

She imagined the family that wallpapered the basement. They may have been exiles, like Baba Zhenia, or wartime evacuees. There might have been a bed in the corner and a woodburning stove in another. The baby would be her mother's age now. Raised sleeping in the drawer, eating rationed food, with a picture of the Alexander Gardens tacked onto the wall, and Acmeist poetry: forbidden, invisible, memorized, and whispered into a tight pink child's ear in the basement. She would grow up straight-backed, straining toward the light, the destroyer of ordinary people. Sasha slid a newspaper shred into her sketchbook, like evidence.

It was still in her sketchbook as she dug in the closet, finally coming upon a poster from the Prostuda Regional Art Museum that lay folded under a bucket. Despite a few yellowed creases and water stains, the back of the poster was clean enough to draw on. Sasha barely had time to pin it to her easel when the hollow head of the Venus de Milo rattled on its shelf, and Bedbug burst into the classroom, carrying an old copy of *Young Artist* magazine with a painting of a plaster foot on the cover.

"The egg speech," whispered Katia.

The foot was an early Picasso. From the barely sketched umber background to the expertly placed highlight on the big toe, it looked so casual, realistic, and graceful, it appeared to have painted itself.

"Only when you can paint like this," said Bedbug, holding up the magazine, "do you deserve a chance to attempt abstraction. So far, none of you can paint like this. You people are eggs. My job is to help you hatch."

Sasha easily imagined herself as an egg. An incongruous, mutant one, with hair and moles. Bedbug was wrong about Katia, though. Katia was no egg. If she hadn't been wearing a boy's checkered shirt tucked into rolled-up track pants, Katia would look beautiful enough to be sitting in a daisy field in a television photo-essay.

"Why are you looking at me like that?" Katia whispered.

I'm trying to picture you crying. I'm trying to picture you on the toilet, Sasha thought.

"When you frown, you look like my mother," she said.

"Forget about your mother, Goldberg. That's what you're here for."

Bedbug nailed the *Young Artist* to the wall above the still-life table and stomped out.

"When we all hatch, he'll make chicken soup," Katia declared. "Mmm, *soupchik.* A man like Boris Petrovich can't survive on pickles alone."

Sasha laughed, thinking of the seemingly bottomless cloudy pickle jar that the teachers kept behind the sofa in the front room.

"I think their pickles are dangerous to eat without vodka," Katia said. "Which is too bad, because I'm starving. This smell is pure torture."

The *ponchiki* kiosk attached to the grocery store by GLORY TO THE stayed open well into the evening, and the basement of AFTER EATIN always smelled like frying dough.

"Do you want to go get *ponchiki*?" Sasha asked.

Katia shrugged. "I don't have any money."

"I do," Sasha said quickly. "Let's go!"

Zipping up her mud-caked boots, Sasha wondered how she would get home. The money she was about to spend was her streetcar fare. Five minutes later, she sat next to Katia on the stairs in front of the grocery, a bulging, greasy paper bag of powdered doughnuts between them.

"An embryo!" Sasha exclaimed, holding a curled, lumpy *ponchik* between her thumb and index finger. It was too hot to eat. Now that she'd spent the money, Sasha Goldberg felt giddy, undisturbed. She would walk home. It was a small price to pay for Katia's friendship.

Katia licked her fingers and dipped them into the powdered sugar at the bottom of the bag.

"I can't pay you back," she said.

"You don't have to. Mama gives me money for sweets on Art Studio days," Sasha lied.

"You're so lucky, Goldberg," Katia said, rolling her eyes.

"You're the first one to tell me that."

"Everyone in there"—Katia motioned toward AFTER EATIN—"You all think you are so miserable. You're suffering, I can tell, because you look, um, unusual. But really, *money for sweets*? Let me ask you something: are you a foreigner?"

"I'm not a foreigner!"

"But your father is a foreigner?"

Sasha shook her head. Victor Goldberg emigrated to America four years ago, and Sasha hadn't heard from him since. Perhaps by now he could be considered a foreigner, but back when he still lived in Asbestos 2, he was simply a member of the intelligentsia who had the inconvenience of being black-skinned. Sasha laughed, remembering Victor in his brown fur hat, ski pants, and quilted coat—what foreigner would look like that? Still, she knew that in Asbestos 2 it didn't take much to be considered an honorary foreigner. Ethnic names and nose shapes, eyelid angles and hair textures were important predictors of personality.

"So you're a plain Jew?" Katia asked thoughtfully.

"A plain Jew," confirmed Sasha, deciding that it would be best to omit the particulars. Her last name positively identified her as a Jew; there was no arguing with it. Being a Jew wasn't all that bad. Sasha knew from experience that it was worse than being an Armenian or a Tartar, but better than being a Chukchi, the butt of a million jokes. Still, none of the above was any good, and many people's parents seemed to understand that and take measures. Sasha had seen the class list at AFTER EATIN. Lenya Novikov's father was a Shapiro, and Masha Krukova's father was a Gurevich, so Lenya and Masha had their mothers' surnames. Sasha's mother, however, liked to throw a challenge to society. Sasha remembered Baba Zhenia chiding Mrs. Goldberg when Sasha was about to enter Number 13. *Luba, you can be as stubborn as you want, but spare the baby. Bad enough the child's dark, you want to send her to school with a name like that? What are you trying to do?*

"That alone is not a good reason to be miserable," declared Katia. "Jews live well."

Sasha smiled, happy with the verdict. Perhaps, she realized, her parents gave her a Jewish name to take the focus off *black-skinned*. There were, after all, degrees of undesirable nationalities.

Sasha decided that, in another conversation, she'd let it slip that her father lived in America. Reaching over to sweep the sugar powder off Katia's collar, she noticed that Katia's coat was much too big for her, that it was a fat lady's coat. When Katia stood up, it floated, mantle-like, around her skinny frame, while its sleeves barely reached past her elbows.

They threw the empty paper bag in the bushes by GLORY TO THE and walked back to AFTER EATIN.

"I lied about the money," Sasha said, opening the door to the basement. "I spent my tram fare."

"What did you do that for?"

"It's all right. I'll walk."

"To District 3? I love you, Goldberg!" Katia exclaimed, balancing on the plank over the puddle. Inside, she pressed a stack of coins into Sasha's hand. "Here's your fare back."

"And you?" Sasha asked.

Smiling, Katia sat on the sofa and wiped the sugary corners of her mouth. Sasha remembered her mother sitting there and felt their uneasy resemblance again.

Evgeny Mikhailovich hobbled out of the classroom.

"Where have you two been? You have an hour left to finish your drawings!"

"Evgeny Mikhailovich," Katia said sweetly, "I need three rubles."

Without a word, the old man dug in his pants pocket, sending a trickle of bread crumbs to the floor.

"Three rubles," he repeated, counting out the coins. Then, to Sasha's amazement, he reached over and ruffled Katia's hair with his flat, tobacco-stained fingertips.

4

Like It Used to Be

SPRING CAME EARLY THAT YEAR. BY APRIL, THE ICE ON THE roads had almost melted. Streams of water rushed through the cracks, drilling holes in compacted black snowbanks. By the wall of Secondary School Number 13, where the underground heating pipe came too close to the surface, a few blades of new grass poked through the mud, electric-green like foreign gum wrappers. Shivering in the moist spring air, Sasha Goldberg lined up behind the flag-bearer and watched the PE teacher adjust the strap of her megaphone.

May Day was approaching, and since Secondary School Number 13 still obstinately celebrated Soviet holidays, the students were rehearsing their annual Marching in Formations Competition. It was only nominally a competition; the marchers mostly attempted to outdo each other in dragging their feet, sighing, and jeering. But nonparticipants received a failing grade in physical education, and for that reason alone, the May Day Marching in Formations Competition limped on. Sasha preferred the competition's tedious rehearsals to the regular PE curriculum, which often included a round of "Kill Goldberg," played with a multitude of rock-hard soccer balls.

The PE teacher, a tall woman in a tracksuit with a haircut that betrayed her secret desire to have been born a hedgehog, tested her megaphone and called for silence. Not a single person stopped speaking.

"Question number one!" continued the PE teacher. "Any artists out there?"

Without the immediate prod to move, the conversations got louder, and the formation started to fall apart. Sasha Goldberg squinted into the sun, wondering if she'd misheard the teacher.

"Who can help with the International! Workers! Day! Decorations?" the Hedgehog barked, turning her head away from the megaphone to sneeze.

Sasha realized that in the past, the elementary military preparedness teacher decorated the schoolyard for the competition. The EMP teacher had left the school last spring, when his class got canceled at the end of the Cold War. Sasha raised her hand and walked out of the formation to the middle of the asphalted square. The crowd behind her quieted for a second, then resumed its commotion.

"Go talk to the principal," said the Hedgehog, waving Sasha off.

The principal, a reptilian granny in a braided chestnut wig, seemed to awaken from a thousand-year slumber to give Sasha the key to the EMP room, a note excusing her from all classes for a week, and a touching request to *make it like it used to be.*

Sasha Goldberg could hardly believe her luck. In the EMP room, she checked the inventory of paint and unearthed a large sponge, five half-decent brushes, and a plastic bucket. She wondered why the EMP teacher hadn't bothered to steal the supplies before he left. She'd definitely take some burnt ochre and white to AFTER EATIN.

"I fucked his sister!" a high voice declared in the yard outside. Somebody else laughed. "The harelip!" the voice continued. "Eh, fuck that cunt, I said. Lesbian harelip! Lesbian harelip fucking toothpaste pussy!" The laughter got louder. Sasha looked out the window. The rehearsal was over. Little kids flooded the schoolyard; older ones huddled on the porch, lighting their cigarettes. Some school authority must have decreed that it was finally warm enough to have recess outside.

Sasha Goldberg opened the gun cabinet and took out an AK-47. Like the other guns in this room, this one was real, but its firing mechanism had been disabled. In elementary military preparedness you learned how to clean and assemble a gun but not how to shoot one. Presumably, in the event of WWIII, someone else would be doing the shooting. Sasha came up to the window and aimed the gun at the crowd. It felt good to stand hidden behind two panes of glass, invisible from the outside. Sasha wondered if a week would be enough for people to forget about her, to find a new bottom for their hierarchy.

She returned the gun to the cabinet and began to lift the paint cans onto the teacher's desk. It occurred to her that her first "serious" drawings had been works of propaganda: produced in multiples, arranged for maximum impact. She made them after her father left.

Victor Goldberg disappeared when Sasha was ten years old. She had gone on a fourth-grade excursion to Prostuda, and when she returned, Mrs. Goldberg met her by the school gate. Sasha couldn't stop talking. In Prostuda, her class walked along the boulevard to lay flowers on the Grave of the Unknown Soldier, and afterward their teacher took them to a movie theater with a café on top, where they drank grape juice through plastic straws (Sasha had saved the straw) and ate tiny salami sandwiches. They also visited two museums: one had art in it, and one had stuffed animals, balalaikas, and a teapot that Lenin had used in exile.

"The Ethnographic Museum." Mrs. Goldberg smiled. "I've been there."

She helped Sasha bring her bag up the stairs and unlocked the apartment.

The first thing Sasha noticed was that the room's only window looked different, its square uninterrupted by the usual black plastic rectangle on the ledge.

"What happened to Papa's radio?"

Mrs. Goldberg smiled calmly. Sasha looked around, confused. The room looked immaculately clean. Fresh daisies stood in a pickle jar on the table. There was one pillow on Sasha's parents' bed. Opening the armoire to hang up her coat, Sasha noticed that all of her father's clothes were gone. Mrs. Goldberg sighed and left the room. Sasha followed.

"What happened? Where is Papa? Why won't you tell me?"

"I have no idea what you're talking about, Sasha," sighed Mrs. Goldberg.

"The radio, the clothes, his shoes, what happened?"

"Sasha, I have no idea what you are asking."

"Did he run away?"

"Who?"

"Papa."

"Sasha, I really don't care for your tantrums."

Over the next few days, it became apparent to Sasha that her mother was going to pretend her father never existed. Fortunately, Mrs. Goldberg's plan to eradicate all traces of her husband contained significant loopholes. For example, there were common-use objects. Aluminum forks in the kitchen. A shoehorn in the bottom drawer of the wardrobe. The doormat, the plunger in the bathroom, the apartment keys. Sasha remembered holding the worn wooden handle of the shoehorn and thinking, *He touched this. He must come back. It's his shoehorn, his plunger, his keys.* She let her mother know that she knew. She had a father, Victor Semyonovich Goldberg, and he left. Mrs. Goldberg looked at Sasha with a mixture of pity and impatience.

"I know!" Sasha yelled. "He left because you're such a bitch, you're so mean to him all the time, and when he gets back, I'm leaving with him!"

Mrs. Goldberg remained calm. "Go stand in the corner, Alexandra."

Sasha searched for more evidence. If her father had died a horrible death and her mother was just trying to protect her, surely there would be something, letters, photographs. But Mrs. Goldberg's desk drawers contained nothing. Sasha saw that her mother had combed through her drawer as well, looking for artifacts, and flew at Mrs. Goldberg with clenched fists. On the top shelf of the wardrobe there had been a shoebox of photos—Sasha's baby pictures and a picture of her parents on their wedding day. The shoebox was gone.

Sasha felt a dual loss, a bottomless sense of betrayal. Not only was her father gone; now she knew that her mother was crazy. It was as if a protective bubble of childhood had suddenly burst, spewing Sasha headfirst, unprepared, into reality.

The explanation arrived in the form of Vera Ivanovna Zaitseva from the third floor. Tetya Vera was a kindhearted, two-hundred-kilogram creature with thin hair and swollen ankles. Sasha liked her crystal chandelier and the needlepoint portrait of Brezhnev that Tetya Vera's daughter had made in third grade. So she was happy when one day, after school, Tetya Vera invited her over.

"Want some tea, *detka*?"

"Thank you."

The Zaitsevs had gold-rimmed Chinese teacups with blue fish, and Sasha wasn't about to refuse.

Tetya Vera brought in a teapot, buttered a thick slice of bread, and tiled it with sardines.

"Here." She watched Sasha chew for a while and sighed. "Your mama is a very proud woman."

Sasha nodded, happy to have a mouthful of sardine sandwich.

"It's understandable."

Sasha kept chewing. She didn't find it understandable.

"She doesn't want you to be upset."

"Can I have more sugar?" Sasha asked, anticipating a lecture about tantrums. Tetya Vera, who lived directly below the Goldbergs, could hear every step they made, and Sasha assumed she was probably disturbed by all the screams and stomping.

"Your papa asked me to give you a letter," said Tetya Vera, causing Sasha to take a huge gulp of tea.

"Dear Sashenka," the letter began, "I must leave as I'm no longer able to endure the oppressive regime we all suffer under. Your mother and I had long discussions about making the move together, but as it turns out, I must go alone. I left while you were away to make it easier for you. I hope the Iron Curtain will soon open, and I'll be able to see you again. I will do everything in my power to make it happen. You're a smart girl, and you know my reasons for leaving. . . ."

The letter went on about politics, Chernobyl, anti-Semitism, and the impending political and economic catastrophe that Russia was bound to become. Rolling her scalded tongue, Sasha skimmed the political part. Victor Goldberg had terrible handwriting. "Kisses," it said at the bottom, "your papa."

"Your papa," Tetya Vera uttered mournfully, squishing Sasha's head against her soft paisley bosom, "has run away to the enemies."

Sasha Goldberg didn't need comforting. In fact, she was elated. A father in America. There weren't many things more glamorous than this. She thought she was about to become one of the rare blue-jean-wearing kids in Asbestos 2. Her father would send her bubble gum, a translucent ball with glitter inside, a pink eraser that smelled like strawberries. All those items Sasha had glimpsed on a classmate whose second cousin had been a security guard at the Russian Embassy in Belgrade. According to Victor Goldberg, that cousin was a KGB pig. One time Sasha yelled at him, "Can't *you* be a KGB pig? I need a pair of sneakers!" Now she had a new respect for her father. He didn't need to become a KGB pig. He'd found a better way.

She thanked Tetya Vera and handed back the letter.

"Oh, you can keep it, *detka*."

"Mama will take it away."

"Well, you can come and read it anytime, then. Anytime."

Sasha watched the letter disappear into the bottomless pocket of Tetya Vera's housecoat.

"Do you have any pictures of Papa?"

"Maybe," said Tetya Vera. "Let me see."

She bent down and groped under the sofa but couldn't reach very far underneath. Sasha Goldberg had to help her drag out several boxes of photos. They sifted through smiling faces with carefully arranged beehive hairdos, some older, browner pictures, a faded color snapshot of a baby. Finally, they found a group photograph of several men leaning on shovels.

"This was at a *Subbotnik*. We were cleaning up the yard. You weren't born yet."

Victor Goldberg stood at the left edge of the picture, one of his shoulders cut off by the frame. He was laughing. His hair stuck out in clumps, looking like rays of a black sun against the white sky.

"I'll keep it with the letter," said Tetya Vera.

Sasha started coming over every week to visit the letter and the photograph. Soon, she'd memorized the letter and didn't look at it anymore. But she couldn't get enough of the picture. She drew her father's face in the back of her math notebook until she could do it with her eyes closed. At school, she drew him from memory. One day, she chose the best likeness of Mr. Goldberg and put it under her mother's pillow. Mrs. Goldberg said nothing. Sasha figured her mother never found the drawing. She taped another one to the mirror and waited for Mrs. Goldberg to come home. She remembered watching her mother walk past the mirror, waiting for her to notice.

"Nice," Mrs. Goldberg finally said. "You're getting very good at drawing faces, Sasha. I don't want you taping stuff to furniture, though."

"I thought you'd like to look at Papa," said Sasha.

Mrs. Goldberg gave her a tired look. "Take it off, please."

Sasha didn't move.

Mrs. Goldberg peeled back the tape and held out the drawing to Sasha. Sasha folded her arms on her chest.

"I don't know, Alexandra, why you choose to drink my blood when I'm tired from work. Does it taste better that way?" Mrs. Goldberg sighed, crumpled up the drawing, and let it drop on the floor.

Sasha hated her mother for refusing to go to America, for leaving her father no choice but to go alone, for trapping Sasha in drab Asbestos 2, where six months out of the year the sun barely came out, where the toys and adults were ugly and children were mean.

The next day she taped portraits of Victor Goldberg to every surface in the room and left, letting her mother discover the damage. When she returned in the evening, the pictures were gone, and the room looked immaculate again. Mrs. Goldberg sat in the kitchen with a cup of tea, reading a book.

"I know everything. Papa is in America!" Sasha cried. "He wanted to take me with him, but you didn't let him! He wanted you to come, too, and you didn't. Is that stupid or what? How much dumber can you be? Do you like it here? I hope you rot to death in your stinking library!"

Mrs. Goldberg pulled Sasha onto her lap. "Is that what you think?"

"Let go of me!"

"Sasha, either you listen to me now, or this conversation is over!"

Sasha ran to her room and slammed the door. It was all useless. A few days later she realized that she couldn't remember her father's face anymore. All that came to mind was a collection of pencil strokes crossing the lines of graph paper.

Although Sasha's drawings of Victor had been as powerless as a peace poster above a schoolyard brawl, she noticed that they managed to infect all of her subsequent work with their desperate, mechanical aggression. At AFTER EATIN, it was a drawback. Dipping a huge brush into the EMP teacher's can of red paint, Sasha Goldberg realized that for this job, it would be an asset. She'd compensate for her lack of skill with a swift and sure hand, turning the backs of old EMP manuals into cheerful Soviet-style monstrosities. She'd make the Asbestos 2 Secondary School Number 13 just *like it used to be* when Sasha first arrived here with stiff nylon bows in her hair, clutching her father's hand.

5

Barrel People

"WHAT'S WITH THE COSTUME?" KATIA ASKED WHEN SASHA came to AFTER EATIN wearing a navy blue skirt and a white blouse with an open book emblem on one sleeve.

"We had our Marching in Formations Competition," Sasha said. "Doesn't your school have those?"

"Not anymore, I guess," said Katia, pointing at Sasha's cuffs. "I used to chew on those buttons, too."

The special-occasion uniforms' soft aluminum buttons invited chewing.

"What are we doing today?" Sasha asked.

The still-life table stood folded against the wall.

"Bedbug is, you know, '*sick*,'" said Katia. "So E.M. is looking for something new for us to do. I think he's bored."

"GoldBERG! I need help getting Igor out of the closet!" Evgeny Mikhailovich yelled from the corridor.

Before he died in a prison hospital and was donated to the school, Igor had been a woman, but a really tall one, and as a skeleton he was a pain to carry around. Parts of him always came loose and rattled to the ground. His entire right arm was gone, but Evgeny Mikhailovich said it was unimportant due to the symmetrical nature of human anatomy and instructed the students to draw Igor as if he had both arms for the added challenge.

"Are you free this Sunday?" Katia asked, watching Sasha drag Igor to the middle of the room.

"Yes, why?" panted Sasha.

"We're having a party for my brother Alexey's eighteenth birthday. I'm not sure what's there to celebrate, other than the fact that he can now go to adult jail. I can't stand Alexey's posse of amateur drunks, but I have to help Mama. She's going out of her mind over this. Come keep me company." Katia winked. "You'll get to see how real Russian people have fun."

Sasha Goldberg rolled her eyes. "I've been to birthday parties before," she said, trying to hide her elation.

"Fine, then. Sunday, at five." Katia wrote down the directions on a piece of graph paper. "And don't tell your mother where we live."

"Why?" asked Sasha.

"Be-cause," Katia said, "if she finds out, she won't let you go."

Sasha Goldberg nodded in a meaningful way, even though she had no idea what Katia was talking about. Back at her easel, she looked at the piece of paper.

"Three to the end of the line, right behind the tobacco kiosk, straight to the power lines, right on the path until the hole in the fence. Go through the hole and turn left. Climb a hill. Keep left of the landfill. You'll see number one from the road. We're in number two." There was a smiley face at the bottom of the page.

Sasha wondered why Katia had asked her to keep this secret. There was nothing unusual about the directions. Not many streets in Asbestos 2 had names, and the few named streets merged effortlessly with unnamed paths and shortcuts. Although all the apartments in town had been privatized, the land still belonged to the People, and people cut corners, trudged through ravines, crossed landfills, and sneaked through bushes, endlessly optimizing their journeys. When people slept, their footprints, iced over or filled with liquid mud, shone in the moonlight. On clear nights silver threads connected the school to the liquor store, the liquor store to the asbestos pit, the pit to the morgue, and the morgue to the Conversation Point, drawing a predictable diagram of daily life in a place unsuitable for living.

Even the name of the town was an afterthought. Built in 1937 as an administrative center for the Gulag, Asbestos 2 was originally called Stalinsk. Back then, it had only two streets, Stalin Street and Lenin Street. The streets converged on Labor Plaza, in front of the District Soviet, the first brick-and-stone structure built in this part of the country and to this day, with its neo-classical portico, the fanciest building in town. Prisoners built the Soviet, and Baba Zhenia used to say there were a hundred people buried in its foundation.

"Why did they kill them?" Sasha remembered asking.

"Oh, they didn't kill them. They just didn't feed them," Baba Zhenia had said. It was an important distinction in her eyes.

Stalinsk grew with the camp system, and streets were named after Yezhov, Beria, and Dzerzhinsky. After Stalin's death, stagnation set in. Khrushchev came to power, and most of the camps closed. Yezhov and Beria disappeared from history books, and the street signs quietly came down. Except for Stalin Street, which became the Prospect of Anti-Imperialists, there wasn't the budget or imagination to rename the streets. Numbered districts and zones seemed more practical. Sasha Goldberg considered her street elite, because it did have a name, although Sasha had to admit it was only a partial kind of name, Third Road Street. There was also Second Road Street, First Road Street, and plain Road Street.

By the time asbestos was discovered in the ground of the town's southeast suburb, it was the last Stalinsk in the union, sorely needing a new name. The choice seemed obvious. Asbestos 2 was named in honor of Asbestos, a larger town in the Ural Mountains, where asbestos was also mined, the weather was milder, and one could occasionally buy beef in stores.

The year Sasha Goldberg was born, an old labor camp in eastern Asbestos 2 was reopened, renamed Strict Regime Colony Udarnik, and filled with felons. The Udarnik felons were being reformed at the asbestos mine and then paroled to be further reformed at the asbestos mill. The felons' families followed the felons into town, and their straw-haired children filled the schools. There was housing, food and water, vodka and beer. Occasional exiled dissidents and descendants of the postwar shipment of "landless cosmopolitans" provided the necessary culture. Back in Soviet times you could sometimes buy flavored toothpaste, and even in 1993 the power station still produced enough electricity to feed the bulb in the clip-on lamp above Igor's smooth skull.

Sasha folded the paper with Katia's directions, put it in her pocket, and, trying to ignore the wires holding together the loose vertebrae, began to draw the skeleton's battered spine.

On Sunday, Sasha Goldberg stood in front of the mirror in Baba Zhenia's ratty garter belt with yellowed plastic clasps and wished for a pair of tights. According to Mrs. Goldberg, there were no tights as far as Moscow. Something had happened to the national supply of tights, something similar to what had happened to salt and matches the year before.

"Where are you going?" asked Mrs. Goldberg.

"To a birthday party," said Sasha.

"Need a gift?" Mrs. Goldberg was in a good mood. She danced over to the wardrobe, opened the drawer at the bottom, and got out a box of chocolates. The box had one dented corner. Sasha knew it had been in the drawer forever, waiting for a recipient. Nobody in Asbestos 2 seemed to eat chocolates. People got them as bribes and presents, checked inside for bills and personal notes, and passed them on. Sasha thought about the people who had nobody to bribe, like the head of the District Soviet or the director of the mine, about all that stale chocolate they must eat. Mrs. Goldberg slipped the box into a net bag and helped Sasha fasten her stockings.

"Here, wear this," she said, giving Sasha her best sweater: purple imitation cashmere with butterfly sleeves. Sasha put on the sweater, squeezed into a pleated plaid skirt, fastening the button to the buttonhole with a piece of string for extra waist room, and clipped white plastic pineapples to her earlobes. Mrs. Goldberg nodded approvingly.

"One more thing!" she said, opening her makeup bag. Sasha winced. She hated the feeling of powder on her face, and the hard plastic mascara brush seemed like a dangerous thing to let near one's eyeball.

"Stop blinking!" commanded Mrs. Goldberg. "Oh, never mind!"

Mrs. Goldberg looked at Sasha with squinty eyes, as if Sasha were an ill-conceived painting that she should have abandoned a long time ago, but instead obsessively overworked. Sasha knew that feeling. Staring at her boots to avoid further conversation, she put on her coat, grabbed the box of chocolates, and ran out the door.

Walking toward the bus stop, Sasha remembered that, as a toddler, she had been fascinated by the contents of her mother's makeup bag: a stub of a pencil, a tube of lipstick, an eyelash curler, a nail file, and something that looked like a miniature spoon with a plastic mother-of-pearl handle. She used to line them up, stroke their smooth surfaces, inhale the buttery fragrance of the bag's cracked, laminated liner. Now it occurred to her that her mother's beauty tools were pretend art supplies, dinky and ineffective in comparison with her own real ones.

The bus made a circle and drove away, enveloping Sasha and her pineapple earrings in a cloud of diesel exhaust. Because it was Sunday, the tobacco kiosk at the end of the road was shuttered. Sasha thought she could hear insects buzz, but then she saw power lines above the trees and remembered that it was too early in the year for bugs. The forest in front of her was still leafless but already faintly green, like a tinted black-and-white photo.

She reached the power lines and walked along the clearing under the wires. The towers that had looked so elegant from a distance turned out to have elephant legs of riveted steel. Sasha looked at the moving clouds behind the closest tower and pretended that the huge thing was slowly falling toward her. She knew she was working herself up but couldn't help it. When she was small, she would dangle both her legs out the window at night, imagining what it would be like to jump, in her mind already jumping, falling, five floors down, into the rustling, moist treetops.

By the time Sasha Goldberg found the hole in the fence, she had completely terrified herself. Sweaty and out of breath, she ran up a hill to the landfill, expecting to see houses down below, only there were no houses. The dump continued, seemingly, for kilometers, disappearing in the fog on the horizon. First, Sasha thought she had made a mistake. Then it occurred to her that she'd been lured, that a murderous orgy was about to take place, that maniacs were lying in wait behind the raspberry bushes, ready to turn her into a "naked headless body of a young girl," the kind of thing that always pops up in landfills.

Her mind raced ahead to Mrs. Goldberg's trip to the morgue, and to the headlines in *Asbestos Truth*, when she noticed that the dump had several distinct parts. Beyond the soccer-field-sized heap of household trash there was a junkyard, dominated by a rusted cistern truck. Looking farther below, Sasha saw eight large concrete half-pipes that lay evenly spaced at the foot of the hill.

Something moved next to one of the half-pipes, and a moment later a gray dog ran out in front of it. The dog barked in Sasha's direction, and Sasha was about to turn around and run when she noticed the dog's chain. Then she saw a clothesline with some sheets and finally a large "1" painted on the side of the closest half-pipe.

Heart thumping in her throat, Sasha Goldberg ran down the hill. When she reached number two, she saw that its front end was capped off with boards. In the middle, there was a door, and a stoop made of four cinder-blocks. Inside, men's voices bellowed an old song.

> . . . *There's someone comin' down the hill.*
> *For sure that's my sweetheart!*
> *He's got a camouflage shirt,*
> *It's gonna drive me out of my mind. . . .*

The men howled with drunken sarcasm. Their voices sounded sweetly familiar to Sasha, as if she had heard them once in early childhood and had completely forgotten them until now. She heard the sound of breaking glass and then laughter. The song stopped. Sasha Goldberg took a deep breath and knocked on the door. The door opened, and Katia's head appeared, letting out a cloud of fried fish smoke.

"Sashka! You! Come in."

Sasha followed Katia inside, squinting in amazement into the dim interior. Afterward, she was angry at herself for looking so shocked. Did she expect the room to become square, to suddenly expand into another dimension? It must have been the furniture, the way it fit into the cylinder. An imposing china cabinet leaned forward into the pipe at a precarious angle. At the top, it was fastened to the wall with a steel cable. A plastic baby doll with matted hair sat on top of the cabinet. It, too, was tied to the wall. Or maybe it was tied to the ceiling. Sasha saw evidence of an attempt to symbolically distinguish between the walls and the ceiling here: garish green and orange wallpaper covered the bottom of the room, leaving a two-meter stripe of bare gray concrete at the top.

Men of various ages and in different stages of drunkenness sat around a table in the middle of the room. Above them, a single lightbulb hung on a wire, orbited by a weblike construction of string, tin, and broken glass. A draft slammed the door behind Sasha and made the light sway slightly. The glass fragments cast multicolored shadows on men's faces, making them look evil and slightly ridiculous, like highway robbers from a German fairy tale.

A fat woman in a red polyester dress walked up to the table, holding a frying pan with sizzling fish.

"Mama, this is Sasha," said Katia.

The woman gave Sasha a red-cheeked smile.

"Natalia Egorovna," she said. She looked like a bloated version of Katia, except her hair was piled high on top of her head in a complicated hairdo that Sasha's own mother would consider abominable. Sasha blinked the smoke out of her eyes and put her box of chocolates on the table.

"Ah, Sashenka . . ." said one of the drunks vaguely, and then, more forcefully, "Move over, you goats, let the lady sit down! Katiusha, give her a glass, please, and tell Mama we're getting low here!"

And they were. Five empty vodka bottles stood on the table, and one lay on the floor. Sasha wondered how long they'd been sitting here.

"Alexandra Alexandra . . ." a fiftyish man with a pockmarked face started into a song, but stumbled and, laughing through his nose, winked at Sasha. This was the first time anyone had ever flirted with her, and even though the man's skin resembled Mrs. Goldberg's pumice stone, Sasha felt her cheeks get hot.

Natalia Egorovna gathered the empty bottles and replaced them with three full ones. Someone filled Sasha's glass. Sasha had never tried vodka before, but now she was determined not to show her inexperience. She took a giant swig out of her glass and let the vodka trickle down her throat like some awful but inevitable medication. The men cheered, "To health, to health!"

Sasha wiped her eyes, swallowed another gulp, and felt something pleasantly expanding inside her rib cage.

"What are you doing, Sashka?" Katia asked quietly.

"What?" Sasha grinned, lifting her nearly empty glass. She was already here, at a drunken party in a half-pipe at the dump, being called a "lady" by a man older than her parents, so what choice did she have? Sasha Goldberg tried to assimilate, play by the rules of the place. It was the most natural thing to do. But there was genuine concern in Katia's voice.

"That's enough, take it easy. Your people don't do this, you can get sick."

Here it was again. Sasha's "people" vs. Katia's "people." A while ago, Sasha had decided that when she turned sixteen and got her passport, she would take her mother's maiden name and become Alexandra Victorovna Nechaeva. To hell with Goldberg. But now she was angry, a reluctant recruit in her mother's battle with *lowlife*.

"*Chauvinistka!*" she admonished loudly, already feeling as drunk as she'd ever felt.

"Ah, shut up, Sashka." Katia's voice was grave, bristling with disapproval. "These old goats have been here for three hours, guzzling vodka. They are experienced. They can keep it down. All of my brother's idiot friends are already gone, sleeping it off in the junkyard. But hey, it's my brother's eighteenth birthday, so naturally Mama spent all our money on booze. I wish I had a family like yours."

"Don't," said Sasha. She realized that she had forgotten all about Katia's brother. "Where is your brother?"

"Oh, he's here," said Katia. "Want to meet him?"

They got up and walked past the china cabinet into the far end of the pipe. Katia parted a quilted curtain and flicked on the light. Behind the curtain, a boy in a plaid shirt and brown polyester pants lay face down on a canvas folding cot. His bare feet and skinny ankles shone white in the smoky room.

"Hey, birthday boy. My friend Sasha wanted to see you. Are you still conscious?"

The boy shrugged. His shoulder blades were almost touching under the plaid flannel.

"You need a pot?" Katia teased. "Sash, wait up out there for me, would you? I'm gonna help Alexey."

Sasha noticed a picture tacked on the wall above the cot. It was a portrait of Katia, done in scratchy black charcoal on butcher paper. In the portrait, Katia was looking straight up, as if in prayer. There were deep shadows in her eye sockets, and the sinews of her neck looked like stretched black cables.

"Oh, he drew it," Katia said, catching her glance.

Alexey rolled over on the cot and looked up at Sasha with an apologetic scowl. He was tall, and his hands were big and pale like aluminum shovels. Unevenly cut dark hair was plastered with sweat to his bluish white forehead. In the tight skin just under his eyebrows there was an expression of suffering that in certain Russian faces looks like pleasure.

"He used to go to AFTER EATIN," said Katia, pointing at Alexey the way a docent at a regional museum points at a stuffed eagle. "Evgeny Mikhailovich made all sorts of fuss about him. 'Alexey is a genius in need of a rescue!' he used to say. According to the old man, my brother was on the way to becoming the next Rubens."

"Did you like Evgeny Mikhailovich?" asked Sasha.

"Hand grenade, my hand grenade!" Alexey sang through his teeth, his eyes full of inward concentration.

"My brother here," continued Katia, "is a nihilist. A drunk nihilist. Come, Sasha."

She grabbed Sasha firmly by the wrist and dragged her back toward the party. Alexey followed the girls with his eyes, a razor-thin smile on his lips.

"He made this, too." Katia pointed to a collage of eggshells and disembodied doll parts on an old road sign, leaning against the wall. "And the lampshade over there. He's so good with his hands, if only he had a brain."

"What's this?" asked Sasha, pointing at a copper relief of a bosomy woman in a Russian folk outfit.

"My father made that, he was also good with his hands. This is supposed to be Mama. It's an idealized version of Mama."

"Where is your father?" asked Sasha.

Katia shrugged and made a gesture with her fingers like something evaporating.

"Mine escaped the oppressive regime," said Sasha.

"Yeah, that was what mine did also, probably." Katia laughed. "Don't they all?"

Sasha had been perfectly serious in quoting Victor's one and only letter. She'd never questioned it before. Whatever large, amorphous thing oppressed her father had nothing to do with her. But now she wasn't so sure. Sasha suspected Katia knew things, the way adults knew things, from the *inside*.

Katia grabbed a bottle of vodka off the table and headed for the door. Sasha followed. Outside, a single blood-red stripe of sunlight seeped through the trees. The girls sat on the stoop, passing the bottle.

"Drink slowly," said Katia.

Sasha noticed that the dump didn't smell that bad, only of rusted metal and moisture.

"Depends on the wind," said Katia. "We won't be living here long. Although that's what they've been saying since before I was born."

"How'd you end up here in the first place?"

"My parents came from a village in the Valdai *oblast'*. They worked at the collective dairy farm there, and Mama says it was miserable. A bread truck came once a week with nothing but bread, soap, and vodka. Very few young people were staying in the village. My parents and a few of their friends volunteered to go build the Baikal-Amur Railroad. Mama says their group was cursed. The government trucked them up here, along with three hundred other volunteers, but the railroad never came this way. These pipes, they're an improvement. Mama told me they started out in tents. The winter she had my brother, they were still in tents."

"Out here?"

"Yeah, some people walked to town and got arrested there for vagrancy. Some died or went insane and then died. We have a little graveyard, right here in the dump. Alexey takes care of it. I'm not into that sort of thing."

"Your parents had your brother in a tent?"

"No, my father dug a trench, like a bunker, and then the government brought these. . . . We call them barrels. Have you heard of 'barrel people'?"

Sasha nodded. Until this moment, she'd thought the expression "barrel people" was a generic Russian name for the homeless, but now it seemed that the expression belonged to Asbestos 2, and she was sitting at its source.

"That's us. Soon, they say, we'll get apartments in town. You know the joke about a guy who waited for thirty years to get a TV and for twenty years to get a refrigerator? So finally they call him and say, 'This Wednesday you're getting your fridge!' and he says, 'Oh, Wednesday is bad! My TV is being delivered!'"

"But that's old Soviet shit. Couldn't you rent a place in town or something?"

"Who has the money? Mama drinks. Alexey's the only one working."

"Where does he work?"

"He was a watchman at the heating plant, last I checked. Not that it matters. He hasn't been paid for four months."

"Does he go to school?"

Katia laughed.

"I'm the only one crazy enough to travel to school from here. My brother quit after eighth grade. Mama was a garbage lady at AFTER EATIN and GLORY TO THE for a while, and that was how we found the Art Studio. Alexey didn't last there, either, even though he has enough talent for both you and me."

Sasha nodded.

"He got expelled for stealing the art history lady's perfume and drinking it right there in class! He figured he'd drink it in the dark, during a slide show. Well, perfume, you know, smells! The art history lady was hysterical. She began to rant about brass-knuckled glue sniffers and declared that Evgeny Mikhailovich had to choose between her and Alexey. The old man practically cried after he kicked my brother out. He said he could have sent Alexey to the Repin Lyceum in Moscow, but instead my asshole brother had to fuck it up. He and Mama, they're weird that way. It's like they're devoted to this dump. They get by, get drunk, scavenge for discarded toys to decorate the graves of people they barely knew." Katia's voice was strained; she was searching for the right words. "It's like they're in a hurry to get to their own graves. Maybe it's all the lead in the well water here. I read an article about it, how it affects the brain."

"But you're not . . ."

"Maybe lead only affects some brains," said Katia firmly. "I'm counting days until I'm out of here. Next year, I'm going to Elita."

"What's that?"

"Don't you ever listen to the radio? *'Discover a star inside—Eli-ita!'*" sang Katia. "It's a modeling school in Prostuda. I've sent them pictures and they said if I decided to come I wouldn't have to pay. At first."

Sasha stared at the ground. She didn't know what to say. According to Mrs. Goldberg, trade schools in general were for lowlifes, and modeling schools were the worst because that was where the lowlifes went to become prostitutes. Children of the intelligentsia didn't leave school after eighth grade. It was a given that Sasha would endure another two years of Number 13 and then go to college. Preferably college in Moscow, St. Petersburg, or, at the very least, college in Krasnoyarsk. Mrs. Goldberg insisted that Sasha would have a *future,* and Sasha knew with some certainty that in a few years she would be striding past the granite facades of a big city, propelled into success by the force of her mother's determination. The idea of someone her age having to create her own future had never occurred to Sasha Goldberg.

"What about AFTER EATIN?" she asked quietly. "Are you going to quit, then?"

The door opened and a man fell out of the barrel.

"Oy!" yelled Sasha, jumping out of the way. The man pulled himself up to his knees and fell again, this time face first into the mud. Sasha imagined the splash his cheek would make and heard it a fraction of a second later.

"See? I can't stand this anymore." Katia stepped over the man's legs and opened the door. Sasha could hear the party winding down inside, laughter turning to moans and hissing curses.

"Mama," yelled Katia, "Uncle Vadim's out here. Tell Alyosha to bring him inside before you go to bed! I'm walking Sasha to the bus!"

There was no answer. Katia guided Sasha back to the path. In the dark, the junkyard looked like the *Titanic* on the ocean floor.

"What time is it now, anyway?" asked Sasha. She was starting to worry.

"About quarter past ten," said Katia, glancing up.

"How do you know?"

"The stars," said Katia. "Alexey taught me last year. It's easy here, the towers are like clock hands, they point at different stars at different times. If you stare at the power lines long enough, you learn things."

The girls ran down the hill toward the bus stop. Sasha Goldberg, who had never stared at anything long enough to learn anything, smelled the new grass and the night air and felt a connection to a world entirely outside herself.

Half an hour later, the headlights of the bus floated above the hill. Sasha was the only passenger. She sat down in the back and tried to look at the sky, but all she could see in the light of the fluorescent tubes were reflections: chrome poles slightly warped in the window glass, a defunct ticket dispenser, a backward sign imploring healthy passengers to give up their seats to invalids, and her own dark face, flanked by two plastic pineapple earrings.

She had violated her curfew before and knew what to expect at home. Mrs. Goldberg would be waiting in the corridor in her floor-length nightgown. She would regard Sasha with loaded silence and, after making sure that her daughter had seen her, would slowly turn around and disappear into her room, leaving Sasha to agonize overnight about her upcoming punishment.

The bus barreled through blackness, all of its loose parts rattling and screeching whenever a wheel hit a pothole. Sasha grasped the handle in front of her seat and pretended to steer the bus, the way she used to do when she was little. She thought about Alexey's drawing of Katia's face, the easy authority of its lines. There was no softness in the portrait, no hesitation, as if each movement of the charcoal, each change in pressure, was predetermined, absolute. Did Alexey know what he was doing? "Good with his hands," Katia had said. Sasha was sure that no one else in AFTER EATIN could make a picture like that. She certainly couldn't.

Sasha looked at her hands: pink palms creased with brown, fingertips knobby and swollen from too much nail biting. She imagined Alexey crushing a lump of charcoal with his thumb, pressing it into the paper. She attempted to remember his pale face, the span of his shoulders under his checkered shirt. His *good* hands, which channeled a wisdom Sasha was able to witness but couldn't understand.

She whispered his name. The final *xey* sounded like a scythe in wet grass, the sound of the coming summer. Grateful for the tightness of her long-ago-outgrown bra, Sasha closed her eyes, slipped her hand between her legs, and let her body have what it wanted.

Getting off the bus on a deserted, dimly lit Third Road Street, Sasha noticed that she didn't feel any guilt or fear. Mrs. Goldberg, white-gowned and bursting with disaster, hung on the fringes of her consciousness like a disgruntled ghost.

6

Tristia

LUBOV ALEXANDROVNA GOLDBERG OPENED THE WINDOW
and peered into the naked treetops below. It was nearly eleven at night and
Sasha still hadn't come home. Mrs. Goldberg made every effort to remain
reasonable. She didn't want to be like the other mothers, who, at the slightest
provocation, opened up their brains to a ghostly parade of hypothetical drug
addicts and rapists, murderers and cannibals. These were the same women
who believed in poltergeists; who, when they had a toothache, put their tubes
of toothpaste in front of their TV sets to be energized by charismatic healers.
Lubov Alexandrovna drew a sharp distinction between herself and women
like that.

The hour hand on the tin clock in the corner snapped out of its stupor,
sending a pinecone-shaped weight down with a jerk. The clock needed to be
oiled. Lubov Alexandrovna realized that she'd forgotten to ask Sasha where
she was going. At least the girl looked nice for a party and hadn't forgotten a
gift. With a child like Sasha, it was a rare day when you managed to avoid
embarrassment.

Lubov Alexandrovna closed the window and turned the latch. Listening
to the silence in the apartment, she unraveled her braid and found the hairbrush. The brush was full of Sasha's hair, curly and wiry, the color of burned
sugar. Mrs. Goldberg's heart momentarily sank, and she breathed deeply,
trying to turn her anxiety into straightforward, punishing anger.

Mrs. Goldberg decided not to wait up for Sasha, not to say a word when the little slob finally walked in the door. She sat down on the bed, brushed her golden mane until her scalp hurt, and changed into her nightgown. The clock made an attempt to chime, then choked and stopped. Mrs. Goldberg got under the covers and lay flat on her back like Sleeping Beauty, waiting for symmetry to do its magic. But the brown stain on the ceiling stubbornly hung in her field of vision, and death-sleep never came. She was still wide awake when she heard the bang of the downstairs door and Sasha's pounding footsteps in the stairwell.

The following morning, Mrs. Goldberg tried to wake Sasha up for school, but the girl just grunted and went back to sleep. She slept with her arms up over her head, as if begging for a stay of execution, just like her father used to. Lubov Alexandrovna watched her sleep for a minute, then put on her slippers and went to the kitchen to make breakfast. Cracking an egg on the edge of a dented aluminum bowl, she admitted to herself that she hardly had the energy for the caustic conversation that Sasha's curfew-breaking behavior occasioned. Lately, every time Mrs. Goldberg had attempted to punish Sasha or direct her or simply talk to her, she felt as if she were hammering on an eraser. She used to get the same feeling from talking to Victor.

Lubov Alexandrovna Goldberg didn't like to admit mistakes, but she made an exception for her biggest one, her former husband. She remembered seeing him for the first time fifteen years ago, on a gurney in a hospital corridor. His arms lay alongside his body like two thick gauze sausages. She walked past him carrying a stack of books, and he cried out after her in a wet, shaky voice, "Where did you get those? Did you know my parents? Where are you going?" She assumed he was crazy.

The books had come from the Asbestos 2 Central Library. Then twenty-eight years old, Lubov was already the head librarian, and she could *get* books. Even in Asbestos 2, people of influence needed to adorn their bookshelves, and by getting books, Lubov was able to get shoes and underwear, Polish makeup, East German clip-on earrings, sausage and cheese, cucumbers in the spring, sometimes coffee, and even, once, a banana. She knew that she was partly responsible for the state of Asbestos 2's libraries, dim, rarely visited places filled with Brezhnev's missives and multiple copies of the *Virgin Soil*

Upturned, where almost all lightbulbs, doorknobs, pencils, and remotely readable books had been pilfered, but she felt that she had no choice. She had her place in the economy.

The day she first saw Victor, she was on her way to see if two volumes of Maupassant and a *Treasures of the Hermitage* folio could proffer her some local anesthesia. Her grandmother, Baba Zhenia, was going to have three toes amputated due to diabetes the following day, and Lubov was determined that the operation be painless.

"*Zabud'*, Lubochka. Forget about it," Baba Zhenia had said when Lubov walked into her hospital room and plopped a stack of books on her bed.

Baba Zhenia prided herself on her stoicism and liked to deflect Lubov's efforts on her behalf with tales of do-it-yourself dentistry and do-it-yourself appendectomies of her camp days. At eighty-six years old, she mostly relied on old stories for conversation, and when she wasn't feeling well, her stories got older. The day of her surgery, she leaned forward on her bed and revealed that her twice-removed uncle had been a member of the People's Will Society and supposedly helped make the bomb that killed Alexander II.

"Remember, Lubochka, we're the descendants of the original Russian intelligentsia!" she croaked. "What's a few toes? *Erunda!*"

Baba Zhenia, Evgenia Nicolaevna Nechaeva, had spent the first half of her life in the thrice-renamed city of St. Petersburg, Petrograd, Leningrad. In 1941, she arrived in the Siberian swamp the same way as other members of the intelligentsia: in a cattle car. She was a Wife of the Enemy of the People. Her husband, a university professor who perished the year before, was the Enemy. When Baba Zhenia was arrested, the Germans had just invaded Ukraine, and the Nechaevs' twenty-four-year-old daughter Anna volunteered to go to the front.

Through the war, Baba Zhenia lived in a log cabin with eight other Wives of Enemies. She worked at the sawmill and waited for news from her daughter.

The war did something to the order of Anna's life. In 1949, she showed up on Baba Zhenia's doorstep drunk, with baby Lubov wrapped in dirty rags. This was the story Baba Zhenia didn't like to tell. Lubov faintly remembered the cabin, the mattresses on the floor, the Wives of Enemies' boots and shawls. Her mother disappeared for weeks at a time, but Baba Zhenia had always been there.

Lubov Alexandrovna slid the fried egg onto a plate, put the pan in the sink, and turned on the water. A cold stream hissed on greasy iron. The water smelled like chlorine, as it did every spring. Lubov Alexandrovna remembered the first time she heard the word *vodoprovod*, indoor plumbing. She was four years old, and they had just moved to Third Road Street. Lubov had thought *Vodoprovod* was a name of a fairy-tale monster. She still associated the word with her mother, a frightening weight pushing against the door of their new apartment. *Babulya, there's a dead body!* Baba Zhenia tried the door, peeked through the crack, sighed. Lubov remembered her grandmother's wide behind, swollen feet stepping on the backs of worn slippers, as the old woman dragged Anna's lifeless shape through the corridor toward the spectacular, shining bathroom. Anna smelled of stale gutter water, like the floor of an outhouse. Lubov remembered hiding her face in the folds of Baba Zhenia's skirt, wishing her mother gone. The following winter, Anna Nechaeva died of pneumonia.

Lubov Alexandrovna took a fork from the drying rack, picked up her plate, and went back to her room to eat. Sasha was still asleep, her mouth agape. Mrs. Goldberg decided not to wake her up yet, to have breakfast in peace.

She remembered the second time she saw Victor. She was coming back to the hospital on the day of Baba Zhenia's surgery. A few elderly patients sat on a bench by the main entrance, feeding bread to a pack of large, woolly dogs. One of the animals turned its head to Lubov, and she gave it a nervous smile. The dog's irises were blue, like morning snow, with black outlines. Lubov couldn't imagine how the babushkas on the bench dared to let the wolfish, unpredictable creatures eat out of their hands. All that slobber. To avoid the dogs, she made a wide semicircle and walked on a mud path between a cluster of utility buildings. Huge tar letters spelled MORGUE on one of the walls. The word was underlined with an arrow.

"That's to boost the patients' morale," someone said behind Lubov's back.

She turned around. The crazy boy from the day before was sitting on a stack of boards, awkwardly holding a cigarette in a bandaged hand. He had black, closely cropped hair. His face looked jaundiced, and he had unusual features. Lubov couldn't begin to guess his nationality.

"What are you doing here?" he asked.

"I was just going around. I don't like dogs."

"I'm afraid of dogs, too. Do you have a match?"

"I'm not afraid," corrected Lubov. "I just don't like dogs. And I don't smoke."

"Well, I'm terrified of dogs," said the boy with a little laugh. There was an edge in his voice, as if he'd just arrived on this planet and was learning his way around. Lubov felt strong and wise. Perhaps she should have been a nurse. It would be her job to bandage his thin wrists. She wondered what his wounds looked like.

"Listen, about the other day," he said, "I'm sorry. My parents, they both died, and I could swear they had those books in their apartment. I wasn't feeling well, I got confused."

Lubov was startled by the normalcy of his apology. "I work at the library," she said, beginning to lose interest in the conversation. "Tell me what you want to read, and maybe I could get it for you. What's your name?"

"Victor," the boy said. "They weren't my real parents," he added quickly, "and after they died, I lived at the orphanage."

The normalcy abated. Lubov studied Victor's face. He had dark pits under his eyes and dry thick lips. His gray hospital shirt was buttoned all the way up.

"There is no orphanage here," she said.

"No, not here. In Moscow. Here, I was in the army. Then I got . . . hurt. So."

Lubov Alexandrovna Goldberg finished her egg, pushed away the plate, and got up to dress. That one word, Moscow, the mark of difference, and his interest in books, had proved enough to make her lose her mind. She'd been both naïve and desperate. Then again, by Asbestos 2 standards, Victor didn't turn out to be so bad.

Lubov Alexandrovna thought about a boy named Vova who used to take her dancing in high school. She still saw him around, now a beefy man with graying hair. He had his name tattooed on his hand, a letter on each hairy knuckle. An eagle on a thick gold chain soared through his chest hair. He wore sweat pants with stirrups and, on weekends, stood in line at the beer kiosk with an empty pickle jar. It seemed to Mrs. Goldberg that even as a young girl she'd been able to predict Vova's future. It had been a relief to get rid of him when she left to go to college in Krasnoyarsk.

In retrospect, Lubov Alexandrovna considered the five years she spent at the Krasnoyarsk Institute of Culture the best five years of her life. She'd loved ancient philosophy and Latin classes, late-night parties with red wine and guitar music, amateur productions of Bulgakov's plays, and hand-sewn *samizdat* books with pale carbon-copy pages. She remembered a succession of dull Marxism-Leninism lectures that she spent copying the forbidden poems of Osip Mandelstam into a small notebook on her lap.

There was just one disappointment. The Institute of Culture educated music teachers, mass entertainment organizers, and librarians, and was almost entirely man-free. Lubov baited aging professors with her spontaneous Akhmatova quotes, the shimmering waterfall of her hair, and her ability to move in high heels as if barefoot. But the professors were burdened and cowardly. They shrank away, citing their *complicated lives,* a phrase that usually described tiny apartments with large, fierce wives inside.

After college, Lubov received a job assignment at the Asbestos 2 Library and returned home. Vova came by a few times, but by then it was clear to Lubov that she wanted nothing to do with Asbestos 2 men. She couldn't stand the smell of beer. She wasn't ever going to eat fish off newspaper. She had decided to stay strong and pure, away from the gutter that had swallowed her mother.

Fastening the collar of her blouse with a silver brooch, Lubov Alexandrovna remembered the lonely years she'd spent at the library before Victor came along. It was during that time that she learned Mandelstam's *Tristia* by heart. Her favorite poems in the cycle were about death: both physical, personal death and the death of culture, the collapse of civilization. In their mournful pitch Lubov found a soundtrack to her misery, her thwarted desires.

She used to wander the stacks, dreaming of a man without tattoos. He would be a stranger to Asbestos 2, a scientist perhaps, passing through town on a work-related trip. But all she found between the bookcases were straw-haired Asbestos 2 children with ballpoint pens, drawing penises, beards, and moles on Tolstoy and Chekhov.

No wonder, the day she'd stumbled upon Victor outside the hospital, Lubov decided to give fate a try. To get anywhere in Asbestos 2 one had to resort to unconventional means. A dark, book-loving Muscovite, an approximation of her fantasy, was sitting on a stack of boards by the MORGUE sign. He was smaller and younger and perhaps not all there in the head, but he was right there in front of her, available for an experiment. Lubov took a step toward him and trusted her future to a dead poet.

"'At a terrifying height a wandering fire, / But is this how a star glimmers, flying?'" she began.

"Petropolis," mumbled Victor, as if replying to a password. "My father had the first edition of *Tristia*. He said he hid it in the kitchen cabinet all through the thirties."

Lubov Alexandrovna liked to remember that at that very moment the clock on the District Soviet had struck twelve times, although she couldn't be certain if that really happened. But what did it matter? The past was pliable. Often, the past was the only thing she could control.

"I have to go," she told Victor.

"Please don't leave," he cried, gripping her forearm with both of his bandaged hands, his arms bent awkwardly at the elbows.

Lubov Alexandrovna remembered looking into his darting, wet eyes and feeling like a snake about to swallow a mouse.

"I'll be back tomorrow," she'd said. "I'll bring you something to read."

The following week Victor Goldberg was discharged. The volumes of Maupassant and the Hermitage folio, each bookmarked with fifty rubles, had gone to a hospital psychiatrist, and Victor no longer had to return to the army. Lubov had invited him to stay with her until he got better. She hired a car to bring Baba Zhenia and Victor to Third Road Street. She remembered sitting in the front, cross-legged and victorious, while the old lady and the young man shared the back seat in awkward silence.

Mrs. Goldberg carried her breakfast plate back to the kitchen, turned on the light in the corridor, and began to quietly untangle her coat from the mess of the neighbors' clothes. She decided not to wake Sasha, let her oversleep. The child needed to learn *to take responsibility for her actions.*

"Mom!" the door to the Goldbergs' room opened with a screech, and Sasha stuck her disheveled head into the opening. "What time is it? The clock's broken!"

"We'll talk tonight, Alexandra," Mrs. Goldberg said icily, picking up her purse.

"Oh, go to the devil!" spat Sasha. "Do you *practice* looking at me like this, or does it come naturally?"

Lubov Alexandrovna slowly raised her eyebrows. Sasha shot her a disgusted look and disappeared into the room. Mrs. Goldberg checked for her keys and wallet, unlocked the door, and left the apartment.

Getting on the bus, she noted with some surprise that Sasha did manage to make her angry. She briefly imagined washing her hands of her daughter. Let her break her own firewood; learn from her own mistakes. After all, no one could be stopped. Baba Zhenia had tried.

"All I'm telling you, Luba, is to be careful," she'd said the night Victor came to stay with them. "This boy is just surviving. He'll latch on to anyone who feeds him and doesn't abuse him. Luba, do you think he loves you?"

"Babulya, he read *Tristia,* and that's—"

"Luba, he's eighteen! Just a child, an orphanage child. I know orphanage children. Damaged, Luba, is the word. Broken. Eighteen and a suicide! He'll write his own *Tristia* for you to get out of whatever hell you've just rescued him from. And then he'll turn around and find a better place to go and forget all about you. You mark my words, Lubochka."

Lubov and Victor celebrated their honeymoon by not speaking to Baba Zhenia for a week. Victor didn't seem to want to talk to anyone then, and Lubov wanted to punish her grandmother for her arrogance. Baba Zhenia had been lucky to remember a time when one could do things in proper order and with dignity. In 1976, in Asbestos 2, Lubov Nechaeva had no such luxury, so she made do with what she had. In the end, everything turned out the way Baba Zhenia had predicted. Victor had received a surprise letter from an American researcher, one thing led to another, and a few months later he was gone. All Lubov could do was eradicate his traces; mop up the eleven years they'd spent together and get on. The neighbors nodded their heads, as if they'd known all along what was going to happen. In Asbestos 2, men didn't last. By middle age, most succumbed to vodka, disease, divorce, or industrial accidents. Sasha was the only person surprised by her father's impermanence.

Mrs. Goldberg got off the bus and walked to the library. Unlocking the front entrance, she surveyed the surrounding landscape: a lonely excavator moved back and forth in a field of mud; a row of leafless saplings lined the horizon. In Osip Mandelstam's view, Asbestos 2 would be a postapocalyptic place. It grew out of the demise of civilization he mourned in his poems. The regime that killed the poet and millions of others, and nearly killed Baba Zhenia, went on to build this ugly little town with a miserable name.

The poem that she'd read to Victor by the hospital wall was about Petrograd during the Revolution, the death of a great city. Lubov Alexandrovna still remembered it by heart:

> At a terrifying height a wandering fire,
> But is this how a star glimmers, flying?
> Transparent star, a wandering fire,
> Your brother, Petropolis, is dying.

> At a terrifying height earthly dreams burn,
> The green star is glimmering.
> O, if you are a star, a brother to water and sky,
> Your brother, Petropolis, is dying.

> A monstrous ship at a terrifying height
> Is rushing ahead, spreading its wings—
> Green star, in splendid poverty
> Your brother, Petropolis, is dying.

> Above the black Neva transparent spring
> Has broken. The wax of immortality is melting.
> O, if you are a star, Petropolis, your city,
> Your brother, Petropolis, is dying.

Mrs. Goldberg had visited Leningrad, now once again named St. Petersburg, and knew that it hadn't entirely died. At least its bones were still there. One could imagine members of the intelligentsia surviving behind the unwashed windowpanes of Leningrad's historic facades. But they were there, and she, Lubov Alexandrovna Goldberg, by the power of her residence permit, dwelled in Asbestos 2. Could anyone blame her for wanting to stay, as much as possible, at a terrifying height, in unattainable Petropolis?

She'd hoped, just a little, that Victor might get her there. That they would create a life apart and above the realm of mud and vodka. By having a child with Victor, Lubov Alexandrovna made sure that her daughter would be instantly different from the lowlifes. But was the difference skin-deep?

Mrs. Goldberg heard children's voices downstairs and got up to meet a school group. Waiting for the teachers to shush the children, she worried about Sasha again. What was the girl doing at the party last night? Lubov Alexandrovna imagined the fat fool on some lowlife's leopard-spotted sofa, listening to the awful "Alain Delon" pop song that was everywhere these days.

Mrs. Goldberg checked her reflection in a glass door and walked down the stairs to the lobby. The children fell silent.

"Who can tell me the rules of the library?" Mrs. Goldberg asked.

Several hands went up. Mrs. Goldberg pointed at a blond boy in the front row and rubbed her temples, trying to stop the throbbing melody of *Alain Delon doesn't drink eau-de-cologne* from reverberating inside her brain. Something needed to be done to keep Sasha from sinking in the proletarian soup of Asbestos 2.

7

Belomor

"WAR AND PEACE: THE OLD OAK AS A SYMBOL OF REBIRTH."

"War and Peace: Natasha Rostova as a Symbol of Life."

"War and Peace: The Peasants as . . ."

The Russian literature teacher sighed and squatted to pick up a piece of chalk, exposing the varicose veins between her nylon knee-highs and the black wool pinafore she'd worn since before any of her students were born. Rema Nikolaevna was as old as her name, an acronym for Revolutionary Electrification of the World. It was rumored that she had a sister named Turbine. There was nothing revolutionary or electric about Rema; like most literature teachers, she was the embodiment of ennui. Today, she had a new blouse. Unlike all of her other, urine-colored blouses, this one was blue. Sasha Goldberg put her head down on her desk and wondered what it meant.

A large clock above the board said 11:38. For what seemed like an hour, Sasha had been waiting for one minute to pass. She looked sideways at her deskmate. Yura was one of only five boys in a class of thirty, and the other girls considered it unfair that Fatberg was sharing a desk with him. Sasha felt a thin affinity with Yura, who was good at math and nonabusive, but she didn't care for boys her own age. Most of them were a head shorter than she—puffy, creamy babies. The ones who were as tall as Sasha had zits and greasy hair and collected something stupid, like bottle caps or naked-lady key chains.

Sasha Goldberg wanted a man. She had read Hemingway, and she knew what to look for. Closing her eyes, she allowed herself a glimpse of Alexey's body on the cot, then glanced at Yura again. She would let him choose the essay topic. Yura picked up the pen with his freckly, ink-splattered fingers and began to write. So the Oak it would be.

"Riding through the countryside, Prince Andrey noticed a dead oak tree," wrote Sasha, thinking of Alexey again. She'd never been in love with anyone real before. Most of her previous lovers fit between the pages of a book. She was in love with D'Artagnan in fourth grade and in fifth with Mr. Rochester from *Jane Eyre*. She had admired the profile of F. Scott Fitzgerald on the title page of *The Great Gatsby* and stole two slick-haired black-and-white faces from the Stepanovs' movie star postcard collection. Alexey Kotelnikov presented special challenges, since he was actually there, moving around in the real world, accessible by public transportation. If only she were brave.

Glancing at Yura's paper, Sasha wrote quickly and sloppily. She resented the old oak. She was annoyed with Prince Andrey for sticking his small bony hand through two hundred years and pinning Sasha down to her plywood chair alongside other prisoners of Russian literature. Grudgingly, Prince Andrey got down to his rebirth business, the old oak grew leaves, and the bell rang, at last. Sasha Goldberg slapped her essay on Rema's desk, dropped the books into her bag, and ran out of the classroom.

"Easy, Hippo!" someone yelled after her, but Sasha didn't slow down. Weighed down by the two cans of paint she'd taken from the EMP room, she ran as fast as she could down the stairs. The echo of her heavy steps felt like repeated slaps in the face. She couldn't remain another second in this building.

It was too early to go to AFTER EATIN. The basement was probably still padlocked, and Bedbug was still at home sipping pickle juice. Sasha Goldberg walked fast, pretending she didn't know where she was going.

An hour later she was walking through the dump toward the barrels. In gray daylight, the place looked less frightening, but uglier. Sasha noticed that the original forest had burned down here. The new growth consisted of anemic, twiggy birches and large patches of underbrush. Here and there, a tall, charred tree was still standing.

The wind picked up, and Sasha smelled rotten potatoes, burned tires, and wet paper. It was a domestic smell, magnified, no different than the smell of her own building's garbage. It reminded Sasha of her mother, the eternal

Cinderella, pulling the handle of the garbage chute with one crooked pinky. Sasha thought about turning back.

"Hi!" Alexey said, rounding a thicket of raspberry bushes. "Looking for Katia?"

"No," Sasha replied, startled.

"Well? Are you looking for me?"

Sasha Goldberg's entire blood supply collected at her hairline.

"Uh. I was just going. Back."

"I'm going to work. You taking a bus?"

They walked together in silence. At times, Sasha had to run to catch up with Alexey. *Like a fat snail,* she thought with disgust, sweating inside her coat. At the bus stop, Alexey finally turned around.

"You smoke?"

"No," said Sasha, and immediately regretted it.

Alexey shrugged and lit a Belomor.

"Want to sit down?" he asked, pointing at an aboveground gas pipe by the ditch.

Sasha gestured weakly toward the sign on the pipe. DO NOT SIT ON PIPE NO SMOKING! Alexey sat down on the pipe and stretched his legs. He had a cold sore on his lower lip, and when he touched it with his tongue, Sasha Goldberg forgot to breathe.

"Why try to control everything?" Alexey asked, smiling.

Sasha noticed his blue-gray eyes, his high cheekbones. There was a patch of dark stubble on his chin. Instead of a coat, he wore a wool army shirt with the epaulets torn off. Sasha felt weightless and light-headed, a metal shaving next to a huge magnet.

"Maybe I'll have a cigarette, too," she said.

Alexey took a pack of Marlboros out of his front pocket.

"These are for girls. Girls like filtered smokes."

Was this a test?

"Actually, I like Belomor better," Sasha said.

She inhaled too fast and gagged on the bitter smoke. She tried not to look at Alexey in case he was laughing, but he wasn't. He took the cigarette out of Sasha's lips and stomped it into the mud, and when Sasha caught her breath he was looking at her again, with his steady, empty eyes.

"You like me?" he asked.

Sasha didn't think this would be so easy.

"You have . . . interesting hair," Alexey said, taking one of Sasha's ringlets and winding it around his index finger. Sasha bent her head toward his hand until his wrist touched her cheek. With his free hand, Alexey unhooked the collar of Sasha's coat and unbuttoned her shirt. The precision of his movements scared Sasha Goldberg. She didn't mean *this*. Prince Andrey never unbuttoned anybody's anything. They stood facing each other. Sasha smelled the wool of Alexey's shirt, last night's vodka in his breath, and grasped her collar closed.

"You can kiss me," she said gravely, keeping her eyes on his mud-splattered tar boots.

Alexey lifted her face and kissed her carefully on the mouth. His lips were cool, and his stubble hurt Sasha's cheek. Sasha kept her mouth closed, her eyes wide open.

They missed the bus and returned to the dump.

In the junkyard, they sat, facing each other, inside a giant tire, barely speaking. Sasha had an idea of what lovers were supposed to say. She wanted to talk about having been lonely, about her unhappiness until now, but every time she opened her mouth, Alexey tossed a thistle at her. The thistles hung in Sasha's hair, caught on the fur of her coat.

"You look like a forest witch," said Alexey.

"A witch of the junkyard," retorted Sasha, giving up the idea of a meaningful conversation. Alexey smiled and ran his finger along the edge of her lips.

"I have to be at the EATIN in an hour," Sasha said.

"I'll walk you."

Back at the bus stop, Sasha Goldberg sat down on the DO NOT SIT pipe, letting Alexey pick thistles out of her hair. When the last one was out, they kissed again. This time Sasha opened her mouth, slightly. Their teeth clashed, and Alexey laughed.

"Will you draw me?" Sasha asked.

"Come back, and I will."

"I love you."

Alexey stopped laughing. The bus rolled by, the driver not noticing them. They jumped off the pipe and ran after it, waving their arms. The bus screeched to a stop, and Sasha climbed aboard.

"Didn't you have to go to work?" she yelled out the window.

"Work? Eh, maybe tomorrow." Alexey shrugged, waving the driver on.

At AFTER EATIN, Sasha took the paint cans out of her bag and waited for Bedbug to notice. She had burnt ochre, white, and cobalt. She was sure that even in his most sour mood, Bedbug wouldn't be able to hide his appreciation.

"Where did these come from?" Katia asked.

"I'm the director of propaganda at school," said Sasha, peeling red latex film off her skin. "Damn." The dried paint was pulling all the hair out of her forearm.

"At my school, they make us work in the cafeteria," Katia noted glumly.

"I get to paint instead of going to class," bragged Sasha. "After I did the May Day banners, they wanted Donald Duck in the second-grade recess area. Then Physichka asked me to paint Isaac Newton on her wall."

"His wig must be a headache."

"My favorite part is the apple tree he's sitting under. All those leaves, all those apples! It's a month's worth of work, during which I get to skip physics. An apple fell on his head, and he discovered something, remember?"

"Gravity, idiot." Katia tapped herself on the forehead with the end of her pencil.

Sasha smiled, searching Katia's face for her brother's features. Who cared about gravity? Gravity had always been there. More important things had happened to Sasha Goldberg in the last two weeks. It seemed that she and the population of Asbestos 2 Secondary School Number 13 had finally achieved a détente. Now that Sasha was mostly left alone, her years of fear suddenly seemed indistinct and remote, like infancy. Sasha could find no explanation for this, other than that she was a different person now. The fact that she'd kissed a man was certain proof of her metamorphosis.

She sat down at her easel and glanced at Picasso's foot on the wall. At the time of the foot, the artist had been fourteen, exactly her age, but Sasha didn't feel discouraged. She knew that she faced obstacles unimaginable to Picasso. She'd never painted with oil. The students at AFTER EATIN used cheap children's watercolors, mixing in white wall paint to make them opaque. They painted with scratchy plastic brushes on stained butcher paper that their parents brought home wrapped around salted herring. But these were just challenges to be overcome, and Sasha Goldberg had plenty of time.

She sat on a lopsided wooden stool, contemplating the eternity in front of her, feeling a species apart from her mother, from Bedbug, from Rema, from Picasso. She was a winner by birthright. Picasso, foot or no foot, was dead, and Asbestos 2 adults, with their greasy suits, mended socks, and varicose veins, were rushing to join him in the grave.

Sasha Goldberg was not going to repeat their mistake. She sat at the beginning of a straight road to happiness never previously achieved by anyone—the kind of happiness Sasha didn't bother to imagine in detail but knew would be hers.

"I have to show you to Alufiev."

"Who's that?"

"You'll see."

Alufiev lived in barrel number six. He was tall and pear-shaped and smelled of turpentine. His blueberry eyes looked lost in the thick lenses of his glasses.

"Good girl," said Alufiev, closing the door behind Sasha and Alexey. "Very nice girl! Come visit old Alufiev!"

Save for a dirty cot in the corner, Alufiev had no furniture in his barrel. Icons in various stages of completion lay on the floor and lined the walls. Alexey plopped on the cot, pulling Sasha down with him. Alufiev muttered something and shuffled out the door.

"Alufiev, he's world-famous," said Alexey.

Alufiev shipped his icons to a vendor in Moscow who sold them to foreign tourists on Sparrow Hills Observation Deck. Alexey explained that after painting the icons, Alufiev worked their surfaces with steel wool and a hot iron to make them appear authentic. Sasha hardly listened. All she could focus on was Alexey's hand, which was now firmly on her waist.

"What does he do with the money?" she asked distractedly, wishing she wasn't wearing her thick coat.

"Stuffs it in his pants. Literally." Alexey tapped himself on the forehead. "He went nuts after his wife died. He doesn't have a fat ass. It's all cash, compressed in there. Ask him, he'll tell you."

"He tells everyone? Won't he get robbed?"

"Nah. Who's going to rob him—me? He loans me money whenever I ask. Besides, he's been like this since the eighties. I reckon his ass is full of worthless rubles."

Alufiev returned with an aluminum flask, three chipped enamel mugs, and a loaf of black bread.

"Now, boys and girls!" he said, rubbing his large hands together. He smiled at the flask and expertly poured even amounts of vodka into each mug. "Za zdorovye!"

"Za zdorovye!" replied Sasha, downing the shot in one desperate gulp.

Alexey drank his too, let go of Sasha, and sniffed his sleeve for a chaser. A yard drunk, thought Sasha. It wasn't too late to leave. By the time she got home, the buzz would wear off, and the smell would disappear. Alexey would never find her. Most likely, he would be too lazy to look. He was exactly the type of man her mother taught her to despise and fear. She pictured him sleeping under a bench, smelling like sour bread. And here she was, Sasha Goldberg, a fat, gullible idiot, sitting on a nasty cot drinking vodka with a couple of bums. Grown men. Sasha started to get up.

"What's the matter?" asked Alexey. There was a watery, demented happiness in his eyes, the kind of look Baba Zhenia used to get shortly before she died. Sasha couldn't walk away from the beauty of his face.

"Nothing," she said. "I'm just hot." She took off her coat and sat back down. Alufiev poured another round and muttered about having to dig up his saints.

"He buried some last year, to see how they age," said Alexey.

"Don't burn the house down, detochki." Alufiev stumbled out the door, leaving Sasha and Alexey alone with a dozen narrow Byzantine eyes.

Alexey latched the door behind Alufiev and sat back on the cot.

"Aren't you going to EATIN today?"

Sasha shook her head no. She appreciated what he was doing, giving her an escape route. Alexey shrugged and took her hand.

"Katiusha," he said, "will tear my head off."

Sasha laughed.

"Did she warn you about me?"

"Yeah. She said you can tell time by looking at the stars."

"Aw. How romantic!" Alexey's sarcastic voice was squeakier than his regular voice, and Sasha Goldberg didn't like it. He took her wrist and lay back on the cot, pulling her on top, and she felt his heartbeat through the fabric of their clothes, which alone was enough to send her own heart flying through the roof of the barrel, to the top of the power lines. She would've been content to lie like that forever, but Alexey gently pushed her up.

"Okay?" he whispered, and Sasha nodded, not knowing what he meant. He unbuttoned her blouse and pulled down her bra. Her breasts rolled out on either side, cold and smooth like lumps of cookie batter. Sasha instinctively hugged herself, covering them up.

"What's wrong?" Alexey's voice was suddenly hoarse and gravely serious.

Sasha was surprised at how close her excitement was to fear. She continued to hold herself until Alexey reached over, got her blouse, and covered her up.

"It's okay," he said, hugging her. Sasha heard disappointment in his voice, and it hurt her pride because she knew it was disappointment Alexey tried, but failed, to hide.

"Turn around," she said. "Don't look."

She took off all of her clothes and folded them by the foot of the cot, making sure to hide her ugly garter belt inside the skirt. The cool chemical air of Alufiev's barrel felt nice on her skin. Nobody, except her own parents, had ever seen her naked. She took a step back, stood up straight, and sucked in her stomach.

"Look now."

Alexey turned around and smiled.

"Don't be scared," he said. "Want a blanket?"

"No," said Sasha. The prospect of using Alufiev's blanket seemed worse than just standing there naked.

Alexey undressed in a hurry, took a step toward Sasha, and stopped, noticing the look on her face.

"You've never seen a naked man before, have you?" He laughed, raising his arms. "Go ahead, stare!"

Sasha Goldberg couldn't reconcile Alexey with the bizarre animal thing protruding from the middle of his body. It was moving, shrinking away from Sasha's shocked gaze.

"Close your eyes," Alexey said, "and keep them closed."

Sasha Goldberg squeezed her eyes shut and waited for pain.

Afterward, they lay side by side and smoked, like lovers in a French movie. Sasha felt accomplished: she had done it with a man, and now she was managing okay with a cigarette. The kerosene lamp cast a deep, warm glow on concrete walls, and Alufiev's saints were now dark, faceless silhouettes. The only reliable icon of childhood, the Mickey Mouse on Sasha's coat, lay crumpled in the corner, silenced by two centimeters of brown fake fur.

She must have fallen asleep, because the next time she saw Alexey, he was kneeling in front of her, fully dressed, touching her on the shoulder.

"What?"

"Get up, it's late. You've got to go home."

Sasha yawned. "Now?"

"Now. Come on, get up. You don't want to get in trouble."

Coward, thought Sasha. After what they'd just done, what did it matter if she got home on time? Sasha dressed slowly, gazing at Alexey with heavy-lidded eyes. But he busied himself with Alufiev's junk and never once looked up. On the way back, he held Sasha firmly above the wrist.

"Are you mad?" asked Sasha when they got to the bus stop.

"No," Alexey said. "I'm just thinking, maybe . . ."

"Can I come tomorrow?"

"I don't know."

"What did I do wrong?"

"Nothing. It's just, you're . . . How old are you?"

Sasha was terribly offended.

"Why do you ask how old I am when I love you?"

Alexey shook his head. Sasha pressed her face to his chest and stayed there until the bus rattled up the hill.

Under the buzzing fluorescent tubes, everything looked crisp and resolved. The strands of wet fur reclaimed their shapes on Sasha's sleeves, the knitted pattern returned to her knees. It hurt to sit. Sasha decimated the fingernails of her left hand, then her right hand, and sucked on the bloody nubs.

She was still Sasha Goldberg, Sashenka. Escaped, unscathed. She was relieved to be making curfew, happy to be sitting in a brightly lit bus on the way to civilization, to be leaving behind the moist thicket, the dump, the barrels, Alexey's sex, and Alufiev's refugee eyes. She would never go there again.

The following afternoon Sasha Goldberg, wearing her mother's red lipstick, stood at the edge of the dump and watched Alexey tinker with a generator outside number two. She told herself that she would only watch and not come near, but when the dog noticed her and growled, she didn't hide.

"Hello again," said Alexey, walking up the hill.

"Hi."

"Come on." He led her to the rusty flatbed truck in the junkyard.

"Do you love me?" asked Sasha.

"Yes," he said, sitting down. The truck was the color of dry blood. "Here, take this."

"What are these?" asked Sasha, accepting a pack of pills. There were four rows of them, seven in each row. The top row was half empty. Above, days of the week were marked in English. Poison, thought Sasha Goldberg. He would drug her and rape her and kill her.

"They are . . . so you won't get pregnant."

"How do you know this works?"

"I don't know."

"What do you know?"

Alexey smiled, as if Sasha had just said the funniest thing.

"Nothing. I don't know anything. I know my name." He seemed very happy to admit it, as if it were a philosophical stance. *Nihilist*, thought Sasha. Thanks to Turgenev, she had always imagined nihilists smoking pipes and wearing linen coats. Pipeless and dressed in a dirty white undershirt, Alexey wasn't quaint enough to be a nihilist. *Animal,* thought Sasha.

"How many do I take?" she asked.

"I dunno. Take two. Just to be sure."

Since the days of the week marked on the package seemed somehow significant, Sasha swallowed two pills lined up under "Friday," pulled off her sweater, and lay back on the warm, velvety rust. When Alexey was inside her, she opened her eyes and watched the changes in his face, the look of amazement in the tight skin underneath his eyebrows, and his empty eyes, unfocused and unseeing.

8

Managers and Prostitutes

MAY 25, THE LAST DAY OF THE SCHOOL YEAR, WAS ALSO THE
last day at the Art Studio. Bedbug had asked his students to come early to
help clean. When Sasha arrived at AFTER EATIN, he was already in the classroom, wrapping a tub of clay in layers of cellophane patched with electrical
tape. A boy and two girls squatted on the floor with razor blades, scraping
paint drips off the linoleum.

"Walls, Goldberg," Bedbug said, pointing at the drawings and reproduc-
tions that he'd tacked up over the year. "I want to take those down in case the
place floods."

Sasha pulled the tacks out of the wall and lay Picasso's foot on the table.
"Boris Petrovich," she asked mockingly, "do I have the right to attempt abstraction now?"

"No," deadpanned Bedbug. "When you're done with the walls, go outside and clean the storm drain. *Umnaya!*"

Clever, indeed. Lifting the metal grate that covered the drain, Sasha
wished she hadn't mocked Bedbug. The drain stank. Sasha held her breath,
plunged both of her hands up to her wrists into the muck, and scooped out the
rotten leaves. Something soft was stuck in the pipe at the bottom of the grate.
Sasha grabbed it and yanked, realizing too late that she was pulling on a dead
pigeon. For a second, she held the bird's head in her hand and stared.

"Sasha!"

Sasha dropped the head.

"Katia, *privet*. I have to wash my hands," she said haltingly, and ran inside.

Rinsing her hands in the Art Studio's filthy bathroom, Sasha Goldberg realized that she dreaded talking to Katia. She didn't have words for what she did with Alexey. Sasha lifted her palms to her face. Her skin still stank like the drain. She took out her pocketknife and began to clean under her fingernails.

"Boris Petrovich!" Evgeny Mikhailovich's voice boomed outside the bathroom door. "Are we ready to unplug?"

Bedbug yelled something from the classroom.

"Katinka," said Evgeny Mikhailovich, "come help me move the lights."

Sasha waited for their voices to disappear, washed her hands with soap, and opened the door. She was hoping to sneak outside, but Evgeny Mikhailovich and Katia were in the front room. Sasha leaned against the corridor wall, unsure of what to do.

Evgeny Mikhailovich sat on the sofa, wrapping cords around hoods of clip-on lamps. Katia stood on a chair and stacked the lights on the shelf. They worked silently for a while, and then Katia said something that made Evgeny Mikhailovich look up.

"You can't be serious!" he said. "Think about your future!"

Katia shook her head.

"You, of all my students! Just another common idiot!" bellowed Evgeny Mikhailovich.

"Evgeny Mikhailovich, if you don't stop yelling at me, I will leave, and you can climb up here yourself and stack these lights," Katia said calmly.

"Go, who's stopping you?" spat Evgeny Mikhailovich, turning beet-red.

Katia got off the chair and picked up her sweater.

"Wait!" yelled Evgeny Mikhailovich.

Ignoring him, Katia tied the sweater around her waist and walked out the door.

Evgeny Mikhailovich picked up a dead lightbulb from the sofa and hurled it to the ground.

"What's going on?" Bedbug stuck his head out of the classroom.

Sasha shrugged.

"Kotelnikova is moving to Prostuda to become a prostitute!" squealed Evgeny Mikhailovich.

"Goldberg, go sweep up that glass," ordered Bedbug.

Sasha grabbed the broom from the closet and walked to the front room, feeling like the sacrificial animal she was.

"You!" screamed Evgeny Mikhailovich. "Another future prostitute! All they want to be these days are managers and prostitutes. Prostitutes and managers. What happened to artists? Goldberg! Do you want to be a manager or a prostitute?"

Sasha began to sweep the floor, trying not to miss shards of glass among the tangles of extension cords. A pencil rolled out from under the shelf, and she picked it up.

"What the hell *is* a manager?" huffed Evgeny Mikhailovich. "At least I know what prostitutes do. . . ."

"You know what, Goldberg?" interrupted Bedbug, reaching for a bottle of vodka on the shelf. "Go home."

"Really?"

Bedbug nodded.

"Go home, everybody!" he yelled toward the classroom. "Come back in September. And don't forget your drawings!"

Walking out of the basement behind the others, Sasha felt like crying. Even though the scene was nothing out of the ordinary, and even though she'd known that Katia would be leaving, suddenly Sasha felt certain that when she returned in September, AFTER EATIN wouldn't be the same.

"Evgeny Mikhailovich," Bedbug admonished behind Sasha's back, "these are children. You'll have parents in here complaining."

"And I'll send them to the devil's grandma! They're raising prostitutes!" squealed Evgeny Mikhailovich.

Sasha paused on the stairs, feeling light-headed. It seemed wrong to simply leave and not come back for three months. The drain cover stood up against the wall where she'd left it, and Sasha decided to put it back. Pulling on the slimy rusted grate, she glanced down at the dead pigeon and threw up. It felt good to puke because it was an excuse to cry. Crying and puking at the same time felt doubly good. Bedbug poked his head out of the basement, then reappeared with a glass of water. Sasha wiped her mouth on her sleeve and drank. She would have liked to keep crying, but her tears dried under

Bedbug's concerned stare, and moments later she couldn't remember what had made her cry in the first place.

"You're a good girl, Goldberg," said Bedbug, awkwardly patting her on the shoulder. "Unfortunately, everything is falling apart."

Sasha didn't feel well for the rest of the week. Finally, the following Sunday, she dragged herself out of the house and went to see Alexey. It was suddenly hot. The humid air felt heavy and still, and once Sasha was away from the road, she could hear the constant buzz of mosquitoes competing with the noise of the power lines. She found Alexey sitting on Alufiev's stoop, whittling a tree root. He was making a woman.

"I missed you," he said when Sasha joined him. "Anything happen?"

Sasha was pleasantly surprised that he noted her week-long absence. "I was sick," she said.

"Katia asked about you. She went away, you know. She said you should come visit her in Prostuda."

"Where is she living?"

"She said she'd be sharing an apartment with other girls from her school. I have the address."

Sasha watched Alexey work. The root woman had a swirling mermaid tail, and was naked on top. Lanky and long-haired, she seemed to be Sasha's opposite in every way. Sasha realized that she lacked the lines and shapes that would lend themselves to being whittled out of a root. Still, the sculpture made her inexplicably angry.

"The *school?*" she asked glumly.

"Yes, Elita."

"People go to Elita to become prostitutes."

"Yeah, I know it happens. But my sister is beautiful. She's going to be a model."

With a few deft moves of the knife, the root woman received a face: a straight roman nose, thin lips, and narrow eye slits.

"How do *you* know?" Sasha thought she'd asked a rhetorical question, but Alexey had an answer.

"Mama worried about her, so she went to a clairvoyant."

Sasha Goldberg stared. More than anything, she wished for this to be a joke.

"What kind of a clairvoyant?"

"There's a woman in town that reads tea leaves."

Sasha laughed.

"She's been accurate in the past," Alexey explained patiently.

"Alexey, you're not *serious*," Sasha began, and then stopped, feeling exhausted. If her words were rocks, she was throwing them down a bottomless well. Still, she had to try.

"What do some woman's tea leaves have to do with Katia?" she began slowly. "You understand that this is superstition. It's crazy, Alexey."

"You never know," Alexey said thoughtfully, admiring his sculpture.

"But how are these things *connected?*"

Alexey shrugged. Looking into his eyes, Sasha felt as if she were staring into a dual abyss of ancient stillness, where everything was connected: tea leaves and prostitutes, sex and clogged drains, Bedbug's rotten teeth and dead pigeons. It was a place where everything had already fallen apart and then reconstituted into new shapes, fantastic and useless chimeras.

Sasha shook her head, feeling nauseated again. Alexey tossed the sculpture under a tree, leaned over, and kissed her on the mouth.

At home that afternoon, Sasha pulled her drawings and paintings from the top of the armoire and spread them on the floor. She had no idea if any of them were good, although she recognized the clearly terrible ones.

"Mama, do you think I have a chance of getting into the Repin Lyceum for tenth grade?" she asked when Mrs. Goldberg came home from work that night.

"I'm sure of it, Sasha!" Mrs. Goldberg declared. "I'll do what I can."

Sasha wondered what her mother could do besides paying for postage to send her work to Moscow. Still, Mrs. Goldberg's irrational striving was a nice antidote to Alexey's fatalism. *Tea fucking leaves!* Even as a young child, Sasha had no patience for magic. At one point, her intolerance for proper fairy tales limited her reading choices to saccharine accounts of Lenin's boyhood and blood-soaked children's war stories. At least the author of *Hand Grenade in a*

Fur Hat didn't require his readers to put up with talking pikes, kissing frogs, golden eggs, and other arbitrary and ineffective means of salvation. Clairvoyants worked for the truly stupid and truly trapped, and Sasha guessed that Alexey was the latter. But what if he was both? Sasha Goldberg couldn't allow herself to think like that.

Mrs. Goldberg circled the room, picking things up and setting them down again. She looked as if she were about to break into song.

"I worried about you so much, *detka!*" she said excitedly, taking Sasha's head in her hands and kissing her on the forehead.

"Enough, Mama," ordered Sasha. She felt transparent and foolish. When she was little, her mother liked to peer into her eyes at bedtime, checking for lies. *I can read them,* she used to say. Sasha remembered the feeling of Mrs. Goldberg's cold palms squishing her cheeks. What did her mother know now?

After Mrs. Goldberg went to the kitchen to make dinner, Sasha made two separate piles: one of paintings, another of drawings. The paintings were all right, she decided. The fluid medium took the edge off her heavy hand. But the dark, murky drawings looked like mini-battlefields. Each bore the evidence of a technical struggle: here, the aftermath of a skirmish between Sasha Goldberg and three-point perspective; there the bloody gore she'd made of Theseus's nose; the white drape she'd killed with excessive shading. Sasha squinted, hoping that this carnage would be invisible to strangers' eyes.

9

Subject Matter for Future Paintings

ALL SUMMER, THE SUN HUNG IN THE SKY UNTIL ELEVEN EACH night, repaying its winter debt to the town. The mud paths dried and cracked. A warm wind played with cheesecloth curtains in open windows, and the Goldbergs' apartment buzzed with flies. On the days when the landfill smell became intolerable, Alexey borrowed Alufiev's bicycle for Sasha, and they rode away from the dump to a cleaner forest nearby. Barely speaking to each other, they fit together like a pair of unborn twins, effortlessly and irreversibly, which seemed to be enough for Alexey. But the stasis of the summer made Sasha restless. The days ran into each other, leaving her mind crowded with questions. By the end of the summer, she wanted to know if Alexey had other girls, if he would ever return to school, whether he would go to Moscow with her if she got into Repin. He always gave the same answer, "I don't know." Sasha suspected he was being honest but wished he'd try harder.

"So," she said, "what do you like about me?"

"Everything," said Alexey after some consideration.

"Like what?"

"Um, your face, your hair, your eyes, your lips, your collarbone, your elbows, the vertebrae in your spine, your fingers, your breasts, your stomach . . ." Alexey swallowed and pulled Sasha closer. "Should I keep going?"

"Shut up!"

"I'm serious."

"Do you think I'm beautiful?"

The pause hurt.

"Yes." Alexey finally said. "I know you like those words, but I don't. They don't mean much. A view is beautiful, a flower is beautiful, a girl is beautiful. I love my life, I love my country, I love my girlfriend. Yeah. Does it make you happy?"

"So you'd do anything to avoid cliché, even if it means not saying anything to each other, just fuck like a couple of animals!"

"It's just a waste of time, saying things like that. Time is better spent fucking."

Sasha sighed, remembering her mother's almost daily monologues about the impossibility of dealing with lowlifes.

"Time! Since when is your time so precious? All you do is lounge around in the dump! You don't even go to work anymore. What do you do?"

"Today I patched the roof on Alufiev's outhouse. Want me to show you? There's plenty of work around here."

"So you quit your job to patch outhouse roofs?"

"No, I quit my job because last week two recruiters came there looking for me. I don't want to go to the army. Not now. A guy I know got sent to the Caucasus."

"They found you at work?"

"It was Mama. She told them where to find me. I haven't been staying at home since spring, but Mama thinks the army would straighten me out. Katia used to egg her on before she left. She was upset about you. Didn't like what I was doing to her little friend." Alexey's voice went up into its sarcastic, squeaky range.

Sasha Goldberg put her hand on his crotch and kept it there until he was hard, and they collided in a patch of muddy dandelions as if it were their last time together.

On Wednesday morning, Lubov Alexandrovna Goldberg painted her lips, tweezed and penciled in her eyebrows, and put on her gold earrings with teardrop rubies. The previous evening, she'd called Evgeny Mikhailovich to ask for a meeting. She'd told him she needed his advice, and he'd invited her to come by the Art Studio.

Mrs. Goldberg lingered by the armoire, finally settling on a light blue cotton dress with a round collar and a pleated skirt. She put it on and smiled at the mirror, pleased with herself. With her hair gathered in a loose bun, She thought she looked attractive yet modest, reminiscent of the women from Evgeny Mikhailovich's youth.

Walking past the aluminum fence toward AFTER EATIN, Lubov Alexandrovna worried slightly about the old man's state of mind. He hadn't recognized her on the phone and seemed to barely remember Sasha. She wouldn't put it past him to chase her away or forget about their meeting altogether. Still, Mrs. Goldberg had to try and fulfill her maternal duty. She felt encouraged by a glimpse of ambition in Sasha, by the eagerness she'd seen in the kid's normally stony, deceitful eyes. As a mother, she had to seize the moment. Her instincts suggested that the old man had to help her somehow. After all, who else could she ask?

She found Evgeny Mikhailovich in the courtyard. To her relief, he had gotten over his amnesia.

"Of course, the lovely lady!" he exclaimed, extinguishing his cigarette on a tree trunk. "Have you decided to let me paint your portrait?"

A red-haired mutt with a coiled tail bounded up the basement stairs and began to sniff Mrs. Goldberg's feet. She curled her toes uncomfortably, regretting that she wore sandals.

"*Foo*, Ryzhk!" shouted Evgeny Mikhailovich. "Looks like we'll have a puppy in here for the kids next year. Nice doggy and, most importantly, never hungry. Who knows what he eats?"

"Evgeny Mikhailovich," interrupted Mrs. Goldberg. "Sasha would like to try getting into the Repin Lyceum. Do you think she has a chance?"

"The Repin? In Moscow?" Evgeny Mikhailovich frowned. "She hasn't been here a full year. It's too early to tell."

"Sashenka really wants to be an artist," Mrs. Goldberg said quickly. "I brought her work."

"Aha." Evgeny Mikhailovich groaned reluctantly. "Would you like to come inside?

The old man appeared genuinely surprised that the lights still worked in the basement. After helping him clear a heap of drapes and dried flowers from the table, Mrs. Goldberg unrolled Sasha's drawings, and, just as she'd done last January, weighed them down with a bottle of Georgian cognac.

Evgeny Mikhailovich acknowledged the bottle and began thumbing through the drawings. The top one was of a plaster head of Athena. Mrs. Goldberg remembered how proud she'd been when Sasha first showed her the drawing. But now she could see all the things wrong with it. She could only hope that the sculptor was to blame for Athena's strangely menacing pout. The goddess appeared to be upset because her helmet sat askew on her head, threatening to fall forward. The drawing was dark and overworked. In places, Sasha had erased too much, destroying the paper and creating indelible swatches of gray muck. It looked as if, while trying to do her best, Sasha ultimately couldn't wait to *get the damn thing over with.*

"She wants to be an artist?" repeated Evgeny Mikhailovich. "You want me to be honest?"

"Perhaps you could recommend a private instructor. Over the summer . . . ," began Mrs. Goldberg. The old man shook his head. They stood in silence for a while, until finally Evgeny Mikhailovich started to laugh.

"Here is honest!" he said, taking down a stack of papers from the shelf. "Hercules! David! Some crap! Crap! Crap! Here!"

He handed Mrs. Goldberg a drawing. This other Athena looked nothing like the empty-eyed monster of Sasha's making. Whoever drew this one understood light and proportion. Mrs. Goldberg sighed.

"She wants to be an artist? Let her be an artist, then!" declared Evgeny Mikhailovich, taking more drawings down from the shelf and pressing them into Mrs. Goldberg's arms. "What are you waiting for? Take these, pick the best ones, and send them in!"

"Whose are they?"

"What's the difference? Someone who could draw but didn't want to be an artist."

"Evgeny Mikhailovich, you can't be serious."

"Take them, take them, dear. What use are they to me? Goldberg, eh? Nice girl, Goldberg. I know people in Moscow, I'll make some calls. I want to go to my grave knowing that *somebody* wanted to be an artist. Do you care for a drink?"

On August 26, Sasha Goldberg stopped at the top of the hill. Below, Alexey was talking to two men. One of the men wore a suit, another an army uniform. The man in a suit wrote something in a notepad. Alexey was naked from the waist up, his hands covered in mud. He scratched his head, looked around, and ran. From where she was standing, Sasha Goldberg silently cheered for him, but he was strangely slow, as if he didn't really want to escape or thought he couldn't. Although he was taller and thinner than the men, they caught up with him very quickly, seized him on both sides, and led him into a green van parked between the trees.

Sasha knew her way to the *voenkomat*. There was only one in Asbestos 2, a squat brick building with a fenced-in yard. Bald-headed boys, still dressed in their civilian clothes, paced the yard. Sasha wasn't the only one hanging on the outside of the fence. A girl in a denim miniskirt passed a lit cigarette to her boyfriend, while another couple was kissing through a hole in the chain-link. There were pink grooves on their faces where they pressed against the wire. Both girls wore orange lipstick, both seemed older than Sasha. *Vulgar,* said Mrs. Goldberg on the inside of Sasha's head.

Alexey was nowhere to be seen. Sasha suspected that, given a chance, they'd garble their farewell. Alexey would remain opaque and irreverent, and Sasha would be seething inside, at him and, mostly, at herself, for not loving him enough. She would say something trite because she was supposed to, and Alexey would laugh. It was better not to see him. She'd given him her address, and he'd promised to write. Aghast at her own coldheartedness, Sasha Goldberg admitted to herself that she looked forward to a paper version of Alexey.

She lingered by the fence, contemplating the diversity of ears on the boys inside the *voenkomat* yard. There were large, floppy ears and ears whose skin was tightly stretched over knots of cartilage. There were pointy ears, lobeless ears, ears with folded tops. The ears seemed pathetic to Sasha, as if their shapes predicted the boys' deaths.

After an hour in the yard, an officer led the boys to a canvas-topped truck. The girl in the miniskirt and the kissing girl huddled together, crying. Sasha thought their cries sounded fake, like the exaggerated weeping of hired mourners at an ancient funeral procession. She felt like crying, too, but for the wrong reasons, for all those sickening, pearly ears, and because the sun was a red ball about to disappear between the buildings.

She decided not to take the bus and instead walked home, taking short-cuts through unfamiliar yards and alleys. One of the buildings had a wooden swing set in front and a flower bed surrounded by penguin-shaped trash cans. Sasha thought it would be fun to live in this building. She sat down on a swing and kicked up her feet. The swing squeaked. By the time Sasha was flying high above the ground, the squeaks became unbearably loud. Sasha dug her toes in the sand and got off. She felt seasick, too old for playgrounds.

Suddenly she was moved to tears by Asbestos 2's twilight ugliness. The buildings and telephone wires were now lopsided silhouettes against the orange sky. Taking the widest possible steps, Sasha Goldberg pounded her boots into the drying mud and bade farewell to her childhood, her first love, her hometown. She could practically feel those things shedding detail, transforming into neat, convenient abstractions, as if her mind were a well-packed suitcase.

Sasha felt a pleasant nostalgia for all things past and things she hoped to leave behind. She was about to turn fifteen. If she was lucky, by next summer she would be living in Moscow, attending the Repin Lyceum. She allowed herself to pretend that her life up until now was a memory, combed through and preserved to be used as subject matter for future paintings. She would be exotic among the Muscovites.

> *A girl from Asbestos 2.*
> *Made love in a half-pipe.*
> *Among unmarked graves.*
> *Descendant of the repressed intelligentsia.*

Among unmarked graves was the line Sasha Goldberg liked best.

She imagined herself on a granite riverbank, shielding a cigarette against the wind, gazing into the distance. There would be a man in a worn leather jacket behind her, an older man, perhaps a professor. His black hair would blow in the wind.

For someone as young as you, your work is amazing.

At home, Sasha went to bed right away but couldn't fall asleep. She tried to picture Alexey lying on a bunk somewhere. The vision was generic, uninspiring. Although she'd seen him just a few hours before, she already couldn't reassemble his face from her memories of its various parts. This realization made her feel momentarily guilty, but no amount of guilt was able to keep her mind from drifting back to the imaginary Moscow riverbank. She would make paintings replete with longing: receding figures in shadowy doorways, empty rooms, rooftop views. The pictures would hint at dark secrets, and no one would need to know that Sasha didn't have any.

Sasha bounced out of bed, found her sketchbook, and walked to the kitchen. A thick envelope with her drawings inside lay on the table, ready to be mailed. Sasha frowned, thinking of just how awful those drawings were. She wondered why her mother had looked so hopeful, so upbeat. Still, it felt nice to give in to her mad determination.

Sitting down on the floor with her back against the fridge, Sasha began to sketch. The graphite in her cheap pencil was full of rocks. The rocks scratched the paper. Sasha wanted to make dark lines, but the pencil was too hard, and all she could get was a pale silvery gray. Powerful light from the bare lightbulb rendered the Stepanovs' chipped coffeepot, a dish rack, and a sink as solid as real life, an antidote to nostalgia. One of the neighbors was making cottage cheese. Clumps of curdled milk hung over the sink in a cheesecloth bundle. The regular drip, drip, drip of draining liquid interrupted Sasha's train of thought. She closed her sketchbook and went to bed, and while she slept a baby girl inside her grew translucent pink fingernails.

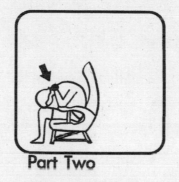

Part Two

1

ESL

"I LOVE YOU, HONEY."

"I love you, too."

For a second after Neal leaves for work, his morning smells, Aqua Velva and Listerine, linger in the white rectangle of burning air, and then the air conditioner kicks in with a loud hum and the door must be closed. Sasha turns toward the dim interior of the living room, eager for a moment of temporary blindness. All too soon, her eyes adjust to the darkness, and things present themselves: a bag of Tostitos on the kitchen counter, dark plastic wood paneling on the wall behind the TV, stucco worms on the ceiling.

Sasha picks up the TV remote and turns on *Hunter*. A woman with a perm rolls over a car, holding a gun in her outstretched hands. Later, the woman and Hunter are in bed, but they won't have sex because they're partners. When Sasha spends an entire day watching TV, she tells herself she is learning English, which is true. After nine months of watching, she can follow *A-Team* pretty easily, and *Sesame Street,* all except for the jokes.

She remembers that today is her ESL class. The day promises a pleasant succession of chores. She'll have to shower, take a bus, decipher unfamiliar voices. Not until Sasha joined Neal in Arizona did she realize what a luxury it was to simply *see* other people. She must be careful of these pleasures, though. A week ago in class, she allowed herself to look at a Mexican boy in a threadbare white T-shirt, and later that night, when Neal woke her up for sex (Neal is fond of soft, under-the-blanket, middle-of-the-night fucking) she inadvertently screamed. It was Neal's fault, really, because he woke her up with a suffocating, CPR-style kiss. Still, Sasha guessed that her classmate had gotten into her dreams and the stark contrast between her dream and the clammy reality of Neal's mouth had contributed to her reaction. She felt disappointed with herself. Up until last week, she believed she was immune to Neal's affections.

Pouring herself a bowl of Rice Krispies, she hopes that her immunity is still mostly intact.

Outside, the huge sun hangs in the sky like the homicidal white balloon from *The Prisoner*. Sasha waits for the bus in the four-inch-wide shadow of a telephone pole, half hidden from the street. In a city where no one walks, the motorists sometimes celebrate the unusual occurrence of a pedestrian by flinging objects. So far, Sasha's had an ice cube and a soda can thrown at her. Neither hit, and Sasha didn't say anything about it to Neal, afraid that he would insist she stay home during the week. Sasha knows that to Neal, her use of public transportation is an unusual and potentially dangerous hobby, a third-world anachronism he wishes she'd give up. Not that he's ever offered to teach her to drive or let her use a car.

Refrigerated air inside the bus feels like an electric shock. Blinking away the black afterimage of the sun, Sasha feeds a dollar into the fare machine. The bus is nearly empty. The other two passengers have Down's syndrome and identical pink lunch boxes marked with their names. One is pensively sticking her finger into the other's mouth. Sasha stumbles to the back of the bus and sits down.

A half hour later she walks across the parking lot to Paradise Valley Community College. The ESL class is free. The teacher, Mrs. Rugg, has bangs that explode upward from her forehead like a tidal wave and a Michael Jackson tattoo the size of a dinner plate on her back.

In the beginning of class, Mrs. Rugg writes on the board: "Why did I come to America?" followed by three choices.

a. To escape religious oppression.
b. To seek a better life.
c. To visit family.

"To seek a better life" copies Sasha, not because the answer applies, but because the other two don't apply at all. All the Mexicans choose the same. Most of them look as if they had just come from digging ditches. The Vietnamese grandma in the back ignores the question. She's there for the air conditioning.

Sasha turns around and sees a new girl behind her write, "To escape religious oppression." She's a white girl, with long brown hair and unevenly cut wavy bangs. A Russian girl?

"We have a new student today," says Mrs. Rugg when everybody is done with the exercise. "Please introduce yourself to the class."

The new girl gets up.

"My name eeez . . . ," she begins, and even before she says "Mareeena," Sasha Goldberg feels discovered, exposed, and brought back to life, all at once. She resolves not to speak to Marina. Her resolve lasts for forty-five minutes and evaporates as soon as the class is over. Chewing her pen, Sasha paces outside the classroom and waits for Marina to finish arguing with Mrs. Rugg.

Marina is trying to convince Mrs. Rugg to move her to an advanced ESL class.

"I shall come for Thursday. I'm high level," she says, inviting Mrs. Rugg to see her notebook.

Sasha smiles. *Surzday.* She hasn't heard it said this way since she left Number 13's English classroom over two years ago. Mrs. Rugg promises to test Marina for an advanced class, and the girl stomps out of the room with a satisfied look on her face.

"*Privet,*" Sasha says as she walks by.

Marina whips around, stares at her for a second, and keeps walking.

With a lopsided smile, Sasha repeats her greeting.

"Oh, you." Marina laughs. "You don't look Russian."

"Meet me: Sasha Goldberg, a real-life Russian *negritianka,*" experiments Sasha, giddy to use the dormant muscles of her tongue.

"Welcome to America!" laughs Marina. "Here you can be anything you want to be! Any type of poor immigrant, I mean. You are a poor immigrant, aren't you? Not some *Novy Russkiy* on vacation in this hell? I can't stand *Novih Russkih.*"

Sasha shakes her head. No, she isn't a *Novy Russkiy*.

Downstairs, Marina unlocks her bike from the rack and walks with Sasha to the bus stop.

"What kind of a question is that, 'Why did you come to America?'" she rages. "Who can possibly answer it? Because Donetsk sucked? Because our neighbor was a Nazi and spray-painted swastikas on our door? To taste *corn-flakes*? In search of adventure?"

"What about religious oppression?"

"I have to say that to indulge my paranoid father. He says Mrs. Rugg could be an INS informant. I'm sure if he saw you, he'd take you for an INS informant, also."

"I don't get it." Sasha smiles, savoring the sound of Marina's voice. Each Russian word feels like a break-in, a crime against her carefully maintained mental twilight. How many hours of *COPS* and *All My Children* will it take to restore it?

"My family's visa is expiring," explains Marina, apparently deeming Sasha too clueless to be an INS informant. "So we're applying for asylum. Officially, we're here to escape religious oppression. That's what's on the application. In reality, we're here to seek a better life. And to visit family. We live with my uncle Gary, who came here two years ago. I think he was the first Russian in Phoenix. He's an explorer type, like Columbus. You're Jewish, right?"

Sasha nods, wondering how she managed to last nine months without this voice, how she'll manage until the next class.

"So you know all the hoops. Or did you come here with a *status*?"

"It's different for me," says Sasha. Marina speaks of the immigration process with the fluid abandon of a pensioner discussing her blood pressure with her fellow *babushkas*. Sasha doesn't even attempt to comprehend what she's talking about. "I'm here with my fiancé," she adds.

"You're engaged to an American?"

"Yes."

"Lucky!" Marina's expression grows remote, as if she's finished with Sasha, as if Sasha *is* the American and not just engaged to one.

They see the bus at a distance, floating on a cloud of dust. More than anything, Sasha wants to miss it, but tonight Jasmine Garden has the $4.99 buffet, and Neal has made plans to go out.

"My bus," she says carefully, trying to sound casual.

"See you next time." Marina waves, biking away.

Sasha Goldberg walks past the WILL WORK FOR FOOD lady, sits down at the back of the bus, and watches Marina through a perforated decal of a newscaster's head on the window.

The white carcass of an old ice-cream truck seems to have sprouted in a garbage-strewn field of Bermuda grass. Sasha and Marina use it for shade. Through the truck's shattered windows, Sasha can see the flat rooftops and the adobe walls of Marina's apartment complex, the Palisades.

The Palisades used to be a motel. A large wooden sign, PALISADES MOTEL VACANCY, still stands near its driveway, with MOTEL VACANCY painted over. The rest of the Palisades landscaping consists of a kidney-shaped swimming pool filled with dirt, an artistically placed boulder, two palm trees, and a broken soda machine. During the monsoons, rainwater collects inside the machine, and at dusk meaty brown water bugs exit its bottom in pairs and promenade by the pool.

"Did you ever notice that those roaches can fly?" Marina asks, stretching out on the ice-cream truck's floor next to her books. "Last week, one smashed into my forehead. I ended up with a bruise!"

Marina is reading *Lolita*. She has two copies of it, one in English, one in Russian. *So determined to self-educate, even in this weather,* thinks Sasha. Under her bed at the Palisades, Marina keeps a stack of Ivy League brochures. Someday she wants to sit on a bright green lawn, surrounded by dignified architecture with turrets. Scholarship is Marina's favorite word. Sasha memorizes it by imagining a white cruise liner, with Marina waving from the deck.

Marina's face glistens with sweat, and her long hair makes swirls in the dust every time she moves. Two warped tennis rackets lean against the truck's back door. Sometimes, after their ESL class, Marina and Sasha go to the park on Tatum to play tennis, but today it's too hot again. Every morning for a week now, there's an egg on TV, frying on the sidewalk. "Hot enough to fry a dog's brain!" says the announcer, advising viewers not to lock their pets and children inside cars.

"Whoever named this place Paradise Valley," Sasha says with a yawn, "had a cruel sense of humor."

"Do you want to go inside and get a drink?" Marina asks, peeling herself off the floor. "Hopefully Zina and Ilya are gone. Lately, every conversation they have turns into a brawl. I feel like I'm living in a fucking mine field. This morning, Zina had a crying fit, and Ilya almost slapped her but reconsidered and yelled at me instead about making my bed. As if it matters in this shithole."

Sasha doesn't say anything. She thinks Marina enjoys her parents' misery too much.

Marina, her little brother Petya, and her parents live with her uncle's family, four people in each bedroom, plus a senile grandma, who sleeps on a cot by the fridge. Sasha believes there isn't anything really wrong with Marina's parents, two formerly happy people, now at the end of their ropes. Marina's uncle Gary drives an illegal cab and is rarely home during the day. Petya goes to high school, and Marina's parents clean houses for cash and argue in front of the TV in their spare time. Grandma spends her days by the window, talking to a dead palm tree outside.

"Is it time to pack?" she asks when Marina opens the apartment door. In the other room, Marina's mother and father quiet down for a second, then resume screaming at each other in theatrical whispers.

"Babushka, don't jump," Marina commands affectionately. "It's me."

The old woman eyes her with mistrust and turns her attention to a plastic crate of mismatched silverware on the table.

"Zina has a yard sale habit," explains Marina. "As Americans call it, shopping therapy. Sometimes she gets carried away, and Ilya lectures her about the mo—"

Marina's father emerges from the other room, slamming the door on the way out as if to announce that he is past the point of decorum.

Sasha plasters herself against the wall and fixes her eyes on a stain on the carpet. She knows it will only take Marina's father a minute to rediscover hospitality, to turn back into *Dydya Ilya who must bear things cheerfully.* This time, however, it takes longer. With a grim look on his face, Marina's father approaches the table and begins to rake through the contents of the silverware crate.

The metal racket brings Marina's mother out of the bedroom. Tetya Zina has the oval face and shapely hair of Chagall's Bella, but her eyes are small and round, closely set, and they lend her face a perpetual look of fear. Her nose is red from crying.

"You'll cut yourself, Iliusha," she says meekly.

"Now, what's this, I ask you?" Marina's father growls. He picks up an object made of two knobby metal rods, connected at the top with a rusted hinge. "You bought it, you tell me!"

"It was free," Marina's mother mutters. "I swear to you, they gave it to me for free."

"It's a nutcracker," explains Sasha, hoping to ease the tension in the room. "You put a nut in there and squeeze. I think it's broken, though—"

"*Nado Zhe!*" interrupts Marina's father. "A special thing to crack nuts with. *But why?* Everyone already owns a pair of pliers!"

Nobody in the room knows the answer to this question. Marina pushes a cold can of President's Choice Cola into Sasha's hands and motions toward the door. Her father slumps in his chair, twirling the limp nutcracker by one of its rods.

"*Psychushka,*" Marina says once they're outside.

Sasha pops her soda can and shrugs. These scenes notwithstanding, she secretly wishes she were Marina's sister and lived there, too. Suddenly she remembers something and looks up at Marina with alarm.

"What did your grandma mean when she asked if it was time to pack?" she asks. "Are you moving somewhere?"

"She said what? I don't even remember. Don't pay attention to Babushka. She is always moving in space and time. That's how she adapts. She's an *inner* immigrant."

"That's what I've been trying to do," Sasha says cautiously, marveling at how perfectly this describes her desired state of mind. "I want to be an inner immigrant."

She feels as if she's just divulged her biggest secret, but Marina stares at her without comprehension and starts to laugh.

"Do you want to immigrate to the mall?" she asks. "It's air-conditioned."

"No, I'd better get home," says Sasha, unexpectedly relieved at Marina's lack of understanding. "Maybe next week."

That night, Neal is in the mood. He wanders around the room naked, dimming the lights, lighting the candles. The candles have names: Vermont Spring, Cinnamon Splash, Apple Tart. Sasha pretends Neal's erection is a pink shiny nose, sniffing the scents. By the time Neal climbs on top of her, the bedroom smells like Walgreens. Sasha holds her breath and counts the slats in the mini-blinds on the bedroom window. When Neal takes a long time, she squares the number. He's never taken so long that she'd have to cube it.

"You want a matzo and peanut butter sandwich?" Marina asks.

"What's matzo?" Sasha is sitting at Marina's family's dining table, which is really a metal patio table with a hole for an umbrella in the middle. Normally it's covered with a vinyl tablecloth, but today the tablecloth is in the wash. Sasha sets her paper on a swatch of painted surface between two rust spots and reviews her ESL homework. Mrs. Rugg is fond of personal essays. This time the topic is "My Family." Sasha wonders if Mrs. Rugg brings her students' essays home and shows them to her own family for fun.

"Matzo is a big Jewish cracker," explains Marina, pointing at a stack of boxes on top of the fridge. "That's what we've been mostly eating since April. We eat everything in season. Jewish Easter is in April, and afterwards we get leftover matzos from our synagogue. And last December, after Thanksgiving, the Food Bank lady brought thirty expired pumpkin pies. You wonder why my father and Uncle Gary are so fat. They ate them all: breakfast, lunch, and dinner; pie, pie, pie."

Across the table from Sasha, Marina's grandma wakes up in her plastic lawn chair.

"Pie, pie, pie," she repeats with a smile.

"Maybe she wants a Jewish cracker," Sasha says.

"Grandma has Soviet dentures. She eats peanut butter with a spoon. Right, Babushka?"

The old woman ignores Marina, turns to the window, and begins to complain to her palm tree. She can't understand what she is doing "in this remote hamlet," when she has a perfectly good apartment in Kiev, right in the center.

"Twelve Pushkina, apartment three. Turn right at the arch. But don't forget, right at the arch, because if you turn the wrong way, you end up in this cul-de-sac and Levik, you don't want to be late."

"He'll be right on time, Babushka." Marina promises. "Right, Sasha?"

Outside, she explains that a German bomb destroyed 12 Pushkina in 1941, and nobody knows who Levik was.

"Maybe Grandma's high school boyfriend? Whoever he was, he is probably in Baby Yar, together with Great-Grandma and her seven children."

Sasha rubs her eyes and jingles the change in her pocket. What can she say to this?

"They hadn't built the gas chambers yet." Marina keeps on. "Instead, they lined people up on the edge of a pit, and shot them row by row, each row of dead Jews falling on top of the previous row of dead Jews. The earth moved for days afterwards because people were still alive."

"Right. I saw that on TV," says Sasha.

She didn't like seeing naked dead people bulldozed around, their flyaway limbs falling at impossible angles. "Come on, let's get ice cream," she prods, feeling thin-skinned and overwhelmed. "I can't spend all day here."

Sasha has heard the story before. Marina's grandma was away in college in Saratov, and when she heard what happened she didn't believe it. She was trying to find her family years after the war and refused to visit the mass grave.

Sasha and Marina walk to McDonald's, buy vanilla soft-serve cones, and sit on the thin strip of grass outside. Across the street, COURTESY CHEVRO-LET, made up of myriad lightbulbs, blinks on and off in the middle of a giant stucco arrow. Marina licks her ice cream silently, with a theatrical frown on her face, and Sasha waits for a punch line because she can tell Marina isn't finished.

"Grandma's youngest sister, Nechama—Ninochka, they called her—she was a baby, and you know what the Germans did?" Marina asks, biting into her sugar cone.

"No." Sasha shakes her head. She feels stripped of all the immunity she's built up over the past months, and it makes her angry. "Why do you go on about this stuff? Is your life so boring you need to dredge up dead babies you've never even seen? Peanut butter on matzo isn't tragic enough for you?"

"Well, it *is* my family's history," Marina insists.

"So write it down for Mrs. Rugg," Sasha says with a sneer. "I bet you'll get to read it aloud in class."

Marina looks both amused and offended, but she's on a roll. "Anyway," she continues dreamily, as if recounting a scene from a movie, "the Germans had the moms hold the babies high above their heads so that at precisely the same moment they could be killed by two separate snipers. Just picture it."

Sasha notices that her ice cream is melting and dripping all over her knees. She rubs the milky drips into her skin, picturing.

"It's like holding a bag of water," she says.

She knows something is happening to her face, because Marina is suddenly next to her, over her. Marina's soft hair brushes her cheek.

"What? What did I say?"

2

Ingres and Kupid

Dear Nadia,

I lay with an ice pack between my legs when Mama came into the room. She was carrying a small brown package and a larger white one. The white package had a face. "Meet your baby sister!" Mama said. I didn't pay much attention to you at first, just being happy the pain was over. You began to scream, and Mama carried you away. I unwrapped the brown package. There was a slab of halvah inside. I was laying on my side, gnawing on halvah, when the power went out. I didn't think much of it at first, but it stayed out overnight, and all the donors' milk in the Birthing House must have gone sour. It was barely sunrise when the nurse wheeled you into the room on a plastic tray. You were screaming.

"Feed her," the nurse said.

I pulled the blanket up to my neck and shook my head.

"I know, I know," said the nurse. "Just this once. I'll show you how. Or would you rather she starve to death?"

You took my breast right away. You were so small, but you knew what you were doing, so smart. Your hair was still stuck together with my blood. The next day, Mama got some formula at the market and said not to worry about you anymore, to get some sleep. She paid dollars to the nurses for the blue pills, and I signed some papers. It was Mama who named you Nadia.

After we brought you home Mama quit her library job and started work-

ing night shift at the asbestos mill. I went to school during the day and took care
of you at night. At first, you cried for hours on end, so much that I wanted to kill
you. Instead, I cried right along with you, from being so tired. I rocked you and
walked you around the room, but as soon as I stopped moving, you began
screaming again. Then I couldn't take it anymore. I climbed into your crib and
nursed you, and we both slept until daylight. In the morning, my whole body
was sore from being curled up in the crib, but I didn't feel crazy anymore. The
next night I brought you to my bed. I put you by the wall, so you wouldn't roll
off. You turned your head to me, with your eyes still closed, looking for milk.
That night I realized that I had no future away from you. Your feet felt like hot
silk against my skin, and your eyes were delicate upward slits, and your lower
lip turned inside out when you sucked.

All those things are now holes in my heart.

The night before I left, you had a fever. You cried and fussed. In the middle
of the night, I went to the kitchen and mixed up a bottle of warm sugar water.
You drank the water and fell asleep with your mouth wide open. Your breath
smelled like stale candy. I couldn't fall asleep that night. I wondered if you
would die without me.

"I changed my mind. I want her back."

"Sasha, we've discussed this before. I won't let you ruin your future. Especially now."

That morning, Sasha came back from the Milk Kitchen with government milk for the baby and found her mother waltzing around with Nadia. There was a thick envelope on the bed—Sasha had been accepted to the Repin Lyceum High School for the Arts in Moscow.

"How did you swing this?" asked Sasha, remembering the drawings she'd sent in for admission. They seemed even more awful in retrospect. "Did you let somebody paint your portrait? What else did you let them do?"

"Look whose cow is mooing!" exclaimed Mrs. Goldberg, making a sweeping hand gesture toward Sasha's lower body. She made those gestures a lot in the past months. At first, Sasha used to look down, to see if her fly was unzipped. By now she knew that the gesture was only meant as a judgment of her moral character.

"I'm not going."

Mrs. Goldberg put Nadia back in her crib and grabbed Sasha's hand.

"Please don't make it difficult on me."

"I'm not going, I can't leave the baby."

Mrs. Goldberg peered into Sasha's eyes. Sasha could see every pore on her mother's nose, and the places where Mrs. Goldberg was letting her tweezed brows grow in accordance with fashion. Nadia squealed from her crib.

"In a year," whispered Mrs. Goldberg, "you won't know her from any other kid."

Sasha Goldberg hit her mother's face with her soft, heavy fist. It was like hitting a squirrel, a brush of light fur, a touch of warmth, negligible weight flying backward. Although Sasha didn't hit very hard, Mrs. Goldberg sat back on the bed, bleeding out of both of her narrow nostrils. In the silence, Sasha heard the scrapes of neighbors' slippers on grimy linoleum outside the door.

Three weeks later Lubov Alexandrovna arranged for Dyadya Oleg to drive Sasha to Prostuda and put her on the train. By evening, Sasha's breasts got hard and hurt. Lying on her bunk with her face to the wall, she was happy to have the pain. It took her mind off the milk that was being wasted, soaking into her sweater, souring. In a few hours, Sasha's sweater smelled like the folds in the baby's neck. She took it off and stuffed it into the waste slot in the lavatory. By the time the train got to Moscow, her milk was all gone.

Were Sasha Goldberg a criminal, she'd be the type who gets her jail term reduced for good behavior. Now that she was already at the Repin, she had nothing to gain by being disobedient. Mrs. Goldberg had leaned into the window of the car: "You're talented, Sashenka, you have a future. All this trouble will be last year's snow to you in no time." Sasha decided to give her mother the benefit of the doubt.

She bought two squirrel fur brushes and attended an orientation.

The Repin Lyceum's large, crumbling building resembled the Asbestos 2 District Soviet. Like most Stalin-era buildings, it was painted cheerful cadmium yellow, but its whitewashed portico stood surrounded by scaffolding. Rumor had it that sometime in the eighties, a piece of cornice broke off and fell on a student's head, leaving her brain-damaged.

With the front entrance permanently closed, the students filed in through the side of the building into a narrow corridor. This part of the school reminded Sasha of AFTER EATIN the most. It had the same smell of plaster dust, the same uneven floorboards and dim electric lights. Enormous mosaics and frescoes lined the walls. Too large to move and too nice to destroy, they were left behind by the graduating students of monumental propaganda. In the older ones, peasants listened to Lenin, workers in aprons clutched hammers to their masculine chests, scientists bent over microscopes. The newer ones were brighter and more ambiguous, full of elongated female figures swirling translucent scarves. Their abstract backgrounds resembled rows of icicles.

The classrooms upstairs were different from AFTER EATIN. Daylight streamed in through enormous filthy windows. In each room, easels were arranged in a wide circle around a central pedestal. On the second week of school, Sasha walked into her classroom and saw an actual naked lady perched on the edge of the pedestal above the giggles and whispers.

The first lesson was a linguistic one.

"The word is nude! I don't want anyone saying naked!" exclaimed the drawing teacher, Lev Borisovich, pointing his frail, warty hand at the old lady's breasts.

The roomful of teenagers died laughing.

Sasha had known that around art, naked people were called nude, but coming from Lev Borisovich's mouth the distinction sounded hypocritical. The old lady was *naked*. Although she was sitting centimeters away from a space heater, she looked cold and aggrieved. She kept glancing at a paper bag next to her. Sasha guessed that inside was a bottle of liquor. She had a feeling that she'd seen the old woman before.

For the warm-up exercises, Lev Borisovich instructed the model to assume three-minute-long poses. In one, she lay on her back with her peeling leathery feet up in the air; in another, she sat hunched like a Neanderthal making fire, her deranged blue eyes peeking out through a curtain of thin gray hair. In between the poses, she put her lips to the brown bag and swallowed her drink without enthusiasm, like medicine.

"Up on one leg, Lida, please. We're almost done."

The old lady stood on her right leg, extending her left one like a grotesque parody of a ballerina. Looking at her straining calf and neck made Sasha sick. She wished the old lady would just get dressed and go home with her bottle.

"Good job, what's your name, uh, Goldberg," Lev Borisovich said approvingly, patting Sasha on the shoulder. "Goldberg has captured the movement!"

You, too, thought Sasha. *You, too, should go home.*

Socially, the class was split between the Moscow kids and the out-of-towners. The Muscovites were better dressed and mostly talked among themselves. A lot of them knew each other from previous art schools. Some apprenticed with the same Repin professors in preparation for admissions. Sasha didn't like the Muscovites. She felt helpless, irrational disdain for their ripped jeans and long hair, their casual mentions of foreign bands, and their inside jokes.

The out-of-towners seemed more approachable. Sasha recognized them right away by the way they looked around themselves, the way they tried too hard, by their fanatical devotion to their work. She tried to find that devotion within herself but instead felt lazy and stupid. Last year's snow wasn't melting. All of the out-of-towners appeared somewhat lost and shell-shocked, but Sasha felt that she was the only one entirely adrift.

"What's your last name?" Lev Borisovich asked again the following week.

Sasha looked at him, confused. She thought Lev Borisovich knew her last name by now.

"I asked you your *last name.*"

"Goldberg."

"Aha! So your last name isn't Ingres! Why do you fancy yourself a master of the contour drawing?"

The class giggled. By now, they'd all been subject to Lev Borisovich's high-minded abuse. There was a fair amount of sympathy in their laughter, but all Sasha could hear was humiliation. Repin wasn't AFTER EATIN, Moscow wasn't Asbestos 2, and Sasha Goldberg was falling apart. At night, the baby cried in her dreams. Every morning, she woke up feeling damaged, like a twitching animal with a broken spine, that she herself was scared of. Now she was wondering how much of it her classmates could see, and how long it would be before they pounced on her. She reminded herself that these were nice kids, the hyper-achievers, but still, walking through corridors, entering the bathrooms, passing by a vacant lot outside, she wondered, where would they be waiting?

"I asked you to work on the structure!" continued Lev Borisovich. "Build the frame! Locate the rib cage! Everyone, I want you to come over here and see what *not to do*."

Sasha couldn't see the frame or the rib cage. The model was an obese man, a pyramid of smooth hairless rolls. A permanent erection was the only part of him that had any structure. Glancing at the drawings around her, Sasha sketched a rib cage, a spine, and collarbones over the white expanse of the man's body. Lev Borisovich was at the other end of the room now, and Sasha hoped he wouldn't come around. She knew he was no different from her AFTER EATIN teachers, a harmless old man whose worst insult was to call her Ingres. Why did she hate him so much?

She couldn't bring herself to complete the drawing. Instead, she tried to draw the baby's face in the empty corner of her paper. She drew the round cheeks and forehead, the pointy chin. The drawing didn't look like Nadia. It didn't look like any baby, just somebody's generic idea of what babies look like. Sasha stared at the drawing. She'd been holding the baby in her hands all night, dream after dream. She nursed and changed her, she watched her face, first red from crying, then smiling, then sleeping. Why, then, did her hands only remember a picture-book stereotype? Next, she tried to draw her mother. Then Alexey.

A woman.

A man.

Two nobodies stacked on top of each other, missing only a house with a chimney and a gabled roof. The real people stayed hidden somewhere, away from Sasha's reach.

She was just beginning to erase the drawings when Lev Borisovich tapped her on the shoulder.

"How's our Ingres? What's *that*?"

"Let me just erase this," Sasha said.

"Goldberg, what do you think you're doing here?"

"Drawing," said Sasha.

"Goldberg, you're a student of art! You're in a life drawing class. *Life!* What are these *babskie shtuchki*? What's next? Fairies? Little angels? Stepashka the Bunny? This isn't preschool! You're to treat your work with respect!"

"I can erase." Sasha shrugged, wishing a stroke on Lev Borisovich.

"This is ruined. Go next door and get a new paper. You're starting over."

The paper drawer in the classroom next door was empty. Sasha considered going back and telling Lev Borisovich, but instead she ran down the stairs. Hurrying past the mosaics toward the exit, she wondered what was stopping the mammoth panels from falling and squashing her like a bug. She glanced up at the workers' and scientists' enormous heads, each four times the size of her own, and felt the last of her energy drain away. Would she be expected, in three years, to climb a ladder and make one of those herself, add another frail Pushkin, another long-waisted Muse to the dusty crowd? She wouldn't be able to do it. *They couldn't make her do it.*

By the end of November, Sasha Goldberg stopped going to class. She spent days in her dorm room, reading the old issues of *Woman Worker* and *Burda* her roommates left lying around. Some days she only got out of bed to go to the bathroom. It was just like being sick. Sasha had an idea that one day she would get up and go back, but she didn't know when. Nobody seemed to notice that she was gone. It was taking her delinquency a long time to trickle down the lyceum's complicated system of class rosters and grade reports.

Sasha lay on her bunk and read about Hot Latin Lovers, knitting techniques, and cucumber face masks, trying to crowd out the memory of Nadia's tears and Mrs. Goldberg's persimmon blood. In one of the magazines, there was an article about a girl who met her American husband through Kupid's Korner Bridal Agency. Sasha had seen their ads in the metro.

There were two photographs with the article, one taken in Red Square, another in Disneyland. The woman, Ksenia, was tall and blond, and her new husband, Joe, heavyset and dark. You could see a tuft of black chest hair above the collar of his shirt. In the Red Square photograph, Ksenia held a small girl in her arms. The girl had pink knee socks and a pink bow in her wispy blond hair.

It appeared from the article that Joe first won Ksenia's heart when he brought her daughter a huge stuffed bear (inset: small child hugging a huge stuffed bear). In the Disneyland photo, the girl, now older and fatter, was sitting on Joe's shoulders. There was a sidebar framed by a design of interlocking pink hearts: "Dream of Meeting an American? It's easier than you think!" At the end of the sidebar there was Kupid's Korner's number.

Sasha Goldberg sat up in bed, thinking about the foreigners she'd seen in the metro. They were recognizable even from the back, by the way they sprawled out in crowded trains, by the ease of their postures, by their loud, unselfconscious laughter. Even when sober, the foreigners laughed like drunks. Sasha admired their forest-green fleece vests, their huge alabaster teeth, and especially the way their eyes skimmed over Russian crowds, only occasionally lighting up at the sight of a gypsy urchin with an accordion or a street photographer's muzzled bear cub. In the foreigners' indifferent wire-framed eyes, one could be neither beautiful nor ugly, neither a hippo nor a black-ass, but merely a molecule in a gray mass, a background to their experience.

Just being unseen was thrilling enough. Could one of those messy-haired young men with a complicated backpack and a camera around his neck actually fall in love with Sasha Goldberg? Was it a matter of simply going to a bridal agency? Sasha fantasized about lying next to her American on an impossibly vast hotel room bed and telling him about Nadia. She didn't bother thinking about the language of their conversation, but she liked to imagine that he would want to adopt her child. He would arrive in Asbestos 2 with his loose joints, easy generosity, and a few adorably garbled Russian words, a true freak, a beautiful alien.

"*Zdravstvuyte!*" he'd tell Mrs. Goldberg, pronouncing every last silent consonant.

Even her mother wouldn't be able to resist such a person.

Sasha Goldberg kicked back the sheet, put on her pants, and went down to the lobby to find a pay phone, feeling alive for the first time in weeks.

The Kupid's Korner people were friendly, though Sasha wasn't their type—neither a "Scandinavian Beauty" nor a "Snow Maiden with a Warm Heart." Oksana, the girl who wrote Sasha's profile, suggested peroxide. Then she reconsidered and said Sasha should just go as is, and they could advertise her as "A Lady with a Raisin." Vika, who owned Korner, vetoed the raisin, saying it wouldn't sound good in English. They finally settled on "Passionate Dark Beauty."

Oksana also told Sasha to lie about her age. Korner had their own lady at the notary, and the girls got whatever ages they wanted put on their birth certificates. Most everybody lied, some up, some down. Oksana told Sasha to lie up.

"It's legal for you to sign up," she advised," but you don't want to end up with some perv who's looking for a sixteen-year-old wife."

Vika, the owner, was thirty. In the early years of Perestroika, she met and married an American guy who was teaching English at the Pokrovskaya Language Academy, the one with the "Learn from the Natives!" TV commercial. Jim was short, pale, and bony, with hair shaped like three biscuits. He had a philosophy degree from Ohio State and a fear of speaking in public. He rarely addressed the class. He mostly faced the board, filling it up with sloping lines of heady, awkward script. He often paused and used the side of his palm to erase parts of his work because he couldn't spell to save his life. Jim was the first American his students had ever been within touching distance of. All the girls in the class were in love with him, his casually faded Levi's, his politeness, his flat r's. But Vika was the one that got him. She was still proud of it, six years later, even though after they moved to the suburbs of Cleveland, Vika discovered bigger and better Americans, left Jim, and moved to New York.

Now she was married to Paul, a strikingly handsome French guy, a consultant with PricewaterhouseCoopers. When Paul got transferred to Moscow, Vika started Kupid's Korner to help other women have her life. Sasha almost never talked to Vika, being just one of the girls. Oksana told her Vika's story.

Oksana became Sasha's friend, and she was straight with her.

"Keep your expectations low. Remember, a husband isn't a luxury, but a form of transportation!" she said.

Vika wouldn't have approved of such talk. She tried to keep cynicism to a minimum. She strove to make Kupid's Korner a deluxe agency. Its catalog contained almost no broken English, and instead of three-month fiancée visas, the Korner provided its girls with year-long student visas, allowing the men a longer "courtship period." According to the paperwork, Kupid's Korner's brides traveled to America to study at the Grand Canyon Institute for Global Initiatives, a struggling vocational college in Utah that Vika used for visa support.

In the glamour shots for the Korner's catalog, Sasha Goldberg wore a miniskirt, platforms, and a red feather boa, like half the people in the "under 25" category. The Korner only had a few outfits.

Two months later Oksana told her to show up at a Kupid's Speed-Dating Event.

"Don't dress like a slut," she said. "That was just for the pictures, for private viewing. The assholes usually bond during these trips. They won't go for a slut in front of their group."

Kupid's Korner rented a high school auditorium for the event. By the time Sasha showed up, feeling like a stilt-walker in high heels, the room was full of girls. Six men were seated up onstage at a long folding table. Around the perimeter of the room, just under the ceiling, plaster bas-reliefs of famous authors peered down from white-painted medallions.

Fyodor Mikhailovich Dostoyevsky squinted his beady eyes in Sasha's direction. Sasha remembered devouring *Crime and Punishment* in two giant gulps; two feverish, sleepless nights. Now she was sitting in a room full of real-life Sonechka Marmeladovas, painstakingly made-up, reluctant whores at the beginning of their journeys. Would there be a Raskolnikov for each of them? Sasha wanted to teach Fyodor Mikhailovich's plaster head a lesson. What that lesson was supposed to be, Sasha wasn't sure. She looked at the stage and sighed. Compared to the men up there, Dostoyevsky was a looker.

Above the table Sasha saw a bald head, a cowboy hat, another bald head, a mustache, a baseball cap, and a combination of a mustache and no chin. Below the table there were white sneakers, white sneakers, white sneakers, cowboy boots, dress shoes, and white sneakers. The men held laminated binders with the girls' statistics. A Soviet-era tablecloth with a golden fringe cast a red tint on their faces, making them look embarrassed.

The interviews started. The girls ascended the stage in order, talked in front of each of the men and left the stage on the other side. Oksana spotted Sasha in the last row and came over.

"Are you just going to sit here? You're overestimating the fuckers' attention span." She grabbed Sasha's arm above the elbow and yanked her out of her seat. "Don't be shy, now. I'm just trying to help you."

Sasha Goldberg straightened her skirt and walked toward the stage.

That night, Oksana showed up at Sasha's dorm.

"You've got a da-ate!" she sang, plopping down on the bed. "With Neal Miller. What, you don't remember him? I cannot believe you don't remember him."

"Stop making fun of me or get the hell out of here," said Sasha. "Is he the one with the mustache?"

"No, the bald one, at the end of the table. Not so bad, actually. Says he's a technician at Intel."

"Whatever that is. How old is he?"

"Thirty-eight."

"*Gospodi!* Did he know Churchill personally?"

"What did you expect? Besides, Churchill was British and Neal is American. Maybe you should try to remember that."

"All the same to me," sighed Sasha.

"That's precisely the point, Goldberg. Think of it as a basic economic transaction: he pays us, you pay him, you get what you want out of it at the end. Its best to overlook the details: age, looks, nationality"—Oksana laughed—"sex . . ."

"Do I have to pay? You guys didn't say I had to pay, because you know I don't have any—"

"Money? No, you don't have to pay money. But you will pay, sweetie. You will pay in a million different ways. . . ."

"*Zatknis'*, Oksana. Be thankful you don't have to do this!"

"Well, I was wondering why *you* have to do this. You are at the Repin Lyceum! Do you really think your life's so bad? The Over-Forty Category I can understand. But what people like you are doing at the Korner, I have no idea."

Sasha kept her mouth shut about the magazine article that had brought her to Kupid's Korner in the first place and about her imaginary American. The men at the speed-dating event had looked hunched over and pre-occupied, almost *Soviet.* They sweated, they had mustaches, they sat *in line,* they lacked the intangible Americanness Sasha had counted on. Still, perhaps it would manifest itself during the date. Since she didn't remember Neal Miller, Sasha Goldberg had preserved a modicum of hope and resolved to meet him.

The day of Sasha's date, Oksana came over again, bringing clothes and makeup in a large plastic bag. Sasha decided to submit to the dress-up, to hide her ambivalence.

"This is important," Oksana said. "I'm going to do your hair."

She brushed Sasha's hair away from her face, gathering it in the back with a zebra-striped velour scrunchie.

"For a Jew, you sure look like a Negro," she mused, raking through Sasha's bangs with a fine-tooth comb. "These won't stay down."

Sasha felt self-conscious and violated, the way she'd felt at medical check-ups as a kid. She felt personally responsible for her bangs' behavior.

"Close your eyes . . . ," commanded Oksana, hosing Sasha's head with Secret hairspray.

Sasha gagged on the bitter, pungent aerosol.

". . . and your mouth," said Oksana, gluing Sasha's bangs down to her forehead.

The look was conservative-yet-flirty. Oksana opened the plastic bag and produced a white shirt hemmed with lace, a maroon knee-length skirt, sheer pantyhose embellished with tiny red hearts, and a black blazer. Miraculously, everything fit.

"Unbutton the top two buttons," Oksana said, and Sasha obeyed.

"Are you sure?" she asked, looking down at the dark space between her breasts.

"Leave it, Goldberg! I know what I'm doing."

Sasha sat in a chair while Oksana did her face.

"Don't squint!"

"You sound like my mom."

"Just wait until you see yourself," Oksana said. "You're going to love it."

After the makeup was done, Oksana told Sasha to close her eyes and led her to the mirror.

"Okay, look now!"

Sasha opened her eyes and didn't recognize her reflection. Without all the hair sticking out, her head looked tiny on her enormous padded shoulders. The black platform boots made Sasha stand lock-kneed, chest forward. She was a disaster.

"Beautiful! Practice smiling!" exclaimed Oksana, hanging a heart-shaped silver pendant in the dark triangle of Sasha's cleavage.

Sasha blinked and touched her face. The blue metallic eye shadow on her lids looked like an extra pair of eyes, and her face was several shades lighter than her neck.

"There isn't face powder in this country to match your skin," conceded Oksana. "Maybe we could wipe that off."

After returning Sasha's face to its original color, Oksana outlined her lips with a dark lipliner and filled them in with lipstick, making them look thinner. With new lips Sasha looked older, her expression prim and disapproving.

"Just smile, will you? It's a date, not a funeral!"

Sasha smiled obediently and, while Oksana wasn't looking, quietly moved the scrunchie, allowing some hair to fall on her shoulders. She definitely looked twenty, the age on her fake birth certificate, if not thirty or forty. She looked poorly assembled from spare parts. A suede appliquéd crane peeked around the side of her blazer, its rhinestone eye twinkling in the vicinity of Sasha's nipple.

"I didn't realize you were so tall, Goldberg," said Oksana, gathering the makeup into her bag. "I should've brought you flats. Good luck!"

Neal paid for the date, and Kupid's Korner arranged it. It was at a place called Brevno, just off Red Square. That day there had been an all-meat buffet. Oksana had warned Sasha not to eat marrow or brains, it grosses Americans out. Eat stuff that's breaded and square.

After two pints of beer, Neal Miller covered Sasha's hand with his and told her that in all his life he had never met anyone like her. He said that American women didn't treat their men right, and that what he knew about Sasha (from the Kupid's Korner's profile) promised the opposite. Although he'd known her for twenty minutes, he felt as if they had known each other their whole lives.

Sasha nodded, impressed with herself for having enough grade school English to grasp the general gist of Neal's monologue. Neal bent down to gaze into her eyes and fumbled with his bag, panting. Sasha caught a whiff of an old-man's breath. Finally, he found what he was looking for—a gray box with a ring in it. He tried to put the ring on Sasha's finger, but it wouldn't go past the first joint.

"Shit!" mouthed Neal.

"Not problem." Sasha Goldberg tried to smile. "Maybe repair?"

The child question never came up due to the language barrier.

When they got up from the table, Sasha extended her hand, but Neal ignored it and kissed her on the lips.

"He smelled like he'd been drinking perfume!" she told Oksana afterward.

"It's aftershave, dummy. Did you just fall off the moon?"

Neal's time in Moscow was up. The next day he flew back to Phoenix, and Kupid's Korner proceeded to complete Sasha's paperwork.

May Day recess coincided with Nadia's first birthday. By then, Sasha Goldberg had been warned by the Lyceum *she'd better spend the break in the studio, or else.*

She gave her art supplies to her roommates and packed her clothes. After Korner, after Neal, she'd had enough. She was going home to her baby. On the way to the train station, she went to the market and spent what money she had left on an imported velveteen alligator. Its tag said "My Pal Al." When you pushed on Al's nose, it said something in a foreign language. Its belly was a rattle, its tail squeaked, its feet made a crunchy noise.

Mrs. Stepanova opened the door. Sasha could hear Nadia in the kitchen, chanting, *Nonononono.*

"Luba, Sasha is here!"

"Sashenka! We didn't expect you so soon. Is the school all done?" asked Mrs. Goldberg, taking Sasha's bag. "Come, see how Nadia's grown."

Nadia thrashed in Sasha's old high chair, trying to get out. She was wearing a vinyl bib with a picture of a fat, orange-topped mushroom.

"My baby," Sasha Goldberg mouthed soundlessly, "come to mama."

"Sasha," Mrs. Goldberg said in a weary voice, "please don't start."

Sasha took Nadia out of the chair and kissed her on the face. The baby was heavy, awkward to hold. Sasha couldn't believe how much she'd grown. But she smelled the same, sour milk and warm skin and pee. Sasha Goldberg stroked her downy hair, trying not to cry. From the corner of her eye she could see Mrs. Stepanova behind the glass-paned door, an illusion of tactfulness.

For a minute, Nadia was quiet, stunned. Then her face became a grimace, and finally she wailed, stretching her arms toward Mrs. Goldberg.

"Amamaa!"

Mrs. Goldberg took her from Sasha, who continued to hold on to the baby's back, stroking, touching. With a precise, grown-up gesture, Nadia swiped away her hand.

"Let go, Alexandra," said Mrs. Goldberg. "Don't act like a child. Nadiusha, this is your sister Sasha. It's all right."

Nadia peeked at Sasha, but continued to cling to Mrs. Goldberg.

"I brought you a toy," Sasha said helplessly. She dug through her bag, clawed out the alligator, and shoved it toward Nadia. Nadia looked at the toy, at Sasha's tear-streaked red face, and began to wail again.

"You scared her, Sasha. Give her time, she doesn't know who you are."

Sasha detected a hint of victory, *I told you so,* in her mother's voice.

"So, how is school? Tell me about Moscow," Mrs. Goldberg asked over tea. Nadia sat on her lap, eyeing Sasha with suspicion.

I hate it. I'm home for good. I've come to be with my baby. Please, Mama, don't you understand?

"I . . ." Sasha paused.

"Sasha?" said Mrs. Goldberg. "No more scenes, all right? If you want Nadia to like you, don't push her. She knows who her mother is. You are a *child.* You are welcome to take care of her, play with her. By the time you return to Moscow, she'll love you. She may even remember you next year. But she doesn't need any *trauma.*"

Sasha opened her mouth again.

"Or," said Mrs. Goldberg, "I can arrange for you to stay in Moscow over the summer."

Sasha sipped her tea. Lubov Alexandrovna set Nadia down on the floor and walked over. Sasha leaned her face against her mother's striped housecoat and closed her eyes. Above her head, Mrs. Goldberg's voice sounded remote and droning, like a political speech on the radio. *The future, your own life, in Moscow, need to study, college, when you get married, when you're older, on your own two feet, when I die.*

Except for an hour of semidarkness between sunset and sunrise, the night was as light as the day. Sasha Goldberg couldn't sleep. She wondered if her love for the baby who so clearly didn't need her was a sickness, a perversion. Like a phantom limb hurting.

She got out of bed and walked to her mother's room. Nadia lay in her crib with her butt up in the air, grinding her head against the side of the pillow. Sasha moved the pillow and felt the baby's breath on her knuckles. Mrs. Goldberg lay asleep on her back, her arms straight alongside her body. She was the spot of light in a blue room, pink luminous skin, golden hair, like a Renoir painting. Sasha Goldberg picked up the alligator from the floor, set it inside Nadia's crib, and tiptoed out of the room.

Out of the window of a bus she watched the sun rise above the asbestos pit. She noticed that the trucks were all gone. The pit looked abandoned. *When did this happen?* Wrapped up in her misery, Sasha didn't think much about what it meant.

Back in Moscow, she called Kupid's Korner. Her visa was ready.

A week later, Sasha Goldberg, age sixteen and a half, dragged her bag from the back seat of Oksana's pink Fiat and waved from the curb. "Don't forget, drinks are free on Delta International!" were Oksana's ever-so-practical last words. "Enjoy yourself, Goldberg!"

Sasha did as she was told. After her fourth bottle of airplane Merlot, she discovered the poetic imagery of the safety instructions card. She especially liked the neatly dressed woman bobbing in calm water on her floating seat cushion, a noncommittal smile on her lips. Sasha smiled back at the tiny woman. She knew that where she was going, she would be spared from speaking, made to learn a code, a nonsense language. Sasha hoped that muteness would infect her brain, spread from the outside in.

She folded the safety card, stretched her legs, and tried to fall asleep. In oblivion, Neal Miller walked on the burning pavement to his freshly washed Saturn and drove to the airport, a plastic rose on the passenger seat.

After the initial kiss, Neal didn't insist on a conversation. On the drive from the airport, Sasha Goldberg read the signs outside the car window: TACO BELL, PARTY CITY, CAMELBACK CHRISTIAN FELLOWSHIP, WENDY'S, RALLY'S, TEXACO, JACK IN THE BOX, 7-ELEVEN, ALBERTSONS, LOS ARCOS, SEARS. She felt weightless and hollow, as if instead of Neal's car she was trapped in a falling elevator.

At first glance, Phoenix wasn't much to look at. The landscape's biggest feature seemed to be the lack of specifics: nothing was especially dilapidated or overgrown; no major shape strayed from a variation of a prism. On either side of the street, Sasha saw stretches of cinderblock walls, and behind the walls, off-white stucco houses with mushroom-shaped vents on their flat roofs. At certain intersections, the walls and the houses suddenly stopped, replaced by huge stores or even more enormous dirt lots. At a distance, a cluster of tall buildings stood wrapped in a brown haze, but roads dominated the scenery: straight, wide, impossibly even, flanked by equally perfect, empty sidewalks. Sasha leaned her forehead against the window glass and imagined that aliens had abducted the people here, while the wind from their spacecraft killed and mangled the plants, leaving an occasional squat cactus, a crooked palm tree, an evergreen hedge. Suddenly the car tilted and headed toward the sky. Sasha giggled in terror.

"This is a freeway," explained Neal.

Clutching her plastic rose, Sasha Goldberg realized that she'd inadvertently chosen the perfect place to erase herself.

Only it wasn't that easy. Sasha's desired deathlike trance was constantly sabotaged by Neal's diametrically opposite agenda: having made his investment in a young bride, he was finally ready to be happy. On Neal's birthday, they went to Red Lobster. Neal was in high spirits, talking about his Intel stock options. The beer he was drinking made his cheeks and nose beet-red, like Santa's; orange crumbs of breading hung in his mustache. Sipping her piña colada, Sasha allowed the ubiquitous song about the wind beneath somebody's wings to lodge its fishhook into her brain and wondered if she would ever get used to this. That was when she thought of a very different plan, simple and far-fetched like hope. In America she might find her father. Someone to fix what happened, to tell her what to do.

Almost as soon as Victor Goldberg disappeared, the fact of his existence was eclipsed by the improbable story of his vanishing and by his absolute silence thereafter. Sasha had forgotten the last time she actually missed her father, the last time she thought of him as a person rather than an absence. Now, attempting to reconstruct him in her mind, she had a feeling that she ended up with the wrong set of memories, as if the important ones were misplaced somewhere, just out of her reach.

Lying in bed next to Neal that night, Sasha remembered the winter of the rabbit coat; her parents' shouting whispers in the dark. *Ask somebody. I can't do it. I've never even seen it done. I'll show you. Then you do it.* Sniffles. Silence. Victor had said something about being afraid of blood. "Afraid of blood?" her mother mocked. "Next you'll be afraid of compote!" Sasha remembered watching her father through the window in the morning. He stood in the snow next to a newspaper piled with dead rabbits, and since all Sasha could see from above was the round top of his fur hat, she couldn't tell if he looked scared.

Anyway, there hadn't been much blood. Dyadya Oleg, the upstairs neighbor, hung each rabbit upside down, slit it down the middle with a sharp knife, and easily pulled off the skin. Without fur, the rabbits looked ridiculous, like tiny naked ladies. Dyadya Oleg wrapped them in newspaper and shoved them in a net bag. Dyadya Oleg raised rabbits in his apartment and killed them as soon as the weather was cold enough to hang them outside his window for storage. He needed the rabbits for meat and gave away the pelts to the neighbors. (Dyadya Oleg had no use for them, his family already outfitted by previous generations of illegal rabbits.) That year, eight-year-old Sasha needed a new coat, and that was why Victor stood outside with a kitchen knife, scraping the pelts.

Afterward, Mrs. Goldberg made Sasha a rabbit coat by attaching the pelts to an old flannel dress. Victor turned out to have been right, he couldn't scrape the pelts very well. Sasha's coat stank through the winter and rotted by spring. Sasha remembered pulling out clumps of fur and gluing them to matchboxes to make toy squirrels.

One night, Mrs. Goldberg was putting the squirrels away when she found a live mouse among them. Sasha remembered that her father had somehow caught the mouse and was holding it gently in his hands, the animal's fleshy tail flailing between his thumbs. After flushing the mouse down the toilet, Victor stayed in the bathroom for a long time. When he finally came out, his face all red and splotchy, Mrs. Goldberg grabbed his messy graying Afro with both hands and kissed him on the forehead. *My sweet city boy,* she called him, as if drowning a mouse in an apartment toilet were an act only rugged rural people could perform dispassionately, as if she herself routinely slaughtered much larger creatures.

Listening to Neal smack his lips in his sleep, Sasha wondered if all of that had actually happened. In a white-walled Arizona bedroom among the smells of fabric softener and synthetic apple pie, her memories of her father seemed improbable and confusing. Had he really been crying in there for that mouse? Had he really immigrated to America? Sasha felt as if she were ten years old again, trying to solve an old riddle. Yes, she had a father, Victor Semyonovich Goldberg. He lived here, in America. But what else did she know? And how would one find a person, anyway, in a huge country like this?

During the day, Sasha had no energy to puzzle over Victor. She continued training herself to exist parallel to Neal, to empty herself out, little by little. She almost enjoyed sitting on the hood of Neal's car with his buddies Terry and Bruce, watching Fourth of July fireworks from the river bottom.

She liked Neal's English, his expert pronunciation of the language's glitzy, utopian endings: -ings, -tions. These were the two sexiest things about Neal: his English and his driving. Sasha tried not to remind herself that both of those skills were as natural as breathing to an American. Sasha wished she could drive and liked speaking English. It still consisted of nonwords, random stand-ins. Sasha wondered if the English words would someday begin to sound real, inextricably attached to what they described, the way they were in Russian. For now, every word she said felt like a lie, and lying was easy. Neal complimented her on her progress.

"Allie," he said, "you're a fast learner."

According to Neal, in America Sasha was a dog's name, and Alexandra was just too long. Sasha was just beginning to like her new name when Marina came along and ruined everything with the sound of her voice.

3

Greyhoundland

"WELCOME TO THE CAVE," SASHA SAYS, PUSHING THE DOOR.

Marina squints. "All the houses here are like this: squat and dark."

"To conserve energy. They live in the dark to save money."

"I detect an anti-American sentiment," says Marina.

"All I'm saying is why do they live here in the first place? Whose idea was it to build the city here? You can't open the windows, you can't go outside for five months."

"Are you telling me this is worse than Siberia?"

"Objectively speaking, no," concedes Sasha.

Marina thinks Neal is rich because he has his own house, but Sasha suspects he isn't. Except for a blue recliner covered in towels, the TV, and the bed, there's hardly any furniture in the house. The carpet is stained and pilled up, and the plastic wood paneling on the walls bulges out in places.

There is a fireplace in the corner, and in it Neal keeps a plastic log on a spit. When you flip a switch, the log rotates, and three red lights glow from underneath. A yellowed, crumbling box, part of the log's original packaging, sits on the mantel next to a golf ball clock.

Neal has other stuff, too, but he keeps all of that locked in one of the bedrooms. He keeps Sasha's passport there, too, along with other important documents. When Neal opens the door, Sasha Goldberg sees stacks of tapes, old computer parts, and a rolled-up American flag leaning against the wall. She's never gone inside. Every day, before he kisses Sasha goodbye, Neal locks that bedroom. Sasha thinks he's following some advice he read in a Kupid's Korner handout. She wonders what's left to steal: a Domino's fridge magnet? A unicorn ashtray? Still, Sasha lives in the kind of house Marina and her mother only get to clean.

Marina eyes the towel-covered chair suspiciously, then takes the plunge and sits down in it, pulling the wooden lever on its side.

"La-Z-Boy!" she exclaims in English, her body nearly horizontal. "You'll love it at Levitz!"

"Do you want tea or coffee?" Sasha asks.

Marina lets go of the lever and rights the towels.

"Did you ever tell Neal about Nadia?" she asks in a conspiratorial half whisper.

Ever since Sasha told Marina about the baby, she's had a feeling that her life has become a prize addition to Marina's collection of gruesome curiosities, along with Marina's grandmother's executed siblings, the deformed children of Chernobyl (*I saw the seal-boy with my very own eyes*), and the recent circumcision of her fourteen-year-old brother (*The Youth Group leader talked him into it! He wore a strawberry carton over his crotch for two weeks!*). Still, Sasha enjoys shocking Marina a little, giving the PBS-loving virgin new material for a book she intends to someday write about her immigration experiences (*Eto takoy surrealism!*).

"I told him I wanted her back," she explains, filling the teapot. "I said that I was only fifteen when she was born, and that I wasn't thinking straight when I gave her up. Except I forgot that, thanks to Kupid's Korner, Neal thinks I'm twenty-one. 'Calm down,' he said. 'Be realistic. It's water under the bridge.' Just like my mother. She said, 'Last year's snow.' Proverb water torture."

Marina shakes her head. She's huddled in the chair now, her eyes glistening in the dark like a cat's.

"He told me someday he and I may have a child together," Sasha says. "That shut me up pretty well."

"Fuck!" Marina exclaims in English.

"*Da*, fuck!" echoes Sasha. She and Marina love the English word fuck. It's so flexible and infinitely applicable. "Neal harbors many strange notions.

Last night, we get back from Bridal Barn, and he begins to complain that the bathroom is dirty. All right, I say, I'll take care of it. Then he goes and shows me my Kupid's Korner profile, which says that I love to clean. Sometimes I look at Neal, and he appears normal enough, and I wonder, how can he believe this *ohinea*? Who the fuck *loves* to clean? Besides, Mama never let me near housework. Children of the intelligentsia don't clean toilets. Until they fuck up, their life consists of mathematics, literature, and art." She laughs. "You should know that."

"Don't forget piano and chess," sighs Marina. "Zina cries when she watches me clean. We clean Uncle Gary's boss's house every two weeks. He has nine kids and his house is a toxic dump of food and shit and everything in between. So, we're both squatting on the bathroom floor, Zina by the tub, me by the sink, and she looks over at me and starts crying!"

"I've never seen my mother cry," Sasha says. "Well, once. She cried when she found out I was pregnant. She walked in on me in the shower. Next thing, she was crying. 'Who died?' I asked. She grabbed the towel and began to beat me. Then she dragged me to the clinic, where they told us I was too far along to have a safe abortion."

"Why are you laughing? You're crazy." Marina shakes her head.

"I just felt like such an idiot. And my mother acted like one, so unlike herself. Even though she is shorter than me, I never think of her as small. But when she was beating me with that stupid towel and crying, she looked so tiny and fragile. It was as if she were temporarily replaced by an average human. Well, after we came from the clinic, she became herself again and didn't speak to me until Nadia was born."

"You're exaggerating."

"Yes, but not much. We communicated on a mundane level. Sort of like a prison guard and an inmate. Once she informed me that childbirth was similar to being run over by a train. She must've forgotten, because in reality it's more like being turned inside out, like a sock." Sasha pauses, watching Marina's face. "BOO!"

Marina screams, then begins to laugh along.

"Well, Zina cries all the time," she complains. She seems eager to change the subject. "She looks like a fucking bulldog. Yesterday my uncle got into an accident, and now he has to pay to get the cab fixed, and Zina starts . . . Wait, Sasha, I completely forgot!"

Sasha pours the tea. "What?"

"My uncle says you may have access to Neal's money."

"What are you talking about?"

"My uncle says you probably have a joint bank account, for INS evidence. What if there is, like, thousands of dollars in there? Half of it is yours!"

"You talked to your mafioso uncle about me?"

"He is not a mafioso, he's a cabdriver." Marina sounds offended.

Sasha shakes her head. She doesn't remember if they have a joint account. After she came to Phoenix, Neal took her to many air-conditioned places, where they sat on plastic chairs with chrome legs. The plastic chairs stuck to Sasha's thighs. Papers were signed. Sasha knows that the place where they made her undress and cover up with a paper sheet was a doctors' office. One of the other places may've been the bank, but probably not. As far as the INS is concerned, Sasha is about to graduate from the Grand Canyon Institute for Global Initiatives.

"I don't think Neal has to do any of that stuff before we're actually married," she says.

"All right, forget what I said," says Marina, opening the freezer. "Wow, star-shaped chicken fingers! No ice cream?"

"Nuggets," corrects Sasha. Through the kitchen window, she sees an orange horizon, the beginning of a dust storm. She has enjoyed her performance in front of Marina, but the words are sticky. The things she can never say, and hasn't let herself feel, cling to them and rise to the surface. Sasha panics, and her palms begin to sweat. She shouldn't have brought Marina here. It's like bringing a living person into the afterlife, completely unnatural. She never should have told anyone about Nadia.

"Fingers. Nuggets. Same thing," laughs Marina.

"You should go," Sasha says. "Neal will be home soon."

"I want to meet him!" Marina whines jokingly.

Sasha hopes that the look on her face will be enough, that she won't have to speak.

"All right," Marina says, backing toward the door. "I'll see you in class."

Sasha Goldberg opens two cans of Hormel chili and pours them into the pot, per Neal's instructions. Neal is disappointed that she can't cook, but Sasha has a feeling that as long as she performs what he jokingly calls her "sacred wifely duty," he doesn't mind eating canned chili.

Neal must be headed home by now. His commute is twelve and a half minutes long. He says that he timed it when he purchased the house. When for some reason the drive takes longer, he comes home upset and talks about taxpayer dollars. At first, Sasha imagined Taxpayer Dollars as a villainous cowboy type, a kidnapper on horseback. Now she knows that the phrase has to do with the politics of highway construction. Sasha pours grated cheese over a tortilla, folds the tortilla in half, and shoves it in the microwave. Neal likes to have a beer and a quesadilla when he first gets home.

There is a newspaper on the kitchen counter. Sasha picks it up to look at the pictures; reading in English still feels like a chore. This time, however, the article holds her attention. It is about a woman who took her kids out on the front lawn, poured gasoline on them and herself, and lit a match. The kids' names were Rocky, Stormy, and Chance. Stormy died, and the woman was arrested. Sasha stares at a photo of the mother, preburn. She is fat and has no teeth. Sasha wants to know why the toothless woman set her children on fire, but the jump page is missing.

Sifting through the pile of ads for the rest of the story, Sasha feels the same way she felt when she first learned to swim or ride a bicycle: as if a force that is both inside and outside herself is carrying her forward, keeping her up. So now she's learned to read. Sasha Goldberg realizes that against her most sincere wishes, a part of her remains alive, learning, like those dumb cancer patients who keep doing their homework and laughing at clowns despite the tubes sticking out of their noses.

In the living room, a Bounty commercial comes on TV. A child takes a swipe at a glass of cranberry juice and sends it flying off the table. The commercial reminds Sasha of her Asbestos 2 neighbor, Mrs. Stepanova. When a syndicated column by a nationally famous healer began to be published in *Asbestos Truth*, Mrs. Stepanova started cutting out the column and soaking it in a jar of water. She left the newspaper strips in the jar overnight and drank

the water in the morning. This was how Mrs. Stepanova cured ingrown toe-
nails, warts, migraines, and indecision. Sasha smiles, remembering how she
used to sneak into Mrs. Stepanova's room, nudge her magic jar toward the
table's edge, and run away before it fell.

Sasha watches the quesadilla spin in the nuke like some hypnotic device.
With each spin, she becomes more and more sure of one thing: she will never
see Neal eat this quesadilla. Scenes of a deadly car accident flash before her
eyes, and she relishes them for a second, before realizing that there is a more
straightforward path to her goal: down the hall, past the laundry room, to the
locked bedroom.

Jiggling the shiny yellow doorknob, Sasha feels like the woman from
Hunter, purposeful and sexy. The panic she's been feeling all afternoon is
gone. She remembers Neal's toolbox under the sink and runs back to the
kitchen.

It takes her seconds to find a screwdriver, a minute to disassemble the lock.

The room is a mess of office supplies and cardboard boxes. A wolf's head
in a black frame leans against the wall, each hair in its mane separately air-
brushed. Sasha begins to dig through the boxes. Old hard drives, a comic
book collection, a rubber Halloween skull mask. Sasha feels defeated. She is
about to give up when she finds her passport in the bottom drawer of a black
filing cabinet.

Besides the passport, the drawer contains photos of Sasha and Neal dis-
playing affection, a receipt for the engagement ring, the engagement ring itself, and Kupid's Korner's *After the Honeymoon: How to Get a Russian Wife and
Keep Her Too* brochure.

Sasha stuffs the passport and the ring in the pocket of her jeans, throws
a few of her things into a plastic bag, turns off the stove in the kitchen, and
leaves the house. Outside, the dust storm has begun. The air smells of dust
and fuel, like the heating vents in the Moscow subway. The wind throws a
handful of sand into Sasha's eyes. She walks to the corner, then begins to run,
squinting against the flying debris. Soon a drip of water the size of a fist
smashes against the top of her head. She runs under the 7-Eleven awning and
sits down on a fiberglass dragon by the door.

In Asbestos 2, this time of year, the sun never goes down. Dusk is followed by dawn and the children inadvertently play hopscotch till midnight. Watching the shimmering wall of rain crash over the awning, Sasha feels sorry for herself and exhausted. She doesn't want to do another thing, but she has crossed the line and now has to keep moving. The rain ends as abruptly as it started, and seconds later the sun is bearing down again. Dry patches appear on pink stucco.

Sasha takes a bus to Marina's apartment. The door is open, but Marina isn't there. The grandma appraises Sasha with her one live eye. Sasha says hello to her and sits down at the kitchen table. The lemons and leaves on the vinyl tablecloth are bright around the edges and scraped white on the top. A few minutes later Marina arrives from Circle K with two foot-long Slim Jims and a liter of orange Squirt and stares at Sasha.

"What are you doing here?"

Sasha stares back at her, grinning.

"You left Neal," suggests Marina.

Sasha nods. She likes to hear Marina say these words. *She left.* She feels strangely untroubled, drunk on her own daring. Still, she suspects she should be afraid of something, perhaps the police. She knows that taking her own passport isn't a crime, but stealing the ring may be. Undoubtedly, there is a crime somewhere in what she's done.

"You're like that poor old Jew." Marina laughs, handing Sasha one of the Slim Jims. "You know, the one whose life stinks, so he goes to the rabbi for advice, and the rabbi tells him to buy a sheep. The old Jew buys the sheep, and it eats all his food and craps all over his house. So he goes back to the rabbi and the rabbi agrees that he should sell the sheep. 'How are you doing now, old Jew?' the rabbi asks. 'Great, rabbi,' says the old Jew—"

"'It's so nice without the sheep!'" laughs Sasha.

"So what are you going to do, now that you're without the sheep?" Marina asks on her way to the kitchen.

Sasha stops laughing. She didn't think it through this far.

"Are you going to go back?"

"To Neal?"

"To Russia," Marina yells over the noise of the fridge. "Do you want Squirt or this gross cream soda from Saint Savior's pantry?"

Sasha bites into her Slim Jim and washes it down with Squirt. For a second, she pictures herself living with her mother and her "little sister." Yes, just to hold Nadia again, to feed her, to watch her sleep, she will go back. She will get a job at the asbestos mill or at the grocery store. But certainly Mrs. Goldberg will never agree to this arrangement. Strings will be pulled at some Provincial School for the Second Chances, and Sasha Goldberg, the slightly tainted child of the intelligentsia, will be shipped off again in search of a worthy future. Sasha remembers the baby's hand pushing her away and realizes that she doesn't want to go see Nadia only to lose her again. If she can't have Nadia, she's better off far away.

"No," Sasha says. "I don't really want to go back. If I can stay, I mean."

She'll find Victor. She suspends her doubt and imagines that her father is rich. Together, they'll get Nadia from Mrs. Goldberg, once and for all. A homeless man dressed in burlap rags and colorful ribbons pushes his shopping cart by the window, smiling at Marina's grandma. His teeth are black nubs. Sasha squeezes her eyes shut, feeling superstitious.

"Do you want to stay—here?" presses Marina.

"No." It's a lie, but Sasha knows it's the right answer. Marina looks relieved.

"Because, you know, my parents . . . and my uncle . . ."

"I understand," Sasha says, looking around. There's an unmade bed by the wall and Grandma's special portable toilet with legs in the middle of the room. Sasha wonders where else she could go and pictures herself sleeping on the floor of the abandoned ice-cream truck out back.

"You should stay until tonight, though," Marina says quickly. "Talk to my uncle, he knows people."

They take their glasses of Squirt outside and sit on the edge of the mud swimming pool, waiting for Marina's uncle to arrive in his yellow cab.

Uncle Gary is all stomach, his perfect roundness further defined by a pair of wide suspenders. The other parts of him seem to be added as an afterthought, and Sasha is surprised when his compact bald head appears to have some ideas regarding her destiny. He tells Sasha that he has relatives in Chicago who can host her for a while, maybe even help her find work.

"The Vasilievs have a nineteen-year-old daughter. They're always inviting Marina to come up, but Marina is unwilling to step over her mother's dead body." Uncle Gary winks.

"Zina thinks that if a young girl moves away from her mother, that makes her a stripper. She also thinks college dorms are bordellos, and if a guy and a girl are roommates, they will sooner or later have an orgy," explains Marina.

"Your mother," Uncle Gary says with a frown, "is just trying to keep the family together in difficult times."

"How can I get to Chicago?" Sasha asks. Talking to a grown man in Russian makes her feel like a child again, and the words stick in her throat. "I don't have any money to travel anywhere," she manages.

"How much do you have?"

"Nothing." Sasha stares at the floor.

"What, literally nothing?" guffaws Uncle Gary. "Marina?"

"*Dyadya*, this is an emergency," Marina says gravely.

"My whole life is an emergency," Uncle Gary wails, waving his tiny puffy hands in the air. "I'm a sick old man with too many people sitting on my head."

Sasha reaches into her pocket and gets out the engagement ring. Sighing, Uncle Gary takes it from her and holds it in his cupped palm. He screws up his face, as if he's inspecting a slug, and then digs in his pants pocket and produces a pile of bills. From behind his back, Marina nods her head vigorously, as if Sasha might refuse the money.

"Thank you." Sasha folds the bills between the pages of her passport.

"*Nezashto*," Uncle Gary grumbles reflexively. "I'll give Vitaly a call."

He drops the ring into a dresser drawer, picks up a copy of *The Arizona Republic*, and disappears into the bathroom.

For nothing? Suddenly Sasha has a destination and a hundred dollars, a whole new life. What if Victor is in Chicago?

"Where's Chicago?" she asks.

Marina shrugs. "North of here. Everything is north of here."

"You can take a bus there, a Greyhound!" Uncle Gary yells from the bathroom.

Sasha and Marina drink tea with matzo and chocolate syrup and watch Uncle Gary eat tuna from a dented can. In the absence of proper women (Sasha and Marina don't count, and Grandma is senile), Uncle Gary doesn't bother with table settings. Afterward, Uncle Gary calls his Chicago relatives and then the bus station to find out the schedule. The last bus to Chicago leaves in three hours.

In the courtyard of the Palisades, Sasha and Marina stand facing each other, not knowing what to say. They don't embrace. Hugs and kisses are Marina's least favorite thing about America, all these strangers slobbering on each other. Finally, they shake hands like a couple of secret agents, stiff and Soviet. Sasha wraps the handles of her plastic bag around her wrist and walks toward Union Hills to wait for the Downtown bus.

Dear Nadia,

I'm going to Chicago. This bus is very comfortable. The seats are soft, with tall backs. It's a long trip, but it's all right on a bus like this. For the last four hours I've had the whole row to myself, but I can't sleep because the man across the aisle from me keeps coughing. He looks like he is dying. His face is covered with sores, and when he coughs, his whole body shakes. This morning he wet his pants. Most of the time he stays on the bus, but at some stops he gets off to smoke. It takes him a long time to get off the bus, one trembling leg at a time. The stops are short, and people stuck behind the dying man hiss and swear. People on this bus are angrier than other Americans. Maybe they are not Americans.

"You're too sick to sit here!"

In the middle of the night a new driver gets on the bus and makes the dying man sit in the back by the lavatory. The driver wears steel-toed boots and has a gun strapped to his belt. Sasha can tell he doesn't want to touch the dying man, but finally has to pick him up by the arm and drag him down the aisle. After that, Sasha Goldberg is finally able to sleep.

When she wakes up in the morning, the bus is stopped in a field. There are new passengers sitting next to Sasha, a boy and a girl. Their parents sit across the aisle, in the dying man's spot. The girl asks Sasha something, but

Sasha can't understand what she's saying. The girl shrugs and closes her eyes. Her brother is already asleep. Sasha realizes that she and the girl look alike. The girl's hair is black, braided in cornrows, but otherwise they could be sisters.

Sasha hears sirens outside, and three men in sand-colored uniforms get on the bus. They have a dog, a German shepherd.

"Immigration," sighs the lady behind Sasha. The INS officers move down the aisle. Sasha hears them ask everyone the same three questions but cannot make out what the questions are. The men are two rows away when Sasha finally understands what they're asking.

"Are you a U.S. citizen?"

"Where are you going?"

"May I see your green card?"

Sasha Goldberg sees a shaking hand on her lap and recognizes it as her own. Neal lies in a puddle of blood, Hunter kneeling over him, digging in his pocket for an ID. The idea that something awful has happened to Neal in her absence and that she'll never be able to prove her innocence lodges itself in Sasha's brain like a tumor. *I didn't kill him, I just ran away.* The officers move deeper into the bus.

The girl in the next seat stirs in her sleep. Sasha grabs a sleeve of her jacket and pulls it gently. The jacket is big enough for both of them, but the girl has a handful of fabric in her fist. Sasha pulls harder. The girl, still asleep, relaxes her hand. Sasha slides close to her, under the jacket, and closes her eyes. The immigration men stop for a second in front of their seat and keep going.

The raid lasts half an hour. Sasha Goldberg keeps her eyes closed all the time, but she knows that a family is pulled off the bus. She hears the father arguing, in Spanish, and the baby and mother crying together, their voices disappearing outside. The driver starts the motor, and Sasha opens her eyes, slides back into her own seat. The momentary sisterhood dissolves.

The girl's little brother wakes up and puts on a pair of headphones. Sasha listens to the faint *BOOM SHHA SHHA BOOM BOOM* and thinks about slaves, dragged into a slave ship, all the slaving the kids' ancestors had to do to earn them the right to remain on the Greyhound. She sees herself in an INS uniform, fat butt squeezed into high-waisted pants, boarding the bus to disperse benevolence. *Who cares about your green card? Keep going. Do what you need to do.* She'd probably get fired.

The bus approaches Chicago in the late afternoon. Sasha sees train yards, abandoned factories, and concrete apartment blocks, just like in Asbestos 2, but a lot taller. Some towers are arranged in rows, some in semicircles. There are black stains on their facades, like burn marks. The sky is the color of a bruise.

4

The Unknown Fibers

"Alyo."

"Who is this?"

"May I speak to Vitaly Sergeevich?"

The woman sighs and drops the receiver. She's gone a long time, and Sasha worries that the phone will eat her quarter. Finally, a man's voice.

"Vitaly speaking!"

"This is Sasha."

"Ah, Sashenka! We're expecting you! Where are you? Should I come pick you up?"

"You don't have to. I can take a bus."

"I won't hear of it! You must be exhausted! I'll be there in a half hour."

Sasha wonders how she will recognize him, but as soon as he walks through the door she feels as if she's won a game of Spot-the-Russian. Sasha is unprepared for the sight of Vitaly Sergeevich. Marina's family in Phoenix didn't look like that. The heat relaxed their faces and forced them to wear shorts.

Vitaly Sergeevich Vasiliev is wearing a gray suit and gray leather shoes. By his grimly set jaw, by the tilt of his neck, Sasha Goldberg knows things about him. She knows that in his life, he's washed dishes with Household Soap and children with Children's Soap. That he never wears street shoes indoors. That he has probably, at least once, owned a Seagull wristwatch, that he treats superficial flesh wounds with emerald-green, stinging *zelenka*.

Vitaly Sergeevich navigates the crowd with barely disguised squeamishness, as if people around him might bite, or drool, or do an obscene dance without warning. Sasha Goldberg stands up and walks toward him, but he looks through her. She smiles and waves. No reaction. In the game of Spot-the-Russian Sasha is at level five, the grand prize. For a split second, she feels gloriously American. She wishes she were wearing a pair of baggy jeans and a T-shirt like most people here, instead of an empire-waist peasant dress in crushed rayon. (*You look so feminine*, Neal said, watching Sasha emerge from a Wal-Mart fitting room. He said feminine the way a starving person might say tasty. On the drive home, they listened to Simon and Garfunkel in compassionate silence, four empire-waist peasant dresses in assorted colors in the trunk. *Buy three, get one free.*)

"Hello," Sasha yells in Russian. "Vitaly Sergeevich! Here!"

"Sashenka? Good to meet you! Come." Vitaly Sergeevich blinks away a look of affront. "The car is waiting."

Vitaly Sergeevich's car is a Crown Victoria. It's as long as Sasha Goldberg's whole life. Vitaly Sergeevich talks about the car, how he got it at the police auction, and shows Sasha the interceptor light.

Sinking into the black vinyl seat, Sasha has trouble keeping her eyes open. They drive for a long time. The buildings get smaller, the trees taller. Vitaly Sergeevich turns out to live in a five-story yellow-brick walk-up, and not in one of the apartment towers like Sasha thought.

"Oh! Those are project homes! There are just blacks in there. It's very dangerous." Vitaly Sergeevich sounds offended, as if Sasha had accused him of living with the blacks because of some shortcoming of his. Sasha Goldberg smiles affectionately. Vitaly Sergeevich's blunt racism is as nostalgic as his suit and shoes. It makes Sasha feel weirdly at home.

Vitaly Sergeevich parks the car. There is a reflection in the window next to Sasha's head, a black girl, made blacker by the dark hedge outside. Sasha decides not to say anything unless asked. For now, she'll just be a very dark Jew. Neal never asked. He probably figured Sasha was just one of those Black Russians, the way Marina's neighbors from the Palisades assumed Ukraine was full of Mexicans, asking Marina what language Mexicans spoke in Donetsk.

From the voice on the phone Sasha imagines Mrs. Vasiliev as a stout bowlegged figure, with teased-out hair, missile breasts, and a sequined outfit.

But Margarita Petrovna ("Call me Rita!") is a waif in a thin black T-shirt. She wears her graying hair shoulder-length and floppy, like an American. Sasha doesn't think she's wearing a bra.

The apartment is decorated Russian style, with floral wallpaper and a red Persian rug hanging on the wall. Lace tulle clutters the window frames; a black china cabinet stands in the corner. Rita looks like a bug caught in all this dark opulence.

"Ritochka, set the table!" exclaims Vitaly Sergeevich.

Rita gets a bottle of vodka and three glasses out of the cabinet, some sausage and bread out of the fridge. They drink to health. Vitaly Sergeevich asks about Marina's grandma, and they drink to her health. They drink to good luck with Sasha's immigration. Rita leans her head on her fist like a child, and stares into space. Vitaly Sergeevich gets happier as he drinks. He chases his vodka with raw garlic. Sasha does the same to try to stay awake, but can't keep her eyes open any longer. Vitaly Sergeevich shows her to the futon in one of the bedrooms.

"Rita, where is the guest pillow?"

"In the trash," moans Rita in a languid, seasick voice.

"But I'd asked you—"

"It was old. It stank. I threw it away."

Vitaly Sergeevich glances sheepishly at another bed in the room. There are two pillows on it, but Vitaly Sergeevich doesn't touch them.

"I have an idea," he finally says, struggling into his dirty beige trench coat.

Sasha perches on the edge of the futon, kicks off her slippers, and lies down, arm under her head. Pillow or no pillow, it feels good to lie horizontally after a night and two days on the Greyhound.

She is still awake when Vitaly Sergeevich returns with a large plastic bag, cheerfully bemoaning the stingy candy-bar-like rectangularity of American pillows.

"At least these are soft," he says, digging in the bag.

Rubbing her eyes, Sasha comes out into the living room. "You shouldn't have."

"Nonsense," says Vitaly Sergeevich. "Besides, we all need new pillows. I got four. They were on sale."

Rita examines the pillows, looks at the tags. "Did you see this? It says *unknown fibers.* I'm not putting my head anywhere near these. I'd rather sleep on the floor," she says.

Vitaly Sergeevich looks defeated. "Well, Sasha and I can each have one, then. Right, Sasha?"

"Wait until Lika sees them," hisses Rita, heaving herself up from the chair. Her alcohol breath burns with resentment, like a fuse, but Vitaly Sergeevich doesn't blow up. He just picks up a pillow and looks at it for a long time, as if trying to solve the riddle of the unknown fibers.

In the morning, yellow sunlight streams through the tulle, covering Sasha's bedspread in delicate designs. Sasha wakes up and notices a poster tacked to the ceiling above her bed. A giant curly head on the poster stares at her with its deep-set eyes.

Sasha rolls over and sees a girl, about her age, in the other bed. The girl is leaning on one elbow, reading a book.

"Hi. I'm Lika." She smiles. She's very pretty, with a small upturned nose and long, straight, sand-colored hair. Her shoulders are tan, and when she shifts in bed, Sasha sees her small pointy breasts through her pink cotton undershirt.

Lika seems not to mind Sasha in her room, and she's happy to talk. Sasha gets the feeling that it's a usual thing for people to stay here.

"So where are you from?" she asks.

"Asbestos 2," Sasha says. "It's in Siberia, by Prostuda."

"Crazy name."

"Yeah, well, it's pretty straightforward. Asbestos is all there is."

"How long have you been here?"

"Since last night," Sasha says, immediately realizing that Lika means in America. "A year."

Lika has been in America for six years, all of them in this apartment. She graduated from high school here.

"It's cool, you know, the way you're doing it," she says.

"What?"

"You know, coming here on your own, it's cool. No parents. Nobody tells you what to do, nobody hassles you about coming home on time, or what color your hair is, or whether you've been drinking. Sometimes I feel like I live under a microscope." Lika sighs. "So, you like it here?"

That's an American question. Immigrants never ask each other this because they know the answer will be too long.

Sasha laughs. "It's all right."

"What do you do?"

"I'm just learning English," says Sasha, offering the most uncomplicated truth. "And you?"

"I go to the Art Institute. Just started my second year."

"I used to go to an art school." Sasha's heart begins to race as she says it. Suddenly she feels like an imposter, like she has no right to remember AFTER EATIN.

Lika springs out of bed to show Sasha her paintings. They're beyond awful, full of gray muck and awkward, hesitant moves. In one, a still life, glass bottles straddle the edge of the paper as in a preschool drawing. Of course, thinks Sasha, she hasn't had Evgeny Mikhailovich and Bedbug train her like a circus animal. *If a bear can ride a unicycle, you can draw perspective!*

She allows herself a few mental glimpses of what now seems like pure happiness: the plank over the puddle in the entryway; graphite sheen on the skin of Katia's knuckles; a cloud of cigarette smoke rising toward a stained ceiling.

"What do you think?" asks Lika.

A chicken can paint better with its left leg! Evgeny Mikhailovich would've savaged Lika, scorched her with his onion breath.

"I like this one a lot," Sasha lies, pointing at the least offensive painting.

Next, Lika gets out the photographs. Oh, things they do at art schools here! Sasha imagines showing Lika's pictures to Bedbug, teaching him that there is more to art than *Fruit with Drape* and *Landscape with Birches*.

Lika photographs herself naked. She scratches words into the negative before printing it. "Obsess" over her breasts. "Possess" over her face. The pictures are dark, with a jagged black border. Lika's body looks gray and lifeless, and the scratches are glaringly white.

"Wow," Sasha says. She's never seen art like this. "I think you should be a photographer."

In the living room, the teapot is boiling and Rita is setting out herring with onions for breakfast. The night has drained away her anger. Pale and heavy-lidded, she moves around sluggishly, as if lost in her own ten-square-foot kitchen.

After breakfast Lika takes Sasha shopping at the Salvation Army. The thrift store smells like Marina's house. Afterward, they walk along Devon Avenue. Sasha is elated to be walking on a street full of pedestrians. She smiles at the leafy trees, at a man selling mangoes from a wooden crate. Her time in Arizona seems like a fading nightmare.

Dear Nadia,

I've been at the Vasilievs' house for two weeks now. Vitaly Sergeevich said I was welcome to stay with them, but I think his wife wants me out. Their daughter, Lika, is rarely around.

During the day when the Vasilievs are at work and Lika is at school, I try to make myself useful—I dust and do the dishes. When I have nothing to do I watch Russian TV and read. Right now, I'm re-reading Anna Karenina, *and it's making me sick. I skip the place where Anna sneaks in to see her son. I miss you so much.*

I asked Vitaly Sergeevich if he could help me find my father. He said he didn't know anyone named Victor Goldberg and suggested I go to the library and check the phone books. He said I should start with New York City, because that's where most Russians live. I should have thought of this back in Phoenix! In the Brooklyn phone book alone, there was a whole page of Goldbergs. There was one Victor Goldberg, three Viktor Goldbergs, a Vic Goldberg, and five Goldberg V.'s. Unfortunately, all of the Brooklyn Goldbergs, except for Vic, whose number had been disconnected, hung up on me. Still, after being one of the two Goldbergs in Asbestos 2, it's thrilling to imagine all these Goldbergs living together in one place. Lika says they're unrelated to each other. She says it's a common name. Hearing that our name is common makes me feel patriotic toward the U.S. Another thing that makes me patriotic is the Nearly Free Shoe Warehouse on Devon—all those nice shoes in one place and that new shoe smell . . . not that I have any money. I feel like I owe the Vasilievs for all the phone calls I made to the Brooklyn Goldbergs. Tomorrow, I'm going back

*to the library to look up the Goldbergs in Manhattan, Queens, and, finally,
Chicago.*

*Vitaly Sergeevich said that in the meantime he'd help me find a job, but
he's done nothing so far. He seems to like me hanging around the house. I tell
him I don't want to impose, and he gets angry.*

"Stop talking like an American!" he says.

Sasha Goldberg wrings the mop into the tub and leafs through an old
issue of *The Foreign Land* that Vitaly Sergeevich has left on the bathroom floor.

"Research Shows Children of Vegetarians are Born Retarded."

"Frigid or Sexpot—How to tell by her Purse."

"The Case of the Telepathic Cat."

A color advertisement for orthopedic shoes falls out of the paper and
slides along the tile floor. Vitaly Sergeevich is the only one who reads *The
Foreign Land.* Lika and Rita call it *The Toilet Paper.*

The front door slams. Rita is home. She hangs her worn, suede-fringed
purse on a chair and throws her jacket on the floor. A black hairnet covers her
head like a toy turban. Realizing that she'd left it on, she tears it off her head,
balls it up, and hurls it across the room. It hangs on the corner of the TV con-
sole, marking Rita's territory, her field of hostility. Sasha Goldberg slinks
back into the bathroom.

"What's new?" Rita hollers sarcastically. "What's happening?"

Rita is a lunchroom aide at Devon High. She is angriest after work.

"Sasha, I need to use the bathroom!"

Almost every afternoon, Rita disappears into the bathroom to attack her
skin with tweezers. She always comes out in a better mood, her face dotted
with chalky spots of concealer. Sasha leafs through *The Foreign Land* and waits
for her to emerge.

"Rita, I was wondering if you could . . . ," Sasha begins, watching a bead
of fresh blood swelling on Rita's chin.

"What?"

"Talk to Vitaly Sergeevich about finding me a situation. I can't stay here
forever."

"And why not? Look, we have two whole bedrooms. Together we make twelve hundred dollars! Of course you can just move in! And invite your family. Do you, by chance, have any relatives selling flowers in the streets of Stockholm, about to be deported to Kalmykia? We specialize in these kind of people! The Vasiliev Shelter. Enter, you hungry masses!"

"All I need is a little help finding—"

"Look, young lady. I moved to America alone. When I married Vitaly I was a waitress at the *shashlychnaya*, sharing a room with three other women. Read *The Toilet Paper*! There're roommate ads in there. There're job ads!" Rita throws her hands up.

Sasha nods, realizing that Rita is right. This isn't Phoenix. The Russian papers are full of illegal jobs. Sasha could even try for one of the better-paying, "English Language Required" jobs and make six dollars an hour.

"I have nothing against you," sighs Rita, digging her maroon fingernails into Sasha's arm, "but when I moved into his apartment I thought I would finally get some peace and quiet. As if! As soon as we were married, Vitaly's ex shipped Lika over from Leningrad. Every day I had to step over Lika's little friends, sprawled out in the living room with their keyboards, putting out cigarettes on my furniture. At least you don't drink Robitussin!"

Rita shudders and laughs nervously. A second bead of blood forms on her face and flows into the first bead, making a tiny number eight. Sasha remembers a physics class from ages ago, water in a petri dish, an eyedropper, a glass rectangle.

"Life is a meat grinder, Sasha," utters Rita, stuffing her hairnet into a kitchen drawer. "I'll talk to Vitaly again. The fool ought to use his connections."

By the time Vitaly Sergeevich comes home from work, she's in bed, half a bottle of passion fruit cognac soaking into the walls of her stomach.

Vitaly Sergeevich and Sasha share leftover borscht, relieving the silence with emphatic slurps until a conversation topic presents itself.

"So what did you girls do today?" Vitaly Sergeevich finally asks.

"I talked to Rita about looking for a job. She said I should look in *The Toi*— . . . in the newspaper."

Vitaly Sergeevich looks down at his bowl, and his face reddens.

"I think it's a good idea," says Sasha.

"It's a shame, Sasha. You ought to go to college."

"Vitaly Sergeevich, be realistic. What about my paperwork?"

Vitaly Sergeevich sighs and dumps his bowl in the sink. "Has Lika been home yet?"

"No."

Vitaly Sergeevich shakes his head, looks in the freezer.

"We're out of ice cream!" he proclaims mournfully, and then says in a decisive voice, happy to have found a problem he can solve, "We should go to Dunkin' Donuts, Sasha."

Outside, the wind blows around something that is neither rain nor fog. Dunkin' Donuts is the only place open at this hour. Vitaly Sergeevich buys two sprinkled doughnuts for himself and a hot chocolate for Sasha, and finds a clean table.

"Maybe you could be a good influence on Lika," he says with a mouth full of doughnut, rainbow-colored mouse turds raining down on his tie.

"I can't live with you anymore, Vitaly Sergeevich," Sasha says firmly.

"Any luck at the library?"

Sasha shakes her head.

"Of course," says Vitaly Sergeevich with a baleful grin, "you would have told me if you found him. What kind of father is he, to just . . ."

Sasha grins back, wondering how old Lika was when he left her in Leningrad.

"Of course." Vitaly Sergeevich swallows. "There are circumstances."

That night, Lika stays out past midnight. Vitaly Sergeevich doesn't go to bed, waiting for her to come home, flipping the channels on the TV. At three in the morning, Sasha wakes up to the trial in the living room.

"It's none of your business! I'm fucking twenty years old with my papa hovering over me watching my every fucking step!"

"Angelika, don't swear. As long as you live here—I'm your father."

"Fine, then, I'll move the fuck out!"

Lika runs into the bedroom and slams the door.

"You aren't asleep, are you?"

"No," whispers Sasha.

"Oh, man, what a day," Lika says in English, flipping on the light.

Sasha waits, expecting to hear more, but Lika is quiet, digging in the blue steamer trunk at the foot of her bed.

To make conversation, Sasha asks about the head on the ceiling.

"Jesus, Sasha. It's Jim Morrison. You don't know Jim Morrison?"

"What is he, an actor?"

"He's from the Doors. The Doors. A band?"

"How was I supposed to know that?"

"Oh, never mind. Do you want to hear something?" Lika waltzes over to her tape player.

The music is loud and insistent, like someone trying to tell you something and you'd better pay attention, except that Sasha can't make out the words.

"Sasha, you're an old lady in a girl's body. Just look at you sitting there with Papa, watching your inane crap on Russian TV. Repeat after me: 'Jim Morrison rules.'"

"Jim Morrison rules," laughs Sasha.

Vitaly Sergeevich pounds on the door.

"What?" yells Lika.

"Turn that down, Angelika! A human being has got a migraine!"

"A human being is shitfaced!" retorts Lika, and then, to Sasha, "He always calls Rita a human being when she's shitfaced. It bugs the crap out of me. ... ."

"Nobody calls me a human being when I'm shitfaced!" she screams at the door. "When I'm shitfaced, you lecture me and take away the car!"

Jim Morrison sings about an LA woman. After a minute, Vitaly Sergeevich retreats. Sasha can feel his heavy footsteps resonating in the floorboards.

"So, are you now a Doors fan?" Lika asks. She finds what she is looking for, a small wooden box and what looks like a hollow screw. "You want a hit?"

"All right, I'm a Doors fan," Sasha Goldberg replies in English, thinking that "a door's fan" sounds like something you buy at the hardware store. "But what's with the box?"

Lika rolls her eyes and smooshes something inside the box with the screw.

"Ma-ri-jua-na," she enunciates. "*Narkotiki.* Moral decay. Didn't you learn anything at school?"

Sasha inhales the scratchy smoke and keeps it inside until her ribs hurt, as told. Ten minutes later she's walking on air, giggling, because it's totally hilarious to be four inches off the ground. The space between Sasha and the floor is spongy, unpredictable. She's waiting to crash. Something is stretching the skin of her face into a gum-baring grin. She licks her lips, tries to figure things out, gives up.

"How do you feel?" asks Lika.

"Good," Sasha manages. "Is this going to go away?"

"Oh, totally," laughs Lika. "Take it easy."

They eat roasted hazelnuts from a crystal bowl and look through Lika's photo albums. In pictures, Lika is mostly with her Russian friends from Devon High. There's a picture of a party, two boys with shoulder-length hair sitting on the floor in front of a keyboard. *This is Igor. And this is Frol. He's intense. He's a construction worker and collects guns. The one in a bandanna. And this is Vlad, he was our valedictorian, he studies computers at Loyola.* In the next photo Vlad has his arm around Lika. They're sitting on a green leather couch, next to a vase of plastic flowers.

"Is he your boyfriend?" Sasha asks.

Lika stares at her and laughs, almost gagging on a nut.

"*Fuck no.* I'd never date any of these guys. They're so totally immature. They live with their annoying parents. They're just"—Lika switches to Russian as she always does when discussing lofty matters—"not very interesting people."

She switches back to English. "They're, like, retarded. All they know is get drunk, get stoned, make stupid jokes." Lika laughs, snatching the album away from Sasha, "If you must know, I have a *vozlublenny.*"

Sasha rolls off the bed. She is writhing on the floor, *dying* of laughter. *Beloved.* Sasha thinks of a knight, a tower, some peacocks. *Tristan and fucking Isolde.*

"I'm serious," says Lika.

"Which one is he?" asks Sasha, still laughing.

"Oh, he isn't in the pictures. He doesn't hang out with my friends, they bore him. He's older. He only sees me alone. We have these amazing conversations."

Sasha puffs out her cheeks, trying not to laugh, but her eyes fill with tears.

"Seriously, though," begins Lika, "I know it's kind of old-fashioned to think this way, but don't you believe that you can only have one true love? That you just *know*?"

"No!" says Sasha. Somewhere in her stoned brain there's a reason why, at that very moment, it's important to prove Lika wrong, to cut her off.

"What do you mean?"

"You only think that way," says Sasha. "One day you think it's true love. The next day it doesn't matter at all."

"You don't have to be, you know, cruel."

Ah, Sasha thinks cruelly, *Americans' stretchy definition of cruelty. Far more things are considered cruel here than just, uh, cigarette burns and electroshock.*

Lika grabs a blue silk strap that she wears around her neck and pulls a tiny leather book from under her shirt.

"Made it in bookmaking," she says, pushing the miniature bone clasp with her thumbnail. The book springs open. Inside is a Soviet passport photo of a bushy-browed fortyish man with old-fashioned glasses and a trim beard. He looks like a guitar-playing type, the kind of man who knows at least a dozen songs about mountains and manly solitude. Perhaps he even writes them.

"His name is Andrey. Rita went to high school with him in Russia. He came to stay with us after his divorce. Papa kept worrying Rita would run off with him!" Lika giggles. "Papa and Rita don't know, for obvious reasons. As soon as I move out of here, we're getting married. Can I trust you to keep a secret?"

Sasha stretches out on her bed, suddenly too tired to move, dry lips plastered to her teeth in a spastic grin.

"Does he play guitar?" she asks, gazing into Jim Morrison's Neanderthal eyes for sympathy and reassurance.

"Yes. How did you know?"

Sasha shrugs. Jim Morrison, from his ceiling, congratulates her on her superb knowledge of Soviet stereotypes.

> *Hepy bursday to you*
> *Hepy bursday to you*
> *Hepy bursday dir Reeta,*
> *Hepy bursday to you!*

Three Uzbek teenagers drone, swaying from side to side. With their glossy raven hair and bare midriffs they should be on the cover of *Glamour*, not here in the smoky, dim kebob house. A candle burns in the éclair. Rita is turning forty-five.

This is the *shashlychnaya* where Vitaly Sergeevich first met Rita. It was his idea to come here. Sasha can see that he desperately wants to have a good day. He says nothing when Lika orders four hundred grams of Absolut and stares him hard in the eye. Satisfied with his reaction, Lika doesn't drink the vodka. Vitaly Sergeevich asks for extra glasses and makes a toast.

"To Ritochka. And to our family. May we always be as happy as we are now!"

Lika snorts, but in a good-natured way.

On the way home Vitaly Sergeevich buys Rita a dozen roses. He's the only one dressed up for the occasion. His white shirt is strangely sheer, and Sasha can make out two islands of chest hair shaped like lungs in a medical drawing.

Sitting on the couch with her legs bent under her and carefully controlled disappointment on her face, Rita unwraps the presents. A bottle of French perfume from Vitaly Sergeevich, a handmade ceramic incense holder from Lika. Rita stacks the presents on the coffee table and begs off to bed. Vitaly Sergeevich follows.

Sasha and Lika burn incense on the kitchen counter and listen to their hushed voices through the bedroom door. The argument they're waiting for never begins. Their conversation persists in a calm monotone, and at one point the girls hear Rita laugh.

Her laughter makes Sasha feel strangely alone, left out. Lika busies herself with incense, but Sasha can see her cringe, like an embarrassed child. The velvety stick starts to smolder. Sasha and Lika stare at each other through the smoke, two sober strangers, one a Doors fan and the other not.

"Want to get stoned?" Lika asks.

"Sure," Sasha says eagerly.

Bleary-eyed and dehydrated, Sasha throws on a T-shirt and comes out to the living room. Lika is still asleep, but the older Vasilievs are almost done with their breakfast.

"Good morning," exclaims Rita, jumping up from her seat. "Tea or coffee?"

"Thanks, I can—"

"Oh, no, you sit down!" Rita admonishes, smiling. "Do you want a piece of toast?"

"Thank you," says Sasha, dropping three sugar cubes into the cup of tea that Rita sets in front of her.

"I have good news for you, Sashenka," says Vitaly Sergeevich mournfully.

Sasha looks up at him, but he doesn't take his eyes from her cup, as if determined to fully observe the dissolution of Sasha's sugar cubes.

"I found you a job. You'll do some light housework for a wonderful family. I've known the roaches for years, they do a lot for Soviet Jews. Best of all, they've offered to let you live with them and promised to look into your status."

Vitaly Sergeevich seems relieved to have gotten that out. He smiles sheepishly at Sasha, and Sasha smiles back.

"Thank you, Vitaly Sergeevich! I appreciate it," she says encouragingly. "Why do you call them roaches?"

"That's their last name," sighs Vitaly Sergeevich. "Tarakan."

Rita laughs through her nose, like a kindergartener.

"Mr. Tarakan is a lawyer," mumbles Vitaly Sergeevich. "He could be very helpful with immigration."

"When do I start?" asks Sasha. She likes the lawyer part, although Vitaly Sergeevich doesn't sound too sure. Has he even met this Mr. Roach?

"Today!" exclaims Rita.

"I'll drive you tonight," confirms Vitaly Sergeevich, absentmindedly picking up a stick of salami and taking a huge bite out of it.

Sasha and Rita stare at him silently. Still chewing, Vitaly Sergeevich sets the salami down on the table and gets up.

"Aren't you going to eat your toast?" asks Rita.

"No, thanks. I'm finished!" he yells with exaggerated cheer, stomping out of the living room.

Sasha watches Rita carve the tooth marks out of the salami with a paring knife. Vitaly Sergeevich is now in Lika's room, making noise. Sasha hears Lika shriek, "What the fuck!"

"I never want to see you smoking this stuff in my house! And the walls! Who said you can write on the walls? This isn't a public toilet! By this afternoon, I want this room clean!"

Lika dashes into the bathroom, a streak of pink flesh and Looney Tunes pajama bottoms, and locks the door. Rita wraps the salami in plastic and puts it in the fridge. Vitaly Sergeevich stands in the middle of Lika's room, panting. Then, with unexpected grace, he leaps onto Sasha's unmade bed and reaches up to the ceiling.

Smiling enigmatically, Jim Morrison's head sails through the air like a lowered flag.

By the afternoon, Sasha's things are packed neatly in two black garbage bags. Lika hangs a rune charm on Sasha's neck, and everyone sits down, for good luck. Sasha has the impression that she's about to be shot off into space or sent on a polar expedition, not merely driven to the suburbs.

In the car, Vitaly Sergeevich lights a cigarette, flicks the ashes out the window. The traffic is heavy on Devon, and Sasha has time to soak up the sights: the Salvation Army, the bank, the Dunkin' Donuts. She wants to remember every detail. The collection of landscapes in her head is the only thing she safely owns. Out of the corner of her eye, she looks at Vitaly Sergeevich. He's wearing one of his murky green suits and a maroon tie. The awful colors give his face an unhealthy tint. Sasha tries to imagine what Vitaly Sergeevich had been like before he turned into Vitaly Sergeevich.

A young man with a full head of hair, in a gnarly seventies sweater.

A skinny child wielding a hockey stick in an orderly Brezhnev-era yard.

A fat toothless baby from a 1950s magazine cover, sitting in an enamel basin, one curly forelock sticking straight up.

The baby lifts his dimpled hands, knowing nothing of what his life will become, what his hands will look like covered in graying yellow hair, on the steering wheel of a Crown Victoria. The old man steers the car onto Lake Shore Drive. Sasha Goldberg blinks away her tears and keeps her eyes on the road.

They get off Lake Shore and drive through the forest on a narrow winding highway, then onto a gravel path. The house is half hidden among the trees, a tiny hut, really, with a shiny red roof and whitewashed walls. The Three Bears' house. Sasha can't imagine a whole family living there, let alone needing a housekeeper.

Vitaly Sergeevich stops the car, talks to the man in the hut, and drives on. Sasha realizes that the hut is just a guard booth. They round a grove of pines and see the *real* house—part Tudor mansion, part concrete block with a glass wall. The two incongruous halves of the house protrude into each other as if frozen in the middle of a wrestling match. The Tudor portion has an un-adorned concrete staircase, and the concrete block is partly covered by a Tu-dor roof. The whole thing looks larger than the Vasilievs' entire apartment building.

"So, what do you think?" Vitaly Sergeevich asks.

"This is a huge house!" Sasha exclaims appreciatively, happy that Vitaly Sergeevich is talking to her again.

"It's called the Waterfall House. It's an architectural landmark. It's in guidebooks."

"Where's the waterfall?"

"Under the house somewhere. You'll have plenty of time to find out. Wait here."

Vitaly Sergeevich gets out of the car and rings the doorbell.

A woman in an apron answers the door and disappears back inside. Vi-taly Sergeevich waits at the top of the stairs, nervously smoothing his suit. When the door opens again, Sasha sees a thin woman with a mane of gold and a face that looks like a combination of Kermit the Frog and Miss Piggy. Her painted lips are stretched into an enormous permanent smile. The smile is noncommittal, parallel to the ground. It dissects the woman's oval head into two equal parts, like a crack in an egg. Her legs are long and smooth, and her face makes it impossible to guess her age. The woman glances at the car, beckoning Sasha to come out.

"This Mrs. Tarakan," Vitaly Sergeevich says in English. "Mrs. Tarakan, this Sasha."

"Hello, dear. I'm so glad to welcome you to my home. And *please,* call me Claudette." Mrs. Tarakan pronounces words slowly and clearly, like a pre-school teacher or someone who is used to talking with foreigners. Sasha gets her bag out of the car and submits to her new employer's contact-free hug. A gold chain-mail triangle dangles down from Mrs. Tarakan's neck, tickling Sasha's shoulder blade.

"Good? I go away now," mutters Vitaly Sergeevich, retreating backward down the staircase like a green crab.

1

Operation Exodus

"VITALY TOLD ME SO MUCH ABOUT YOU," SAID MRS. TARAKAN, leading Sasha inside the house. "You're a brave girl."

"Thank you," murmured Sasha.

Brave? Sasha wondered what Vitaly Sergeevich could have said. What did he even know?

Inside, the air smelled like moist concrete and candle wax. The sky-lit foyer opened into a two-story hall with a buttressed ceiling. Despite her high heels, Mrs. Tarakan managed to walk soundlessly on the stone floor. Sasha tried to follow suit, but each step she made echoed under the roof, making her feel like a *Masterpiece Theatre* character.

Sasha stared at the boar skins that hung upside down above each of the hall's four fireplaces. The boars still had their heads. A cluster of medieval weapons crossed in a petrified brawl on one of the whitewashed walls. The Waterfall House looked like a museum. Did people actually live here?

They walked into a bedroom. Here, the luxury was spare: a platform bed with translucent silk canopy stood in the middle of the room, some embroidered pillows lay scattered on the floor. Through the open door, Sasha noticed a huge bathroom with two sinks and a claw-foot bathtub in a glass enclosure. A couple of stylishly exposed chrome pipes ran along the ceiling, terminating at a vintage showerhead. Mrs. Tarakan slipped a gold chain with a Star of David charm into Sasha's hand.

"I want you to wear this," she instructed. "And now, just relax. We're having a party tonight, and I must get ready."

"Thank you," said Sasha. The chain was real gold, but the star itself was brass, just like the one Marina wore in Phoenix.

Mrs. Tarakan showed Sasha to a sprawling leather couch in an adjacent room and left. The couch and a glass-topped coffee table were the only furniture here. African statues lined the walls. Most were at least as tall as Sasha, but the vast white space above made them appear insignificant, like figurines on a souvenir store's shelf. One had a drum, and another was offering its elongated conical breast to a tiny version of itself. For a second, Sasha Goldberg pretended that she shared their shelf. It would be nice to just stand by the wall, mute and dumb. Sasha wondered what Mrs. Tarakan expected her to do during the party.

She picked up a Norman Rockwell folio from the coffee table and tried to interest herself in the dilemmas of knotty-faced imps, but had trouble concentrating. The Tarakans' house reminded her of something she'd read in childhood. Some endless story by Victor Hugo, replete with sweaty stones and secrets. Sasha shivered and put down the book.

Mrs. Tarakan flew in and out of the room, yelling in Spanish at her two maids. Every time Sasha saw her, she was wearing a different expensive-looking but slightly off-kilter outfit. Finally, she returned for good, dressed in a pearly beige jumpsuit and a ten-inch-wide golden belt with scales. The belt looked dangerously sharp, as if it were about to slip underneath Mrs. Tarakan's rib cage and open her up like a can of tomato paste.

"There will be lot of important people at our house tonight. We are having a benefit for an organization that helps people like you. Do you know what a benefit is?"

Sasha knew. She didn't know what "people like you" meant.

A man in his sixties and two young people came into the room. The man wore a Castro suit with short shorts and innumerable pockets. His hair was dyed jet-black. The young guy and girl had handsome faces with heavy jaws and Mrs. Tarakan's mermaid hair. The girl was telling the man in shorts about her new apartment.

"I'm trying to get Jason to move in with me," she said. "I can keep an eye on him."

"No way!" The young man shook his head, laughing.

"Gordon, I told you about Sasha Goldberg," interrupted Mrs. Tarakan. "Sasha, meet Mr. Tarakan, Alyssa, and Jason."

"It's my pleasure . . . ," said Mr. Tarakan, obviously flipping through a giant book in his brain, trying to remember who on earth Sasha could be. Mrs. Tarakan whispered something in his ear, and the flipping stopped. Mr. Tarakan nodded meaningfully. Gazing into Sasha's eyes with a wide benevolent smile, he seemed to be about to speak, but didn't. Instead, he took Sasha's right hand in both of his and held it long enough for Sasha to thoroughly contemplate the nature of the blue space between his teeth and his gums.

Alyssa looked Sasha over with large disinterested eyes. The last rays of sunset illuminated the room, and Sasha felt her vision sharpen in a dizzying, unpleasant way. She couldn't stop staring at Alyssa's orange cleavage. It seemed to have a life of its own, threatening to swallow the gold razor-blade charm on the girl's necklace. Alyssa scratched her chin with her curving pink fingernails, and Sasha noticed tiny metallic spiders glued to each nail's base. She felt an irresistible urge to run and hide.

"Excuse me, where's the bathroom?" she asked, hating herself for the break in her voice, for sounding like a foreigner, for being a foreigner, for being there at all.

"Down the hall, the first door to the left," said Alyssa, and Sasha hurried away, ignoring the echo as best she could. She spent a long time in the bathroom, playing with iridescent soap shells, touching her own face in the mirror for comfort.

By the time she came back out, most of the guests had arrived. Sasha noticed that many women were dressed like Mrs. Tarakan, in fabrics that changed the texture of their bodies in some mad attempt to transcend their species. There was a Moth lady, a Fish lady and a Firefly lady. Old men, homogeneous like black bugs, accompanied these shimmering creatures around the room. Sasha noticed OPERATION EXODUS buttons on their lapels. A tall, stiff-haired woman walked into the room, awkwardly holding hands with two brown children in polo shirts. The room fell quiet. Mrs. Tarakan flew up to the woman and pecked her on the cheek.

"That's Congressman Leake's wife," Mr. Tarakan explained to someone behind Sasha's back. "They just came back from Bangladesh with their adopted children. They also have a baby girl at home."

"Those kids are sure lucky," replied a nasal voice.

"*Tozhe mne*, lucky!" someone declared aloud in the high-pitched, disgruntled Russian of a market haggler. "What's so lucky? Their parents are dead, and he calls 'em lucky!"

Or alive somewhere, thought Sasha, looking around for the source of the voice.

"*Zatknis'*, Mama!" another woman hissed.

They stood by the wall near one of the fireplaces. The mom was a squarish, bowlegged shape that Russian women get from years of carrying and eating potatoes. Heavy gold earrings with sapphire, probably a retirement present from a now-defunct Soviet organization, stretched her wrinkly earlobes. The daughter had beautiful fat lips and almond-shaped eyes, like the People in Ivanov's *The Appearance of Christ to the People*.

Making her way toward them in the crowd, Sasha noticed that the mother absentmindedly reached over and stroked the stuffed boar's rubbery snout. Encouraged by the homey gesture, she approached the women and began a standard immigrant "Where are you from?" conversation, but soon stumbled, realizing that she couldn't them tell anything coherent about herself. A dark-skinned mail-order bride from Siberia. Where did she live now? She wasn't sure yet. As soon as the introductions were finished, Sasha could read the verdict in the old woman's posture, in her distracted eyes. Alla Aronovna was thinking, *trash*.

Alla Aronovna and Yulia were from Kiev. Sasha found out that they had refugee status, a Section 8 apartment, and a monthly Social Security check. Alla Aronovna was proud of the fact that Yulia would be starting at Northwestern in the fall. Sasha could tell that, from the wisdom of her years, Alla Aronovna calculated more or less exactly where Sasha came from, and regarded her the same way she regarded the Bangladeshi children, as a pitiful victim of a world that was not her own. It was apparent from the look of well-hidden squeamishness on Alla Aronovna's peaceful face that if Sasha and Yulia had been kids, they wouldn't have been allowed to play together.

The party moved outside. The maids set up three rows of white plastic chairs on the lawn, and people began to take their seats for the official part of the evening.

"Come, sit by me!" Mrs. Tarakan beckoned Sasha to a chair next to her own.

Mr. Tarakan tested a microphone on a card table draped with a large Israeli flag and waited for silence. Mrs. Tarakan crossed her legs and leaned forward, the elegant golden S of her body culminating in a Kermit head, her eyes barely visible under the bluish, stretched-to-the-limit lids. In profile, Mrs. Tarakan resembled Igor the Skeleton. Her nose didn't seem to have any cartilage. Sasha wondered if she destroyed her face herself. She couldn't imagine a plastic surgeon who'd carve up a person like that. She pictured Mrs. Tarakan in her clawfoot tub, armed with one of Lika's X-Acto knives and a compact mirror.

After the last of the guests were seated, Mr. Tarakan began to speak. Sasha studied blades of grass at her feet. In the light of a flood lamp, they looked uniformly healthy, supersaturated green, like Astroturf.

Sasha heard Mr. Tarakan say "thousands upon thousands of Soviet Jews," "freedom," and "hope." Trained by years of Asbestos 2 schooling, her mind automatically tuned out the speech. At one point, Mrs. Tarakan yanked Sasha by the arm and made her stand up. Sasha noticed that Alla Aronovna and Yulia were also standing and realized that all three of them were serving as examples of Soviet Jews. She got to gloat, briefly, watching Alla Aronovna hide humiliation under her little smile. Yulia remained solemn and beautiful, her expression unchanged.

Following some imperceptible cue, the guests began to applaud, and it was Yulia's turn to speak.

"My mother and I have been fortunate to slip through a crack in the Iron Curtain, to escape anti-Semitism and oppression, but thousands of Jews are still trapped in the former Soviet Union, unable to worship openly. Because of your efforts, many of them will receive the gift of freedom. In the name of all the Jews from the former Soviet republics, I would like to thank everyone present here. You will be in my prayers tonight."

Cheeks flushed, Yulia smoothed her skirt and sat down, prompting another wave of applause. A woman to the right of Sasha dabbed her eyes with a tissue. Sasha couldn't help but be impressed with Yulia's oratory. She wondered if Yulia really prayed, and to what. Suddenly nostalgic for Phoenix, she could almost feel the heat rising from the Taco Bell parking lot where Marina had pompously delivered the news.

"Jews have their own religion, Sasha."

"What, they go to church?" Sasha had asked. She'd never seen a religious Jew.

"No, a synagogue, and the priest is called a rabbi," explained Marina. "My grandma remembers her grandma going to one. Now we go, too, with our benefactors. We sit there, and then they give us food and stuff."

"You pray to Jesus?"

"No, to God."

"To a different god? What's his name?"

"How would I know?" Marina shrugged. "It's all in Hebrew. In their English prayer books, they sometimes replace the o with the dash. So I call him Gd. Sounds sort of Vietnamese."

Sasha didn't blame herself for being confused. If you didn't count Alufiev's icons and the plaster heads in the basement of AFTER EATIN, gods kept a low profile in Asbestos 2. Perhaps they were intimidated by the giant RELIGION IS THE OPIATE OF THE MASSES! banner that spanned the entire length of the coatroom in Sasha's school. It had been there from the time when Sasha didn't know what an opiate was; it hung there the day she found out. It was probably still there, too large to remove, fading to anemic peach.

On TV, Sasha Goldberg had watched the rest of Russia rediscover Christianity: mattress factories and museums were converted back into churches; a silhouette of the Virgin Mary appeared on a slab of beef in a Moscow supermarket; a group of American missionaries cured a blind child at the Prostuda soccer stadium. But Asbestos 2 was too new to have had a church and too small to draw missionaries. Only the fake diamond crosses in the town's teenagers' ears reflected the national obsession with faith.

When the old projector in AFTER EATIN wasn't swallowing slides, it was possible to glimpse gods' dim and scratched visages on the wall. Sometimes the slides were of Jesus, sometimes of an old man with a gray beard. White doves flew through stiff golden rays; the art history teacher talked about intuitive perspective. Religious paintings were discussed in the same terms as still lifes and landscapes. Color, light, composition.

Sasha looked around, wondering when she'd be allowed to sit down. She tried to achieve Yulia's expression, to look pleasant on display, but suddenly felt terribly alone. Looking at the fat couple in the second row, Sasha pictured them going home at the end of the evening. The wife would throw her shoes across the room and plop down on the sofa. The husband would lock himself in the bathroom and sit there with a magazine until his legs went numb and the toilet seat made a crimson ring on his thighs, and then they would both go to bed and put their heads on pillows that smelled like their hair. Even the congressman's Bangladeshi children were probably already used to their maritime teddy-bear wallpaper.

Sasha realized that she'd become complacent at the Vasilievs', because they had seemed similar to her, only a notch above on the food chain. On Devon, Sasha could fantasize about walking into a store and seeing a tall black man arguing with a cashier in Russian. *Do I know you?* she'd ask. And although the phone book Goldbergs offered little hope, at least it was something to hang on to. Vitaly Sergeevich had mentioned that Mr. Tarakan was a lawyer and that he might be able to help Sasha sort out her immigration status. Standing on exhibit in front of the glittering audience, Sasha Goldberg suspected that Mr. Tarakan had better things to do. After all, he was trying to help *all* the Soviet Jews at once.

Mrs. Tarakan motioned for Sasha to sit down. One by one, the guests approached the table and handed checks to Mr. Tarakan. He pushed his glasses down to the tip of his nose and, holding the checks in an outstretched arm, slowly read the amounts.

"Mr. and Mrs. Sidney Shmel, one hundred dollars!" Applause. Mrs. Shmel, dressed in transparent layers that rustled with every move, gave a little wave from her seat.

"Mr. and Mrs. Sarancha, five hundred dollars!" The applause got louder.

"Mr. and Mrs. Svetlyak, seven hundred dollars!"

"Mr. Pauk, one thousand dollars!"

"Mr. and Mrs. James Blocha, three thousand dollars!"

"Mr. and Mrs. Komar, twenty thousand dollars!"

Even though it wasn't really cold, Sasha felt so tired she shuddered every few seconds. She hugged her knees and tried to warm up. The air smelled of freshly mowed grass, food, and perfume. Sasha squinted and watched Mrs. Komar's diamond earrings turn into perfectly symmetrical four-pointed star-bursts.

She imagined the Komars' donation benefiting the Soviet Jews. Thanks to the organization's efforts, the Soviet Jews would get to travel, dazed and sweaty, in airplanes, with their fur coats underneath them in suitcases. On arrival, the young ones would exchange their gold teeth for more becoming white teeth and lose weight, while the old ones would keep their gold teeth and attend English classes to never learn English, and the children would go to school to forget Russian.

Sasha wondered what she'd do if she personally had twenty thousand dollars, if such an amount would constitute a *future* to Mrs. Goldberg's liking. *You're an adult now, Sasha. Nadia deserves to be with her real mother.*

Suddenly an alternate future popped into Sasha's head and refused to leave. *She is a college student, like Yulia and Lika. She owns a futon and a CD tower, her own personal Jim Morrison on the ceiling. In Asbestos 2, Nadia grows into a schoolgirl.*

Jim Morrison's black-and-white head loomed in Sasha's field of vision, obscuring everything else. From somewhere behind the head, Sasha heard Mrs. Tarakan's concerned voice.

"She's falling asleep. Honey, could you show her to her room?"

Jim Morrison disappeared. Sasha got up groggily and followed Alyssa into the house.

2

Foie Gras

Dear Nadia,

I'm in a new place now, living with some rich people in the suburbs. Get this, their last name is Tarakan. Eventually, I'll be put to work, although I'm not sure what my job is yet. Last night Vitaly Sergeevich brought me here, and there was a party.

Afterwards, I slept like a rock and woke up disoriented. Except for a few streaks of sunshine coming through the dirt and weeds outside a tiny window, the room was pitch dark. I got up and tried to find the light switch. Finally, I got dressed in the dark and found the door.

For a second I was sure that the door wouldn't open, and that I would have to spend the rest of my life in the basement, with Mrs. Tarakan shoving bread and water under the door once a day. But the door opened and the switch was right there.

The room was plain except for a watercolor landscape on the wall and an ornate metal box nailed slightly sideways to the doorframe. Sasha made her bed and waited. Soon she heard stomping on the wooden stairs. Mrs. Tarakan, wearing a silk kimono and a pair of clogs, walked into the room and took Sasha upstairs.

"Would you like to see the house?"

They walked through the Oriental room and the African room.

"Ours is a house of collections," said Mrs. Tarakan, pouring granola into rustic ceramic bowls. "See all the animals? Better than the Field Museum. The previous owner killed them all himself. His new wife was a vegetarian, so when they sold us the house, we were able to buy the taxidermy. I don't mind it. I find it serene."

Chewing, Sasha glanced at her twin reflections in the glass eyes of a wall-mounted deer head. The head looked fairly alive. Sasha could picture it, in turn, chewing, drooling all over the Tarakans' terra-cotta tile. Without the drooling, it was certainly serene.

"When Jakey was small, he used to beg for a pet, but . . . Oh I know it sounds strange!" Mrs. Tarakan giggled. "These are better, really. You get attached to a pet and then watch it die. The stuffed ones don't have that problem."

Sasha nodded. She thought it touching that Mrs. Tarakan felt compelled to justify her love for taxidermy to a complete stranger. Looking at the pillow lines on Mrs. Tarakan's pre-makeup face, she thought that even if the house were decorated with cat skeletons and live snakes she wouldn't think it was weird. Sasha Goldberg was prepared.

"When you finish eating, I want you to dust the idols in the African room. Ask Nina to show you where she keeps the feather duster. It's a delicate job. Also, the downstairs hall bathroom needs to be cleaned. Nina and Esmeralda will be here soon, they'll let you know what else they need help with. Oh, and leave your bowl on the table. Nina will take care of the dishes." Mrs. Tarakan touched Sasha lightly on the shoulder and shimmered down the hall. In her cobalt kimono, she looked designed to complement the interior.

A half hour later, Nina and Esmeralda arrived in a station wagon and immediately went about cleaning with such frightening efficiency that Sasha couldn't even pretend to be of any help. She didn't need to speak Spanish to know that by the afternoon both women were annoyed with her. They sneered when Sasha washed the sink and the toilet with the same washcloth, and completely gave up after watching her fold a fitted bedsheet. After that, they pretended not to understand when Sasha meekly offered her services, leaving her to wander the Tarakans' house like an idle inmate.

The house seemed to endlessly expand in every direction. Stairways appeared out of nowhere, narrow passages opened into rooms as big as exhibition halls. Clutching a feather duster like an ID pass, Sasha pushed open a glass door and came face to face with a group of tired, vacant-eyed Soviet people walking toward her on a railway platform.

"Well, *zdravstvuyte*," she mumbled, almost dropping her duster. She had discovered the Tarakans' Russian room.

The photorealist painting took up an entire wall. The people on the platform were rendered in textureless murky green, the color of Vitaly Sergeevich's suit. The man closest to the edge of the canvas suffered from lens distortion. He appeared ready to strike Sasha across the face with his aggressively elongated left arm and *avoska* bag.

On the other wall, Sasha saw a dark grid of whimsical chalky-white figurines and a huge glossy canvas with a disembodied masklike head painted in its middle.

Sasha tried to remember the names of the painters. The Moscow kids at the Repin used to worship these people, the bushy-haired rebels of the 1970s and '80s, who lived at a time when there were things to fight against, when art was a moral endeavor that could land you in prison. Sasha knew that many of the underground artists had become successful in the West, riding the first wave of Glasnost into foreign auctions, but she never thought about where their works ended up.

Except for the barely audible gurgling of the peeing cupid in the swimming pool, the house was as quiet as a purgatory. Outside, a middle-aged Mexican man dragged a black plastic bag through the Tarakans' backyard forest. Watching his methodical, soundless movement through thick glass, Sasha felt sorry for the paintings. Away from the danger and excitement that produced them, they looked misplaced, like a pack of anonymous letters at a thrift store.

Turning to leave the room, she noticed a display case filled with vintage Soviet porcelain. Prickly, aggressive geometric shapes surrounded the familiar goateed profile in the middle of the largest avant-garde soup bowl. Bloodthirsty triangles slamming into unsuspecting circles, piercing red lines, and flying bits made Sasha think of bashed-in heads and up-against-the-wall executions of

Baba Zhenia's time. The Tarakans had a choice collection here. Some of the plates had slogans in angular cursive, lest the violence get too abstract.

"Kick Out the Wedge with Another Wedge!"

"Sober Up and Toil!"

Alyssa Tarakan's high school graduation picture was tucked in between the panes of glass in the cabinet's door. In it, Alyssa still had her original nose. She was wearing a shiny maroon robe and throwing her hands up in the air.

The glossy canvas caught the sun's glare, and the mask-head in its middle seemed to eye the violent dinnerware with scornful suspicion.

"Who Doesn't Work Doesn't Eat."

By late afternoon, Sasha was starving. Mrs. Tarakan was nowhere in sight, and even if she were around, Sasha would be too embarrassed to ask for food after a day of uselessness. She wandered back into the Russian room and stood in front of a large muddy abstraction, watching Nina and Esmeralda unwrap their tamales on the stone bench outside.

A mechanical noise startled her. She turned around sharply and saw a complicated electric wheelchair roll down the rubberized ramp out of the side door like an enormous futuristic beetle.

"Hi."

"Hi," said Sasha, staring. The boy looked almost superfluous to the chair, like a hat on a robot. He had skinny arms and legs, and his hands were flat in the middle, as if something heavy had stepped on top of them and they stayed that way. Two wide Velcro straps, crossed on his chest, held him to the chair, and his head leaned on a black vinyl headrest at an unnatural angle.

"Are you finished staring?"

He had a weird, synthesized-sounding voice. Sasha wanted to tell him that no, she wasn't finished staring. There was too much in this house to stare at, dead animals, dissident art, and now him.

"I'm not staring," she said.

"I'm Jake."

So it was he who wanted live pets instead of the serene ones.

"Sasha." She wasn't sure how to elaborate on that. Should she tell him she worked here?

"So, you're mommy's new toy. Good to meet you."

Sasha decided to ignore the *new toy* comment. Jake was hard to understand, and Sasha couldn't be sure about his mental state.

"Nice to meet you, too," she said. "I didn't see you last night at the party."

"Those things get old after a while. My parents host a lot of fundraisers. Israel, Soviet Jews, the disabled causes. They care. Do you care?"

Sasha shrugged, baffled.

"How old are you?" Jake asked.

"Almost eighteen."

"So we're the same age. I'm finishing high school."

Sasha wondered how he went to school. People like him didn't go to school in Asbestos 2. In fact, they weren't seen at all. If they existed, they stayed inside their apartments all the time, their parents' awful secrets.

"You like these paintings?" Jake asked.

Sasha wanted to tell him that "like" wasn't the right word for it, that the whole experience was like bumping into your best friend at the bottom of the ocean.

"Some of them very much," she said. "Are your parents interested in Russian art?"

"My dad, sort of. Interested in the hype that used to surround it. He'll tell you that he started the collection as an investment, but then he got into it, when he met those bearded guys who'd never been anywhere. He liked paying them money for their works, taking them around. Just wait till you hear about Grisha Bruskin's first hot dog. . . ."

Mr. Tarakan, in his jogging clothes and with a towel over his shoulder, walked into the room.

"Admiring my collection?"

Sasha nodded.

"They are great, aren't they? You know, I bought Grisha Bruskin his first American hot dog! He got off the plane in New York, and I thought he might be hungry, and I got him a hot dog. He'd never had a hot dog before."

Sasha heard Jake's bizarre robotic laughter behind her and bit her lip.

"I don't know what's so funny, Jacob," sighed Mr. Tarakan, resting his arm on Sasha's shoulder, but Jake was already out the door, the noise of the wheelchair's motor receding down the hall.

"Over here is the valuable stuff." Mr. Tarakan pointed at the china cabinet. "We recently had it on exhibit at the Athenaeum. I just got that little fellow, he's worth over a thousand dollars!"

Sasha looked at an unassuming figurine perched at the edge of the middle shelf. It was a standard depiction of a capitalist—a fat man in a tux and a top hat straddling a money bag. This particular capitalist was a saltshaker. His hat had four holes on top, and his face wore an aggrieved expression.

"I was wondering if you could tell me what it says," said Mr. Tarakan, leading Sasha closer to the glass.

A rhyme was scribbled along the bottom of the money bag. Although the writing was beady and faint, Sasha could tell exactly what it said. Baba Zhenia used to whistle the ditty, absentmindedly, for a lullaby.

> *Munch on your oyster,*
> *Eat your foie gras*
> *Your last day is near,*
> *Bourgeois.*

Sasha imagined blurting the words into Mr. Tarakan's face. Would he take them personally? For a brief moment, she pictured the Tarakans gone, and the Tudor portion of the Waterfall House chopped up into a hundred little rooms. What a splendid, sprawling communal apartment it would make, with all those bathrooms! The tenants could fashion coats out of boar skins, burn the sculptures in fireplaces, litter the yard with broken bottles and twisted bicycle frames. The beige couch could easily sleep four children; the claw-foot tub could sleep a man. The contemporary part could be made into the House of Culture or a day care. A rock band would sing "Eighth Grade Girlfriend" in the Oriental room, their amplified voices but a faint echo in the Russian room, where tiny cots would line the walls. Scabby-kneed girls would pour milk for feral kittens into Mrs. Tarakan's rustic cereal bowls, and the little capitalist saltshaker would be liberated, put to good use, salting fried fish and boiled potatoes.

"I can't read that, Mr. Tarakan," Sasha fibbed. "It's Old Russian."

"Oh, well, maybe I can ask someone at the museum." Mr. Tarakan sounded disappointed. He smelled like chlorine, and his arm was growing heavy on Sasha's shoulder. Sasha stood up straighter and waited for him to take it off.

After he left, Sasha picked up her duster and headed toward the gothic archway that separated the contemporary wing from a dark alcove in the older structure.

Inside, there was a wide-screen TV with the sound off. On TV a skinny white lady ran around the stage with a microphone, while several fat black ladies sat in chairs. Some were crying. Looking for a cleaning opportunity, Sasha walked toward the TV until her hip hit something hard in the dark.

"Careful, will you!"

"Oy!" Sasha caught her breath. "What are you doing here?"

"What does it look like? Watching TV."

"Oh, okay."

"Can you do me a favor?"

"Sure, what?" Sasha felt happy to finally be useful.

"Find the remote, will you?"

Sasha groped around in purple darkness, then switched on one of the lamps, but the remote was gone.

"Shit," sighed Jake.

"You want me to ask somebody?"

"Nah, forget it. When José reappears, he'll find it."

"Who's José?"

"My personal care attendant. He's sick today."

Sasha realized this was her chance do something productive in the Tarakan household.

"So, you need any help, then?"

"Nah, I'm fine," said Jake, fixing his eyes on the TV again.

Sasha looked at his pale face in the glow of the screen. He had a thin nose and heavy-lidded dark eyes. There was a scar on his neck, under the Adam's apple. Sasha imagined his body unfurled from its permanent seizure. He would be taller than Jason. He must be the little brother, Mrs. Tarakan's last child.

"Can I ask you a favor, too?" said Sasha.

Jake's eyes darted briefly to her face.

"I'm starving to death." She noticed the alarm in his eyes and corrected herself. "Not literally. I'm just hungry. Can I have some food?"

"Come with me," said Jake, wheeling in reverse, out of the room, the alarmed look still on his face. When they got to the kitchen's marble threshold, Sasha grabbed the black sponge handles of the wheelchair and gave it a push.

"Leave it alone," said Jake.

Sasha let her hands drop, embarrassed.

"Open the fridge."

"Which one?" There were two of everything in the kitchen: two refrigerators, two microwaves, two pairs of sinks.

"What do you want—meat or dairy?"

"Um, just some bread would be fine."

Jake showed Sasha the bread box. Inside, there was a quarter of a stale baguette. The bread was so hard that Sasha had to gnaw on it. Jake sat in his chair, staring into space just past Sasha's head. Sasha realized that an awkward silence was doubly awkward when shared with someone without a moving body, someone who couldn't smooth his hair, wipe the table, open a cabinet door, tie a shoelace. All Jake could do was sit there and avert his eyes while Sasha gnawed.

"So, why there is two of everything?" Sasha asked, giving her jaws a break.

"It's a kosher kitchen."

"What's that?"

"You know, it has a meat side and a dairy side?"

"What for?"

"It's a Jewish thing. 'Don't boil a kid in its mother's milk . . .'"

The image of Nadia boiling in Sasha's milk was so vivid that Sasha almost choked on her bread. It took her a second to process what Jake had just said, that it wasn't some terrible insult, directed at her personally.

". . . it's in the Torah. You know?"

Sasha shook her head. Her nipples still hurt from the notion of milk as a source of pain, boiling.

"The Bible?" Jake kept on. "Do you know about the Bible?"

Sasha nodded. This two-fridge thing, boiling kids, had nothing to do with her. It was just the Bible.

"Where did Mommy dig you up?"

Sasha considered the question. "A friend brought me here."

"Listen, Sasha. I don't know what your story is. But if you get really mad, you come see me. I'll help you. I'll get you out of here. Do you understand?"

"Why would I get mad?"

"Promise that you'll come to me, please."

Sasha was puzzled by the insistence in Jake's voice.

"All right," she said with a shrug.

Jake smiled a tight fake smile and wheeled out of the kitchen. After making sure he was safely gone, Sasha Goldberg opened one of the refrigerators and found a stick of butter. She took a knife out of a drawer, buttered her baguette, and opened the other fridge. In a thin compartment on the door there were bags of sliced lunch meats. Sasha layered membranes of roast beef on her bread and choked it down, squatting behind the fridge door. She thought she could hear Nina and Esmeralda's footsteps. Quickly, she washed the knife in one of the sinks and put it back in the drawer.

3

The Captive of the Talmud

"HONEY, GET DOWN FROM THERE!"

Not realizing she was "honey," Sasha Goldberg kept rubbing the glass.
"Sasha, come on down, Nina can finish this!"

Nina will hate me, thought Sasha, frantically squirting Windex at the sunset and watching it run down the red sky in bubbly rivulets. She couldn't believe Mrs. Tarakan expected her to be done with this mile-wide arcadia door in ten minutes.

"I'm almost finished!" she said desperately. For a week now, she'd sheepishly shadowed Nina and Esmeralda. She was a hardworking and respectful student, and on Wednesday, Esmeralda trusted her with her first serious job, laundry. Sasha carried the hampers to the basement and sorted the clothing, setting aside the "dry clean only" and "hand wash" items. She filled the washer and, while it was spinning, hand-washed Mrs. Tarakan's filmy underwear in a square steel sink. She was proud of herself for finding a small pink bottle labeled "Light Touch Lingerie Soap" in the basket of laundry supplies, for not forgetting to set the dryer on "Delicate."

Esmeralda had seemed happy enough.

"No squeeze," she'd said dryly, noticing that Sasha wrung out something that wasn't supposed to be wrung, but Sasha detected a softening in her voice, a hint of acceptance.

Now she didn't want to lose it.

"Sasha, leave it alone and get down," insisted Mrs. Tarakan. "Don't worry about the door!"

Sasha backed down the ladder.

"Go change into something nice, sweetie. The sun is almost down."

Sasha surmised that the Tarakans were having guests for dinner, and that she would be given an apron to match the other maids.

"Should I put away the ladder?"

"Leave it, honey. Scoot!"

Mrs. Tarakan was already dressed in a pearly pantsuit and pointy-toed turquoise shoes.

In her basement room, Sasha put on her Salvation Army velvet dress and brushed her hair. The dress had a round scoop neck. Sasha took her Star of David necklace out of its box and put that on, too.

"Oh, darling! You look *lovely*!" exclaimed Mrs. Tarakan, throwing her arms around Sasha. "Come, it's time to light the Sabbath candles."

Of course she'd rather light candles than wipe glass. Sasha imagined a huge chandelier that she was to set ablaze and was disappointed when Mrs. Tarakan took two candlesticks out of a drawer. Mrs. Tarakan stuck the candles into silver holders and gave Sasha a box of matches.

"You light one and I'll light the other. Did you do this in the Soviet Union?"

"Sometimes," lied Sasha.

"Do you know the prayer?"

Sasha shook her head. "No."

"Of course not. Just repeat after me. *Barukh atah Adonai* . . ."

"*Barukh atah Adonai* . . . ," repeated Sasha. She had a good memory for words, especially poetry, and her recitation was effortless. Mrs. Tarakan looked on approvingly.

"Hungry?" she asked.

Sasha nodded.

"Come, the dinner is about to start."

Sasha stared at Mrs. Tarakan. Was she inviting her to eat at the table? All week Sasha had been sneaking food. One time she bumped into Jake, and he said that it was all right, that she should help herself whenever she wanted, but she still didn't feel wholly comfortable doing it. Unsure which food the Tarakans wanted for themselves, she'd taken a spoonful here and a bite there.

"Yes, you're eating with us tonight," explained Mrs. Tarakan. "It's the Sabbath, sweetie. Jewish people don't work on the Sabbath."

In the dining room, the table was already set. A large braided loaf lay in the middle, covered with an embroidered cloth. Esmeralda had been working on the bread all day, filling the house with its delicious smell.

"I sent Esmeralda to a kosher cooking class," said Mrs. Tarakan. "She's a fabulous cook."

Mr. Tarakan walked through the door, wearing a golden fez with beaded geometric designs. José wheeled in Jake. Because of the headrest, Jake's plain silk yarmulke sat slightly askew on his head. José righted it, attaching it to Jake's hair with a bobby pin. José wore a dark brown polyester suit, a chocolate shirt, and a rust-colored tie. He looked as if he were meant to disappear against a brown background in some magic show.

Alyssa came next, complaining about the traffic. She wore a floor-length skirt of distressed denim, several heavy bracelets, and a velvet choker. A silver hummingbird-shaped clip miraculously supported the fountain of hair above her head.

"You look nice," she said to Sasha in a casual, familiar voice, as if they'd been girlfriends forever and always commented on each other's appearance.

"Thank you," replied Sasha, turning red. Being included like this, all of a sudden, after a week of invisibility, made her squirm. She realized she should've returned the compliment to Alyssa, who really did look nice, but she'd waited too long by now.

"Well, no Jason tonight," said Mr. Tarakan.

"Honey, he said he was coming."

Mr. Tarakan consulted his watch. Sasha noticed that nobody, except Jake, was sitting down. For a while they stood in silence.

"He does this every time," said Mr. Tarakan. "I don't know why you insist on waiting."

"Gordon, please, let's not fight on a Sabbath. We can begin without Jason if you'd like," replied Mrs. Tarakan. "I'm sure he'll be here any minute."

Still standing, Mr. Tarakan began his prayer. When he was done, the family sat down and then got up again, one at a time, to wash their hands over an antique copper bowl. There was another prayer for the hands. Sasha noticed that all the prayers started with *"Barukh atah Adonai."* She thought about adenoids and long winter colds, the smell of Tiger Balm in stuffy rooms. Mrs. Goldberg used to say that if Sasha didn't stop sleeping with her mouth open, her adenoids would have to be removed. Sasha had tied a scarf around her head at night, to keep her jaw shut.

"Sasha," said Mrs. Tarakan.

Sasha got up, walked over to the marble counter, and stood next to the bowl. Mrs. Tarakan picked up a gracefully dented silver vessel and poured water over her hands.

"Repeat after me."

"I remember it," said Sasha. *"Barukh atah Adonai, Elohaynu, melekh ha-olam . . ."*

She finished the prayer herself, making no mistakes. Remembering a string of sounds she couldn't understand was simple, easier than memorizing meaningful text. The ice-cold water numbed Sasha's fingers, but her cheeks felt hot under Mrs. Tarakan's admiring stare.

"Did you hear that? Did you all hear that? Isn't she *wonderful?*" squealed Mrs. Tarakan.

Alyssa smiled and clapped her hands. Mr. Tarakan patted Sasha on the shoulder, hurried through another prayer, and doled out slices of challah. The bread was sweet and soft. Sasha felt halfway like a star student and halfway like a lucky Ivanushka the Idiot, who had been granted some wish he could neither comprehend nor remember.

"Did you know the prayer from before?" asked Alyssa.

"No, honey, she's from the *Soviet Union*! Isn't that something?" said Mrs. Tarakan. She sounded like a scientist who had just discovered that Sasha possessed a larger-than-expected brain.

Jake glared at his mother. His glare fell across the table like a tree limb, stopping all conversation. *Thank you,* thought Sasha. But he glared at her, too, and for a second his eyes lingered below her neck. Sasha hunched over her plate.

"What's the matter, Jake?" Mr. Tarakan asked sharply.

"Nothing."

Sasha watched Nina turn the corner from the kitchen with a metal serving tray. What would Nina do when she found her inept understudy at the table with the masters? Would she scream, "I don't have to serve *you!*" in the bloodcurdling manner of Soviet waiters? Squeezing her eyes shut, Sasha fantasized about the metal tray hitting her in the head.

But Nina didn't use the tray in an improper manner. She piled food on Sasha's plate and went on to serve Alyssa. Sasha hid her face in the fragrant steam and stared at the apron straps on Nina's back and at her short graying hair. Nina seemed completely unfazed, going about her business. Esmeralda came out of the kitchen with a glass bowl of watercress salad and made her silent trip around the table. Sasha scanned her face for signs of outrage, too, but Esmeralda looked the same as always, tired and mechanically polite.

Nina's key chain was sticking out of her pocket, a fan of Plexiglas hearts filled with children's faces. Sasha tried to picture the apartment Nina went home to every night. She imagined a carpeted room with bright American children's things scattered about: cereal boxes, cartoon T-shirts, crayons, strings of shiny plastic beads. They probably played the kind of music Sasha had heard blaring out of cars in Phoenix and Chicago, loud Spanish songs that rhymed like Russian ones. That was why they didn't care. This was only a job. *This is only a job,* Sasha reminded herself. But what else did she have? What was hers?

She watched the Tarakans' chewing faces in the warm light of the chandelier. The energy she'd felt a few minutes ago, the desire to impress these people, seeped away. Sasha concentrated on the pile of food in front of her. It was her first hot meal this week, and it was good. Several elongated leaves floated in a pool of chicken grease like miniature canoes, and the rice looked like gold. *Herbs* was the word that explained it all. It would be Sasha Goldberg's vocabulary word for the day.

In the morning, Mrs. Tarakan presented Sasha with a palm-sized souvenir Torah, a scroll of paper on an ivory plastic spool. "Denver, 1994" was engraved in silver on either end.

"Would you like to know more about Judaism?" she asked.

"Yes, Mrs. Tarakan," said Sasha. Coming from Mrs. Tarakan's mouth, learning about Judaism sounded like a job assignment. Dust, vacuum, wipe, wash, dry, learn.

Mrs. Tarakan told Sasha about the Torah. She sent José to Jake's room, and he returned with a dusty stack of children's books.

"Jakey!" Mrs. Tarakan yelled into the depth of the house. "Jakey, would you like to join us?"

There was no answer. Mrs. Tarakan ordered José to go get Jake. She explained to Sasha that because it was Sabbath, Jake wasn't allowed to operate his wheelchair.

"Mom, I think I'm a little too old for that," Jake sighed when José wheeled him into the room.

"Well, honey, perhaps you could help me with Sasha. She has a lot to learn."

"Mom, you know what I think."

"Jake . . ."

"You know I don't believe in God."

"Since when? You are much too young to decide what you do and don't believe, Jacob!" Mrs. Tarakan jerked back her head, and her silky golden hair brushed Sasha's cheek. Sasha thought she could see tears in her eyes.

Jake made an obnoxious face and wrapped his fingers around the joystick.

"Don't you dare, Jacob!"

"Get me a pair of working legs, and I won't have to!" he replied, wheeling in reverse out of the room.

Sasha Goldberg played with the waxy paper of her Denver scroll, her downcast face in a solemn mask, concealing her admiration.

Mrs. Tarakan dismissed José and shuffled through the stack of books until she found what she was looking for: a worn paperback with ballpoint pen scribbles on the cover. The book's title was *Jewish Holidays*.

"This used to be Jakey's favorite. Would you like me to read it to you?"

"I can read in English, Mrs. Tarakan," said Sasha, opening the book. Inside, pie-faced children in yarmulkes marched past a schematic tree toward a barnlike structure labeled "Temple."

"'Rosh Hashanah is the Jewish New Year,'" Mrs. Tarakan read over Sasha's shoulder. Tears were now audible in her voice. "'It comes in the fall. God has a big book, where he writes the good and bad deeds of every person in the world. On Rosh Hashanah, God opens the book and decides who will have a happy new year.'"

Every Sunday, Mrs. Tarakan handed Nina and Esmeralda a stack of twenties and two plastic containers of leftover Sabbath food. Sasha was never paid. She told herself this was logical, since the Tarakans fed her and gave her a roof over her head. In the confines of the Waterfall House, she had no use for money. Besides, she reasoned, she had to earn Mr. Tarakan's expensive legal help.

At first, Sasha Goldberg assumed that Vitaly Sergeevich had asked Mr. Tarakan for advice regarding her immigration status, but now she wasn't so sure. Mr. Tarakan never offered to help, and Sasha Goldberg was waiting for the right time to ask him herself. The trouble was, Mr. Tarakan almost never came home, and when he was around, he seemed to make a special effort to ignore Sasha. When forced to look in her direction, he aimed his stare an inch above her head, as if Sasha were a hard-to-see ghost and Mr. Tarakan wasn't sure of her exact location. Sasha Goldberg wondered what she'd done to put him off and couldn't think of anything. She told herself she was imagining things and resolved to talk to Mr. Tarakan.

After a month at the Waterfall House, Sasha Goldberg had learned the contents of the cavernous utility closet, decoded the purpose of the "Toilet Duck," and mastered the one and only proper way to fold hand towels. Next to understanding the functions of various chemicals and an army of vacuum cleaners, the biggest trick was knowing what needed attention and what was already clean enough in the Tarakans' seemingly immaculate house. Nina was an expert at detecting imperfections. After washing breakfast dishes and sweeping the floor, she armed herself with a bottle of leather cleaner and attacked the invisible scuff marks on the side of the couch. Sasha watched her closely. Slowly, Nina and Esmeralda began to treat her as one of their own, except for the two hours every afternoon when Sasha was excused from housework to study Judaism.

Mrs. Tarakan set up a desk for Sasha in the corner of the library. The younger Tarakans nicknamed the corner "Mommy's Yeshiva."

"Where is Nina?"

"Cleaning up the Yeshiva."

"Do you have a paperclip?"

"See if there are any in the Yeshiva."

Mrs. Tarakan didn't seem to mind the name. She appeared almost flattered by it. She decorated the Yeshiva with posters: a Hebrew alphabet, an Israeli flag, the Wailing Wall.

Sitting down at her desk, Sasha remembered a cartoon of a vicious-looking pig on the last page of Mrs. Stepanova's *Asbestos Truth*. The pig had been labeled "Israel." It was devouring a shriveled shape labeled "Palestine." Sasha was admiring the intricate rendering of the animal's snout and lower jaw, and the strange foreign names, when Victor tore the paper out of her hands.

"I don't want this trash in my house!"

"This isn't your *house*," said Mrs. Goldberg calmly. "It's the neighbors' *Truth*. Sasha, put it down."

"What's the piggy eating?"

"A country," said Sasha's mother.

"A territory," clarified her father.

Sasha looked up, dumbfounded.

"A map, Sasha," Mr. and Mrs. Goldberg sighed in unison.

"It's propaganda, Sasha. Eat your food," said Mrs. Goldberg impatiently, reaching over to put a spoonful of currant jelly into the bowl of Sasha's lumpy oatmeal. There was no way Sasha was going to eat that porridge, jelly or not. Her father tweaked the volume knob, hoping to catch "enemy voices" through the howling interference. The enemies chanted the exotic names, too, *Soedinennie Shtati Ameriki. Israel. Sector Gaza.* A jar of water stood on the windowsill, next to the radio. Sasha had been growing a green onion for a second-grade Earth science project.

Now she looked at the posters above her desk and remembered the onion's single sprout, how brilliant it had looked against the snowy darkness outside. Maybe the Torah would take her away from the gloomy Chicago afternoon, save her from the mahogany fortress of the Tarakans' library. She'd lounge on white sand, walk through citrus orchards, ride a camel into the sunset. Sasha leaned back in her chair, allowing the deep ultramarines and luscious oranges of the tourist posters to enter her wide-open eyes and warm up her brain with counterfeit spirituality.

She preferred the pictures to the texts. Although Mrs. Tarakan's copy of the Holy Scriptures contained little archaic language, it was still the most tedious thing Sasha Goldberg had ever read. After two hours at her desk, her mind was a blur of double-voweled names and niggling footnotes. Infuriating details stuck out of the blur like the beginnings of a migraine: virgins lain with against their will, slaves and daughters given to strangers as consolation prizes, people blindly obeying God's mercurial whims.

Mrs. Tarakan outlined the passages that she thought were especially important and quizzed Sasha afterward.

"What do you think this means?" she asked, searching Sasha's opaque, tired eyes for signs of spiritual growth.

They arrived at the place of which God had told him. Abraham built an altar there; he laid out the wood; he bound his son Isaac; he laid him on the altar, on top of the wood. And Abraham picked up the knife to slay his son.

Sasha thought about Isaac, what it would be like to lie there bound, with your own father towering against the sky, about to kill you with the knife. And poor Sarah. Abraham, dumb and obedient as he was, had been smart not to tell her about his little trip.

Sasha Goldberg shook her head.

"I don't know, Mrs. Tarakan."

Mrs. Tarakan refused to give up. "You shouldn't take this literally. It's a parable."

Sasha wished she was still in the laundry room, folding underwear.

"I guess, if you obey God, everything will turn out all right?" she whispered, turning red.

She couldn't tell from the look on Mrs. Tarakan's face if her answer had been satisfactory. Mrs. Tarakan closed the book and checked her watch.

"The electrician left a mess in the Russian room. See if you could clean it up, honey."

Sasha swept up bits of wallboard and colorful wire from the Russian room's floor. The green crowd on the platform followed her every move with their hazy photorealist eyes. Lately, Sasha had become tired of the paintings. The air in the room felt heavy with unused meaning, outdated subversiveness. The mask-head hung in its varnished purple haze like a lone pickle in a jar, ridiculous. The electrician had left the china cabinet unlit. It was now a dark rectangle, the evil dishes barely visible inside.

Sasha looked out the window at the carefully premeditated slope of the Tarakans' lawn, at the peeing cupid. Oscar the gardener walked by in his yellow raincoat. At the Vasilievs', Sasha had armed herself with a dictionary and slogged through Nabokov's *Speak, Memory*—the only English-language book the older Vasilievs owned. Now she realized that, in her mind, Nabokov's bucolic lost world—an idyll of bicycle bells, butterfly nets, and sun-flecked forest paths—had always resembled the Tarakans' backyard. In the latter part of the book, a bloody revolution caused the author's "removal from the unforgettable scenery." The revolution appeared to come out of nowhere, like a tornado or an unfortunate loose brick to the head. Before she came to the Tarakans', Sasha hadn't given much thought to the future rebels themselves, the peasants, the proletarians, the "tragic bums" that lurked, unobtrusively, in the brilliant light of Nabokov's memory. Now she felt as if the first chauffeur and the second chauffeur, the butler and the footman, the nameless "girl," the doorman's obese wife, the naked peasant children, and the dirty-footed adolescent Polenka, the subject of the author's early, squeamish romantic longings, were collectively sending her a message. Sasha Goldberg received it into her hands, irresistible like a reflex. Dropping her broom with a thud, she allowed her fingers to curve around the handle of an invisible pitchfork.

"Is everything all right?" Mrs. Tarakan yelled from the TV room.

"Yes, Mrs. Tarakan," said Sasha. "Everything is fine. I'm almost done here."

On Rosh Hashanah the Tarakans took Sasha along to the temple. After weeks of indoor confinement, Sasha was ecstatic to be looking out of the window of a car, even if it was only at trees and occasional mailboxes. Oak Grove Jewish Center turned out to be a tentlike modern structure, a cross between the Moscow Circus and a flying saucer. Surrounded by a vast parking lot, it looked like a Phoenix Baptist church, where Marina's mom would get free canned food.

In the lobby, men and women separated. The temple was full. Mrs. Tarakan and Sasha sat perched on metal chairs in the aisle until a woman in a black suit noticed Mrs. Tarakan and reseated them on a velvet bench near the front.

Sasha couldn't see the rabbi, who was behind the partition, with the men, his voice droning and remote. She was trying to decide what she should look at. The women sat facing a grayish blue wall. Occasionally, Mrs. Tarakan whispered into Sasha's ear. Her hot breath and the smell of her perfume offered a momentary distraction.

Yom Kippur was better than Rosh Hashanah. This time, when they got to the temple, Mrs. Tarakan gave Sasha a booklet with the text of the service in English.

After the evening service, most people went home, but a few stayed. The Tarakans spent the night on the synagogue's floor in sleeping bags. Sasha noticed that among the faithful who spent the night, Mrs. Tarakan was the most zealous. She'd packed foam-rubber mats for Mr. Tarakan and Sasha, but preferred to sleep directly on the tile herself. Mr. Tarakan didn't protest. Apparently this was something Mrs. Tarakan did every Yom Kippur.

José drove Jake home for the night.

Sasha woke up in the morning sore and angry. The cot hadn't made much difference. Her neck was stiff, and she was hungry. If this holiday was about forgiveness, the way it was celebrated didn't put Sasha Goldberg in a forgiving mood.

Mrs. Tarakan tilted her chiseled head toward the synagogue's round skylight, bathing her face in the sun, smiling. Her eyes peeked from under the membranes of their mutilated lids, peaceful and unfocused, like the eyes of a newborn. Holding her throbbing head, Sasha Goldberg walked to the bathroom.

In the lobby, Jake Tarakan was eating a Pop-Tart out of José's hands like a dog. Nursing mothers, young children, and apparently Jake were allowed to eat on Yom Kippur.

"Hey, Sasha!" Jake called. "You look skinny."

It took Sasha a second to put on her pleasant face.

"Oh, look at that evil glare!" exclaimed Jake. "Be on your way, child, lest I tempt you with my Pop-Tart."

José laughed hysterically and dropped the Pop-Tart on Jake's lap. His eyes were crimson, as if it were he who didn't sleep all night. Sasha stormed into the bathroom. When she came back out, José and Jake were sharing a bag of potato chips and a can of Coke. Sasha hurried back toward the frosted glass doors of the auditorium, hoping they wouldn't notice her.

"Hey, Sasha!"

"What?" Sasha let go of the door handle.

"Do you forgive me?"

"You didn't do anything bad to me, Jake."

"Still, I ask your forgiveness, and I forgive you, too. And José forgives me!"

José laughed again. Soda squirted out of his mouth onto the gray industrial carpet. He wiped his face with his sleeve and laughed louder. Jake rolled his eyes.

"Sure I forgive you," said Sasha in her best Yom Kippur voice, grabbing the handle again.

Jake Tarakan reminded Sasha of the fourth-grade boys in Number 13 who liked to trip older girls in hallways and wrestle them to the ground. Except that Jake wasn't little and couldn't wrestle. Instead, he converted the physical manifestations of idiocy into name-calling and juvenile jokes. Sasha wanted to tell him that she was a maid and not his fucking classmate, but precisely because she was a maid and not his fucking classmate, she felt that she could say no such thing.

Inside, the service had already started. Hearing the rabbi's tired drone through the door, Sasha hoped that Jake and José would offer to share their snack, but they didn't. A dark shape approached the frosted glass. A large woman in a blue turban walked to the bathroom, and Sasha went inside.

From the back of the room, she could see Mrs. Tarakan upright in her chair, her hair ablaze in the rays of the sun.

"Tell mom I forgive her, too!" Jake screeched through a mouthful of chips.

Sasha wished she had a TV in her room. Without one, there was nothing to look at, except for the watercolor on the wall. There was something peculiar about the picture: the particulars had been taken away. There was a boat without a name and a seagull without an eye. The cabin had a door without a handle. Sasha missed Jim Morrison's curly head. This place was worse than the Vasilievs', worse than Neal's house. Sasha thought wistfully about the Repin Lyceum, about lively Moscow streets. *Squandered my life for a child who wouldn't know me from a stranger,* she heard herself think. When she pictured holding Nadia in her arms, a warm, heavy bundle, her eyes remained dry. Here, at the Tarakans', she was accomplishing what she'd failed to achieve in Arizona: the pain of being away from Nadia was becoming duller, more like a memory of pain. The Waterfall House, with its inflexible regime of work and ritual, felt like a true jail. Sasha noticed that her yearning for Nadia had been replaced by constant, nagging anger. In a way, it was a relief.

Sasha had approached Mr. Tarakan twice. The first time he told her he was busy. The second time he listened, nodding his head slowly. "Let me work on this," he finally said. "No, I don't need to see your passport yet. Maybe later. I'll let you know." Afterward, Sasha heard Mr. Tarakan and Jake arguing. She thought she heard them say her name but couldn't understand the rest. As usual, Jake had shouted at his father, and Mr. Tarakan replied in barely audible, exasperated bursts.

That was a month ago, after Yom Kippur, and Mr. Tarakan hadn't said anything since. Instead, Mrs. Tarakan began to invite Sasha to eat at the table every night, nudging her to lead the family in prayer beforehand. Sasha lowered her head and exhaled mysterious *Barukh-atah-Adonai*s with as much expression as she could muster, while Nina and Esmeralda served her food. She would gladly trade places with them. In the evenings, before returning to her basement, Sasha watched the maids get into their station wagon and envied them for going home.

Sasha's Denver Torah lay in a coiled heap by the bed. Did criminals "find

God" in jail because the Bible was the only thing they were allowed to read? Sasha felt that God had gotten to her too late, that she was missing whatever nerve endings were responsible for taking Him in.

Sasha stared at the eyesore seascape on her wall, thinking of all the good ways it could be defaced. She didn't come to America to join a *convent*. It was time she talked to the Tarakans as a family. Maybe Mrs. Tarakan could speak up for her. *Really, Gordon, you know people at the INS. You can spare a phone call on the girl's behalf.*

"Mom, she asked you a question!"

"What is it, Sasha?" Mrs. Tarakan dabbed her mouth with a napkin.

"I appreciate you treating me like family, Mr. and Mrs. Tarakan, and teaching me so much. Mrs. Tarakan, you're like . . ." Sasha swallowed. The wad of linguini on Mrs. Tarakan's fork reminded her of the stuff she'd pulled out of the drains that morning. "My mentor."

"What a wonderful thing to say!" exclaimed Mrs. Tarakan.

"But I can't be a burden on you forever."

"Please, don't worry about that. You aren't a burden. You do a lot of good work around here, and you're a pleasure to be with," Mrs. Tarakan said firmly.

"I was wondering," continued Sasha. "Vitaly Sergeevich said that Mr. Tarakan may possibly be able to help me with my immigration?"

"Dad?" Jake piped in like a moderator.

Mr. Tarakan, previously oblivious, stopped chewing and glanced at his wife.

"I haven't had time to look into it," he admitted, sounding like it was the first time he'd heard of Sasha at all.

"I can show you my passport, Mr. Tarakan," Sasha jumped up from the table. "Please tell me what you think. If there is no hope for me to legally stay in the U.S., I should think about returning to Russia, or . . . Wait just a second, I'll bring it up."

"Wait!" yelled Jake.

Ignoring him, Sasha thumped down the stairs to her room and emptied the contents of her garbage bag on the bed. Here it was, a thin red book, slightly worn around the edges. Maybe Mr. Tarakan could do something right away, call somebody, wave his magic Cross pen. Maybe he would even know how to find her father.

"Well, your visa's expired." Mr. Tarakan folded his glasses back into his pocket. "But there's always the possibility of appeal and the asylum route."

"Gordon will work on it," Mrs. Tarakan said with a reassuring smile, taking the passport from her husband and dropping it into the pocket of her linen tunic. "We'll see what we can do."

There was a loud clink. Sasha watched Jake's fork bounce off the edge of his plate and fall to the floor, sending drips of spaghetti sauce flying everywhere.

"Hey," José said softly.

"Nina!" shrieked Mrs. Tarakan. "Jake?"

"This is so fucked up, Mom."

"Watch your language, please."

"Do you want me to say it?"

"Jacob, we can talk later!"

"Adriana. Another fucking Adriana! I don't believe it!"

"Jakey," whispered Mrs. Tarakan, getting up from the table. "Excuse me."

"Jacob, I will not permit you to treat your mother this way!" Mr. Tarakan said without conviction. His hand moved as if he were about to strike the table with his fist, but stopped in midair.

"Fuck off, Dad," retorted Jake, and Mr. Tarakan didn't argue.

Sasha Goldberg ducked her head over her plate. What was this about? She was a nobody, a maid, asking for a little favor from her masters. Why was Jake so upset that his parents may help her become legal? One thing was clear, Jake was to be avoided. From now on she would discuss her future with the older Tarakans, alone.

Two days later, Jason Tarakan finally showed up for a Sabbath dinner. Even Sasha could see that he was stoned out of his brain. His bloodshot eyes darted around the room, as if finding numerous surprises in his own parents' house. Worst of all, Jason came with a girl. Nikki had nubby pink dreadlocks and tattooed arms. She was pretty in an exaggerated, action-figure way—thin and small, dressed in a tight tank top and extra-wide pants that hung low on her hips, exposing the hot-pink elastic band of her underwear.

Upsetting the symmetry of the Tarakans' dinner table, Nikki sat on a folding chair next to Jason and ate as if she'd been starving for weeks. From where Sasha was sitting, she could see Jason kneading her thigh with his left hand. Sasha was pretty sure Mrs. Tarakan could see it, too. Mrs. Tarakan was tense and distracted through dinner, all of her energy channeled toward Jason, and Sasha missed her usual attention.

After dinner, Mr. and Mrs. Tarakan took Jason to the TV room "for a talk." Sasha and Alyssa sat on the couch in the living room, trying to eavesdrop. They heard Mrs. Tarakan say "our circle" and "your type" and Mr. Tarakan say "respect" and "again." They heard Jason say "fuck."

"I want to hear, too!" whined Jake, and José rolled him into the room.

"Shhh!" Alyssa raised her finger to her lips.

"Downers Grove Community College! We take you as high as you want to go!" Jake sang, imitating a commercial.

"Shut up, smart-ass!" hissed Alyssa.

Sasha shrank into the couch and looked away. Since the flying linguini episode, Jake had been trying to catch her alone. Sasha had to admit, she was afraid of him. She was scared of his outbursts, of his twisted body. The rules of civil behavior didn't seem to apply to Jake. Thankfully, he was easy to avoid without seeming impolite. All she had to do was walk up the stairs and pretend not to hear him. Now she hoped Jake wouldn't harass her in front of his sister.

Nikki was the last one to get up from the table and come out to the living room.

"Your parents are . . . pretty neat," she said, breaking into a giant smile. She seemed proud to have completed a sentence.

"They aren't my parents," said Sasha.

"Sasha is a slave," piped in Jake.

Sasha Goldberg froze. Nikki stared at Jake, then at Sasha, and laughed hesitantly.

"No, really."

"Shut up, Jakey!" said Alyssa.

"She is a captive of the Talmud!" Jake said in a low, warbling voice.

"Holy Jesus!" Nikki glared at Sasha.

"Take it easy, Jake," said José. He rolled over his consonants like he was sucking on a toffee.

Sasha stared down at her knees, twirling a loose thread of her skirt.

"Nikki, do you have a smoke?" Alyssa asked.

Nikki nodded. Sasha watched them leave, wishing she could go along.

"Sasha, I need to talk to you," said Jake.

Sasha shook her head.

"You're crying."

Sasha bent lower and wiped her tears with the back of her hand. It was important to calm down by the time Mr. and Mrs. Tarakan reemerged from the room.

"I'm sorry," said Jake.

Sasha nodded.

"Sasha, look at me!" Jake's voice was breaking, making him sound like a little boy.

Sasha realized that she didn't have to look at him, that there was nothing he could do about it, either, stuck in his wheelchair on the other side of a glass coffee table. She could tell that Jake was in the kind of mood that would make a normal person get into her face and grab her by the chin. Keeping her eyes down, she heard him start his wheelchair and saw the edge of the table rock slightly. He was ramming his footrest into it, and the table was slowly inching toward Sasha, about to hit her in the shins. She jumped up and stepped away, narrowly avoiding the moving glass edge.

"What's your problem?" she shrieked in Jake's general direction, grateful for the English phrase that had conveniently popped into her mind. "What do you want from me?"

"I need you to listen," said Jake.

"I don't have to listen to your insults! I'm not *your* slave!"

She was almost out of the room when she heard a crash behind her back, the sound of glass breaking on stone. Jake must've pushed the glass tabletop off its textured concrete foundation.

"The hell did you do, man?" Jason bellowed happily, glad to be off the hook.

Nina will clean it up, thought Sasha, running down the basement stairs. *I don't work on the Sabbath.*

That night, the sound of shattering glass reverberated through her dreams. Sweating inside a felt tree costume, she stood in the middle of the Russian room and dropped Mr. Tarakan's revolutionary dishes on the stone floor, while Jake cheered her on from across the pile of porcelain shards. She woke up smiling.

The following day, Jake stayed away from her. Somebody had cleaned up the glass and carted away the concrete stump.

4

Mr. Tarakan

MR. TARAKAN STEERED HIS SILVER LEXUS OFF THE FREEWAY, drove past McDonald's and the Chevron station, and rolled down his window. The air smelled like dirt and wet pine. Mr. Tarakan always looked forward to this stretch of the road, with its gentle turns and tranquillity, occasionally punctuated by a passing car. This was his zone of decompression, between Chicago and home, but today the air didn't feel right. The pine smelled too intense, as if the forest had been doused in one of Nina's cleaning solvents. The smell made Mr. Tarakan sneeze, and he rolled up the window. Perhaps he was getting sick.

He turned the wheel sharply to the left to avoid a fallen branch. Twenty years ago he'd hit a deer here in the dark. Alyssa and Jason squealed in the back seat, Claudette cried. He got out to inspect the damage. One of the headlights had been destroyed. The wounded animal scampered into the forest. Mr. Tarakan remembered squinting at the swaying treetops. He'd never noticed how tall the trees here were, how black the forest. He was scared. He'd lived in the city all his life. What was he doing, buying a house he could barely afford, in a place where large animals were allowed to roam freely?

Claudette tapped on the glass, snapping him out of his stupor. Alyssa had turned on the cabin light, and he saw the back seat of his car littered with toys and coloring books. Jason was falling asleep again, doubling over his ratty Snoopy. Mr. Tarakan remembered driving home that night, his hand firmly on his wife's knee. In his head, his dead mother droned in Yiddish about the inevitability of disasters.

When he met Claudette, she had been a temp at Kozel, Kozel & Tarakan. Mr. Tarakan liked to watch her from his desk. He liked the curve of her neck and the place where the soft polyester of her blouse was slightly raised over the hooks of her bra. Occasionally she'd look around as if she were forgetting something, the expression on her face both flustered and defensive. Mr. Tarakan took a vacation, and when he returned, she wasn't there anymore, her desk occupied by a stocky woman in a powder-blue pantsuit.

He found her number and called her that night. She couldn't go out, but she invited him to come over. She lived on the West Side, in the kind of neighborhood that in Mr. Tarakan's opinion would've benefited from complete demolition. At first he thought he had the wrong apartment. Children's voices sounded from behind the door.

"Skunk!"

"Sponge head!"

"Poop head!"

"Mom, he used a bad word!"

Claudette poked her head out of the door.

"Uh, you're . . . on time!" She gave a nervous laugh.

She was pulling a sweater over a black silk slip.

"We were just cleaning up!" she exclaimed, shutting the door in his face.

Mr. Tarakan rang the bell again. This time she let him in. He had to step over a tangle of children's coats and boots by the door.

"See?" said Claudette, looking around wildly. "I always make the same mistake. I start cleaning this place from the back of the apartment. I make the beds. I put the toys away. I never get around to this." She laughed, bending over the couch to shove aside a pile of dry laundry. Mr. Tarakan could see the entire length of her leg under her slip. "Come in and sit down. Can I make you a drink?"

Mr. Tarakan surveyed the kitchen. The dishes were piled higher than the faucet in the sink. A pool of soggy cereal was congealing on the counter. Two golden-haired children, a boy and a girl, sat on the sticky linoleum in their underwear. Just looking at them made Mr. Tarakan feel cold. He picked up the coats from the floor, hung them up, and lined up the boots by the wall.

"Just sit down." Claudette sounded irritated. "I can do this myself."

He took off his suit jacket, rolled up his shirtsleeves, and started washing the dishes. It was exciting in a way, an adventure. Like volunteering in a soup kitchen, dirty work. Claudette fluttered around him, picking up odds and ends and setting them back in place. The children resumed their argument. Suddenly his antiseptic downtown condo didn't seem sufficient. He'd need a house in the suburbs. Claudette would have a cook and a maid. The children would have a nanny.

It was his idea to have another child. Claudette hadn't wanted any more, but he insisted.

During the first years of his life, Jake practically lived in the hospital. At times, he didn't look like a kid at all but like an extension of the machines, a *place* to plug in the equipment, marked by a bit of pale skin, a tuft of dark hair sticking out from under a wool cap. At first, they only worried about his heart defect and the hole in his left lung. The objective was to keep him alive. The CP diagnosis seemed like an afterthought, just another nasty surprise. They almost ignored it, even though the doctors were fairly certain that Jake would never learn to speak.

He was recovering from another surgery in a medically induced coma, his chest rising and falling with the rhythm of the ventilator, when Claudette first said she wanted a nose job. It seemed shocking at the time, but later Mr. Tarakan understood.

Every time Jake had a surgery Claudette would have one, too, on her face. When the boy returned from the hospital, his mother greeted him swaddled in gauze, drainage tubes sticking out all over. It was like a penance she was paying for her son's pain. Jake, who did learn to speak, uttered his first sentence at age three.

"Mommy scary!"

"Scary as shit!" confirmed Jason.

"I will not permit you to speak of your mother that way!" howled Mr. Tarakan, grabbing his golden-haired stepson by the meaty bicep.

Jake laughed from his stroller.

By the time Jake started elementary school, there was nothing left of Claudette's face. Mr. Tarakan was beginning to worry that she might pay someone to gouge her eyes out. He fought revulsion every time he kissed her frog-mouth and took special care not to touch the gruesome scar tissue behind her ears. He was preparing to take her doctors to court when Claudette discovered religion and philanthropy. Then God had sent Adriana, a new cause, an ersatz child.

Mr. Tarakan stopped in the driveway, climbed out of the car, and stood still for a second, allowing an enormous sneeze to rock his body. He was definitely getting a nasty cold. He noticed that the front of his suit was wrinkled, and one pant leg had somehow turned up, exposing a black sock and a strip of shockingly white flesh. He checked his hair. On windy days his comb-over tended to dislodge itself from his skull and stand up like a black fin. On days like this, when he was unwell, Mr. Tarakan felt puny, dwarfed by the giant pines in his own front yard. He got his briefcase from the front seat and went inside.

Jake was in the backyard, talking to Claudette's latest project. This new one wasn't nearly as pretty as Adriana. She looked almost . . . black, which made no sense. Mr. Tarakan remembered standing with Adriana on the steps of the courthouse after the trial, waving at the crowd of women below, smiling for the cameras. He was the hero of all domestics, a champion for human rights. Adriana clung to his arm, leaned her head on his shoulder. Her hair smelled like apples.

This new one was older, cautious as a stray dog. She put up a show for Claudette, but every time *he* went near her, she bristled, all clenched fists and pouting clumsiness.

Through the glass wall Mr. Tarakan watched Sasha kneel in front of Jake. The wheels of his son's chair grazed the concrete rim of the pool. Mr. Tarakan dashed toward the door, stopping at the last moment. They were only talking. He ought to tell Oscar to drain that pool already. Why did they have a pool that nobody used? For the viewing pleasure of migratory birds, for Jason's drunk friends to stumble into in the dark? *It's dangerous*, Mr. Tarakan thought angrily, watching Sasha's every move. The vision of Jake falling upside down into the pool burned in the back of his brain.

They seemed to have a lot to say to each other. Jake was smiling. Mr. Tarakan tried to read the look on Sasha's face, but she was bending her head low, scribbling something with a pen. All he could see was the shapeless back of her red bubble jacket and the muddy soles of her sneakers. There was something childishly reassuring about the girl's large feet, the inward-pointing toes. Mr. Tarakan stifled a sneeze and walked briskly into the bedroom.

Sunlight filtered through sheer rust-colored curtains, bathing the room in a warm glow. Claudette had an understanding of light and space that he admired. Mr. Tarakan felt grateful to her for surrounding him with beautiful things. He opened her carved teak jewelry box and found a key to a lacquered chest in the corner. Claudette was a lover of exquisite notebooks. The chest housed stacks of her unfinished diaries. Each journal was blank, its first page ripped out and discarded. Mr. Tarakan lifted the books out of the chest and set them on the floor. The covers reminded him of the trips they'd taken: the unicorn tapestry, a bumblebee pressed into handmade paper, a golden embossed Buddha, a safari scene. One journal was bound in thick, buttery leather. He remembered Claudette getting it at the Leonardo da Vinci exhibit. Finally, at the bottom of the chest, Mr. Tarakan found what he'd been looking for, a thin book the color of a scab.

Mr. Tarakan piled the journals back into the chest and returned the key to the jewelry box. Holding Sasha's passport with two fingers, like a dead rat, he hurried to Jake's room. José extinguished his joint, waved away the smoke, and, pushing with his legs, rode an office chair to the door.

"Oh, Mr. T, that you?" he said, surprised.

"Here." Mr. Tarakan sneezed. "When Jacob reappears, give it to him."

5

Oxygen

"I'M SORRY ABOUT THE OTHER NIGHT."

Sasha whipped around, startled. Between the cupid's gurgling in the pool and the rustle of the leaves she was raking, she didn't hear Jake's school bus in the driveway.

"My parents are sending me to a shrink."

"A shrink?"

"You know, a psychologist."

"Oh," Sasha regained her composure. Outside, in the yard, with his green backpack hanging from the handles of his wheelchair, Jake didn't appear intimidating. Sasha reminded herself that she could walk away from him at any time.

"I need to ask you something," Jake said. "What do you think you're doing here?"

"Raking."

"Right. I meant, what are you doing in this house? What do you want?"

"I work here, I'm trying to stay in the U.S. I have to live *somewhere*. I can't believe you don't get it. You should be thankful you don't have to . . ." Sasha stopped herself.

Jake laughed. "Sit down. I can't see you against the light."

"Just tell me what you want. I have work to do." Sasha crossed her arms and kept standing. It was better to tower over him.

"There was another one before you," said Jake, squinting into the sun.

"Another one?"

"Her name was Adriana. She walked three miles on the highway. She said she was sixteen years old. She had no papers. Some Romanian higher-up, who was renting the house up the road from here, brought her from Romania and had been mistreating her. Apparently, she did everything in his house: cleaned, cooked, watched the children. She said she worked around the clock and never had enough to eat. She showed up on our doorstep with this huge swollen arm. She said a ladder fell on her a few days before, and the Romanian didn't take her to the doctor or anything, just made her keep working. Her arm was broken in two places. My parents became outraged. There was a trial. My father represented Adriana for free. The Romanian got off on some diplomatic immunity shit, but he got transferred somewhere else. He also had to pay Adriana a settlement. My parents offered to be her legal guardians, and she stayed with us."

Sasha leaned the rake against the wall and sat down on the lion-footed bench.

"Thanks," said Jake. "Adriana took care of me when I was little. She did all the shit work, but still she was happy at first because nothing was as bad as what they did to her at that Romanian's house. I mean, Mom fed her and took her shopping. She got to go to high school. Mom even made Alyssa take her out when Alyssa got a car.

"Still, when Adriana turned eighteen, she wanted her money, and she wanted out. She wanted to go to college, and Mom couldn't let that happen. When Adriana went to a guidance counselor at school about it, my parents stalled on her money and hid her papers.

"What I'm trying to say is, they aren't about to let you go."

"But I don't have any money," said Sasha.

"It wasn't for the money, my parents are rich enough. Mom just *collects people*. She should adopt a baby and get it over with. Or just do charity, volunteer at a fucking Boys and Girls Club. Instead she has you. Do you like playing Yeshiva? Adriana was a nice girl; it took her two years to lose her mind. You don't seem like a patient type, although your job's easier."

"Two years?" Sasha shivered. The lawn was littered with leaves again, no use raking in this weather. She zipped up her jacket and looked at Jake. The edges of his lips were turning blue. For the first time, Sasha noticed his teeth, two straight white rows. She couldn't believe the Tarakans bothered to torment Jake with orthodontia, with all the things wrong with him.

"What are you looking at?"

"Nothing," Sasha said quietly. A gust of wind threw a cluster of dry leaves on Jake's lap, and she instinctively reached to swipe it away. "What happened to her after two years?"

"She got deported." Jake said, looking down at a place on his Levi's where Sasha's hand had just been.

"Your mom got tired of her?"

"No. Mom *loved* Adriana. Same way she *loves* you. After Adriana missed all the college deadlines, Mom bought her a pink canopy bed. Nine-year-old girl stuff, really. You wait."

"But I'm from *the Soviet Union*!" Sasha exclaimed in Mrs. Tarakan's syrupy voice. "I might *appreciate* a canopy bed! I thank you for your warning, Jake. I'll ask about my passport tonight. If I bother your parents enough about it, if I tell them what I want, they—"

"No, they won't." interrupted Jake. "They'll just sit on your papers indefinitely. Don't you get it? Mom wants to keep you."

Sasha nodded weakly, trying to imagine where in the house her passport might be hidden. She heard Mr. Tarakan's car in the driveway. The sun was setting now, and the trees around the house appeared as a solid dark wall. Would she become another undocumented girl trudging through this forest between mansions?

"Why do you care what I do?"

"The day she got her canopy bed, Adriana came home from school and made me stop breathing," Jake said evenly.

Sasha pushed her knuckles against the edge of the bench, until the pebbles in the concrete dug into her skin.

"I was, like, ten or eleven, and I didn't go to school that year, because for most of it I was on oxygen. That was before my last lung surgery. My parents hired tutors to come here, but Adriana took care of me most of the time. She fed me, checked my homework, and then tweaked with the oxygen tank and watched me turn blue. She told me not to tell or she'd kill me. She probably didn't mean to kill me, but I was a little kid and I totally believed her. She told me she was sick of my shit and of this house." Jake spoke in an airy monotone, as if telling somebody else's story. "I've seen what happens when toys turn on my mother."

Sasha Goldberg shook her head. Her passport was gone, her future was uncertain, the damn yard still had to be raked, but at that instant the most upsetting thing was being taken for a torturer.

"Are you afraid of me?" She hated how her voice shook, like she had something to hide.

"No. Yes. Not of you, but of her, yes. Even though she's in fucking Romania, I'm still afraid of her. For a while Adriana was the scariest thing in my life. I mean, I couldn't even eat because I was just living in fear. They put a tube in my stomach. She told me she wanted her money and papers and that it was up to me. But see, nothing is up to me. It's not up to me to lift my head.

"The girl was *crazy*. I remember some lady, a friend of Mom's, was over. She mentioned that her cat died. That night Adriana made up a whole story about how *she* killed the lady's cat. I took it all very seriously. . . ."

"So what happened?"

"So I had to have this other surgery. They put me under, and when I woke up, the first thing I saw was this red-haired nurse tweaking with my IV. For some reason I decided it was Adriana. I had this idea that she came to the hospital to finish me off. I was still halfway delirious, and I lost it. The nurse got my parents, and I told Mom everything. Adriana had another trial. She got convicted of child abuse, went to jail for a while, and then got deported. Mom took it hard. She said Adriana betrayed her."

Sasha laughed abruptly and covered her mouth.

"Yeah, funny," sighed Jake. "Why do I waste my childhood trauma on you? You're probably running from some gulag. What's your problem? I don't see any cigarette burns."

"Bad things happened to me, but they were my own fault," Sasha said. "Not cigarette burns. No, nothing like that."

"If I get your passport, do you have a plan? Like a place to go?"

Sasha shook her head. "No place to go here. Only . . ."

"What?"

"My father lives in America."

"Great!" exclaimed Jake. "Where?"

"I don't know. I tried to find out."

"Oh. Do you know what city, at least?"

Sasha shrugged.

"State?"

"I don't know."

"You know his name, right?"

"His name is Victor Semyonovich Goldberg," said Sasha, realizing she'd never said it aloud before. Papa had been a reedy, skittish mouse-mourner, but his name sounded solid and important, suitable for a reliable, well-heeled man.

"There's a pen in the front pocket of my bag," Jake said. "Write it down."

Reaching behind Jake's chair into his backpack, Sasha glanced at his fingers and thought that he couldn't possibly use a pen.

"They have note-takers for me at school," Jake said wearily, catching her eye. "Write his name on my hand."

"On your hand?"

"That way I won't lose it," he explained quickly.

There was a barely noticeable break in his voice, a plea.

I don't mind touching you, Jake. There was no way to say it.

I want to touch you.

Sasha knelt in front of the chair and took his right hand in hers. She had to firmly grasp his wrist to keep his palm from turning down. His skin was smooth and cool, damp in places where his hand touched the plastic of the hand rest. Sasha scribbled "Victor Semyonovich Goldberg" in the middle of his palm and folded his fingers around the name.

"All right," Jake said slowly. "I'll do a Web search, try some different spellings."

Sasha let go of his hand.

He was going to do something with a computer. Sasha had never used a computer. The Vasilievs didn't have one, and Neal kept his in the locked room.

"I'll let you know if I find anything," said Jake, turning toward the house.

"Thank you very much," Sasha said stiffly. After Jake was gone, she picked up the rake and continued to comb the lawn, saying, "Thank you very much, thank you very much," until it sounded relaxed and heartfelt. She raked the yard until it was almost dark, and the floodlights turned on under the patio roof. A harsh wind pulled apart the piles of leaves as fast as Sasha gathered them, but she enjoyed the meaningless dance of raking and the wind on her face. She didn't want to go inside. In the house, her idiotic optimism would bounce off the walls, wilt in the sobriety of the Yeshiva, make the idols laugh. Here, the wind patiently carried away even the most far-fetched hopes, leaving Sasha feeling pure and unjinxed.

"Jake?"

"Miss." José rounded the corner, letting the door slam behind him, "Mrs. T is calling you."

"Tell her," Sasha caught her breath, "I'm coming."

José dashed across the lawn.

Sasha stepped back. "What?"

"You lost this," José said, pressing Sasha's passport into her hand. "Put it in your pocket."

Sasha opened her mouth to speak, but in two giant leaps José was by the door again, waving from a semicircle of yellow light.

Sasha stuffed the passport into her coat pocket and ran into the house, fighting a manic grin.

It was like running down the stairs and thinking you were at the last step, but there was one more drop-off, a jarring void. Jake and José weren't at the dinner table.

"Where's Jake?"

"In his room. He has the SATs tomorrow," said Mr. Tarakan.

"A test for school," clarified Mrs. Tarakan, smiling at Sasha's alarmed face. "He's worried about it. I think that's why he's been acting so strange."

After the SATs, Jake got the flu and didn't come out of his room for a week. On Friday, Sasha cornered José in the hallway.

"He's fine," José said, using his foot to close the door behind him, his hands busy with a tray of food.

Sasha told herself that she could wait. On Saturday evening, she listened from the Yeshiva as Mr. and Mrs. Tarakan got dressed for an Art Institute fundraiser. She could hear their muffled voices and the water running, Mrs. Tarakan's heels on stone, and finally the front door.

There were only three people left in the house now. Nina, Esmeralda, and Oscar had gone home. Sasha walked upstairs, feeling her way up the dark staircase. The hallway still smelled of Mrs. Tarakan's perfume, fermented oranges with a hint of nutmeg.

She knocked on Jake's door twice before José appeared in a cloud of smoke. Sasha could hear *Saturday Night Live* in the background.

"Hey . . . ," José said with a smile, waving the smoke away from Sasha's face.

"Let her in, pothead!" yelled Jake.

José let Sasha in and stood there, holding the door open.

"Close the goddamned door!" Jake yelled again, and José did.

Sasha saw the empty wheelchair in the middle of the room, and a hospital bed by the window. Jake lay in bed, looking no worse or better than usual. Sasha walked toward the bed, unsure what to do.

"There's a chair by the desk," said Jake. He was wearing a gray T-shirt with a ripped-out collar. A white bed sheet covered his legs. "Did my parents take off?"

Sasha nodded.

"Look at the paper tomorrow. They're sure to be there, in the Living section, flashing all their sixty-four teeth at the photographer, looking like the living dead."

"Are you stoned?" Sasha laughed, pulling out the chair. She was happy to sit down, to be facing Jake. She knew if she kept standing she would try to guess what his body looked like under the sheet, and he'd know what she was thinking.

"Me? No, I can't smoke. José's stoned."

"You want some?" José asked. Without taking his eyes off the TV, he extended a large glass tube in Sasha's direction.

"What's that?" Sasha asked. The object resembled a vase from the contemporary wing.

"It's a bong," sighed Jake. "You don't want to smoke weed. You want to know about your father."

"Did you find him?"

"No."

Sasha tried to hide her disappointment.

"Thank you. And thank you for getting my passport back."

"I had nothing to do with it. It was Dad, heeding some call of conscience. You can leave whenever you want now. Let me know if you need money."

Sasha nodded.

"Look, I'm sorry I couldn't find your father," said Jake. "There are Goldbergs on the Internet, it's a common name. But no Victor Goldberg plus Russia."

Sasha nodded.

"Are you sure his name's Victor?" asked Jake.

"He's my father. I know his name."

"There was one Goldberg that kept popping up when I typed in "Goldberg" and "Russia." He had a different first name. Could he be a relative of yours?"

"I don't have any relatives. My grandparents, Semyon and Raya, died when—"

"Semyon. That was it, Semyon Goldberg. When did you say he died?"

"Before I was born. My father was just a kid."

"Was your grandfather a scientist?"

"I don't know. An engineer, I think."

"José, help me."

José put a tiny keyboard under Jake's right hand, attaching it to his wrist with a brace.

"Is this him?"

A black monitor hung above Jake's bed on a telescopic arm. Afraid of another disappointment, Sasha gave the monitor the briefest glance and saw her grandfather. There could be no mistake. She remembered this very photo hanging above her bed, in between the bookshelf and the pile of skis in the corner. People always said that Semyon looked like the poet Alexander Blok. In the picture, he had full, unsmiling lips and dark, furrowed brows. When she was little, Sasha used to be afraid to sleep under his face, and now she realized with surprise that her grandfather had been a handsome man. After Victor left, Mrs. Goldberg replaced the photo of Semyon with a drawing of the real Alexander Blok.

The picture disappeared beyond the top of the screen. Jake was scrolling through the text now. Sasha saw formulas and graphs.

"'Soviet technological advancement in WWII,'" read Jake. "Apparently, your grandpa was an inventor. He won the Lenin Prize. I wonder if that's a lot of money. You didn't know anything about him at all?"

Sasha shook her head. "Let me see the picture again."

Jake scrolled back to the picture, and Sasha saw what she was looking for. Two fold lines crossing just below Semyon's nose. The missing corner. Sasha grabbed Jake's hand, and the photo fluttered off the screen.

"Let go, you're pushing the buttons!" said Jake. "The guy has been dead since the seventies. So what if someone's studying him? How does this help you?"

"This photo belonged to my father. See how it's been folded? My dad carried it around with him in the army. It hung in my room for years."

"Are you sure?"

Sasha nodded.

"Well, Victor isn't mentioned anywhere on the site. Let's see who wrote this paper. Oh, look."

"'Heidi Goldberg,'" read Sasha.

"Is she a relative?"

"No. It's not even a Russian name."

"Look, here's her e-mail address. Want to send her a note?"

"Yeah, but . . ."

"What?"

"Can you maybe write it for me? Make it sound . . . nice."

"Dear Mrs. Goldberg," typed Jake. "The photograph of Semyon Goldberg that you use to illustrate your paper (http://www.newschool.edu/sovietstudies/goldberg.html) belonged to my father, Victor Semyonovich Goldberg. I'm trying to get in touch with him and wondering if you have his contact information. I appreciate your help, Sasha Goldberg."

"Say 'Alexandra.' More official."

"You don't have to sound official," laughed Jake. "Send?"

Sasha nodded, her ecstatic mind busy grafting her father onto her grandfather, turning him into an American scientist, a suit-wearing man, a commander of a lecture hall, an owner of a house with stainless-steel appliances and a knife set.

"How can I thank you?"

"Want to play Strip Scrabble?"

"Jesus!" José rolled his eyes.

"Jesus can play, too!"

"What's strip Scrabble?" asked Sasha, turning red.

"Well, we take turns and a person with the lowest score takes off one item of clothing . . ."

"I know what 'strip' is. What's 'Scrabble'?"

"Oh." Jake laughed. "A word game. I was just kidding. We don't have to play Strip Scrabble. Strip Scrabble is for lecherous nerds. Although, given your ancestry . . ."

"My father was adopted."

"Well, that changes everything!" Jake exclaimed sarcastically. "We *definitely* shouldn't play Strip Scrabble."

Sasha glanced at the monitor.

"Nothing yet," Jake said. "It may take a while. Unless she's sitting in front of her computer, waiting for you to write."

José lit the bong and showed Sasha how to inhale. *Bong Scrabble Heidi Scrabble Bong Heidi,* thought Sasha, holding her breath to absorb the smoke and the new vocabulary through her lung walls. Things were happening again. Sasha felt flushed and giddy. Stoned, she dared to stare back at Jake for as long as she wished, letting the silence stretch and compress time. His hair was coal-black against the pillow, his eyes shining, deep brown.

"I'm going to bed." José yawned, turning off the TV. "You need anything?"

"She may not write today. I'm sure she'll write tomorrow," Jake said.

He sounded tired, and Sasha remembered that he wasn't stoned. How long had she sat there? All she had to do was go out the door and . . . She tried to think it through. Walk past the Russian room, past the menacing pickle head, through the African room with the idols silhouetted against the window, past the gloom of the Yeshiva down to the basement, flip on the light, see the dead seascape, black garbage bag at the foot of her bed, the four white walls.

"Are you okay?" Jake asked.

"This is strong stuff." Sasha giggled, shivering. "I don't want to go. I'm scared. There's something in the dark. God, or something. In the Yeshiva. It'll snatch me."

"Yes," Jake said gently. "I feel that way all the time here, and I don't even smoke. Do you want a blanket? There's one in the closet. There's a glass of water on the desk. Have some, you'll feel better in a half hour."

Sasha got the blanket out of the closet and returned to her chair. Every edge in the room was in focus. The plastic rail of Jake's bed, the black phone cord, the parallel lines of the miniblinds threatened to slice her eyeballs.

"Do you want me to turn down the light?" Jake asked.

Sasha nodded, shaking. Stupid drug.

With a push of a button, Jake dimmed the lights.

The room was completely dark when Sasha woke up. The clock on the desk said 3:10. In its red glow Sasha saw the side of Jake's sleeping face. Quietly, she got up from her chair and tiptoed toward the door.

"Sasha."

"I didn't mean to wake you," she whispered hoarsely, "I'm okay now. I'm going downstairs."

"Don't leave." Jake sounded still half asleep, all the abrasiveness drained from his voice.

"Your parents . . ."

"Come here."

Sasha retraced her steps and stood by the bed.

"Touch me."

Sasha put her hand on his forehead and moved it down, over his eyes, nose, and mouth and down to his neck, to the collar of his T-shirt. Feeling his body tense under the sheet, she bent over the bed rail and kissed him. His lips were hot and soft. Sasha felt his lashes brush her cheek as he closed his eyes. They kissed until Sasha's back was sore from bending over.

"Jake, have you ever been with a girl?"

"Uh . . ."

"I've seen you looking at me."

Jake swallowed. "I'm sorry I offended you."

"Do you want me to show you?" Sasha pulled her shirt off over her head and unhooked her bra.

"You don't have to," Jake protested weakly, without taking his eyes off her.

"I want to."

"*Touch me.*"

Sasha lay down next to him and touched him under the T-shirt. He had smooth skin and small hard nipples. His chest was a map of scars. Sasha traced a line of hair from his navel under the elastic of his boxers and held him in her hand. That was all it took. Startled, Sasha stared at the stain spreading on the sheet. When she looked back at Jake's face, he was crying.

"It's all right," Sasha said quietly.

"I'm sorry," Jake sobbed, turning away. "You should go. I'll get José."

Sasha took his hand and kissed his fingers. "I like you. Don't make me leave. I can do whatever José can do."

"It isn't your *job.*"

"Jake."

"Please, go."

In the basement, Sasha got under her blanket in her jeans and T-shirt and lay there wide-eyed and shaking.

How do you love someone whose body is another person's job?

I was a mail-order bride. For a year, I lived with a stranger. Fucking meant fifteen minutes of endurance, of holding my breath three times a week. Not much to complain about, no rape. I even learned to enjoy it by the end, Neal a tool between my legs, Alexey's face, what was left of it, safely hidden under my lowered eyelids, a pathetic, last-ditch antidote.

You don't have it in you to exploit me, Jake. I know what I want.

When Sasha finally drifted off to sleep, almost at sunrise, she dreamed that the eyeless seagull had somehow dislodged itself from its seascape and was thrashing in the corner just above her bed.

6

True Love

"LET'S HELP LITTLE BEAR MAKE A PIE!" AN ELECTRONIC VOICE squealed from the bedroom. "A pie, ie, ie, ie."

"Ben, sweetie, quit clicking on the same spot, it drives Mommy crazy!" yelled Heidi.

The computer went silent. Heidi shifted on the couch, kicked a Clifford the Big Red Dog puzzle out of the way, and leafed through the remains of last Sunday's *New York Times*. She knew that if they had a TV she'd spend an entire day watching soaps, Oprah and Jerry. Shortly after Ben was born, Victor carried the TV out to the curb. It'd been Heidi's idea to get rid of it, but now she missed the comfort of the tube's drone.

"Let's help Little Bear make a pie!" the electronic voice suggested again, snappy with static, inanimate cuteness.

"Ben, you're done!"

Heidi slowly got off the couch, waited out a leg cramp, and stormed into the bedroom.

"I'm sorry, I'm sorry!" Ben chanted, wrapping his entire body around the monitor in a desperate, protective gesture.

Heidi reached between him and the keyboard and pressed command Q. The music stopped. Ben stared at the empty desktop, crumpled in his chair, and began to wail.

Watching him grind his head into the back of the office chair in a halfhearted, too-much-time-indoors tantrum, Heidi hated herself. She'd let the poor three-year-old play with the computer for hours.

"I want juice!" gasped Ben.

Heidi glanced at the screen. It was three in the afternoon. The kid was probably starving. Heidi used to have a sixth sense for Ben's needs: she knew when the boy was hungry; she also woke up the minute he did, even if he lay quietly in the other room. Piercing a juice box with a plastic straw, Heidi wondered when they'd lost this precious telepathic bond.

She set a PB&J sandwich next to the remains of Ben's breakfast and returned to the couch. Throwing away the leftovers required too much effort.

"Don't touch it, that's yucky," she shouted when Ben started fishing a shrunken Froot Loop out of the rainbow-tinted milk.

While Ben ate, Heidi finished the sports and business sections, the TV guide, and the obituaries. With nothing left of the paper, she felt a familiar, all-encompassing rage. She wanted to die. She needed a shower. Perhaps she could salvage what was left of the day.

"Want to go to the bookstore?" she asked, getting up.

Ben sniffled and nodded. "Will you read me three books?"

"As many as you want, baby," said Heidi.

Ben stood up in his chair and leapt into her arms. Heidi felt the warmth of his palm-sized butt through his Curious George underwear and realized that all day she'd been trying not to cry. Nothing scared Ben more than his mother's tears.

Heidi dug in the hamper for a bra. She hadn't done any laundry in two weeks, so when she found a pair of clean matching socks on the floor of the closet it felt like a victory. She didn't bother to shower. Sensing his mother's limits, Ben dressed himself and didn't wiggle when Heidi bent down to tie his shoes.

The brownstone stoop was plastered with wet leaves, and Heidi gripped Ben's hand tightly. She enjoyed the concentration required to keep him from slipping. Degraw was a wind tunnel. Heidi unfolded the stroller and slowly pushed it against the wind, uphill to Court Street.

"Blue," said Ben.

The streetlights had just turned on, and Heidi realized that Ben was talk-

ing about the color of the shadows on the wet sidewalk. The boy had an un-
canny ability to see colors. Heidi wondered if this ability was somehow linked
to his tone deafness. She liked to think that she could track the development
of her son's little brain and delighted in its unconscious choices: talking
before walking, dinosaurs over trucks, color over sound. When Heidi was
pregnant with Ben, Victor would put headphones on her belly to expose "the
baby" to classical music. Now he liked to joke about suing the makers of the
headphones. The only song Ben ever learned was "Jingle Bells." He sang it
year-round in an earnest monotone devoid of melody or meter. Heidi bragged
to other mothers about Ben's eye for color, but his defiant, out-of-season
chants secretly made her the most proud.

By the time they got to Barnes & Noble it was almost dark. Heidi always
felt better at the end of the day. She felt accomplished for getting out of the
house, for braving the cold. Guiltily, Heidi preferred the brightly lit Barnes &
Noble to the small community bookstore next door. Here, nobody cared
when Ben tore apart the books or spilled juice on the carpet. Blowing on her
hands, Heidi unwrapped Ben's scarf and followed him to the kids' section.

When Heidi and Ben got home, Victor was already there, clearing dishes off the
table. Heidi smelled the Middle Eastern takeout he was reheating for dinner.

"I'm sorry the house is a mess," she mumbled.

"It's okay," replied Victor. "Good thing you didn't marry a Russian."

It was a long-standing joke with Victor and Heidi. Russian men, Victor
said, insisted that their women serve them hand and foot, while wearing
heels. Victor was proud of not being "a typical Russian man." Perhaps because of his disdain for "typical Russian men," he had no Russian friends.
Heidi knew that he was proud of that, too. He didn't seem to miss the company of people who spoke his language, and he never spoke Russian with Ben.

It often seemed to Heidi that her husband's main accomplishment had
been paring himself down, testing the limits of his own blandness. As if he
were born, fully grown, in Terminal 3 of JFK Airport, only to become a thoroughly conformist, uncomplaining dental technician.

Every evening, when Victor came home from work, Heidi experienced a
bout of amnesia and panic. "Who are you?" she was tempted to ask. "And,

next to you, who am I?" Ben alone was fully real, undeniable. Using the boy as a guide, his dark curls, his warm hands and voice, Heidi reconstructed her husband, carefully imagining the hidden Victor. Every day, it was harder to do. The panic persisted into the night, and every word out of Victor's mouth threatened to turn it into hate.

It bothered Heidi that she didn't know any more about Victor than she had eight years ago, when he emerged from the JFK immigration line, rumpled and disoriented, wearing dirty brown polyester slacks. She asked about his suitcase, and he told her that he didn't have one. To her dismay, he also didn't have a place to stay or any money for a hotel. Heidi laughed and rubbed her forehead. When she'd sent Victor an invitation form, she'd assumed it would be a mere formality, a small favor. She'd sent these forms twice before to secure visas for her Moscow friends. Both of those friends had stayed with their relatives in Brighton Beach. Heidi never expected Victor to drop into her lap like this. Of course, he was welcome to stay in her apartment, she told him. He looked harmless, and she had a spare futon. This would be something to tell her friends about.

In the cab, she attempted conversation, pointing out landmarks and interesting-looking people, even making jokes in Russian. Victor nodded and smiled with his lips only, his eyes fixed on the back of the cabby's head.

"How long will you be staying?" asked Heidi.

"I'm not going back to Russia," he replied, finally turning to face her.

"You're going to defect?" murmured Heidi, trying to process the implications of his announcement.

Victor nodded. "I'm going to apply for political asylum," he said.

"Oh," replied Heidi. They were nearing her street. Fumbling for the fare, she tried to think of tactful ways to withdraw her invitation but couldn't come up with any. By the time she paid the driver, Victor was asleep, his mouth falling open. Heidi woke him up and helped him out of the car. He reeked of sweat, and she held her breath.

On her way to the bathroom that night, she watched him sleep: his lean arms hanging over the edge of the futon, his white undershirt glowing in the neon light from the sign outside, his Afro like a dark halo on the pillowcase.

As inconvenient as his presence was, Heidi found it thrilling. Here was her own refugee camp, her underground railroad. She felt alive with purpose. First thing in the morning, before Victor even woke up, she was on the phone with the Hebrew Immigrant Aid Society, investigating the asylum procedure.

Small things had to be worked out. Victor had one change of clothes— two pairs of polyester slacks and two long-sleeved polyester shirts, all in muddy Soviet earth tones. He wore each outfit for a week. By Friday, Heidi's living room filled with the smell of his body, and on Saturday he took a shower and washed his clothes in the sink.

Heidi wondered how she could bring it up to him about showering more often. She also wanted to offer to take his things to the laundromat but couldn't think of a tactful way of doing so. Finally, tired of Victor's wet shirts dripping on her whenever she went to the bathroom, she called HIAS again.

The following week Victor had an appointment with a social worker, a bossy Russian woman by the name of Mrs. Volk. Heidi listened from the waiting room.

"This is America. They don't wash their clothes in the sink," said Mrs. Volk, handing Victor a bag of donated clothing. "Have your host show you a laundromat. Here's some change for the laundry. Shower every day, or Americans will think you stink."

Say it like it is, Heidi thought appreciatively. From then on, Victor showered every day. A week later, Mrs. Volk paired him up with a volunteer family who took him shopping. A stick of deodorant and a new toothbrush appeared on the edge of Heidi's sink.

During the day, Victor watched TV. Heidi was impressed by how quickly and effortlessly he learned English. Soon she started leaving him grocery lists, and he bought their food while she was at school. Heidi's friends teased her about him, asking her every week if she was sleeping with her refugee. Heidi got mad, but she couldn't help looking at Victor with different eyes than when she first met him.

"How old are you?" Heidi asked him one night over dinner.

"Thirty," said Victor.

"Did you have a girlfriend in Russia?"

Victor's face registered such shock that Heidi regretted asking him.

Maybe it was a provincial thing, this modesty. Muscovites didn't mind talking about their girlfriends. Or maybe he thought Heidi was hitting on him and didn't like her.

"Once," said Victor.

"What was her name?"

"Lubov."

"Did you . . . love her?"

"No." Victor wasn't going to say any more on the subject.

"Well, I just broke up with someone," said Heidi. "His name is Eric. He's a musician and a total asshole." She laughed. "In fact, everyone I've dated lately seems to be a total asshole."

Victor listened politely. He had that nod-and-smile immigrant look on his face again. The subject was obviously embarrassing to him.

"Want some wine?" asked Heidi. She hated the tension that always settled over them in the evenings, when the TV was off and they were alone together, a man and a woman, total strangers. "Let's put on some music."

Heidi put a tape into the tape player and pressed the button. A whiny guitar sound swelled and fell, and a harmony of nasal girls' voices began to plead and complain in an imaginary language.

"This is my friend's band, Pillowhead. Like it?"

Victor nodded. He agreed with everything.

"That was how I met Eric. He was a guitarist for Selfish Vegan. Selfish Vegan is getting pretty big now. Pillowhead opened for them, and after the show my friend introduced me to Eric—"

"What's a vegan?"

"Oh, it's a person who only eats plants—no meat, no dairy. . . ."

"A starving person?"

"Well, no. You can be a vegan and have a healthy diet."

Victor laughed. It was the first time Heidi ever heard him laugh.

"What?"

"The band names. Funny."

"Well, yeah, they're meant to be ironic." Heidi felt slightly defensive, and at the same time happy that Victor finally laughed. She didn't know then that the band names would be one of the very few things that ever made him laugh, that he would never like the music of Pillowhead or the Vegan, preferring to listen to Bach at a subaudible volume. She had no idea that Victor would be sulky and boring around her friends, that he would forever remain blind to her culture, whether out of contempt or simple inattention, Heidi would never know.

That night they drank wine and Heidi rattled off the names of the bands she knew, making Victor laugh again and again, until they were sufficiently drunk to sit on the couch side by side and look through the pictures of Heidi's visits to Moscow.

"I have something to give you." Heidi jumped up, suddenly remembering. She dug through her drawer for a small stack of photos and photocopies she'd set aside more than a year ago.

"The third one from the corner," said Victor, caressing the glossy surface with his thumb, "is my room."

He peered closely at the photo of a yellow facade, as if hoping to see inside his childhood home through the black rectangle of the window.

"Did you go by there when you were in Moscow?" Heidi asked.

"No." Victor looked up at her as if she'd said something brilliant, something he hadn't thought about until now. "I should have. I . . . forgot."

"Look at this," said Heidi, handing him a copy of another photograph. The photo depicted an official event. In the background, men and women in suits sat around two long banquet tables under a GLORY TO SOVIET INDUSTRY! banner. In the foreground, Semyon Goldberg was shaking Nikita Khrushchev's hand. Raya, with a fox wrapped around her neck, stood beaming by their side.

"This is the first time," said Victor.

"What?"

"First time I see my mother since she died," said Victor, shaking his head.

Pleasantly tipsy, just a sip away from *very drunk*, Heidi leaned back on the couch, watching him. It seemed to her that this was the first time she mattered in somebody's life. Up until then she was raised, educated, entertained, a passive participant. A researcher of obscure topics, a casual lover of assholes, a consumer of culture and fashion. And now look, she'd *resurrected a man's mother*.

"You can have all these," she said.

"You put plastic. You saved," Victor said appreciatively. "Plastic," he repeated, holding up an old photo of Semyon by its sleeve. He sounded as if putting a picture in a plastic sleeve were an act of love.

"Well, it's an old—" Heidi started, feeling Victor's lips on hers. Drunk on her own relevance, Heidi did her best to ignore his halitosis and the plastic sleeve that was now between them, poking her in the ribs. In retrospect, she would say she enjoyed the kiss. The following day, she discreetly asked Mrs. Volk to take Victor to the dentist, eliminating the last obstacle that stood in the way of *true love*.

"Want some food?" Victor asked.

Heidi wasn't hungry, but she took some of Victor's rice and a slice of cucumber for Ben.

After Ben's bath, Heidi took him to bed. The boy liked to fall asleep with his arms wrapped around his mother's neck. The warmth of his embrace, his sweet wet breath, always put Heidi to sleep, too, and often she stayed in Ben's room until morning, curled up next to him in his blue plastic race-car bed, fully dressed. But this time she waited Ben out. When he loosened his grip, she climbed out of bed and walked into the brightly lit hallway.

Victor was in the hallway, too. Was he just walking by or had he been hovering behind Ben's door, waiting for her?

"I think I'm going to do laundry," Heidi said, still squinting and groggy.

"Now? Why don't you do that stuff during the day?"

Heidi was sure that Victor was about to say something about the two-day-old pile of dishes in the sink and the overflowing trash can that had begun to stink, and about how he, Victor, couldn't imagine what Heidi did all day because the house was a disaster and nothing in it had changed since he left for work that morning.

"I hate to make the baby sit in front of those god-awful cartoons in the laundromat for two hours," said Heidi's peacekeeping reflex.

Heidi herself, had she been free from reflexes, wouldn't have minded a fight right now. Fighting was preferable to sex, better than the claustrophobia of her husband's sagging body on top of hers. After a fight, she would take the laundry, grab her Walkman and a few old tapes, and flee, feeling self-righteous and justified to enjoy her freedom.

The music had to be treated with caution. The tapes were mostly of Selfish Vegan's and Pillowhead's live performances, and sometimes Heidi thought she could hear her own laughter in the din between the songs. Every time she allowed these ghosts from her previous life to mingle with the sight of Ben's and Victor's everyday things, Heidi experienced a terrifying animal confusion, the kind of feeling one gets from walking backward on a moving escalator. She never listened to these tapes at home anymore, and in the laundromat she would take special care to sit with her back to the machines, to avoid glimpsing Ben's firefighter PJs through the porthole. Then, for the duration of a washing cycle, she would disappear inside herself and be happy.

"Just drop the laundry off tomorrow, and I'll pick it up after work," said Victor, and Heidi could clearly see that there wouldn't be a fight.

"I've really got to take care of this mess," she said guiltily. "Will you wait up for me?"

Victor shrugged. Heidi knew that when she came back, he would be asleep. He had to get up early for work the next morning. Victor Goldberg manufactured dentures. He preferred working in daylight to achieve the most natural look and color.

"I'll be back in no time. Love you," she added, slipping away with her back to the wall to prevent touching.

It was almost one in the morning when Heidi returned home, but she didn't feel tired. She made a cup of tea and set it down on the pile of papers next to the computer. The pile of papers was Heidi's never-to-be-finished dissertation. She still taught her science and totalitarianism class at the New School, but deep inside she believed her academic career to be over. Since the end of the Cold War, nobody was interested in the Soviet Union anymore. Her class was an elective, and she was down to one session a week.

She was slowly turning into an overeducated housewife, now almost completely reliant on Victor's income. She was becoming a stereotype. All she needed was an expensive handbag hand-stitched from vintage upholstery. A store selling them recently opened around the corner from their apartment. A tiny temple of wearable irony, it was called Found Objects. Hot-rod leather wallets handmade by *real prisoners* were lined up in its window display like ancient artifacts. Every mom in the neighborhood sported something from Found Objects: a wallet, a purse, a T-shirt coyly embroidered with an image from a 1950s advertisement, the markings of the upper-class tribe. Nostalgic for her punk days, when being fashionable meant going to an army surplus store in an Albuquerque strip mall, Heidi bitterly resisted the trend. She had a queasy feeling that she was living a lie, that she accidentally ended up with someone else's life while her own was waiting just around the corner, unused and unlived.

Heidi turned on her computer, yielding to the compulsion to check her e-mail. As long as she could stop herself from going to Yahoo, from searching for old boyfriends and high school math teachers she'd had crushes on, she'd get enough sleep.

She had new mail. The subject was "Semyon Goldberg," and the sender was Jake Tarakan. Trying to remember if this Jake Tarakan was one of her students, Heidi opened the message.

She read the message several times. It had to be a scam, an extortion scheme of some sort. Heidi thought about the dangers of the Internet the newsmagazines liked to expose in their long, sensational stories: invasions of privacy, credit card fraud, stolen bank accounts, perverts lurking in teen chat rooms. But why target their family? What was there to extort?

Heidi pushed back her chair, walked into the bedroom, and sat on the edge of the bed, listening to her husband's rhythmic snores. She would talk to Victor in the morning, just in case.

7

Rates of Exchange

IN THE TARAKANS' LIBRARY, SASHA GOLDBERG SET A CHERRY-wood dolphin down on the glass table and rubbed her eyes. She could see the elongated reflection of her head in the dolphin's shiny red back. Another, identical dolphin was waiting to be shined. Sasha squirted oil soap on a piece of cheesecloth and began rubbing its snout.

The dolphin's protruding forehead looked familiar. Sasha remembered the thrashing eyeless bird in her dream. Did all animal representations share this particularly unpleasant, hypercephalic look? Sasha wished she could stop noticing these things. She'd been awake since five in the morning, watching the interior of the house develop out of the predawn dusk. It took all her energy to protect last night's feeling of euphoria and tenderness from the iron spikes of the medieval armoire and the suspicious stare of the dead boar, from the eagle-headed fireplace accessories and artful clusters of tea candles.

By the time Jake appeared, the house had won. Twin cherrywood lozenges had altered the meaning of Sasha's experience like quotation marks. Was she allowed a moment of freedom last night, or had another exchange taken place?

Washed the floor in the Russian room in exchange for a bed to sleep on.
Scraped the gunk from in between the hallway stones for a bowl of granola.
Wrapped Mrs. Tarakan's summer shoes in tissue paper for a turkey sandwich.
Replaced a type D vacuum cleaner bag in exchange for a pack of tampons.
Pretended to read the Torah for a plate of pesto ravioli.
Helped Jake Tarakan jerk off for an Internet search.

"She wrote back," Jake said from the doorway.

Sasha couldn't bring herself to look at him, but she knew that he'd given some thought to the way his voice would sound.

"What did she say?" she asked cautiously, assuming it was bad news.

"She said that there must be some mistake because Victor Goldberg is her husband and the only child he has is Ben, age three and a half."

"Husband?"

"Sincerely, Heidi Goldberg," Jake said in a shrill feminine voice.

"Ben?" Sasha stood up straight, letting the dolphin drop on the table with a resounding thud.

"Careful."

"What is this thing, anyway?"

"It's a bookend."

"What's a *bookend*?" Sasha asked, looking at the gathering clouds outside. She remembered a blue cloudless sky from another day. They were coming back from a trip to the lake. Her father held her by the armpits between two train cars while she sprayed diarrhea all over screeching steel plates. Afterward, he carried her back to her seat. Groggy and limp, Sasha put her head on his shoulder and pretended to sleep. "It's the water," said Mrs. Goldberg. Her father's red checkered shirt smelled like sand and sweat. It was Sasha's first memory of him.

"Calm down," said Jake.

"So I polish ends of books while my father goes around marrying *Heidis* and having *Bens*?"

"I sense a problem with names."

"Did you even believe me yesterday?" Sasha asked slowly. Jake's dull, automatic sarcasm felt like a betrayal. It was what Sasha needed. She'd betray him right back.

"About?"

"About the photograph! That it was my grandfather? You didn't, did you? Tell me!" Cradling the dolphin in her arms, Sasha blocked the door.

"You know what you look like? You look like a deranged fisherman with a trophy," Jake laughed.

It was his *fucked-up laughter* that led Sasha to discover the meaning of blinding rage. Jake disappeared. Instead, Sasha saw thousands of dollars' worth of rubber and metal, his mechanism. Its six fat wheels looked like sections of a dismembered caterpillar. With a queasy fascination, Sasha wondered about the functions of the chair's various parts, its levers, buttons, and brakes, and about other things she'd seen in Jake's room. The tools of José's *job*.

She glared at the place on Jake's chest where the belts crossed.

"Did you think I just made it up to impress a . . ."

"Cripple? A gimp? A freak? An invalid? A special person?" Jake recited quietly, his eyes narrowing with hatred. "I think you need help with your vocabulary on this. Now, why don't you tell me something I don't already know?"

Sasha looked away, then down at her hands, at the dolphin. She wanted to hide her face, to bolt out of the door, but the silence in the room felt like a stranglehold.

"Jake, I'm sorry," she muttered finally.

"Forget it, Sasha. What I came to tell you is that Heidi is a college professor in New York. Her home address is listed in the White Pages. If it's outdated you can always find her through the university. My parents and I are going to Chicago this weekend. You can go then. I'll leave all the information on my desk for you. I can even *buy* you a plane ticket."

Sasha stood still, trying not to breathe. It was her own special way of facing attacks, developed in grade school. You absorbed the impact, demonstrated the infinity of your cowardice, denied the attacker the pleasure of resistance.

"José will show you how to walk out of here so that Larry the security guy doesn't notice," Jake added, twisting his mouth into an evil grin. "He can also give you a fucking *tour* of my room, answer all of your questions."

"I don't have any questions," whispered Sasha.

"Yes, you do."

"What, you read minds?"

"Just the most primitive ones," Jake said, wheeling past her out of the room.

Sasha put down the dolphin and covered her face with her hands. Jake's words rang in her ears like a diagnosis. She knew she had a primitive mind because there was always something just beyond her grasp, things she could feel but couldn't understand. Things she lost before finding.

A key turned in the front door. Sasha heard the rustle of paper bags and seconds later Mrs. Tarakan fluttered into the library. In her gym clothes, with a ponytail poking out through the back of her baseball cap, she looked like an oversized, underfed child.

"Oh, these look much better!" she exclaimed, stroking one of the dolphins. "Could you throw an English muffin in the toaster for me?"

"Sure," Sasha managed with her trembling mouth. She was suddenly grateful for the primitive nature of her mind, for its sturdy, walled *compartments*. "Do you want jam or butter?"

8

The Real Story

IN BOROUGH PARK, BROOKLYN, VICTOR GOLDBERG SET HIS cup of coffee on the stairs and unlocked the lab. He didn't need to be here now that it was almost dark. He couldn't work in artificial light, but he couldn't bear to go home, either. He finished his coffee and cleared his desk. Dentures in various degrees of completion lay lined up on a narrow metal shelf.

"She's here. Now what?" Victor asked them. The dentures kept quiet. Some were clamped shut in vices.

Victor Goldberg loved his job. He was a dental technician to the stars, a man well known in his field, whose skill was compared to that of a jeweler. The best Manhattan dentists sought Victor out for their most difficult jobs, their most famous clients. He had made a diamond-encrusted partial bridge for a rap star and had recently worked for Hollywood, making dentures for horror and vampire movies.

Victor had no idea it would turn out this way, when years ago Mrs. Volk presented him with a stack of vocational school brochures. All the directions his life could have taken.

Nursing assistant
Refrigeration repairman
X-ray technician
Network administrator
Dental technician

"There are also four-year colleges," said Mrs. Volk, eyeing Victor skeptically. That was what Heidi had wanted him to do, but Victor chose the path of least resistance. From the first day, he liked the dental lab; the company of the silent, headless mouths.

All the disembodied teeth he worked with made him think of the Holocaust. Occasionally, he allowed himself to daydream that his past life, his first wife and daughter, were victims of some large sociopolitical catastrophe that he couldn't control. But Sasha was no Anne Frank. Alive and growing, she made herself at home in his nightmares: her thick curls, yellow skin, baby teeth, permanent teeth, baby fat, nascent breasts. She tore holes in the knees of her tights and wore out her boots but, overall, remained. Victor Goldberg couldn't make himself forget the real story.

Asbestos 2 stood frozen in winter black-and-white when a letter arrived from Moscow. It was addressed to V. S. Goldberg in careful, overly correct cursive.

"What is this?" Lubov asked.

"I have no idea," he said, tearing the envelope.

Respected Mr. Goldberg,

I am an American historian, studying Soviet science. While interviewing your father's colleagues, I found out that Semyon Goldberg had a son, and I was very fortunate to be able to locate you through government records.

The Moscow Aviation Institute and specifically your father are the subject of my dissertation. I would appreciate any information you can share. In exchange, I can avail you of the images of your parents that I have been able to find in the archives of the Institute. I would prefer to interview you in person, but my resources do not permit travel to Siberia.

I'm anxiously awaiting your reply. Perhaps we may work together.

Respectfully,

Heidi Parkinson

"Vitya, this is it."

"What, Luba?"

"This is our ticket out of here," said Mrs. Goldberg, smoothing the letter and folding it in two. "This Heidi will help us move to America."

Victor Goldberg bit his lip. *Give it back, this is mine,* he was tempted to yell, like a child. Again, she was taking things out of his hands, scheming. This time it was his parents, his past, turned into a *ticket.* He said nothing. He'd learned long ago it was useless to argue.

"Respected Mr. Heidi," dictated Lubov, "I regret your lack of resources. Perhaps you can assist me in traveling to America. I have a wealth of information to share with you, and I have always wanted to visit your beautiful country."

"What wealth of information?" asked Victor. "I barely knew my father. The only meaningful conversation we ever had was one time in sixth grade, when he told me about women. A real man needs at least one mistress, he told me. I think I blocked out the rest. What I know about his work, I learned from the *Science Hour.* I'm sure they have it archived somewhere."

"What does it matter, Vitya, what you do and don't know? You can make something up for the American. Personal things. *My father never forgave Hitler. My father especially enjoyed Uzbek regional delicacies.* . . . But you're right. We should bait this Heidi, give him something real. Go get Semyon's photo."

"No. You know it's one of the few things—"

"Go bring the picture, Victor."

A reply arrived within a month. Heidi thanked Victor for the photograph and enclosed an invitation form for a visitor's visa. "I'm looking forward to your visit," she wrote. "Please let my friend know when you plan to travel, and she will get in touch with me." There was a Moscow phone number at the end of the note.

Like most Jewish families in the Soviet Union, the Goldbergs had discussed emigrating, but their conversations always had an apathetic, theoretical tone. Lubov was worried about losing her job if she became an *otkaznik,* and while Baba Zhenia was still alive, there was no question of going because the old woman was intent on being buried in Russian soil.

This time, Lubov appeared convinced that she'd discovered a shortcut. The mysterious Mr. Heidi offered a way to bypass the usual treacherous route to America that involved Israeli visas, long waits, and resettlement camps.

Victor was amused at his wife's almost religious belief in Mr. Heidi's hidden potential, his untapped influence, his magic *blat*.

Lubov took Heidi's invitation to the Prostuda OVIR office herself, only to find out that the form was meant for Victor alone. Unless her name was mentioned in the paper, Lubov had no basis for an exit visa.

"This can't be true, Vitya," she raged at home. "These people are incompetent. We're a family. Of course we have to travel together!"

The next day, she took Victor to Prostuda with her. She also took a box of Bird's Milk chocolates, with a hundred rubles tucked inside. The whole way to OVIR Victor dragged his feet like a sulky child, and when it was their turn to enter the office, he slumped against the wall and allowed Lubov to present their case. The middle-aged, one-eyed woman at the desk didn't look incompetent. In fact, her monolithic posture and her stiff, maroon suit suggested an unshakable institutional power.

"What do you want from me, woman?" she said, ignoring the box of Bird's Milk on her desk. "This is your husband's invitation. *He* can apply for a passport, not you. Even if I lay my bones down for you, you won't get a visa from the Americans. You have no basis! Besides, I don't see a problem here. This is only a vacation. A couple weeks in America, and you'll have your husband back in Asbestos 2." The clerk paused, then grinned and winked. The lids of her empty eye gaped and closed like a fish's mouth, revealing some pink flesh inside. "Look at it this way—he'll come back with gifts. And I have one word for you, woman: TAM-PONS! If there is one thing I'd ask my husband to bring—"

Forgetting the chocolates, Lubov grabbed Victor by the arm and stormed out of the room.

"Ah, hysterics!" sighed the clerk. "Next!"

Lubov considered the matter closed, Mr. Heidi's magic ticket canceled. But Victor Goldberg couldn't help trying on the possibility of a solitary future like an invisible suit. With each passing day, the suit fit better and better, until one day Victor yielded to the temptation to make it real.

"I think I might apply for a travel passport after all," he told Lubov over breakfast.

She met his announcement with steely, incredulous eyes.

"It was your idea," he said.

"You *are* just planning to travel, right? There and back? Vitya, we can't afford such a trip."

He fumbled with his teacup and didn't reply. Remembering the OVIR clerk's fish-mouth wink, he trusted Lubov to know what he meant.

"You are not going to abandon us," she said.

"You don't love me," he tried.

"You don't even know what love *is*, Victor," she said. "You don't have a will of your own. All your life you've been bobbing around like a turd in an ice hole, sticking to whatever happens along."

Victor began to laugh. He laughed until his sides hurt, until Lubov's pearly lips began to stretch and tremble. "Ice hole!" he repeated hysterically, pointing at the thick layer of hoarfrost on the windowsill. "Who's in the ice hole, *vedma*?" For once in his life, Victor Goldberg felt as if he *did* have a will.

He left when Sasha was away in Prostuda. At the last moment he wrote her a letter and left it with the downstairs neighbors. He chose his words carefully, tired newspaper words, whose meaning had been rubbed away by millions of eyes and ears.

At the American Embassy in Moscow, he leaned across a gray plastic counter and handed his passport to another clerk. Young, slender, and sternly polite, this clerk possessed both of her eyes and projected a wholly different kind of institutional power.

"Do you intend to remain in the United States beyond the time period indicated in your visa?" she asked.

Victor shook his head, but the clerk seemed to be waiting for more.

"Here, look," Victor said, getting a photo out of his wallet. It was a picture of Lubov holding Sasha. Lit from above, Lubov's face looked gaunt and angular. With her hair in a bun, she resembled an aging ballerina. Sasha, about six years old in the picture, looked like her usual self: a blur for a face, a halo of curls, two smudgy highlights in the blackness of her eyes, an automatic "here comes the birdie" smile. Victor pointed. "This is my wife, and this is my daughter. They're staying behind."

The clerk smiled. "Have you ever been a member of the Communist Party?" she asked.

"No." Victor Goldberg smiled back.

Outside, he reached in his wallet for a subway pass and realized that the picture of Lubov and Sasha was gone. It must have fallen on the floor during the interview. Victor considered going back for it, but by then two lines had formed in front of the embassy. At the end of each line, people were jostling and screaming at each other, attempting to figure out who belonged in which queue. An embassy security guard stepped out of his booth and began to admonish the crowd through his loudspeaker. Victor doubted that the guard would let him back in to retrieve a picture. After a moment's hesitation, he jumped off the curb and, with a strange sense of relief, briskly walked away from the embassy. Suddenly he felt ravenously hungry. He found a *pelmennaya* and swallowed two bowls of potato dumplings with sour cream, barely bothering to chew.

Victor waited for his visa in a small hotel room in Izmailovo. He spent most of the time sleeping and never once thought to visit parts of the city familiar to him from childhood. He was content to emerge on the other side of the clouds without memories, a new man, still young at thirty. He hoped that the series of errors that was his life would somehow be corrected.

Mr. Heidi turned out to be a skinny girl dressed in corduroy. Her earnest blue eyes beamed compassion, and she held his mother's face in her delicate white hands. Just like before, with Lubov, Victor didn't have to do any work. He died, he had been reborn, Asbestos 2 lost its geographical reality, flattened into a myth, a thing only Victor knew or imagined.

The problem was that New York City was full of Russians, their singsong voices like stabs in the back on the subway, in the streets, in the stores. There were Russian hairdressers and nannies, nurses and bank tellers, pharmacists and construction workers. Even the Styles section of *The New York Times* featured Russians: platinum blond, swaddled in fur, encased in leather, terrifying.

At first Victor only met people from Moscow and Leningrad, Odessa and Kiev, but after the Soviet Union fell apart it seemed as if every village in the former USSR had sent an ambassador to New York to hound Victor Goldberg. He was sure that sooner or later Asbestos 2 would send its own.

When Victor didn't see any Russians, he had the blacks to worry about. Just last week he saw a girl Sasha's age on the subway. She looked like a hippie or an artist, with long untreated hair and a thrift store tweed skirt. Girls like this, the ones who didn't *dress* black and didn't straighten their hair, were Victor Goldberg's preferred means of self-torment besides the Russians. He stared at the girl all the way to his stop, trying to read her lips over the noise of the train. She was whispering something to a white boy with a green mohawk. Covered in cold sweat, Victor was convinced he heard her speaking Russian.

He fantasized about buying a clean, spacious house in a quiet suburb, free of both Russians and blacks, but Heidi said she would never leave the city. So Victor prepared himself for the inevitable.

The night before, he'd hastened to reassure Heidi, to deny things after she'd showed him the e-mail. He even made up a story about a deranged co-worker and mused about possibly calling the police. Heidi appeared relieved. She'd assumed the note was a scam. How long would it be before Sasha presented herself in flesh and blood?

Victor Goldberg put on his jacket, locked the door, and walked down to the subway. On the train, he leaned his face into his hands and tried to picture his daughter as an adult. Instead, in the darkness of his cupped palms, he saw a gargoyle face of retribution: half Heidi, half Lubov. Heidi wearing Lubov's heavy amber necklace. Lubov berating him in perfect English.

They were the ones Victor had used. They'd offered themselves to him, and he took what they had to offer. It was different with Sasha. When she was little, he'd taken care of her. For ten years, he shielded Sasha from Lubov's insane version of love. Maybe his daughter, of all people, would understand how tired he'd been all his life.

Victor wondered how long Sasha had been in the U.S. Did she just come here? Or was she by now settled, the way he was, into the pleasant pace of American life, punctuated by easy work, easy shopping, and too much food? Maybe she'd arrived tired, just like Victor, too tired to ask questions, dig into the past. Victor had instructed Heidi not to answer her e-mail. He hoped that Sasha's interest was cursory, genealogical. He hoped that she would give up. Someday in the future, he could see writing her a long, polite letter and sending some photos. Sasha would write back and they'd reminisce about their first experiences in this country, toss back and forth the iridescent flecks of capitalist society's inherent humanism that both of them had since learned to take for granted:

Could you believe the pre-sliced bread?

And those cheese squares that are designed to fit the slices of bread?

The free plastic bags in grocery stores?

How about pizza delivery?

Toilet paper in public restrooms?

Remember being startled when a bus driver wished you a nice day?

Victor Goldberg liked to make lists. They helped him to organize his thoughts in a predictable, calming manner. The first thing on the list always related to the last, and things that didn't fit in could be forgotten or filed away for a future list. The F train came out of the tunnel and began climbing the bridge over the Gowanus Canal. Victor could see his building's rooftop from the train and the landlord's swing set in the backyard. The Goldbergs didn't have access to the yard, and every time Ben asked if he could play on the swings, Heidi replied with her irritating joke: "Yes, baby, when the revolution comes."

Victor peered out the window, slack-jawed and distracted. His thoughts of Heidi made him forget the list he was making. He stared at the old billboards on factory roofs, at smokestacks and the gray clouds reflected in the canal. For an instant, he felt as if he were back in Asbestos 2. Sasha was Ben's age, and Victor had to begin all over again.

The train went back into the tunnel and entered a station. It was Victor's stop, but he didn't move. The plastic seat under him and the smudged metal handle next to his head suddenly appeared to be essential for his comfort, impossible to give up. With a strange thrill, Victor listened to *please stand clear of the closing doors* and watched the train doors shut. Then he leaned back in his seat and, ignoring the fact that an hour later he'd have to get off at the last stop in Queens, began to snore.

9

An Element of the Landscape

ON FRIDAY AFTERNOON, SASHA GOLDBERG STOOD BY THE glass wall and watched the Tarakans get into their van. Squinting against the drizzling rain, José rolled a green suitcase down the driveway. Mrs. Tarakan leaned against the side of the car, giving last-minute instructions to the gardener and the security guard. She looked like a long-stemmed mushroom under her oversized red umbrella.

Jake sat under the awning, waiting for José to lower the lift. Looking at his pale profile made Sasha feel obscenely strong and meaty. She pressed her body to the glass, her mind already in New York.

Jake had been avoiding her all week, and it was all right with Sasha. She wondered if he was the one with a primitive mind. Always telling the truth, wanting the truth, hurling his truth at people like rocks. What did he really know?

Like your mother, I have a child.

Like you, I know what it's like to be a freak.

At night I dream about touching you again.

Oscar opened the van's hood, and José bent down and began to poke at something inside. Mrs. Tarakan held her umbrella over them, letting her own hair get wet.

The rain came down harder. A stream of water ran along the edge of the roof and down Jake's arm. His sleeve and hand were getting soaked, but he didn't move. Sasha realized he was in a different chair, a lighter, all-manual kind. His feet were planted awkwardly on the ground, and his face looked rigid with the effort of keeping himself upright.

There seemed to be something really wrong with the van. Jake glanced at his hand as if it were a foreign object, something he'd just found sitting there. A torrent of water was now crashing into it. Sasha ran out of the Russian room into the hallway and threw open the front door, almost colliding with José.

"All right," he said, tilting Jake's chair back and lowering it down the ramp. "Ready?"

"My jacket's all wet," complained Jake.

"I'll take it off in the car," replied José.

"Goodbye," Sasha said to their backs.

José turned around, smiling. "God bless."

Sasha couldn't see Jake's face. Halfway across the yard, his arm slid off the armrest and hung by the chair's wheel. His fingers curled slightly, and Sasha hoped that he was waving.

She waited until nightfall before going into his room to retrieve the envelope on the desk.

Back in her basement, she opened the envelope to find a computer printout of a Brooklyn address and phone number, a plane ticket, and two hundred dollars in cash. Sasha shook the envelope upside down. There was no note. She stared at the printout, trying to extract personal meaning from "345 Degraw #1, Brooklyn, New York." Maybe it was in the spaces between the lines, in the width of the margins, the curves of the font. She'd practically written Jake's note in her mind. All he had to do was type it up, but apparently he just wanted her to leave, was *paying* her to leave.

Sasha Goldberg wasn't going to let him disappear like that, drown in the murk of her memory, like Nadia and Alexey, like her mother and father. A vague approximation of his face wouldn't become a new subject of her compulsive doodling.

She tiptoed back to his room and flipped on the light. She wasn't going to stare at his stupid *equipment*, just steal a photo. She found a stack of yearbooks in the closet and opened the most recent one. *The Oak Grove Falcons.* 1996. Everyone looked long-dead in washed-out black-and-white. Sasha didn't like the dumb earnest smile Jake was making in his picture, but it would have to do. She ripped out the page and shoved it in her pocket.

In the kitchen, she got a new garbage bag and packed in a hurry. The bag was smaller than the one she had before, and Sasha left some things behind: all of her Sabbath clothes, the blue velvet dress, the Star of David. She left through the arcadia door and walked close to the wall, the way José had shown her, avoiding the guard booth. The back of the house's modern wing sat on a small stone cliff, with one corner protruding over the edge. No fence separated the house from the forest around it and the road beyond. Maybe the forest belonged to the Tarakans as well.

Standing at the edge of the cliff, Sasha heard the sound of water and noticed a stream below. The stream was narrow enough to jump over. Sasha dangled her feet off the edge of the cliff, slid down toward the stream, and walked past the protruding concrete corner toward the highway. Suddenly the gurgling sound got louder, and a second later a shower of cold water poured on Sasha's head out of the pipe in the house's foundation.

"Chiort!" cursed Sasha, jumping away.

She had to laugh to keep herself from crying. After months with the Tarakans, she had finally discovered the Waterfall House's waterfall. She felt shaky enough without being pissed on by an architectural landmark, but the damn house couldn't resist exacting its final revenge. Sasha pulled off her wet sweater and tossed it into the bushes. Her jeans mostly escaped the damage, but her sneakers were soaked because when she dashed away from the waterfall, she ended up stepping into the stream. Shivering, Sasha groped in her bag for a jacket. She wished she had an extra pair of shoes.

She scampered up the hill to the highway and began to run, trying not to give in to a childish fear of darkness. Nothing to be afraid of here, she reminded herself. This was a rich people's forest.

Last time Sasha had seen this road was in late September, on the way from the temple. Now the trees stood bare in the moonlight. Drafts of wind dragged brown clumps of leaves and mud along the edge of the road. Sasha had watched the leaves turn yellow and the sky turn gray through the Tarakans' glass wall. She had helped Oscar rake the lawn and drain the pool. Three mornings ago, Oscar turned off the fountain, and Sasha watched the dripping water turn into an icicle on the end of the cupid's plaster penis. But only now, on this road at night, did she fully realize how long she'd stayed in the Waterfall House, and how happy she was to leave it.

She kicked the leaves with the toes of her sneakers, thinking of Heidi. Blond. Old? A university professor. Sasha tried to think about her father, but the presence of his deluded American wife flattened him into a theoretically possible but incomprehensible concept, like a black hole or gravity. Like sleeping with Jake.

At last, the road merged with a larger one. There was a gas station and a McDonald's, and above, a raised freeway. Two cars zoomed by, spraying Sasha with mud. She stepped back from the road and found her passport. Marina's number was written lightly in pencil, on the last page. At the gas station, Sasha called collect.

"Sashka!"

"*Privet!*"

"How are you? Uncle Vitaly said he got you a job!"

"Yeah, well. I quit it. Do you know anybody in New York? I need a place to sleep tomorrow night."

An hour later a cab dropped Sasha off at O'Hare. Her flight wasn't until eleven. Shaking with giddy excitement at choosing her own food, Sasha bought a large coffee and an apple Danish. This was the moment she'd been waiting for, her third escape, an instant of perfect anonymity. She was nobody's pet Soviet Jew, just an element of the landscape, a girl in the airport. Sasha propped her wet sneakers against the radiator and spent the rest of the morning watching the black silhouettes of planes move sluggishly against a purple sky.

part four

1

In the Old World

THE LIPMANS, WARTIME FRIENDS OF MARINA'S GRANDMA, lived in Coney Island. A white high-rise on a block of dingy brick projects, the Golda Meir Senior Residence was easy to find. Smoothing her hair, Sasha Goldberg got out of the elevator and walked along the maroon-carpeted corridor to the Lipmans' apartment. The whole corridor smelled like boiled cabbage, as if all the elderly inhabitants of the residence were collectively making *schi*. Sasha rang the bell and waited. Finally, the apartment door opened just a crack and shut again before she had a chance to speak.

"Naum, there is a *negritianka* at the door—we should call downstairs!" said a wobbly voice.

"Ludmila Evseevna, it's me, Sasha Goldberg—Marina's friend . . . I called earlier!" Sasha yelled in Russian, pressing the bell again.

"Ah, Marinochka! Luda, what are you—blind? It's Marinochka!" a man's voice exclaimed, and the door flew open.

Two tiny old people stood smiling in front of Sasha, their problem with her race apparently solved by her language. They didn't think she was a *negritianka* anymore. Now they seemed to think she was Marina. Sasha wondered if she should set them straight. She would only be here for one night, two at the most. Maybe it was best not to complicate things.

Naum Moiseevich wore an old Soviet suit jacket over a fleece shirt that boasted Citibank's involvement in the March of Dimes. He had a ruddy face and knotty, trembling hands covered with blue veins. Ludmila Evseevna, although tiny and hunched over, looked younger than her husband, perhaps because her hair was dyed an aggressive shade of magenta.

"You've grown so much!" boomed Naum Moiseevich. "You probably don't even remember us!"

"Of course she doesn't, think with your head, Naum! She was just two years old when she saw us last."

"It's nice . . . to see you again," said Sasha, deciding not to insist on her true identity.

"Do you remember you scared her, Naum!" continued Ludmila Evseevna. "You scared the child! You hid behind the *soonduk* and jumped out at her, you never use your head, with all your jokes! You scared the child!"

Laughing happily, Naum Moiseevich disappeared into a tiny kitchen.

"Take off your jacket, Marinochka, let's have some tea! How's Papa? How's Grandma?"

Desperately thinking of things to say about Marina's family, Sasha stuck her toes into a pair of beaded silk *tapochki* too small for her feet and studied the room. There was a stack of lacy pillows on the couch, a poster of kittens in firefighter uniforms on the wall, two straight rows of gold-rimmed teacups in the china cabinet. Sasha could tell that her visit was an event in the Lipmans' lives, a welcome interruption in their routine that made them almost giddy. She regretted coming over disheveled and empty-handed.

Ludmila Evseevna cut up salami and opened a can of sardines.

"These are Italian!" she bragged.

Naum Moiseevich poured tea. The kettle trembled in his hand, knocking against the delicate edge of the cup.

"Careful, Naum!" shouted Ludmila Evseevna, and then to Sasha, "Speaking of being careful, you have to be really careful around here. Long as you stay with us, I don't want you coming home after dark. There are Negroes everywhere. Criminals. Just yesterday, Rimma Iosifovna from the third floor let one of them help her carry her grocery bag. *Ha!*"

"They are drug addicts," said Naum Moiseevich, making a faint shooting-up gesture at his elbow. "I read in *The Foreign Land* that addiction is a disease—"

"You also read that computers can read your mind," interrupted Ludmila Evseevna. "The point is, ours is a nice, prestigious building. All our neighbors are intelligentsia. But the neighborhood . . ." Ludmila Evseevna pointed at the window.

"It's nice in the summer. We have swimming—" piped in Naum Moiseevich.

"*Tfu*, swimming!" spat Ludmila Evseevna. "Naum, tell Marina how many times you've been robbed."

"Twice."

"One of those times a kid on a bicycle pushed him, and he broke his arm. They're bandits. Even their children are bandits. It's in the genes. A week doesn't pass without someone being beaten, purses stolen." The old woman's voice grew tearful. "I tell Naum, why did we ever leave Minsk?"

Sasha looked out the window at the ocean. A large ship hung on the horizon. It seemed to hover in the gray space between the water and the sky. On the boardwalk, groups of stout elderly women in luxurious fur coats walked and sat on benches. Some wore fur hats that matched their coats. Sasha imagined that the first thing they'd done in the Land of Plenty was exchange their meager life savings for the *shubas* of their dreams, *shubas* to showcase on the American boardwalk.

No wonder they got mugged, these poor God's dandelions, with their furs and careful makeup, starched collars and "axle" rings of coppery Soviet gold. Trapped at death's door in government housing with nothing to their names, disconnected from their past, they were free to go out of their minds in seaside isolation. No wonder *The Toilet Paper* pandered to them with bizarre race theories and stories of alien abductions. Sasha wondered if the Lipmans had followed their children to America, and whether the children ever visited them at Golda Meir.

"Negroes let their kids run around with no hats on! In the middle of winter!" Ludmila Evseevna lifted both of her hands toward the ceiling, as if to say that she'd given her final verdict, presented decisive evidence.

Sipping her tea, Sasha felt coddled and scalded at once, guilty of not wearing a hat and of being a Negro, both. She was happy when, after tea, the old people begged off to bed. As soon as she was alone, Sasha turned on the TV and found a Russian channel. The programming seemed to have been designed to trick the audience into thinking they were still in the Soviet Union, circa 1965. Once in a while, a colorful and loud furniture commercial interrupted the all black-and-white lineup. An ancient May Day Concert segued into a 1930s musical about a boy's love for his tractor. One-third into the musical Sasha gave up and went to the shower.

By the time she came out, a newscast replaced the musical. "In the Old World" said the banner at the top of the screen.

Sasha put on a clean T-shirt and sat down to watch the news.

"We are here in Moscow, where people are able to enjoy a lot of Western conveniences," said the anchorman. The TV showed two women in leather jackets laughing over pizza at an outdoor café. "New shops and restaurants are opening their doors every day, cell phones are becoming commonplace."

Sasha poured herself a glass of water, watching with interest a crowd of well-dressed pedestrians on Tverskaya Street.

"But in other parts of Russia, the situation is far from rosy. Our correspondent has now returned to her hometown to see how it's faring in the current economic climate."

"Yes, Sergey," said a female voice. "This is Ekaterina Veselova, reporting from Asbestos 2, a small town in the Prostuda region, which has become the latest victim in Russia's economic tragedy."

"Marinochka? What's the matter?" Ludmila Evseevna croaked from the other room, and Sasha guessed that she'd shrieked, although she didn't remember screaming. *And the glass.* She didn't remember the glass of water slipping out of her hand onto the kitchen counter. It must have made noise.

"Nothing is the matter," Sasha stammered, blotting the wet counter with a kitchen towel. Her own voice sounded unfamiliar, as if she were speaking in a dream. The TV played a Brezhnev-era song about a strange man who *voluntarily* moved to Prostuda. A boomerang graphic flew across the screen. Sasha dropped the towel and ran back to the living room.

It was now night on TV, the near-constant Arctic night of Asbestos 2. Katia stood in front of the District Soviet, gripping a microphone in her mittened hand, unchanged despite her new name. Her eyes were tearing up from the cold. Sasha had forgotten what that weather felt like on your teeth and eyes. Now, kneeling in front of the TV, she felt the stinging, bone-breaking cold, as if the temperature in the Lipmans' apartment had suddenly dropped to Asbestos 2 lows. Sympathetic tears streamed down her cheeks, and she wished for the freezing wind to dry them. More than anything, she wanted to be standing in that darkness, next to Katia.

"The town's livelihood depended on the production of asbestos. The mine had become depleted, and Asbestos 2 felt it firsthand," said Katia. Puffs of steam exited her mouth with every word. "When the pit closed, the town lost its last source of income. Unemployment is now nearly ninety percent. The library and the hospital have been closed for a year. Most schools are still open, but the teachers haven't been paid for seven months. In the summer, vegetable gardens sprout between apartment blocks. The population is abandoning the town. Not everyone, however, has a place to go."

The newscast cut to another location.

"This used to be one of the nicest apartment buildings in Asbestos 2," said Katia, craning her neck toward a brick building behind her. An entrance door was open, and Sasha could see a pile of snow in the vestibule. The camera panned away from the building, and Sasha recognized the yard. The swing was now missing a seat, but the penguin-shaped garbage cans and ornate benches still poked out here and there from under the snow.

"Lets go inside," said Katia, walking up a dark staircase.

She knocked on several doors, getting no answer. Some doors stood ajar. Someone off camera shone a flashlight inside the unlocked apartments, and Sasha saw an abandoned bed frame, a pile of rags in the corner, and a man's boot. Finally, a woman poked her head out of a fourth-floor apartment, inviting the crew inside.

The apartment was nicely decorated, much fancier than Sasha's old place. There was a TV in the corner and a round dining table. The wallpaper had a pattern of small pink roses. Two girls, wearing fur coats and wool socks, played on the daybed in the living room. Sasha saw steam coming out of their mouths when they breathed. The camera focused on a mountain of frozen condensation by the window.

"The residents of Asbestos 2 receive electric power two hours a day," explained Katia.

The woman pointed at a drum stove in the corner of the room. Sasha remembered that this kind of stove was called a *burzhuika*. It didn't belong at the end of the twentieth century. It belonged in a documentary about the blockade of Leningrad, in a darkened classroom with a hissing projector. A reliable indicator of hardship, the *burzhuika* stove called to mind other stark, black-and-white images from the history class: a woman in a shawl pulling a sled through blinding white snow, a tiny, tightly swaddled corpse on top of the sled.

The children on TV were in color. They were smiling for the camera, holding up their dolls. Sasha exhaled. The girls' mother explained that she had no money and no relatives to go live with, but had enough potatoes and pickles to last through the winter. Katia asked about the water supply. The woman said that during the two hours the power was on, the pump worked, and water reached the second floor. There was an empty apartment there, and she sent the girls down with buckets.

"It starts out brown and tastes of melted snow," she said, nodding at the stove. "We boil it."

"The federal government has been threatening to entirely disconnect power to the town for nonpayment of bills. However, the local military authorities object. There are two army bases in the suburbs of Asbestos 2. Both are being considered for closure. With the military gone from the region, the future of this town will be written on water with a pitchfork. This is Ekaterina Veselova, reporting from Asbestos 2."

A blue boomerang obliterated Katia's face, and Sasha reached to touch the screen. How could she just disappear like that, without telling Sasha what she needed to know?

Surely her mother had found a way around this. Sasha trusted Mrs. Goldberg not to drink snow-brown water, not to subsist on pickles and potatoes. She couldn't picture Lubov Alexandrovna and Nadia swaddled in layers of clothing, huddled in front of an oil drum stove. *Children of the intelligentsia don't wear coats indoors.*

"Independent Television has pledged to assist the family you just saw with relocation, housing, and employment," said the Moscow studio anchor. "Now the world of sports. . . ."

Sasha turned off the TV and let the sleeper sofa fall open with a loud bang. She was suddenly furious with Katia. That pretty face, the pipe-bred genius, a Moscow TV correspondent at nineteen! Some people got what they wanted. Others had accidental children, drank tea with purple-haired racists in Coney Island.

What if, during her last trip home, Nadia hadn't pushed her away? What if her mother had let her stay? Sasha would be another unemployed eater of anemic ditch-grown vegetables. In the end, she was lucky to have a mother like Lubov Goldberg.

Sasha lay on the sofa, staring at a clown-headed cookie jar on the counter. Suddenly she regretted running away from Neal. If she were to do it again, she'd tolerate Neal all the way to INS and then all the way to the bank. She'd stay away from the likes of Marina and Jake, the free ones. She'd trade her selfish loves for Nadia's future.

Children of the intelligentsia don't exchange love for money.
Children of Asbestos 2 don't return home empty-handed.
Did her mother know this when she pushed Sasha out?

Sasha realized that she didn't care what Victor looked like, and whether he loved her, or why he was hiding. She just hoped that he was sufficiently rich. She didn't need a father. She'd survived without a father for eight years. What she needed was legal residency, work, and money. When she became legal, she would take her money back to Asbestos 2.

Dear Nadia,

America has done its job. I don't dream of holding you anymore, or of taking you away from Mama. I hardly remember you, but I know what you need. You will have food and clothes. You will also have light-up sneakers and cherry-flavored vitamins, cartoon bedsheets, and a dollhouse with tiny furniture. I will hold you from a distance with soft teddy bear arms, I will talk to you with singing greeting cards. I will become your means of survival.

A digital clock next to the cookie jar flooded the countertop with the red glow of 10:43. How many interminable minutes were in one night? Sasha willed herself to sleep, but her eyelids refused to close. They seemed to be the only light part of her, fluttering up while the rest of her body felt weighed down with sandbags.

She dialed the number in the morning, before the old people woke up.

"May I help you?"

Victor's voice sounded comically deformed. Sasha forgot to expect an accent. He was her long-lost father in America. He sounded just like any other Russian.

"Papa?"

"I'm sorry . . ."

"I'm looking for my father, Victor Semyonovich Goldberg."

A murmur, a click, a shrill dial tone. Sasha puffed out her cheeks, furious.

She couldn't wait any longer. She dressed quietly, rode the elevator down, and walked along the ocean to the subway. Except for an old man in a tracksuit doing tai chi by the bench, the Boardwalk was empty at this hour, its benches, railings, and garbage cans floating in the fog like a mirage. The man doing tai chi stared at Sasha as she approached, then quickly walked away. Sasha grinned into the wind, for the first time completely happy to be a big black girl in an ugly coat. Wow, she was capable of frightening the elderly. She liked Coney Island.

In Heidi's neighborhood, the streets were alive with people. A pretty child in a lavender raincoat jumped up and down on the sidewalk, trying to catch the corner of an Italian flag in front of a pizza place. Her nanny was trying on street-vendor sunglasses, two for five dollars. Noticing with dismay that a beggar in front of the deli wore her jacket, Sasha asked the sunglasses vendor for directions and ran down Court Street to Degraw.

She saw them from the corner. They were coming down the stoop: a woman, a man, and a little boy. The woman was tiny and birdlike, the man tall and fat. The kid broke away from the parents and jumped down the stairs two steps at a time.

Sasha stood still. A man who was most likely her father stood on top of the stoop, unfolding a stroller. Sasha couldn't see his face.

The woman wore dark jeans, a vintage green jacket fringed with orange shag, and no hat. Her curly blond hair was cut in a childish bob. She had a young face, but moved like an old person, in halting, stiff jolts.

The boy hugged a parking meter and held on. After pleading with him, the woman peeled away his hands and dragged him to the stroller. The man approached, and the child stopped flailing. In his snowsuit and boots, the boy had seemed half the size of his mother, but in his father's arms he was small and pliable. The man lowered him into the stroller and snapped the belts. Sasha tried to remember her father doing that with her, but they didn't have strollers, they had prams, bright orange and navy blue, with large wheels and no belts. Sasha looked down at her size ten sneakers and laughed. Trying to imagine herself in a pram was absurd.

The woman took over the stroller. The man kissed her on the cheek, waved to the boy, and began to walk away, downhill to Smith Street. The woman turned the stroller around and pushed it uphill, toward Sasha's corner. It was slow going; the child was obviously heavy. Sasha sat on somebody's stoop, half hiding behind a huge plastic Jack-o'-Lantern. She waited for the woman and the boy to pass, then followed close behind, listening. Soon she heard the woman call the boy's name, *Ben,* a final confirmation.

Sasha kept her distance, waiting for an opportunity to speak. Heidi crossed Court Street and walked a few blocks to a playground nestled inside a hospital courtyard. She let Ben out of the stroller and opened the playground gate. Sasha lingered by a newspaper stand on the sidewalk, trying to collect her thoughts. This Heidi was small and brittle-looking, she decided. She could be made to listen.

Heidi sat down on the bench and scanned the playground for familiar faces, her accidental friends, the playground moms. They always talked about the same things—eating habits, sleep patterns, and potty training—but Heidi didn't mind the predictability. In fact, she couldn't get enough of these conversations. Everything she said about Ben was layered with sly hints at her son's brilliance, and afterward she felt embarrassed, as if she'd been bragging, but the other mothers didn't seem to mind. Perhaps they, too, had been bragging, but Heidi didn't notice. She had a hard time paying attention to other people's children in Ben's presence.

Sometimes in the early evenings, working mothers in gray wool coats and pressed pants, hands laden with bags from Manhattan stores, entered the playground. They fumbled with the iron gate, unfamiliar with the latch. The nannies put on smiles and dusted off the kids before handing them over.

Heidi watched the working mothers with a mixture of pity and envy. She was sure they didn't know their children the way she knew Ben. Then she thought about their lunch breaks in Manhattan cafés, their *adult* conversations. They probably never felt as if they might disappear and no one would notice, the way Heidi had been feeling, lately, all the time.

Today, the playground was almost empty. Two nannies with sleeping infants sat on one of the benches, sharing a bag of Cheetos. Beyond basic politeness, Heidi didn't talk to nannies. She assumed they didn't want to discuss the children of their employers. One time she asked a nanny about her own children. The woman told Heidi that she'd left her children in Jamaica four years ago to come and work in the U.S. Heidi didn't know what to say. She wanted to tell the nanny that it must be awful, and how she, Heidi, would die if she ever had to leave Ben for that long. But then she thought that saying things like this wouldn't be appropriate and said nothing at all.

From then on, she only talked to women like her, white women in rumpled clothes with expensive British strollers. She told herself she didn't pick them consciously but was ashamed of it all the same. In conversation, Heidi steered clear of topics outside child care. She didn't want to hear about people writing for *The New York Times,* finishing medical school, or publishing novels. While she never would have admitted it to herself, she avoided successful women with the same determination she avoided nannies.

Ben wanted to sit in a baby swing. With some difficulty, Heidi lifted him into it. His feet were getting too big for the holes in the bucket seat. She would have to take off his boots to get him out.

Heidi heard the gate bang behind her back and turned around. Another nanny. A big black girl, in a dirty red bubble jacket. The girl's hair was pulled into a tight ponytail, with a halo of frizz around the forehead.

Heidi gave the swing a push. The girl walked around the iron fence and stood next to her. She didn't have a child. Nor did she have a cardboard box of wholesale candy. *I'm getting mugged,* thought Heidi, still smiling, keeping the fear inside, for Ben's sake.

The girl threw up her arms, palms forward, the way fugitives did on *COPS* to show that they were unarmed, and cleared her throat.

2

The Last Twig

SHE'S SCARED OF ME. **THE THOUGHT IS SO FUNNY THAT SASHA** Goldberg forgets what she's going to say. Instinctively, she lifts her arms up in the air, willing the carefully rehearsed sentences back into her brain.

"You studied Russia, Mrs. Goldberg," she says. "How many black Russians do you think there are? You're married to one. He's my father."

Heidi keeps pushing the swing. The girl's Russian accent instantly relieves her of fear, and Heidi silently chides herself for being racist. *This isn't a mugging, it's a scam,* she decides, chiding herself again, this time for ethnic stereotyping. This chiding is like a mental tic, a sorry placeholder for missing rationality. Heidi doesn't know what to think.

"Look at me!" Sasha is beginning to panic. She hasn't counted on being met with silence. What if Heidi calls the police?

"Keep your voice down, please, you're scaring my son," says Heidi, reassured by a sheepish note in the girl's voice. Perhaps she can get rid of this person. "Look, if you want to talk to my husband, I can give you his number—"

"I already called him. He hung up on me. But I'll call again. I'll call you all the time, if that's what you want."

Reluctantly, Heidi realizes that she ought to take this matter into her own hands. Whatever *this* is, she doesn't trust Victor to deal with it.

"I look like him, no?" presses Sasha.

It occurs to Heidi that if she decided to believe the girl, the answer would be yes. Victor's lips? *Yes.* His eyes? *Absolutely.* As soon as Heidi allows herself to believe, there is no going back. She feels strangely empty, untroubled. It's as if she finally received an explanation. Her life with Victor has been a lie, and now she knows why.

"Do you want to go somewhere and talk?" Heidi asks. "You want some . . . coffee?"

"All right," says Sasha.

Victor's smile. Pulling Ben out of the swing, Heidi thinks about her husband's large hairy ass, his tub of a stomach. She'll finally have the excuse, the motivation, to leave him.

They walk out of the playground and head toward Smith Street. The wind picks up, and Sasha clasps the collar of her jacket around her neck. Heidi notices that her fingertips are chapped and cracking.

"I have an extra pair of gloves," she says. "Do you want them?"

"No, thanks," grumbles Sasha, suddenly feeling exhausted and fragile. She's done so well until now, but this little gesture of Heidi's, this offer of extra gloves, unexpectedly threatens to reduce her to tears.

"Are you all right?" Heidi persists.

"Fine," snaps Sasha, remembering her mother's favorite expression. *Vozmi sebya v ruki.* Get a grip, take yourself into your own hands. Pull yourself up by your own hair, Sasha imagines, like Baron Münchhausen. "I'm just tired."

But Sasha doesn't seem tired to Heidi, not the way Victor was tired when he first arrived. He fell asleep in crowded trains, snored through Heidi's upstairs neighbors' midnight flamenco classes, didn't wake up when the ambulances blared by the bedroom window. One time, Heidi asked him about his dreams, and he told her he didn't have any.

She fell in love with the mystery of him. She liked how her friends kept referring to him as "your refugee" even years after they became a couple. Victor, however, did everything to dispel the mystery. With time, his tragic aura, so essential to Heidi's love, became replaced with quiet, unassuming satisfaction. Victor liked to muse about the miracle of the superabsorbent paper towels, the perfection of Starbucks, the Christlike humility of restaurant waiters, and about the genius of the market economy that was responsible for all the above marvels.

"Only in this country," he remarked after practically every encounter with the world outside their apartment. He didn't seem to notice the particularly Soviet aspects of city life, where the plumbers never called back, and bus drivers saw you running after the bus and peeled away. Heidi joked that Victor lived in his inner Westchester County. She prayed he wouldn't discuss the ingenious nature of a tea bag around her PhD friends. As a foreigner, he was allowed to delight in simple things, but there had to be limits.

It irked Heidi when Victor subscribed to *The Wall Street Journal* and, despite the fact that they had no money, lectured her at length about the stock market. When she started to teach the Soviet technology class, she invited him to speak to her students, and instead of talking about his father, he erupted in an embarrassing anti-Communist rant that confounded a roomful of undergrads. At home after the class, Heidi and Victor had their first serious fight.

"But I don't know anything about my father," said Victor.

"What *do* you know anything about?" yelled Heidi. "Dentures? Capitalism? Didn't you learn anything in your previous life? Can't you be a little more *human*?" Heidi was really ready to kick him out, except for the fact that he looked so miserable, ready to cry. Wait and see, Heidi decided, cradling his graying head in her arms. The following year they had Ben.

"Do you want to go in here?" she asks Sasha.

The café's glass door is plastered with stickers. YOUR ONLY AN OBJECT says one. Sasha holds the door, and Heidi maneuvers the stroller up the steps. Inside, it's dark and mostly empty, but there's a DJ behind a plywood partition. A few young people stand by the counter and sprawl on old couches and chairs. A girl with a bat tattoo on her neck smiles at Ben.

Sasha perches on a lime-green plastic barstool. The music slows down and over it the DJ plays the "I have a dream" speech. Sasha recognizes it from PBS. On a video screen above the DJ booth blurry black-and-white shapes dance to the music. Heidi comes back with two chipped mugs of coffee and a hot chocolate for Ben.

"I can show you my passport," Sasha says, warming her hands on a coffee mug.

Heidi waves her off. "I believe you. How old are you?"

"Eighteen."

"So you were ten years old when Victor immigrated. Did he know about you?"

"Know about me?" laughs Sasha. The weakness she felt outside has passed. Dr. King's voice, mixed with the slow beats makes her feel elated and powerful, like a Doors fan. "I hope he knew about me! We lived in the same apartment."

"He raised you? I wonder why he never . . ."

"Let's go ask him!"

"He had a difficult life." Heidi feels defensive. In a way she's happy that Victor has a secret, that he isn't such a blank slate.

"Oh, and so did I," says Sasha. "And my mom."

"What's your mom's name?"

"Lubov. It means 'love' in Russian."

"I know," says Heidi.

"She's a crazy bitch." Sasha says in English, relishing the worried look that Heidi shoots Ben's way.

Ben is oblivious. He's playing with the coin slot of a pinball machine. A string of sticky drool extends from his lower lip down to the bib of his overalls.

"I'm sick of having a difficult life!" continues Sasha. "I have a baby, his age. I want her to have an easy life."

"You have a daughter? Where is she now?"

"My mother has her," Sasha says, startled by how normal this conversation feels. When she was telling Marina about Nadia, every word brought her back to Asbestos 2, breaking her heart over and over. Not anymore. "Her name is Nadia." Sasha tests herself, dumbfounded by her newly grown thick skin. "Nadezhda. It means 'hope.'"

"I know," echoes Heidi.

"A boneheaded name. You can tell my mother named her."

Heidi remembers the Jamaican nanny and doesn't say anything. She can't understand why these foreigners abandon their children so easily.

"Hello!" snaps Sasha, despising the intricate mix of compassion and squeamishness in Heidi's eyes. "Things are really bad in Asbestos 2, and I want to help. I need to provide for Nadia. I want her to have all the same Elmo stuff, like he does," she adds, pointing at Ben's snow boots.

The boots are from DeeDee's Discount, Victor's favorite store. According to Victor, DeeDee's encapsulates America. It's all there, in one place, in all its plastic glory. Ben seems to agree. He loves the toys that his father buys at DeeDee's: mostly gaudy contraptions adorned with dismembered Sesame Street heads that pop up and make noise. *Elmo loves you!* Heidi tolerates these things at home, but when Ben gets invited to birthday parties, she goes to the Iron Monkey Toy Shoppe and buys something understated, wooden, and Swedish.

"Yes. Of course," she blurts, suddenly ashamed of the class considerations that guide her toy purchases. "I'm sorry, I was just thinking . . . So when did you come to the U.S.?"

"A year and a half ago. I was a mail-order bride."

"Where is your husband?"

"In Arizona," replies Sasha, eyeing the pastries in the glass display. "We never got married. I ran away last summer."

"Are you hungry?" Heidi asks, reaching for her wallet.

"Uh . . ." Sasha realizes that she hasn't eaten anything all day. "Yes. Thank you."

"What do you want?"

"That thing." Sasha points. "Looks like a shell."

The girl's language deficiency makes her sound like a toddler, and for a second Heidi feels an almost maternal tenderness toward her.

"The bear claw," she says. Sasha has no eating manners, just like Victor. Watching her chew with her mouth open, Heidi loses the tender feeling. Victor has always eaten like a starving animal, and over the years at a sit-down job he's doubled his weight. Heidi can barely remember the time when she was attracted to him. Now she has to deal with his female version.

"So, after you ran away," she says, hoping that Sasha would swallow before replying, "what did you do?"

"I stayed with these really crazy people. And then with some other"—she forgets to swallow, and when she laughs, pastry crumbs fly into Heidi's lap—"crazy people. Sorry."

"She spit on you!" exclaims Ben, hanging on the edge of Sasha's stool.

"Shush!" Heidi sounds appalled. "It's all right."

"Very funny, little brother!" Sasha smiles, watching Heidi's face. "Or what should I call him?"

Heidi feels as if someone has just punched her in the chest.

"Just call him Ben," she says. "Until we resolve this issue."

"Okay," agrees Sasha. She feels as if she's won, although she can't quite say which battle.

"Victor should be home by now," Heidi says wearily. "Do you want to go see him?"

"All right."

"Do you want to be alone with him?"

"No, please. I mean, I already know you," Sasha says quickly. She shouldn't have antagonized Heidi. She realizes that she is afraid of finally meeting her father. "He wrote me a letter when he went away," she adds, watching Heidi struggle with the zipper on Ben's jacket. "He left it with a neighbor because my mom would've destroyed it."

"I can understand your mother," Heidi says coolly.

"Nobody can understand her. She's crazy. After Papa left, she didn't seem unhappy. She just got rid of all of his things and pretended like he'd never existed. She gave me a blank stare every time I mentioned him, as if I was making up some *imaginary* father. After a while, talking about him made *me* feel insane."

Heidi lets go of the zipper and looks up at Sasha. Maybe Victor didn't abandon his family after all. Maybe his insane wife made his life hell and then refused to accompany him into exile. Maybe she kept the child from him. Heidi installs Ben in the stroller and pushes him outside. Thinking of Victor in the context of his pain, she feels affection toward him again.

"Look!" Ben jumps up and down in the stroller, pointing at an inflatable ghost that hangs from a fire escape.

Partially deflated, the ghost flails its arms in the wind, as if inviting the passersby to some wild party. Sasha thinks about her father's letter. It's filed safely in her mind, sandwiched between "We Pioneers, Children of Workers" and the "Sad Crocodile Birthday Song," away from her mother's reach. Sasha had always blamed her mother for refusing to go to America. Now she realizes that Victor never said anything about her refusal to come along. "As it turns out I must go alone," was all he wrote.

They walk up the stoop, and Heidi unlocks the door. The lights in the apartments are on. Sasha hears the radio and running water.

"Papa, Papa," yells Ben, bursting inside, "we found Sasha in the street, and I got a hot chocolate!"

Victor Goldberg comes out of the kitchen and picks up the boy.

"Sasha," he says, shaking his head from side to side.

Sasha feels her face stretch into a cartoonish evil smile.

"I know who I am," she says.

Heidi sighs and sinks into the couch, still wearing her coat and boots.

"Life is like climbing a tree," Victor says in English. "No, no, don't laugh. First you have all the branches—all the choices. You climb. There are fewer branches, fewer choices. Then you're clawing up a single twig. It breaks. What did you say?"

"You can always land on your feet, Papa. Or climb down," Sasha retorts wearily.

"You can't go back in time."

They have finished dinner and are now sitting in the living room, Victor on a straight-backed antique chair, Sasha and Heidi side by side on the couch. Victor picks up an address book and begins to doodle on the endpaper, drawing a tree. Sasha watches his sausage-thick fingers around a pen and remembers how he used to cover paper after paper with houses, farm animals, and anything else Sasha asked for.

"Draw a birdie, Papa!" squeals Ben, sliding on his belly onto the coffee table. "Draw a squirrel!"

Victor frowns and puts the book down.

"I have to apologize to you for all those years, for—"

"I don't need your apologies," Sasha says in Russian. "I need you to tell me something. Did Mama refuse to come with you, or did you just leave us?"

"Your mother wanted to come. She didn't get a visa."

"Why?"

"The whole emigration thing"—Victor glances at Heidi—"was really Lubov's idea. But she'd made a mistake. . . ."

"So you just left?" presses Sasha.

"Yes."

"Why?"

"I couldn't take it anymore. Asbestos 2. It was an oppressive—"

"—Fucking regime! You could have gone about it differently, we could have all come here together! It was Mama, wasn't it? You'd had enough of her. But what about me?"

"You were so little. You needed your mother. I thought maybe later. And then I had . . ." Victor gestured toward Ben and Heidi.

"Please," Heidi says with a disgusted grimace. "You could have at least told me."

Sasha watches Victor give a helpless little shrug. He looks almost surprised, as if he isn't sure who he's talking to and why all these people are attacking him. Sasha has seen that look on his face before. He used to stare at her mother like that. As if he didn't know her name. As if she were a particularly aggressive horsefly buzzing around his head.

"Why didn't you at least send us stuff? A pair of tights?" Sasha thinks back to her garter belt, the injustice becoming tangible, material, like worn nylon.

"I sent a package once. Toys. Must've been lost in the mail. Or your mother . . . She said she'd rip up my letters."

"What about money? I'm sure she would've kept the money if you'd sent any."

"I couldn't send Western Union. You didn't have a telephone."

Sasha takes a deep breath. She feels that the conversation is following its own logic, quite apart from how life normally works.

Heidi shakes her head. "Victor, you can't *do* this," she says, coming to Sasha's rescue. "You can't just abandon your old life and start a new one. You aren't Buddha. People have attachments. People take care of things."

Sasha opens her mouth to speak, then closes it again. Her father stoops in his chair, a fat middle-aged man. Prompted by Ben's whining, Heidi opens the freezer and doles out ice-cream sandwiches. Victor consumes his sandwich in two tremendous bites.

"This is what's so great about this country!" he exclaims with his mouth full.

Sasha watches him flick bits of chocolate off his BriteSmile Labs T-shirt, and her anger seeps away, replaced by pity so intolerable it feels like love. It's as if a thick scratchy rope is being pulled through her, entering a tight opening in her chest and coming out in the back, between her shoulder blades. When she was little she thought the soul was a body part. This was where she thought it was, to the right of the heart.

"All I want from you is legal immigration status," she says, holding back tears. "I want to be able to go back to Asbestos 2 and see what I can do for my family."

"We'll start on the paperwork tomorrow," says Victor. He sounds relieved to be facing a specific demand. "If necessary, we'll hire a lawyer."

Khomyak, thinks Sasha. Her father is nothing more than an enormous gerbil, a soft animal. He can't be held responsible. He's barely adapting. Sasha can't resist imagining Victor in a cage full of alfalfa pellets, fussing with his water bottle.

"Would you like to stay here?" asks Heidi.

"Yes, thank you," says Sasha, feeling her mouth stretch into a vindictive grin again. "But you know what? I'm not a maid, and I'm not a free babysitter."

Heidi turns red and waves her arms around like a puppet, as if to say that it would never occur to her to use Sasha that way. Sasha Goldberg appreciates the show.

3

What to Fear

"LOOK, HONEY, I'M DRESSED UP AS A TEENAGE GOTH!"
The day before Thanksgiving, Heidi Goldberg stood in front of the bathroom mirror, giving her wig a haircut. It was a cheap Rite Aid witch wig, long and tangly like Barbie hair, dull black. Heidi cut off the last clingy fibers in front of her face and grinned at the mirror. With super-short bangs, the wig framed her face in a strikingly flattering way. She painted her lips with dark red lipstick and gave herself black eyeliner cat-eyes. Tonight, Pillowhead was playing at the Fire Exit, and afterward there was a party at her friend Melissa's house. It was a costume party, a kind of Halloween-on-Thanksgiving affair that Heidi didn't bother to question.

"Be careful tonight," said Victor, barely lifting his eyes from *The Economist*. "Everyone will be drunk."

"Me included." Heidi wished that her husband would just get off the couch and come with her, that he'd stop worrying about her safety. What good was safety if all you did with it was sit on the couch?

A worn copy of *Motherhood: What to Fear* sat on top of the bookcase where Heidi last left it over a year ago. When Ben was an infant, she used to read it like a Bible, looking to have her fears allayed, strangely happy to have them confirmed. The "Marriage" chapter of *What to Fear* advised couples to go out on regular dates, and Heidi made sure to get a sitter once a week so she and Victor could go out. But Victor was stiff and uncomfortable in restaurants, always worrying that he might ask too much of the waiter. He was subdued and glum at parties, only occasionally unleashing one of his humorless monologues on some other glum person who happened to share his corner of the room. Heidi had a feeling that after the hassle of finding a sitter, after worrying about Ben, and after the money spent, Victor wasn't enjoying himself in the least. Finally, she had given up on dates. A week went by, then a month, and Victor said nothing. He seemed content to stay home with Ben. Since then, Heidi went out alone.

Victor's surprise child emerged from the bathroom. After two weeks, Heidi was still unused to having her in the apartment. The girl took up too much room. Her dirty jacket on the couch, her sneakers by the door, the black garbage bag with her belongings by the coffee table. Heidi wished she could compact Sasha, make her sit quietly in the corner *on top* of the garbage bag. The effort of insincere hospitality left Heidi snappy and exhausted. She was short with Ben and Victor, using up all of her mental energy to be nice to Sasha. After all, it wasn't Sasha's fault. There simply wasn't any room for another body in the Goldbergs' apartment. At least, unlike her father, this new Goldberg came partially assimilated, aware of hygiene and laundromats.

"Wow," said Sasha. "You look beautiful, like in a silent movie."

"Thanks." Heidi blushed, embarrassed by what she'd just been thinking. She liked the directness of Sasha's half-formed English. The kid communicated with blunt efficiency, as if she were afraid to lose the gift of speech at any minute. It was both entertaining and maddening, like the time Sasha interrupted Ben's adorable stream-of-consciousness banter with, "Enough. Now be quiet." Heidi felt like killing her then, but now she was flattered.

"You want to come? You can be a Goth, too!"

She was surprised at how the girl's eyes lit up.

"What's a Goth?" asked Sasha. She said "Gos." Heidi sighed, getting ready for a long night. She'd expected Sasha to refuse and stay home, like her father. She should've known better. After watching Sasha for two weeks, Heidi knew that Victor's lifelessness wasn't a genetic trait. She dug through Victor's clothes, trying to find something black for Sasha to wear.

At the bar Sasha got quickly and efficiently drunk and rocked to the music. Heidi noticed that she had Ben's negative sense of rhythm. She wondered what it would be like to have a daughter, a huge girl with an Afro like this. She thought about Sasha's mother back in Asbestos 2.

The music and three scotch-and-sodas left Heidi relaxed and pleasantly disoriented. At the party, Sasha ate half of a baguette and most of the fancy cheese from the tray on Melissa's coffee table. Melissa worked for a nonprofit and probably had spent half of her paycheck on the snacks. Watching Sasha polish off the cheese, Heidi felt embarrassed, but strangely proud, too.

"So, are you a relative of Victor's?" somebody asked Sasha.

"He's my dad," she replied, and Heidi felt the eyes of her friends on her.

"Well, she just appeared," she said. "Two weeks ago. . . ."

Sasha giggled.

"She came to Arizona as a mail-order bride," continued Heidi.

"Imagine the culture shock!" said a fat woman in a man's suit, her voice sounding muffled from the inside of a rubber Clinton head. A drunk girl in a rainbow wig hung on her elbow, laughing.

"Did you know before—" Melissa began, but Heidi interrupted her.

"Sasha, tell them about the bridal agency!" she commanded. This was the wrong time for serious questions. Before Sasha had come to live with them, Heidi used to call Melissa once a week to bitch about Victor. Melissa was obsessed with her biological clock, with finding a man and having a baby. Heidi felt that no matter what she said about Victor, she had a certain advantage over Melissa, which made bitching easier. Heidi felt as if she were a person with merely a broken leg, complaining to an amputee. But after Sasha showed up, she found herself reluctant to call Melissa. She felt that things were too complex to be bitched through.

"It was called Kupid's Korner. With two K's," said Sasha.

Heidi grinned. Sasha was decidedly presentable. She seemed to understand what this particular crowd might find funny. Victor never had this ability. Perhaps it was because he was a teetotaler. Heidi walked over to the table and poured two large glasses of wine. She was happy that Sasha liked to drink.

"Kupid's Korner got me a student visa to a fake college, so that my fiancé could try me out before he married me. They run a serious operation," explained Sasha.

A lot of people were listening now. They were all in costume. There were several turkeys, a belly dancer, a girl dressed in a Boy Scout uniform, a pregnant woman wearing a cardboard oven over her belly, androgynous twins dressed as a pair of breasts. Heidi felt as if she were relating her life to an Intergalactic Federation–like community, and that here, in this room, what happened finally made sense.

"So, you're her stepmom?" Melissa asked.

"Yeah," said Heidi, taking Sasha's hand. "What's wrong with that?"

"Yeah." Sasha smiled.

After the party, Heidi was starving. Sasha seemed to be up for more food anytime. They sat on plastic chairs at the Happy Dragon and shared a container of pot stickers. The food made them sober, and by the end of the meal they were staring at each other in awkward silence, feeling like strangers again.

When they got home, Victor was still up, sorting through old electric bills and stacking them in chronological order. He nodded at Heidi and Sasha but didn't speak.

"You should have come with us, Vitya," Heidi said. "We had fun."

Victor lifted his index finger and muttered something. Sasha realized that he was counting. She stared at Heidi and twirled her index finger at her temple. Heidi sighed.

"One minute," said Victor. "Fun?"

"Not as much fun as you had," Sasha mocked.

"I'm ready for bed," said Heidi. "Did you take Ben to the bathroom?"

Victor gave her a long glance, nodded slowly, walked to the bedroom.

"Good night!" Sasha yelled after him.

The day after Sasha had come to New York, Heidi threatened Victor with divorce unless he went to see her therapist. Dr. Phillips heard the story of Victor's childhood and promptly diagnosed him as having reactive attachment disorder. She maintained that Victor had an especially severe form of the disease, since it had never been treated. She also said that he had post-traumatic stress disorder and prescriped antidepressants.

Sasha believed that Dr. Phillips deserved a brick through her office window for bestowing fancy scientific names on Victor's cowardice. She hated the way her father slinked away in her presence, as if trying not to take up too much space, not to call attention to himself. When Sasha was around, Victor constantly occupied himself with housework. Perhaps he imagined that if he washed dishes long enough, with his back to the room, when he finally turned around she would be gone. At times, he appeared aloof and disoriented, almost senile. Sasha waited for him to ask her about the rest of her childhood, the time after he left, but so far he hadn't.

Unfolding her futon, Sasha realized that Heidi was the only beneficiary of Victor's diagnosis: she seemed to like him better sick.

For Christmas, Heidi, Victor, and Ben were going to New Mexico to visit Heidi's family. Heidi invited Sasha to come along, but Sasha knew she was expected to refuse.

She was looking forward to being alone in the apartment. She especially looked forward to a week without Ben. She wondered if all children were like him, high-strung and loud. Living with Ben was like listening to an endless instructional video. The boy narrated his own life in a nonstop monologue, telling the room how to mix paints, how to stack blocks, how to attach magnetic train cars to their engine. He expressed his desires with a preemptive high-pitched whine, a warning that he was about to fall apart. Sasha had to stop herself from telling him to stop screeching.

The Goldbergs packed separate suitcases. Victor had his things ready a week ahead of time, his socks and shirts and underwear neatly folded in a small black carry-on. Heidi packed on the day of the flight, haphazardly throwing her and Ben's things into a faded army-green duffel bag. Victor had been sent to Rite Aid to buy Dramamine.

"I want to bring Sniffy!" Ben whined.

"You can't bring him, baby," Heidi said. "He won't fit in the bag."

Sniffy was a fuzzy, dog-shaped bean bag. It was both larger and heavier than Ben. Sasha watched from the couch, anticipating an explosion.

"But Sniffy will get lonely!" argued Ben.

"Sasha will watch Sniffy, honey," Heidi said evenly, groping under the couch for Ben's missing sneaker. "Won't you, Sasha?"

"Sure." Sasha smiled.

"No, she won't!" wailed Ben, pummeling Heidi's face with his fist.

Sasha winced. With Heidi's arm still stuck under the couch, Ben had a height advantage.

"It's not nice to hit Mommy, honey," Heidi muttered.

The admonition earned her another smack on the nose. The sound of Heidi's voice seemed to inflame Ben's rage.

"Mommy doesn't like it when you hit her!" rephrased Heidi, reaching out to hug him.

"I want!" gulped Ben. He sounded as if he were about to suffocate. "SNIFFY!" He lunged at Heidi and tore into her hair.

"Let GO of her!" screamed Sasha. She couldn't take it anymore.

Ben jumped back and stared at her, speechless, his arms hanging at his sides. It was so simple. Sasha smiled at Heidi, but Heidi shot her a withering stare.

"Don't do that again," she warned, when Ben was out of earshot.

"Do *what*? Save you from being mauled?"

Did Heidi *like* being hit? Motherly love mystified Sasha. She thought back to her first days at the Repin, after her milk dried up. She remembered the feeling of being interrupted, as if she'd lost or forgotten something. Maybe Mrs. Goldberg was right when she said that Sasha wasn't ready to be a mother.

"Please, Sasha," mouthed Heidi, smoothing her hair back into a ponytail. "We have a flight to catch. We can discuss this later."

"What's there to discuss?" pressed Sasha. This tone of Heidi's irritated her more than Ben's outbursts. "The Sniffy *issue* is resolved, right?"

"Frankly, Sasha, I think you're the one with issues. I think you have issues with Ben because of what happened to you. And I seriously think that you should talk to Dr. Phillips."

"What exactly do you mean, what *happened* to me?" shouted Sasha. "Besides, do you want two zombies creeping around this apartment?"

The key turned in the front door. Heidi and Sasha glared at each other.

"I'm not sick," whispered Sasha.

"Of course not," Heidi said quickly, lifting her hands as if in self-defense. She didn't sound convinced.

"We should probably call a car," Victor yelled from the hallway, stomping his feet on the doormat. "It's snowing. The traffic might be bad. Are you about ready?"

Sasha dragged Heidi's duffel bag out to the stoop, watched Victor wrestle Ben into his car seat, and managed a goodbye smile for Heidi. After the cab left, she locked the front door, walked to Heidi's and Victor's bedroom, and lay down on their unmade bed. The pillows smelled like her father's dry skin. Sasha closed her eyes and imagined that she was a small child again, playing under her parents' blanket in Asbestos 2. She remembered the light-blue flowered sheet that covered their bed, and a large hole that appeared in its middle after years of use. Mrs. Goldberg had gotten out her sewing machine— a shiny foot-pedaled Zinger with a golden sphinx on the side, that some soldier had stolen from a German housewife half a century before and that somehow made its way to a market in Prostuda—and made the sheet into a set of curtains. When the sun was out, it was possible to see the yard through the curtains' threadbare blue fabric: the sandbox frame, the rusted iron T's supporting the clotheslines, and a five-story *khruscheba* building, identical to the Goldbergs', beyond the muddy soccer field.

Sasha sat up abruptly and rubbed her eyes, feeling restless and queasy. She must have fallen asleep because for a moment she felt that she had in fact traveled back in time and had to repeat her life again. Marina had warned her about nightmares like that.

Sasha got up and made the bed. She needed to find a cash job and move out, she decided. How long could she remain here waiting for the envelope from INS, her whole life organized around the mailman, not unlike Marina's was in Phoenix? The lawyer who helped Victor file Sasha's immigration papers had said that the wait could be as long as one year. By then, the four of them would kill each other.

Sasha Goldberg got dressed and went to the newsstand to buy *The Foreign Land.*

A mature woman, live in, New Jersey, take care of three children, $250/week. Status not required.

Girls up to twenty-five, easy work, status not required.

Subway Jobs. Great Benefits.

Make money reading books! To find out how, send $29.99

Back home, Sasha called the "Subway Jobs" ad. A man picked up, sounding as if Sasha had just woken him up. He wanted money for an information brochure.

"No, thanks," Sasha said, hanging up the phone. Of course this was a scam. She couldn't work for the city without a legal status. She called the "easy work" place and left a message. Most of the other ads were for babysitting jobs. Sasha suspected that she'd be a terrible babysitter. She washed Ben's cereal bowl, wiped the milk off the table, grabbed *The Foreign Land,* and went out to get a coffee.

Like most businesses in Heidi's neighborhood, the Fallen Leaf Café catered to mothers in search of distraction. There was a basket of unsanitary-looking toys in one of its corners, a stack of coloring books and a box of dead markers in another. Sasha sipped her coffee and scanned the job ads again. Perhaps she'd have to become a terrible babysitter after all.

She folded the paper and looked around. Suddenly she saw the description of her career tacked on the Fallen Leaf Café's bulletin board: "Experience Cleaning Lady. Good reference. Call Precious 718 555 3390." The letters in the flyer appeared to be borrowed from various printed sources, as in a ransom note. Sasha was amazed that she hadn't thought of this sooner. A child of the intelligentsia, a painter of fruits and drapes, a high school dropout, after her stint at the Tarakans' she was, most of all, an *Experienced Cleaning Lady.*

By the time Victor, Heidi, and Ben returned from New Mexico, Sasha Goldberg was employed.

The work was easy. The rich in Brooklyn hid their enviable interiors behind narrow brownstone facades. Nobody had a house as big as the Tarakans'. Then there were the apartment dwellers, who seemed pained by Sasha's presence, wracked with guilt at using a cleaning lady in their measly square footage. They tried to make conversation, asking Sasha where she was from, telling her they used to babysit, clean, flip burgers—back in college. Sasha Goldberg liked to watch them writhe in their painful class-consciousness. She could reassure them with a few words, ease their burden, she could say she was also working toward college, but she didn't. She enjoyed being a representative of the world's proletariat in the eyes of her weirdly Marxist employers. This was an unexpected perk, a pleasure the Waterfall House didn't provide.

Sasha took a quarter of her February wages to Maria's House of Hair on Fulton Street.

Maria turned the mountain of frizz on Sasha's head into a cascade of shiny braids, worth every penny. When Sasha got home that night, Heidi clapped approvingly. Victor stared. Sasha could guess what he was thinking, but she didn't want her knowledge confirmed. *Too black.*

I'm only as black as you, as Russian as you, as Jewish as you.

She took her new skirt from the FASHIONS UNDER SEVEN bag and looked at the tag again. "Karma Girl," it said. "100% Acrylic. Size: Medium." *You're normal,* the tag seemed to proclaim. Tomorrow, Sasha Goldberg thought shyly, she'd spend some money on makeup that matched her skin.

Pushing her red granny cart of cleaning supplies over the cobblestones, Sasha Goldberg felt almost happy. Brooklyn was beautiful in the spring, with its blooming magnolias and sudden warm winds, the precursors of summer. This wasn't Asbestos 2, or even Chicago. Seasons didn't ambush you here. They gathered strength gently. They showed *signs.*

At the end of each day, Sasha shoved her cash into a dresser drawer.

At the end of April, she bought *The Foreign Land* again. It was time to look for an apartment.

The Foreign Land was no *New York Times.* In the Real Estate section, people advertised to share a room, to share a *bed.* Perhaps they worked in shifts, thought Sasha. She couldn't imagine strangers actually sleeping together to save money.

Young woman wanted to share an apartment with two others. Own room, prestigious neighborhood.

The building stood on a barren stretch of Avenue U, between a windowless post office and a shuttered store called Raccuglia's Dolce Meats. It was a five-story, modern brick cube. Gold veins snaked through dim mirrors in the lobby, a dusty plastic ficus leaned against the wall. Sasha noticed that the entrance, the gloomy corridors, and the elevator had been retrofitted for handicapped access. The women in the apartment, both named Olga, explained that the building was Section 8 housing now mostly occupied by illegal sublets. The elderly would-be tenants, let 'em perish in peace, were back where they belonged, living at home with their children, while their apartments contributed to their grandchildren's college funds.

Sasha could tell that the Olgas were having a hard time finding a roommate. The gloomy low-ceilinged bedroom had one tiny window and matted dark-blue carpet. The living room was neatly furnished with dumpster finds: a sagging, stained floral sofa, a broken rocking chair, an ancient black-and-white TV. "Shawn loves Jess" was scratched into the surface of the table.

"Let me think about it," Sasha said to the Olgas, unable to make a decision in front of their eager faces. The enormous stainless steel elevator was by far the newest, most cheerful part of the building. Downstairs, Sasha noticed a square button with a blue wheelchair pictogram on the wall. She touched the button with her fingertips and the door swung open.

Running down the ramp, Sasha remembered a story she'd read in the *Times*: "Often, the choice of an apartment is influenced by personal or intangible factors present at the time of viewing: the apartment's odor, fresh flowers on the tenants' table, the arrangement of furniture, the weather outside." A button in the lobby? If Jake ever wanted to, he could visit her here.

Sasha turned a corner under the train tracks, wandered into Leonid's Futon Warehouse, and sat down on a dusty couch. A man in a suit asked if she needed help. He looked like Vitaly Sergeevich. Sasha shrugged, walked out of the store, and headed back to the Olgas' house.

Signing the lease, she felt as if her skull were made of Plexiglas, her foolishness exposed to the world. The odds of Jake Tarakan looking for her on Avenue U were only slightly better than those of D'Artagnan and his musketeers, with their billowing scarlet cloaks, wide-brimmed hats, and swords at the ready galloping down Third Road Street.

"The place looks like a hospital," commented Victor. But he and Heidi didn't question Sasha's choice. By their neighborhood's standards, the Olgas' apartment was a good deal. They got Sasha a futon from Leonid's as a housewarming present.

By June, Brooklyn was floating in the thick heat of a tropical summer. People moved sluggishly on sidewalks, cowered in the thin shadows of awnings. Playground moms sprawled on benches, barely breathing, their all-white outfits revealing tattoos from their previous lives. The children cautiously treaded rubber pavement and avoided metal slides. Sometimes the wind blew moist ocean air over Heidi's neighborhood, but Avenue U always smelled like rotting cardboard boxes.

Sasha Goldberg rolled her granny cart out of the elevator and unlocked the door. There was a message on the machine.

"Sasha, we have a surprise for you!" She could barely hear Heidi's voice over the racket of the Olgas' broken air conditioner.

When Sasha got to the Goldbergs' apartment, Victor was still at work. Heidi handed Sasha the INS letter. She'd wrapped it with a golden ribbon. Tearing the envelope, Sasha loved Heidi. She even loved Ben, who sensed the excitement and began to clap his hands above his head in imitation of some preschool ritual.

Victor accompanied Sasha to her green card interview. At home, Heidi and Ben waited with flowers.

"I picked them," Ben said. "They're coronations! You're a princess!"

The red carnations reminded Sasha of the Tomb of the Unknown Soldier. Hardy and odorless, they mummified rather than wilted, making them perfect for cemeteries. They were the color of her nonexistent country's flag, the color of the mustachioed heroes' blood.

After Victor and Ben went to sleep, Heidi and Sasha split a bottle of Merlot.

"What are you going to do now?" Heidi asked.

"I'm going to Asbestos 2," Sasha replied without delay, her certainty growing with every sip of wine.

They stayed up until three in the morning, resurrecting Asbestos 2. Sasha told Heidi about AFTER EATIN, and about Alexey. Heidi asked if she missed Alexey sometimes, and Sasha said no, and Heidi told her about her high school boyfriend's maroon Camaro, about listening to Led Zeppelin on a mountainside, Albuquerque a quilt of lights below, stitched with freeways.

They opened another bottle.

"You don't respect Victor," Heidi stated, fingering her cracked lips.

Sasha laughed. "What's there to respect?"

"He's such a wonderful, gentle father," Heidi sighed.

"He's a liar," said Sasha, filling their glasses.

"That's your age speaking. Everyone is a liar. I think I really loved him when we first met, and then"—Heidi lowered her voice—"I began to feel stuck. Things that I used to enjoy now make me miserable. After Ben was born, even the music I used to love began to make me feel long dead and buried."

Heidi shivered and reached for her sweater, almost knocking over Sasha's glass.

"Shit, I'm so drunk!" she sobbed loudly.

"Shush, Ben will wake up," said Sasha.

"He never wakes up." Heidi sniffled. "Sleeps like a rock, just like his father! God, when he was a baby, I thought he'd never sleep. He just *screamed* for the first six months of his life. I think it's because of all the interventions, you know, when he was born."

"What interventions?"

"Oh, it was horrible. I wanted this beautiful, natural birth. I wanted to, you know, feel every minute of it, be aware. I wanted a water birth. We were able to get a new room, with a Jacuzzi—"

"What's a Jacuzzi?"

"Oh, you know." Heidi waved her hand in Sasha's face, as if to show that she was too drunk and tired to explain things like a Jacuzzi. "I was in labor for thirty hours. Finally I begged for drugs; that slowed things down even more. I couldn't push Ben out. They tried vacuum extraction, he went into distress, and at the end of it all I ended up with a Cesarean. By then my epidural wore off, and I could *feel* the incisions. I was depressed for months afterwards. I felt so guilty. If only . . . What?"

"They cut you up and you feel *guilty*?" asked Sasha, wondering if she'd missed something. She couldn't understand much of what Heidi was saying, all the medical words.

Heidi shot her a hopeless look. "What was it like—for you?"

Sasha thought about it for a second.

"I had my baby natural," she finally said, startled at how strange it sounded here, in Heidi's universe, like something she'd chosen, like something to be proud of.

Dear Nadia,

The day you were born, Mama and I were sitting in the kitchen. There was fear in my stomach, above you, above the cramps. Then I felt a cramp bad enough to make me forget what I was saying. I laughed when it passed, but Mama knew.

Nine beds in the Birthing House's labor room were empty. I lay down by the window and touched a line of brown stains on the blanket. It must've been shit. Or blood.

Shitblood shitblood. Soon my brain was busy setting shitblood to jingly cartoon music. My whole body was shaking, molars clanking to the rhythm of shitblood. I had to pee.

The bathroom was down the hall. I measured the distance in cramps, bending over every few steps. I still remember the wood grain pattern in the brown linoleum. In the bathroom, the toilet seat hung on a nail on the wall, to be shared between three stalls. It was like a school bathroom: no doors, no toilet paper, but clean. I was taking the toilet seat down from the wall when I felt a cramp that finally made me cry. I squatted by the wall and felt hot liquid on my legs: at first a little and then more and more. It wasn't stopping. They, whoever they were, would kill me for making this mess.

A woman with a mop called me an idiot in a friendly, motherly way.

"Vo dura, kuda zabralas! The hell you doing here? Up, up wif you."

She tried to pull me by the sleeve, but I couldn't get up. Her narrow black front teeth made me feel sick, and I turned away.

"Fine," the woman said, "suit yourself, princess. Lie here till you die."

I lay down on the floor and closed my eyes.

Some time later the woman with the mop returned, accompanied by a man in a stained lab coat. Cursing under their breath, they picked me up on either side and dragged me, like a wounded comrade in a movie, into the delivery room.

"They put me on a high table in the middle of the room," Sasha said, "and tied my feet to these things. . . ."

"Stirrups?" whispered Heidi.

"Then they tied down my wrists."

"Oh, my God," said Heidi. "With ropes?"

"No! What do you think it was—a torture chamber? With strips of gauze. Then they sat down to drink. I couldn't see them because they sat below me. They were toasting the upcoming May Day. The man had plans to go fishing. Maybe he was the doctor. Every time I screamed, the nurse told me to shut up. She didn't say it meanly. I think they were just annoyed that I might be in there over the holiday."

Sasha grinned. She'd been so terrified in that delivery room, but now she was able to turn it into an outrageous story, a slice of Soviet life. Heidi slouched in her chair, looking like a small ruffled bird in her knotty olive-green sweater. She squeezed Sasha's hand with her bony fingers, and Sasha squeezed back, hard, until Heidi's sorry knuckles felt like a fistful of acorns. It occurred to Sasha that she was a powerful monster, capable of inflicting harm. It was time to stop drinking, she realized, or, as Jason Tarakan liked to say, she'd be *driving the porcelain bus* in the morning.

"It didn't take that long," she continued. "After a while they got up and began to yell instructions at me. By then I couldn't even understand what they wanted. I think it was the man who finally pushed on my stomach and forced the baby out of me. And then it didn't hurt anymore."

"What did you think when you first heard Nadia cry?" whispered Heidi.

"I can't remember," said Sasha. Why couldn't Heidi be satisfied with her story? Americans liked to keep all the shit that ever happened to them in precious keepsake boxes, and Heidi was the worst of them all. "I don't think she cried."

"Really?"

"Go to hell, Heidi," laughed Sasha. Suddenly her face felt hot and numb. She stared at the rim of her glass and saw two shiny circles gliding over each other.

Heidi had a hideously offended face on, as if she were a priest and Sasha had just desecrated her church. *The Church of Keepsake Shit*, with congregants' tears for windowpanes. If Sasha didn't blink, her eyes welled up, and the kitchen began to look like a mosaic of luminous shapes. She leaned back in her chair and watched the olive blob of Heidi's sweater sway between the table and the sink.

No, baby, I didn't hear you. They must've taken you away somewhere. After a while, I heard a sound like raw liver hitting a bucket. I thought they were throwing you away because you were born dead, and at the time, it made me happy.

"It's okay to cry," Heidi grumbled. "It's okay to let yourself feel."
"Go to hell, Heidi."

4

The House of Gold and Straw

A PIXELLATED AIRPLANE CREEPS OVER THE NORTH POLE ON the TV screen. Sasha Goldberg saves the tiny bottles of vodka for presents and bribes. After cutting her finger on the edge of a perfume sample, she stuffs her magazine into the seat pocket, drinks four gin-and-tonics, and tries to fall asleep.

The morning finds her in the bathroom line, her face in a barf bag. The Americans in line have toothbrushes and travel-sized tubes of toothpaste, the Russians have bloodshot eyes and unbridled fury. Sasha Goldberg has all of those things. Also, in her backpack, she has a pink windup music box. When the lid opens, the music starts, and a ballerina Hello Kitty twirls on a spring in front of an oval mirror.

The plane lands in Moscow in a thunderstorm. The passengers applaud the pilot and hurry toward the door. An airport attendant guides them past dark offices with outdated computers, behind clapboard partitions, and into a wide stairway where a line is forming. An hour passes before the passport control queue starts to move.

Sasha hears a middle-aged couple in front of her tell another couple about their trip. They have come to Russia to adopt a baby. A tall brunette with a heavy chin accompanies the couple on their trip.

"Sally Ann is our guardian angel," the husband says.

The wife digs in her bag for a pack of tissues.

They complain about the bureaucracy, about having to spend three weeks in

Russia waiting for a court decision. "All that time off work for Carl," the wife says.

The husband passes around the baby's picture. Sasha can't see it from where she is standing. The baby's name is Oleg. A boy. Sasha exhales. The wife explains that "back home" Oleg will become Henry.

"What a *lovely* name," the wife of the other couple says. Her short permed hair hugs her head like a helmet. Strangely, her husband appears to have a matching perm.

"It's such a blessing!" she continues. "You wonder how such precious lambs—"

The guardian angel anticipates the question and cuts her off with a smile.

"Everyone's circumstances are unique," she says, "but the main reason is poverty. Our adoption agency has a special relationship with three orphanages. We do everything to ensure a high standard of care for these children."

Sasha notices that Sally Ann is the only one who appears comfortable. The future parents of Oleg-Henry and the perm couple look worn out and skittish in the dim light of copper honeycomb fixtures. In a half hour, thinks Sasha, they will be robbed blind by taxi drivers, soaked by the rain. The bureaucracy will make them cry. Mother Russia will gather all of its thirdworldness and pour it on their heads like a bottomless bucket of shit. Oleg-Henry will never get to play with his Hot Wheels trucks. Sasha wants to warn the parents, make them understand. But of course nothing like that is going to happen. Rubbing her temples, Sasha wonders if she is losing her mind.

She has a day in Moscow before her flight to Prostuda. The metro looks different. Permanent glassed-in kiosks have replaced the vendors' carts in the underground passageways. One of the kiosks is called Café Manhattan. It sells beer, hot dogs, and potato pierogis.

People look different, too. They're better dressed than Sasha remembers, especially the women. Sasha stares at their five-inch heels, leather miniskirts, enormous earrings, purses with baroque buckles. They stare back. Feeling a hundred blue eyes on her like mosquito bites, Sasha Goldberg gets out of the train. Near the station's exit, a hunched-over old woman sits on a wooden crate with a stack of shawls on her lap. The shawls are black, embroidered with the word CHANEL in all colors of the rainbow. Sasha buys one and ties it on her head peasant-style, hiding her braids.

She takes the metro to the food market. There she buys gifts for her mother: four kilo slabs of frozen meat, a stick of salami as thick as a human leg, chocolate-covered wafer cookies, instant coffee. She's proud of herself for thinking to bring a portable cooler.

The Prostuda flight is full. Tan families carry baskets of fruit and vegetables from their Crimean vacations. Here, nobody bothers with seat belts. Men smoke in the lavatory, and children play under their seats. Sasha thinks that her mother would never let her play on the filthy floor like this.

By the time she gets to Asbestos 2, Sasha Goldberg is exhausted and jittery. Every little thing threatens to make her cry: a faded May Day banner by the District Soviet, graffiti on the walls of the bus stop pavilion, and the mere fact that it's all *still there.* Sasha realizes that she's halfway expected her hometown to be gone or to be unrecognizable. It has only been two years, she reminds herself.

Her apartment building is there, too. The same littered foyer, busted lightbulbs, same reek of rotten potatoes, cat pee, and human pee. This is home. Sasha feels herself immediately settling into it, the way Heidi's cell phone snaps into its charger. She wonders where she has found the strength to live anyplace else.

She runs up the staircase in a few giant leaps, taking three steps at a time. The door to the apartment is ajar. Sasha hesitates, terrified that the apartment will be abandoned, like so many others in the building. And then she hears voices from the inside and pushes the door.

They're sitting in the kitchen. From the corridor, Sasha counts them, one, two dark shapes against the window. For a second, until her eyes get accustomed to light, she can't tell who is who. They appear approximately the same size. Then the shape to the right says Sasha's name, and Sasha recognizes her mother's voice.

The child looks up from her teacup. She has the face of a stranger. Gray eyes peer from under her thick straw-yellow bangs. Sasha Goldberg tries to catch her breath from running up the stairs, but her heart is beating high in her throat. She is utterly unprepared for the sight of her daughter's face.

She looks around the kitchen for the baby she'd left.

Nadia runs to the other side of the table and hides behind Mrs. Goldberg.

Lubov Alexandrovna presses her head into Sasha's chest, laughing. Her laughter runs away from her, turning into schoolgirl giggles, old woman's moans, and finally, into tears.

"Take yourself into your hands, Mama," says Sasha, standing in the middle of the tiny kitchen like an ever-out-of-place monolith.

So here is my award for a long winter's work, Mrs. Goldberg thinks, realizing that her daughter can't return her hug because of all the bags she is holding.

Sasha's arrival coincides with the first warm day of summer. Lubov Alexandrovna can't be sure what date it is. The dates are becoming elusive, now that neither she nor anyone around her goes to work. Pretty soon she'll have to carve the calendar in her wooden doorframe, like Robinson Crusoe.

Since the Stepanovs have moved to Rostov, Mrs. Goldberg and Nadia have the apartment for themselves. The neighbors' rooms stand empty, with only faint negatives on sun-bleached wallpaper to remind Lubov Alexandrovna of their former décor. Privately, Mrs. Goldberg luxuriates in all that space. Watching Nadia twirl a Hula Hoop in the square of light on the floor makes her think about Baba Zhenia's prerevolutionary girlhood, when rooms were so big they had to be called "halls."

Lubov Alexandrovna keeps the apartment clean. *For the future,* she tells herself, for when things get better. When things get better, she'll replace the dirty-green linoleum with gleaming parquet, buy furniture. Mrs. Goldberg has never bought furniture in her life, and the thought of buying furniture usually snaps her out of daydreaming by the force of its sheer outrageousness. The thought of buying furniture illuminates the magnitude of her delusions. Things aren't going to get better. This is no place to raise a child. And still Mrs. Goldberg can't help imagining a black lacquered bookcase in the Stepanovs' former room; an elegant oval coffee table on a Persian rug in the Orlovs'.

They have plenty of clothes; they stay warm. Food is another matter. Lubov Goldberg remembers her first meal of fried bread. It was a fluke. She must've forgotten to get groceries, Nadia must've been sick, she didn't feel like going outside, why else? Now they eat fried bread all the time. The grocery store has closed for good, its glass vitrines broken, then boarded up. When the power goes on, part of its sign still lights up, like some perverse beacon of hope, OCERY.

In the beginning of winter, Lubov Alexandrovna traded some of her jewelry for a bucket of cloudy sunflower oil. Nadia loved fried bread. She liked it crispy, nearly burned. Sometimes Lubov Alexandrovna sprinkled Nadia's bread with sugar, and it earned her a greasy toddler kiss, a touch of colorless eyelashes on the cheek.

The child didn't know that she needed milk, sweet tea seemed enough for her, but Mrs. Goldberg knew. When Nadia got sick, Lubov Alexandrovna feared the worst. Her worry manifested itself in rage. *I told you to wear a hat, I told you not to go into the drafty corridor!* Nadia cowered and cried, chewed on the thermometer's glass tip. *Don't touch that with your teeth!* Thankfully Nadia almost never gets sick anymore. She has no playmates, no one to catch diseases from. As far as Mrs. Goldberg can tell, there are no other children left in Asbestos 2.

Sometimes she takes Nadia to Prostuda to gawk at the food. At the Prostuda central market, you can buy canned roast and potatoes, chickens and fruit, milk and even imported mango nectar in bright orange cartons. But that requires money. Lubov Goldberg spent her last ruble the previous fall, and she's still too young to qualify for a pension.

One time, she took some books to Prostuda and tried to sell them at the market. She didn't sell a single one, but at the end of the day, people gave her change and she bought Nadia a *pirozhok* with meat. The girl was up all night feverish and vomiting. Mrs. Goldberg thought that maybe it was best to stay put in Asbestos 2.

She thought about Sasha, about how she'd tried to breast-feed the baby. Lubov Alexandrovna would come from work and see all those unused bottles in the fridge. The thought of her daughter lying in bed with a baby by her side, like some animal, repulsed Mrs. Goldberg. All that work, wasted. Her daughter, a child of the intelligentsia, lying underneath a boy, lying next to the baby.

She wanted Sasha upright.

For a while, the boy wrote letters. He didn't seem very bright, describing his days in excruciating detail. Mrs. Goldberg read the letters and stacked them under a large group photograph matted on cardboard.

"Workers of the World, Unite!" said the ribbon above the picture, and under the ribbon, "The Class of 1963." In the photo, Luba sat between her math teacher and her Russian teacher, upright and smiling. She'd been beautiful, she'd been full of hope. Her world dissolved so gradually that when she finally noticed it was too late.

She was proud of herself for getting Sasha out of bed, for catapulting her out of Asbestos 2, but Sasha repaid her by disappearing. Lubov Alexandrovna spent countless hours at the Conversation Point, calling the Repin Lyceum, getting the number of a bridal agency from one of Sasha's dorm mates. Nadia screamed in her pram outside the phone booth. Everyone at the Conversation Point screamed. Burly men with tattoos wailed in their booth like lost babies, *Mama, Mama, can you hear me, Mama!,* trying to compensate with the power of their voices for the faulty telephone connection.

Sasha was gone, married to an American, living in Arizona. The bridal agency wouldn't give out the number. America swallowed people whole, Mrs. Goldberg knew that much. She rolled the pram home, boiled Nadia's diapers, hung them out to dry in the freezing wind, and cried herself to sleep.

After two years, things have become easier. Nadia is almost helpful now, almost good company. On cold nights, Lubov Alexandrovna peels back the pile of blankets and climbs into the girl's bed, pressing her face to the back of Nadia's little warm head. Nadia's dirty hair seems to absorb all the smells of the household: the smell of melting ice on windowsills, the dry smell of wallpaper, the smell of frying sunflower oil.

Mrs. Goldberg feels guilty for using a child like that, to warm her hands on, to cry next to. In the mornings, she wakes up before Nadia, combs her hair, and puts on makeup. That way, when the child opens her eyes, she is greeted by a proper mother.

The first thing Sasha notices about her mother is her makeup. It's too bright. Mrs. Goldberg looks like the crazy ladies in the New York subway, and smells like them, too: perfume and rotting feet. Sasha assumes her mother has dressed up especially for her, then realizes Lubov Alexandrovna didn't know she was coming.

Nadia smiles shyly, still clinging to Mrs. Goldberg's leg. She looks healthy. As if sensing Sasha's doubts, Mrs. Goldberg points to a piece of cardboard on the table.

"Look, Nadiusha can already write her name."

My mother taught a three-year-old to write, thinks Sasha.

"Would you like some tea, Sasha?"

Sasha sits down at the table, in her usual spot, and looks around the kitchen, feeling as if she's in a dream. Her mother is talking to her as if Sasha has just come back from an errand, not from a two-year absence.

"I'm going to go get water," says Mrs. Goldberg.

She grabs the kettle and leaves the kitchen. Sasha pictures her mother in somebody's empty apartment, hooking the handle of the kettle around a tub faucet to collect the drips, and wishes she brought bottled water.

"Who are you?" asks Nadia.

Sasha stares at her, startled by this new voice in the room. Nadia speaks like a grown-up: no babyish lisp or dropped consonants.

"Sasha."

"I can write your name."

"You must be very smart," Sasha says, fully appreciating the lameness of her remark and her insincere, exhausted smile.

Nadia bends down over her piece of cardboard.

"I'm a genius," she says calmly.

"Mama tells that to everyone," replies Sasha, feeling irritation rise up in her throat like bile.

She watches Nadia lick the pencil and remembers the baby's compact acorn head and fat cheeks. Nadia's chin is pointy now, and her large white ears move when she breathes. Sasha has known before, but now she really *knows.* This child doesn't belong to her anymore.

Nadia finishes writing and holds up her cardboard. Sasha recognizes the cover of her childhood notebook.

"Your *S* is backwards," she says, feeling suddenly spiteful, about to cry.

But it's Nadia who begins to wail.

"Oh, please," Sasha pleads guiltily. She can't believe she is arguing with a three-year-old over a letter. "Please, don't cry."

Nadia stops making noise and cries silently, in long, gasping sobs. Sasha knows that at Nadia's age she would have cried, too. They are both Lubov Goldberg's daughters, aimed like arrows at perfection. Sasha is grateful to be her mother's failed project. Now it's Nadia's turn, and she feels bad for the child.

"Hey, look! I brought you a present."

Sasha puts the music box on the table. The purple gift wrap has crumpled inside her bag. Sasha wishes she brought some new paper to rewrap the box. She remembers agonizing over the toys at a boutique toy store on Court Street. The store had a bunny music box and a Nutcracker one. Sasha can't recall why she picked Hello Kitty. Now it seems weirdly arbitrary, insufficient.

"Thank you," Nadia says, holding the present in outstretched arms. She is staring at something on the floor. Sasha follows the girl's gaze and notices a bag of airplane snack mix that must've fallen out of her bag.

"You want that?" she asks.

"May I?" Nadia whispers shyly.

Sasha picks up the metallic sack and tears it open. Nadia piles the contents on the table and begins to arrange the individual pieces along the edge. She seems to have forgotten about the music box. Sasha tears off the wrapping paper, winds the crank, and opens the lid. The box begins to play "Mary Had a Little Lamb."

Nadia fingers miniature pretzels, Ritz crackers, Chex, and peanuts, and watches the Hello Kitty spin on its spring. Finally she smiles. Mrs. Goldberg comes back with a full kettle. Nadia sweeps the snack mix into the music box and snaps the lid. Sasha thinks about the pink velveteen lining on the inside getting all greasy. She wonders if Nadia will treasure the tiny snack shapes for years to come, the way Sasha used to treasure her 3-D Olympic postcard and a plastic rhinestone, the precious spoils of poverty. Whatever happened to them? Yawning, Sasha realizes that since there is no water in the apartment, she won't get to shower.

"We should put the meat in the freezer, Mama."

"Freezer?" Mrs. Goldberg exclaims, laughing.

"You still don't have power?"

"Still?"

"I saw a television report in the fall."

"The electricity comes on sometimes. Two, three hours at a time, not enough to have a refrigerator, anyway."

"When's the next time they turn it on?"

"When the lobster whistles on the hill." Mrs. Goldberg shrugs. "We'll have to smoke that meat of yours. Like the Indians. Or eat it all now. She can't have any, though. Meat makes her sick," she says, pointing at Nadia.

"How long do you plan to live like this, Mama?"

"What do you suggest I do? At least I have an apartment here. And when things get better—"

"Better? When's that?"

"Tell me about yourself, Sasha."

"I'm all right. I live in New York."

"What's your husband's name?"

"We're not together anymore."

"Oh."

"I found Papa."

Mrs. Goldberg looks down at her teacup, waiting. Sasha realizes that even now she's too proud to ask questions.

"I lived with him for a while, and now I have my own place. I know that he left us."

"I tried to tell you then, but you didn't want to hear it," Mrs. Goldberg says with a shrug.

"You didn't exactly tell me *sanely.*"

"I was trying to do what was best for you. Haven't I, in the end? Would you be living in America had I not sent you to Moscow?"

"I could have signed up with a bridal agency in Prostuda, Mama."

"But who would pay attention to you? The only reason your husband married you was because you were attending the Repin Lyceum. It's well known internationally."

"Mama, you are so Soviet. Americans pay no attention to that sort of thing," Sasha says, laughing. "He just liked my beautiful face. Maybe he had a thing for black girls."

"You are not black, Alexandra," Mrs. Goldberg's voice is suddenly hushed, as if Sasha said something unsuitable for the child's ears.

"No, Mama, I'm white. Your life is normal. Good times are coming. And the sky is green, with purple polka dots!" Sasha feels her voice falter and stops.

Mrs. Goldberg crosses her arms on her chest.

"Did you come all the way here to mock me?" she asks.

"I came to take my daughter," Sasha lies angrily, sneaking a look at Nadia. The girl is oblivious, playing.

"Nadiusha," says Mrs. Goldberg, "come to Mama."

Without taking her eyes from the music box, Nadia climbs onto her lap.

"When Nadia's older, she can visit you in America," says Mrs. Goldberg, smoothing the girl's hair. "Will you go visit Tetya Sasha in America, *detka*?"

"Is it far? Is it near Prostuda?" says Nadia, disappearing under the table. She's been turning the crank on the music box the wrong way, and it has finally come loose. "The bus makes my belly hurt."

Mrs. Goldberg laughs. Sasha is upset that her mother hasn't even thanked her for bringing the food. She wants to feel the upper hand, wants her mother to beg for help, although she knows Mrs. Goldberg won't.

"I have something for you, Mama," she says quietly, reaching into her shirt for her trump card, five hundred dollars in cash.

The money is warm and smells like Sasha's body. *A rape bonus,* she joked back in Brooklyn, pinning the bills to the inside of her bra. The joke made Heidi cringe. Victor Goldberg sighed. That night, he made a halfhearted attempt to talk Sasha out of going back, and she shouted insults at him.

Sasha slides the money across the table to her mother. For a minute, she thinks Mrs. Goldberg will refuse to take it, preferring to starve rather than allow Sasha her small victory. But Lubov Alexandrovna takes the cash. Sasha watches her tuck the bills into her own shirt. It doesn't feel like a victory. It feels like an organ transplant.

"I appreciate it," Mrs. Goldberg says with her lips only, as if addressing a representative of some faceless charity.

"All right, Mama. Let's eat."

With the humiliation of the money transfer behind her, Mrs. Goldberg seems ready to be entertained. She laughs at Sasha's stories, slaps her hand on the table. Even though they're only drinking tea, Sasha feels pleasantly light-headed and woozy. Soon she notices that Nadia is falling asleep, her eyelids drooping. Mrs. Goldberg looks at her watch. It's eleven at night.

Outside, the sun hangs in the gray haze, unmoving, as if it's three in the afternoon. Sasha thinks about Brooklyn's starless darkness, humid summer nights saturated with orange light and ambulance sirens, with the sounds of breaking glass, with a drunk screaming, "Yuppie dickhead" at the top of his lungs. All of that seems completely unreal now.

Mrs. Goldberg picks up Nadia and carries her to Sasha's old bed. The child leans her head on Lubov Alexandrovna's neck and closes her eyes. Sasha tries to remember being that age, being close to her mother's skin like that, and can't. Mrs. Goldberg lays Nadia on top of the blanket, lifts her blue flannel dress, and pulls down her *kolgoty*.

"Still wears diapers at night," she whispers to Sasha.

"Mom, she's only three. It's normal."

"She is a very smart girl," says Mrs. Goldberg, closing the door.

"She informed me she was a genius. Mama, we need to talk, seriously. Have you thought of leaving? We can try getting you a visa. You and Nadia can stay with me," Sasha says, trying to sound assured, as if what she is proposing is no big deal.

"What about the apartment?"

"Forget the apartment, Mama. You have no one here. Think about it. Papa and Heidi found a lawyer to help me, maybe we can figure out—"

"Heidi?"

Although Sasha can't see Mrs. Goldberg's face in the dark hallway, she realizes that she's made a mistake. Or did she mention Heidi for a reason?

"I can't go through this again." Mrs. Goldberg sounds as if she swallowed something disgusting. "This is my life. This is where I live."

Sasha doesn't argue. She feels as if a huge weight has been lifted off her shoulders. For a moment she is free, and then the weight settles back, twice as heavy, and Sasha slumps over by the coat rack, crying. What does Heidi, with her dumb C-section, know about *guilty*?

"*Nu, nu.*" Mrs. Goldberg smiles, patting her on the shoulder. "*Gluposti.*" Silliness.

"Mama, how long will the money last you?" Sasha asks.

"Five hundred dollars? A year, easily."

"I will come back in ten months. I will also send food packages. There are companies in New York that will ship food anywhere."

Mrs. Goldberg nods, coughing into her fist.

"Take care of her."

"I took good care of you, didn't I?" says Mrs. Goldberg, reaching to stroke Sasha's hair.

"Are you alone in the building?" Sasha asks when they return to the kitchen.

"Oh, no. Tetya Vera is still downstairs, and the first-floor drunks. It's a wonder they're still alive."

"What about my art school? Is it still open?"

"No, that's gone. Evgeny Mikhailovich died last winter. The day of his funeral one of the ceilings collapsed. Nobody's had the energy to reopen it after that. It's sealed now."

"What about Boris Petrovich?"

"*Spilsya.* He was a handsome man," says Mrs. Goldberg.

So Bedbug drank himself to death. Sasha isn't surprised. She tries to decide what's stranger: that someone considers Bedbug handsome or that her mother is talking about a man that way. She wishes she could recall her last time at AFTER EATIN. She thinks of the way parts of New York transform: a parking garage into a condominium, a block of row houses into a pharmacy, Lacy Lucy Underwear Emporium into Ovum, a restaurant where all the food is made of eggs. But Asbestos 2 is a problem in itself, whose only solution is collapse.

"How do you know all this, Mama?"

"Your friend came by a few months ago. Katia, I think. Such a nice girl, lives in Moscow now. Very successful."

"Did she have a TV crew?"

"No, she was by herself. She brought us canned roast and vitamins. She had a very nice camera. Took pictures of Nadia."

Ten days later, Sasha Goldberg watches her mother and her daughter from the back window of a bus. They wave until they can't see her anymore, then turn around and walk home. Despite the rusting scaffolding of the never-finished District Soviet annex behind them, they look like an old lithograph of peasants in their matching kerchiefs. Sasha reminds herself that she will soon come back, but can't stop feeling that she is looking into a distant past, as if the graffitied, filthy bus is the future.

In the Prostuda airport, Sasha digs in her purse for her last remaining rubles to buy a bottle of Fanta and finds a package. It's wrapped in newspaper and marked with Mrs. Goldberg's exemplary handwriting.

> *Sashenka, I was just trying to keep you moving in the right direction.*
> *Love,*
> *Mama.*

Sasha shakes her head, laughing. Her mother has certainly kept her moving. She isn't surprised to see letters from Alexey, still in their envelopes, each neatly opened along the side with a sharp knife. At least he's been writing. Sasha is happy to have something to read on the plane, but the letters are maddening, incomprehensible. If nature could narrate itself it would produce something similar. Alexey seems to lack the urge to generalize and draw conclusions, instead describing events around him in minute detail, without any particular order. One of the letters is about a man who passed out in a pool of his own vomit. Sasha finds out the color of the vomit, its texture and reflective quality, the curious position of the vertebrae in the man's neck. The description ends abruptly with a small drawing of a cross section of a mouth, the tongue and vocal cords replaced by a leaping black cat.

Sasha Goldberg scans the sloping lines of text for meaning and promise until her head begins to hurt.

"The liquor store by the bus station sells candy shaped like eggs, fifty rubles each. There are plastic toys in the eggs. The girl let us eat the melted, flattened ones. I found a pacifier in mine. The pacifier was yellow and required assembly."

Something about becoming a childlike soldier?

"A guy ran off today. They stopped the truck to let us piss, and he ran into the forest. I heard him, but didn't see. They shot after him but he was gone. Arutiunov flicked his lighter all night again, it's like sleeping with a canary in the truck. Had boiled onions for dinner and half-liter of vodka with Seven-Up."

The safety of the makeshift community? The danger of freedom?

"An ear of corn is like a dick with hair on top. Like a drawing of cum. What's it like to have your dick wrapped in leaves?"

He missed me.

Sasha tries to become Darwin to Alexey's nature, Marx to his history. By the time the pilot announces landing, she feels like she's grown a beard.

"At a school building there is a hospital for women with holes in their necks. They talk through holes and smoke through them too. Flaps of skin move like little lips."

Jake had, has a tracheotomy scar.

Thinking of Jake is a relief. Stuffing the letters into her backpack she wonders what Alexey has omitted. Aside from the corn dick part there isn't anything in the letters even obliquely related to her, and it irks her. Maybe all this poetic nonsense isn't communication, but a defense against what has really gone on, the equivalent of covering your eyes and ears and screaming.

The last letter dates from a year ago. It's written after Alexey's discharge from the army. It has an Ulianka, Tula Region address. In the airport, Sasha looks at the map, telling herself she shouldn't, knowing she will.

She rides the metro to the Kurski station, takes the suburban train to Tula, and finds a bus to Ulianka. The bus is broiling hot. Sasha's head is sweating under the CHANEL shawl, but she keeps it on.

In the metro, she's heard two women complain about "the blacks." It hasn't taken Sasha long to realize that by "blacks" the women actually meant the *Caucasians,* the southern intruders on their privileged city. Sasha remembers a chinless, fur-hatted boy from the Repin who used to call the actual, African blacks "negatives."

The village of Ulianka consists of one dirt road lined with wooden houses. The houses stand uniquely lopsided, as if they've tried to disconnect themselves from their foundations and flee the village. Their paint is peeling and faded, and the wooden lacework under each roof mostly consists of gaps. An old lady comes out of one of the houses, and Sasha shows her Alexey's address on the envelope.

"Oh, that's in the *poseyolok*," the old lady says, pointing at a group of low brick buildings at the end of the road. "*Bozhe moi!*" she exclaims, taking a second look at Sasha. "*Negritianka!*"

"Thank you," says Sasha Goldberg, backing away.

"*Ponayehali . . . ,*" sighs the grandma.

On her way to the *poseyolok*, Sasha tries to translate the old woman's lament into English. The single word *ponayehali* means "they arrived over a period of time, in large enough masses as to become an annoyance." *O, the great and mighty Russian language!* thinks Sasha. Here abuse is compact and efficient; two prefixes do the job of a sentence. Suddenly Sasha finds herself missing Brooklyn, where people simply call each other motherfucker.

Built in the field alongside each other, the buildings of the *poseyolok* look like storage lockers. Only the curtains in the tiny windows under the roof and a dilapidated swing set in a puddle of water out front indicate that these are human dwellings. Two girls, about Nadia's age, run up to the edge of the puddle, considering the swing set.

"Get away from there, you'll get your feet wet!" yells one of the girls' mothers.

The mothers perch on a metal railing nearby. They look like teammates in their identical nylon tracksuits, each holding a brown bottle of beer.

Sasha knocks on a reinforced metal door, and Natalia Egorovna Kotelnikova appears on the threshold. She's wearing a lavender polar fleece muumuu decorated with stylized martini glasses and white tennis shoes without laces. She is fatter than she was in her barrel days but essentially unchanged. Sasha can still see Katia's and Alexey's handsome features in her ruddy face.

"Oh, who do I *see*?" Natalia Egorovna bellows theatrically. "Sasha! The American! Lenka, come here!"

A round-faced young woman in fishnet stockings and a denim miniskirt walks out of the kitchen. Her short hair is bleached yellow, with black roots.

"This is Lena, Alyosha's wife," says Natalia Egorovna.

Sasha feels something inside her deflate, like a punctured balloon. But only for a second.

"*Zdravstvuyte*," the young woman says formally.

"Sasha was Katia's friend, back in Siberia. Katia doesn't live here, Sashenka. Stay with us to drink tea?"

Sasha sits down at a small table. The apartment doesn't look any bigger than the barrel, but at least all the walls are straight. A huge flat-screen TV stands in the corner, contrasting wildly with the rest of the meager décor.

"Katia's present," Natalia Egorovna says proudly, reaching for the remote. "Katia is a newscaster. Every time she's on, it's like having her right here. She did well for herself."

On TV, Beavis and Butthead scream at each other in Russian overdub.

"Do you like Beavis?" Lena asks flatly. "I don't think it's very funny."

"It's not," agrees Sasha, and Lena smiles for the first time. The entire top row of her teeth is made of gold.

They sip tea in oppressive silence. Natalia Egorovna wants to know if American men always put their feet on the table, but then runs out of questions.

"This is really good doctor's sausage, Mama," Lena says quietly, sinking her gold teeth into a thick slab of bologna. She seems totally indifferent toward Sasha's Americanness, and Sasha can't help but be a little hurt. She's forgotten bologna's Russian name—doctor's sausage—and now she considers it spitefully. Is doctor's sausage supposed to make people healthy?

"We don't have a phone here, Sasha," Natalia Egorovna finally says. "Do you have a *mobilnik*?"

"No." Sasha realizes that by not having a cell phone she has further undermined her American authenticity in the Kotelnikovs' eyes. She is amazed by how much it bothers her.

"I'm just thinking you should call Katia directly. She doesn't visit here very often. She's busy," explains Natalia Egorovna.

Sasha takes this as a hint that she should go. Besides, she has to catch her plane in five hours.

"So, how is Alexey?" she asks as casually as she can, getting up from the table.

"Oh, he's good. Working construction. By the way, he'll be here soon. Why doesn't he give you a ride back to Tula?"

"Alyosha bought a car," Lena adds proudly.

"Katia helped him buy a car," corrects Natalia Egorovna. "I don't know what we'd do without that girl."

Lena rolls her eyes. "Alyosha makes good money," she says.

Watching the Kotelnikov family tensions erupt to the surface makes Sasha squirm. This is a good time to say goodbye.

"All right," she says, sitting back down. "I'll wait."

An hour later, Alexey still hasn't come home. Sasha sits on the Kotelnikovs' greasy sofa, biting her nails and hating herself. At least she doesn't have to speak. Lena and Natalia Egorovna stare at the TV, transfixed by an episode of a *telenovela*. One monotonous male voice does all the Russian dubbing, but when somebody cries or shouts, Sasha can hear the Spanish in the background, like voices of ghosts. She realizes that she may as well wait for Alexey. If she takes public transportation she'll miss her flight anyway.

In her agitation she doesn't hear the key in the door, doesn't notice Alexey until he is standing directly in front of her.

"Look who came to visit!" exclaims Natalia Egorovna. "You remember Sasha?"

Alexey looks taller than Sasha remembers, stronger. He has a wide workman's face. Scratching his head, he stares at Sasha with a mute look of played-up piety. Just the face Mrs. Stepanova used to make when she drank her supercharged water, bits of newspaper pulp floating in the jar. *Ivan the Idiot*, thinks Sasha. Still, she is captivated by his hands and face. She waits to feel limp and willess, like back in seventh grade. Is this why she has come here, to test her body's memory?

"Actually, I just came to say hello," she says. "I have to catch my flight."

"I'll drive you to the airport," Alexey says slowly.

"Oh, if you just take me to Tula, I'll make it," Sasha lies for Lena's benefit. He'll have to drive her straight to Moscow, and *fast*.

Alexey's car is a dark-blue boxy Zhiguli with a missing window and a puddle of rainwater on the back seat. Alexey slides Sasha's bag past the puddle and opens the front passenger door.

"You've changed," he says, turning the key in the ignition. He looks like a cartoon giraffe stuffed into the laughably small car. Steering with his knees, he wiggles out of his jacket and lights a cigarette. Under the jacket, he wears a yellow angora sweater tucked into high-waisted black jeans. The sweater says WYOMING. His belt buckle is a golden shell.

"You look like God's Fool," says Sasha, all the tension of the last two hours pouring into one sentence.

Alexey laughs. He seems to take it as a compliment.

They drive in silence for a while. Even though she doesn't know her way around Moscow, Sasha realizes that they aren't driving to the airport but instead going back into the city. Concrete apartment blocks give way to older brick buildings, the stores turn fancier, the traffic thicker. Every few blocks, Sasha notices McDonald's golden arches.

"Where are you going?" she asks, panicking.

"I thought you might want to see the city. A car tour."

"My plane leaves in *three* hours," Sasha says. Heidi urged her to spend more money on a ticket with an open departure date, but she refused, buying the cheapest ticket instead. "Do you understand *time*?"

"Time can wait," says Alexey. "Look."

Sasha takes a deep breath and stares out the window.

She's never been in the front seat of a car in Moscow. She always took buses, where the windows were on the sides. Now she notices that every major road in the city leads to a church. Is this what Alexey wants her to see? The golden domes glisten in blue sky at the ends of traffic corridors like Lena's teeth, scattered.

"Your wife is very proud of you for buying this car," Sasha says.

Alexey pulls over to the curb and stops. "I want you to see this."

"What, this?" They're parked in front of a restaurant called the Bear's Den. By the restaurant's door, Sasha sees a semi-abstract sculpture of a galloping horse, artfully twisted out of swirling bronze noodles. It's the kind of outdoor sculpture that makes Sasha wonder why anyone bothered to make it. A tree or some empty space would be easier on the eye.

"I know this artist," Alexey says. "He is like a teacher of mine. I helped him work on this. I wanted to show it to you."

What attraction Sasha felt just a minute ago abates, leaving her tearful with annoyance.

"It's very nice," she says, remembering the scratchy charcoal drawings and garbage sculptures from Alexey's barrel days, the portrait of Katia above his bed. She can't believe he's brought her all the way here to look at this heavy noodle mess.

"Listen, I have to get to the airport. If I miss my flight, I have no money to buy another ticket."

"I missed *you.*"

"What about Lena?" Sasha asks, keeping her eyes on the horse.

She is still afraid that if she looks at Alexey's face, into his opaque gray eyes, her body will attach itself to his like a parasite, and she'll never make it back to Brooklyn. Alexey ignores her question.

"Why do you wear that thing on your head?" he asks.

"People stare."

Alexey unties the knot on Sasha's neck and lifts her shawl, running his hand over her braids. She closes her eyes and lets him kiss her. His hand travels along her hair, touching it gently, but all Sasha feels is heat and discomfort. Her hair is soaked with sweat and her head itches. Her knee is painfully pressed against the gearshift. Alexey's kiss feels too hard, suffocating, wrong.

Sasha turns away and opens her eyes. The noodle horse is still there, but she doesn't need it anymore.

"I wrote to you," Alexey says.

"I just found out. My mother hid your letters."

"You had my child."

"She looks like you."

"I've seen pictures."

"She lives with my mother."

"I know."

"I need to go home."

"*Home?*" his sarcastic voice, which Sasha used to hate, now sounds endearing and pathetic.

"What do you want me to do, stick around and be your second wife? Drive me to the airport."

"I didn't think you were ever coming back," Alexey says quietly, touching her hand. "You're so different from everything . . . here."

Sasha is surprised by the longing in his voice. She realizes that this is the most straightforward Alexey has ever been. He does understand time. Sasha understands it, too, and suddenly time is *all* she understands. She sees Alexey with the eyes of a statistician. She sees an out-of-towner without a Moscow-region residence permit, a second-class citizen with an unloved wife, trapped between vodka, television, and a construction job. No amount of vague poetics and graphomania can keep the trapdoor from closing, the lines of lost drawings from turning into bronze noodles, and Alexey from becoming a face of a public health problem, *a Russian man, life expectancy fifty-something,* looking for an escape in Sasha's hair and skin, in her pathetic two years of *elsewhere.*

Sasha wants to tell him that her difference is superficial. It's just in the texture. *Look at this sculpture,* she is tempted to say. *For all of its bronze macaroni, it's still a bronze stupid horse, on a stone pedestal, like the other countless bronze horses.*

"You used to say 'I don't know' all the time," she finally says. "You were right. There are things I wish I could fix, but I don't know how. I used to think I'd come back to Asbestos 2 and get my baby. I used to love you, and now I don't. Please drive, or I'm taking the metro."

Alexey pulls away from the curb so fast that the back of Sasha's head hits the headrest, and her braids whip around her face. She grabs the dashboard, afraid of what he might do. But once they're in traffic, he drives carefully.

"Where are your seat belts?" Sasha asks.

"I took them off."

"Why?"

"They're a hassle. They get in the way," Alexey explains, switching on the windshield wipers.

The raindrops stretch into brown streaks on the dusty glass.

Looking over his shoulder, Alexey throws his arm around the back of Sasha's seat, and Sasha fights the desire to lean her head into the crook of his elbow. They're making good progress. She'll make her flight.

They pass a Sanyo billboard, and behind it Sasha sees a roadside war memorial: two rusted anti-tank "hedgehogs" on a slab of granite. Beneath the monument, in a cruel rain, a wedding is in progress. The groom in a black tuxedo holds an umbrella over the bride, who is sitting in her frothy white dress astride a wet live camel. The priest has neither an umbrella nor a camel, and his bologna-colored face looks pinched and miserable.

In the airport Sasha tries to hug Alexey, but he remains behind the wheel, staring straight ahead. Sasha gets out of the car, furious at herself for attempting the absurd American "still friends" behavior. Alexey drives away as soon as she shuts the door.

"It is not my fault!" Sasha yells, shaking her fist at a battered Plymouth that takes Alexey's spot at the curb.

These are the things I forgot to tell you.

By the time I found out I was pregnant, I'd stopped expecting your letters. I felt jilted but not really sad—I was looking forward to Repin. But I wanted to get the address of your army unit to let you know that I'd be having a baby, and that my mother would be keeping it. So I went back to the barrel village.

As soon as I got off the bus, I noticed that something was different. The kiosk was gone. There was a bulldozer parked in the grass at the edge of the forest and fresh tracks in the mud between the power lines.

I heard the sounds of engines by the junkyard. There was a flatbed truck and a crane parked in front of the barrels. I couldn't tell what was going on until I saw two men tying steel cable to rebar rings on the roof of number four. I sat down nearby and watched the half-pipes sail one by one through the air. They were still painted and wallpapered on the inside.

I thought about your mother moving into her new apartment, trying out the appliances, hanging curtains. I couldn't picture Alufiev doing the same. Maybe he was still around, hiding somewhere in the forest.

It took the workers all day to get to number two. When they were done I went back to the bus stop. I felt really pregnant then, weighed down and dumb.

I wanted a souvenir, so I went back the next week. The construction crew had moved on to clearing the junkyard. I wondered if the railroad was finally coming here.

It had rained over the weekend, and the barrels' footprints had turned into rectangular pools of mud. I walked around, stepping carefully on scattered boards. People left nothing. I suppose they were too poor to leave things behind. I found a broken bottle, a dented aluminum mug, a length of rusted chain. I couldn't recognize any of it as belonging to you, or Alufiev, or anybody at all. Floating in the mud, the objects looked recently unearthed, like archaeological finds.

I walked over to Alufiev's secret burial spot, picked up a sharp-edged board, and began to dig. At first there was nothing. Alufiev had taken his icons with him, wherever he went. But then the board hit something soft. I put it down and continued to dig with my hands. The thing I found in the hole was a bundle of rotted fabric and plastic bags. I unraveled the bundle. I was happy when it got smaller, no longer the size of a dead infant. I was beginning to think that the bundle was empty when I found the money inside. There were five ten-ruble bills from who knows how many reforms ago. They were large and thin like paper napkins. I'd never seen this kind of money before.

I dropped the bills back into the hole. The wind shifted them around like flower petals.

The bus didn't come for the longest time. Sitting on a gas pipe, I felt the baby move. It felt like a bird flapping, trapped inside of me.

"Home?" you said.

I watched your home sail through the air like a giant eggshell.

5

Four Years Later

SOMETIME IN THE LATE AFTERNOON, THE HALFHEARTED drizzle changed into a fierce November rainstorm, and by the time Sasha Goldberg dragged the trash bags out to the stoop, the gargoyles flanking the brownstone's door were wearing caps of dead leaves. Sasha dumped the garbage into the trash can and checked her watch. She should have told Jonathan to meet her later. Sasha always spent longer than expected cleaning this house because the family that lived here liked to write notes. "Would you kindly mind washing dishes? Many thanks." "Would you look for Isobel's ballet slipper? I'm afraid she threw it behind the dryer. Many thanks." Today, Sasha kindly cleaned the cat vomit out of the guest bedroom rug, many thanks, and now she wondered if Jonathan would be angry with her for being late. If they would get into a fight again.

Sasha had met Jonathan a few months earlier, in the summer. She was working as a studio assistant for her Educational Alliance drawing instructor Anatoly Ivanovich Opekunoff. Mr. Opekunoff was just the type of person who'd spell his name with a double *f*, like some early-twentieth-century exiled monarchist. Twice a week, Sasha took a break from cleaning houses to stretch and prime Mr. Opekunoff's canvases, and at night her nightmares filled with his paintings.

Mr. Opekunoff called himself "a master of the female form." Most of his creations bulged with breasts: hips as breasts, knees as breasts, two rows of breasts down the front. Swollen breastbeasts devoured puny two-headed Anatoly Ivanoviches in epic, sepia-toned canvases.

Sasha felt sorry for the building that housed Mr. Opekunoff, a stylishly renovated former warehouse on the Brooklyn waterfront that was now festering with awful art. Down the hall from Anatoly Ivanovich, a raven-haired woman painted chalky acrylic portraits of a rubber chicken. A grizzled old biker made towers of bottle caps. Glitter-coated toilet plungers figured prominently in the collaborative sculptures of two willowy punks. The artists' statement tacked to their door said that they were dealing with the issues of childhood abuse. What Anatoly Ivanovich's issues were, Sasha was afraid to imagine.

Her least favorite part of her job was the semiannual Open Studio Day, when Mr. Opekunoff's studio inexplicably filled with drunk overdressed French women who called him "Anatole." Sasha couldn't understand where Anatoly Ivanovich had amassed such a following, but he certainly knew how to captivate them. Dressed in a broad-shouldered black tuxedo, he paced the studio, filling the air with words like "passion," "folly," and "desire." It was Sasha's job to ensure a sufficient supply of wine, cheese, and gold-bordered *Atelier Opekunoff* business cards.

Halfway through the June Open Studio Day, Sasha Goldberg fled outside to have a cigarette. She was resting her breast-weary eyes on the Brooklyn Bridge when a boy asked her for a light. He had messy blond curls and a full beard that made his face look especially young. In his vintage denim jacket and plaid polyester trousers he radiated the kind of hipness Sasha Goldberg could never hope to replicate or even approximate. Looking at the ballpoint-pen doodles on his sleeves, she asked if he was an artist.

To her great relief he said no, he just worked at the Other Bean, the fancy chocolatier around the corner. He was also in a band. Sasha asked if he knew about Selfish Vegan.

"I *love* Vegan! You met Eric? He's, like, *God*! How do you know him?"

"My stepmom has been dating him off and on, like, her entire *life*," said Sasha. "I think she's with him again, now that she divorced my dad."

Sasha wondered if all foreigners inadvertently mirrored the speech mannerisms of others, or if it was her own particular tic. Like a perpetual baby, she

learned by imitation. After six years in the U.S., English still felt almost al-
chemical, impossible. Every conversation pulled her out of her muteness
anew, and she followed the other's voice like EXIT signs. Sometimes it was a
happy and effortless journey. Talking to Jonathan, she felt queasy, as if someone had spun her around and let go. Maybe it was just the cigarette.

He had invited her to hear his music, but she had to leave for Asbestos 2
the next day. She had been spending two weeks there every summer, and this
would be her fourth visit. She wrote down Jonathan's number and promised
to call him when she returned.

Fifty kilos of buckwheat, a hundred cans of Spam, twenty sacks of flour, and
twelve tubs of Crisco had been delivered to Third Road Street before Sasha
Goldberg finally recognized her features in her daughter's face.

"Mama is in the garden. She's going to die soon!" seven-year-old Nadia
announced, grabbing at the handle of Sasha's suitcase. It was her lips and
chin, Sasha decided. Nadia had grown at least three inches since the previous
summer. She still had straw-yellow hair and Alexey's gray eyes, but her skin
now glowed like honey against her baby-blue GIRLS RULE T-shirt. Anywhere
but in Asbestos 2, the kid would tan.

"Wait a minute, what did you just say?" Sasha asked.

"Sasha?"

Mrs. Goldberg had cut off her hair. Blinking away jet lag, Sasha stared at
the half-moons of bluish skin above her mother's ears.

"It's easier that way," Mrs. Goldberg rasped, and Sasha screamed.

It took asbestos fibers fifty years to work through Lubov Alexandrovna's
lungs.

"Nobody knew any better," she explained, reminiscing how as a girl she
played King of the Hill on a gleaming slag heap by the mill.

She could only whisper now, and her hoarse voice along with her severe
makeup reminded Sasha of cabaret singers.

"You have snakes," said Nadia.

Sasha's own hair was now down to her shoulders, matted into thick
dreadlocks that she gathered in the back with an elastic band. She didn't need
to cover it anymore. Dreadlocks acquired a Russian name, *dredi.* In Moscow,

they were considered cool, and *Negri* were cool, and so was *heep*-hop. Black bodies twirled and danced in Russian music videos.

Sasha pulled off the elastic and let Nadia handle the snakes.

Mrs. Goldberg rolled her eyes, as if Sasha's hair were indicative of some approaching Armageddon. Sitting in a town with barely any food, running water, or electricity, Sasha wanted to say that her mother picked the wrong indicator.

"Shouldn't you go to the hospital?" she asked instead.

"I will, when the time comes. You go into one of those places and you never come out." Mrs. Goldberg dumped a bunch of whitish carrots into the sink.

"Maybe we could go to Moscow, get you chemo."

Sasha barely knew what she was talking about, but saying these things made her feel better, like she was taking care of business, not just sitting there dumbly watching her mother die. She wondered what was wrong with her. She was losing a mother, but she felt angry, as if she were losing an argument.

"Sasha, what's going to happen to Mama?" Nadia asked that night.

"What do you mean?"

"When she dies."

"She'll go in the ground."

"But for real?"

"That's all I know," Sasha said stubbornly, wondering if Nadia expected her to mention heaven. Even in the face of death, the divine made Sasha think only of taxidermy.

Straight-backed and proud like her grandmother, Nadia intimidated Sasha. Before every visit, Sasha spent days shopping for toys, but Nadia never took them out of their packages. She liked to admire them through the plastic, to keep them tied to the cardboard, trapped in perfection: a Barbie hovering above a two-dimensional armchair, her raised arm forever reaching for a butterfly-shaped hairbrush; a family of teddy bears petrified in a pink carrying case. Sasha wanted to liberate the prisoners, to teach Nadia how to play. If these had been Sasha's toys, they would've been loved, destroyed, and lost.

After Mrs. Goldberg's death, Nadia would be coming to Brooklyn. Sasha admitted to herself that she was afraid of inheriting her. It was like being asked to drive a forklift or speak Japanese. It didn't seem like something she could just fake.

At the end of Sasha's visit, they said their goodbyes at home. Mrs. Goldberg was too weak to walk to the bus station.

"Are you sure you'll be all right? Don't you want me to stay?" asked Sasha.

"We'll be fine, won't we, Nadiusha?" croaked Mrs. Goldberg.

They had been rehearsing. Once again, Sasha watched them repeat their routine. If Mrs. Goldberg passed out, Nadia would bang on the radiator, summoning Tetya Vera from downstairs. It seemed to Sasha that her mother was anxious for her to go away, that she couldn't bear another pair of eyes on her weakness. In the shadow of the District Soviet, Sasha waited for the bus alone, feeling useless, orphaned, and angry at herself because she couldn't cry.

Back at Avenue U, she called Heidi's number, but hung up before Heidi had a chance to pick up the phone. After she'd divorced Victor, Heidi remained close with Sasha. At times, she acted almost maternal, as if Sasha's well-being in New York were her responsibility. Now that Sasha could use the support, she realized that she dreaded Heidi's insistent, suffocating compassion.

An American Spirit cigarette box sat by the phone. Sasha stared at the number scribbled on yellow cardboard. She'd forgotten all about Jonathan during her trip, but now she craved the company of a stranger to save her from waiting alone on Avenue U at night. She was also hoping that as a musician, Jonathan would be able to get her stoned often and for free.

Jonathan's band was called Lecherous Doormen. Sasha wondered if the structure of the name, a noun plus a negative attribute, was an homage to Selfish Vegan. She promised to introduce Jonathan to Eric.

Since Victor had moved out, Eric was constantly on Heidi's couch, half naked with a beer, his pale belly sagging over his low-rise jeans, pierced nipples pointing down like two sad beaks. He was enrolled in three 12-step programs and liked to call himself "has-been" and "washed up." Apparently not to Jonathan.

"Are you kidding? Vegan is, like, perfection itself! You should see how much their old records go for on eBay!"

The Doormen sang about growing up in Michigan, about video games, skateboarding, and teenage confusion. Jonathan tried to explain the lyrics to Sasha, but every time he opened his mouth, she stopped listening. *Do you know Hardees? Commodore 64? Toughskins? Sunny Delight?* She couldn't make herself care. She felt as if she were watching Jonathan through a pane of glass, seeing his lips move in silence.

After months of being his girlfriend, Sasha was still fuzzy as to what an Atari was and how it was different from Nintendo. She stubbornly refused to see the original *Star Wars*, which for some reason plunged Jonathan into despair.

"You aren't interested in me," he complained.

"I just don't care for science fiction," said Sasha.

He was right, she wasn't interested, though she very much wanted to be. By all accounts, Jonathan was hot. Every Friday night, in a cavernous Williamsburg bar, Sasha heard beautiful women with postmodern earrings describe Jonathan as "hot." These were husband-hunting women in their early thirties, with precision makeup and expensively messy haircuts, and Sasha trusted their judgment.

Jonathan looked good onstage, more a dancer than a singer, his body all delicate, broken angles, his beltless pants down at his hips, his vintage T-shirts hugging his concave chest in a maximally sensual way. ELMBROOK JUNIOR HIGH, PETE'S BURGERS, STARSHIP FANTASY ARCADE.

Loving him could have been Sasha's final conquest of America, its culture, its geography as far as Michigan. If only she could stop *picking fights*.

When Jonathan mentioned reading *Catcher in the Rye* in high school, Sasha called Holden Caulfield a brat.

When he talked about growing up the only Jewish kid in his town, Sasha hurried to explain that she had it worse. "But you aren't Jewish!" protested Jonathan, provoking a screaming, breathless lecture. Angrily, Sasha revisited the subject again and again. She even used the phrase "the core of my identity," though it set her ears on fire.

She laid into him for his simple-minded delight in Communist kitsch. They were wandering through a flea market one Saturday, and Jonathan bought her a Lenin pin.

"Don't show me this thing," Sasha snapped. "It reminds me of school-yard bullies."

Was it a matter of their misaligned nostalgias?

"My mother is dying of cancer," she told him that night.

"Oh, my God. I'm so sorry."

"But I don't feel anything."

"Do you want me to hold you?" he asked, pressing his face between her shoulder blades. They were stoned, and he was getting horny.

"No. It doesn't help," said Sasha. Sex with Jonathan made her feel like a pinball machine, a collection of touchdown points. She dreamed of tying him down to the bed, to keep him from moving.

"You can talk to me," Jonathan said before he let go.

Sasha turned away and closed her eyes. Her ears buzzed and her head felt weightless like a Christmas ornament, but when she fell asleep her dreams came vivid and stifling, solid as memories. A tall child with a shaved head stood in a cafeteria line, holding an aluminum bowl in one hand. From the back, Sasha couldn't tell if it was a boy or a girl.

She was never stoned enough to tell Jonathan about Nadia.

She would never admit to anyone that she felt ready to abandon her child again. That, after compulsively checking her voice mail for the news of her mother's death, she stroked the rubbery power button of her cell phone and fantasized about turning it off once and for all. That way, Tetya Vera wouldn't be able to reach her, her mother would never die, and Nadia would forever remain a skinny seven-year-old in a GIRLS RULE T-shirt waving from the top of the stairs on Third Road Street.

In the morning, Sasha Goldberg washed orphanage dreams out of her eyes with ice-cold water. She knew that when she came out of the bathroom, she would have to engage in a conversation about the relative merits of different places to get brunch. She didn't want to seem indifferent, because her indifference upset Jonathan.

Later that day, Jonathan finally met Eric. Heidi hadn't closed the blinds, and when Sasha went outside to smoke, she could see the entire apartment through the window: Heidi in the kitchen, Ben on the couch curled around *Harry Potter*, Jonathan and Eric by the stereo, clutching their identical beer bottles like microphones. Suddenly Sasha was happy. It felt natural to be standing alone in the dark, looking from the outside in. The thick warped glass of Heidi's window was a comfort. Sasha stayed outside a long time, and when Heidi finally came looking for her, she felt like hiding.

When they went back to Jonathan's apartment that night, Sasha told him that they needed to "take a break." He agreed, but now, two months later, he had called her on her birthday. She was touched that he'd remembered. "I missed you," he'd said. "I hope you're feeling better. Want to get a coffee sometime?"

Sasha ran up the subway stairs and checked her phone. Someone had left a message. For a few seconds, Sasha held the phone in her gloved hand, afraid to press the button. She imagined tossing the phone into a trash can. How much longer would it be before she did that? She held her breath and checked the message. It was from Jonathan, who was also running late because "the fucking place flooded again." The Other Bean had sensitive plumbing.

They were meeting not far from Heidi's house in a place called Glow. Sasha opened the door, saw a bulletin board, and dug in her bag for a flyer.

Feng Shui Maids Natural Cleaning
Gentle, effective cleaning
WITHOUT TOXIC CHEMICALS
Safe for Children and Pets
Four years in Brownstone Brooklyn!

Feng Shui Maids had been Heidi's idea. After the divorce, Heidi finished her dissertation, got a new teaching job, and finally succumbed to the culture of her neighborhood. She signed up for yoga classes, joined the Park Slope Food Co-op, and began revising the contents of Sasha's granny cart, replacing Comet with Organic Seashell Tub Scrub and tossing out Mr. Clean to make room for WholeEarth Citrus Soap. Sasha was skeptical at first. She had a weakness for chlorine: if you used enough, you could make the dirt *disappear*.

"Trust me," said Heidi, "just do it for a month."

It was also Heidi's idea to adorn the flyer with a Chinese ink painting of a mountainside stream, to put the name in plural, and to charge an outrageous $25 an hour. Heidi thought Sasha could make even more, if only she wore an unbleached cotton uniform, but Sasha drew the line. She did cleaning, not theater, she told Heidi.

Sasha Goldberg pushed a pin into the corkboard and suddenly remembered hanging her very first flyer in this space years ago. Glow was the new incarnation of the Fallen Leaf Café. The new owners carted away the stained couches and the basket of frightening toys, replacing them with angular plastic tables and chairs. Glow specialized in electric-colored drinks with edible glitter. A blond toddler in one of the chairs appeared to be drinking Windex.

Squeezing into a diminutive orange booth in the window alcove, Sasha glanced at a group of mothers who sat in a circle around a low table. All of them were at least a decade older than she. All were slender, small-boned, and pale, with floppy dark hair. Most carried infants in identical black pouches strapped to their chests. Sasha pictured them bouncing around Glow in their high-tech sneakers like a herd of kangaroos.

She surveyed the tiny feet dangling from the carriers. A bald baby girl wore pink socks with a black design that made it look as if she were wearing Mary Janes. The clever socks reaffirmed the familiar dread in Sasha, made her think of Nadia again. How could she care for a child she feared?

Some of the mothers in the group looked up, and Sasha realized that she'd been staring. She averted her eyes. She was sure that the mothers were silently chiding her for even *trying* to be of the same species as they. *You're missing something, Goldberg,* their looks seemed to say. *We're different animals. Our love dangles on our chests like a parachute, weighs down our shoulders. We instinctively touch its tiny feet to make sure it's still there. Where is your love? What color socks does it wear?*

"Sorry I'm late." Jonathan threw his messenger bag on the chair and looked around. "Oh, my God, Gob Stoppers!" he yelled, pointing at a row of gumball machines in the corner. "And check it out, Nerds! This place's *sweet!*"

As soon as she saw him, Sasha knew it was hopeless, that she'd find a way to start a fight. Jonathan was wearing his Mao T-shirt. The black outline of the chairman's face smiled from the red star on his chest.

"Are you wearing this to annoy me?"

Jonathan's face sagged. "Please don't give me a hard time," he said softly, sitting down. "Why do you care so much about a dumb T-shirt?"

Sasha shook her head. She didn't care all that much, but around Jonathan she wore her half-baked historical sensitivity like a suit of armor.

"Want some candy?" Jonathan asked, digging in his pocket for a quarter.

"No, thanks. This place is stupid. It'll be out of business in a month."

"Come on, have a sense of humor."

Sasha had never met anyone who managed to be so well lit so much of the time. Even on cloudy days, Jonathan attracted slanting rays to his luxurious beard, his cheekbones, and his long fingers, as if nature itself wanted him to star in a Jesus movie. Watching his face in a tunnel of dusty sunlight, Sasha felt anger set in like bad weather, unavoidable and anticipated.

"Do you find it humorous to parade around with a despot on your chest?" she asked.

"Sasha . . ." Jonathan looked tired.

Sasha wondered if he was finally giving up on her. Maybe that was why he wore the Mao shirt. She realized she sounded petty and insane, but couldn't stop. If she couldn't cry for her mother, if she couldn't love her child, the least she could do was stick up for the dead victims of Mao Tse-tung.

"Have you ever starved, Jonathan?"

"Oh, fuck. Have *you*? This is a big load of crap, Sasha. I asked if you wanted to talk, but obviously you aren't up for it. Call me when you want to see me again."

The electric door chime celebrated Jonathan's departure with a jingle.

Sasha Goldberg watched him walk toward the subway and felt as if she were trying to follow someone else's tedious story and could barely keep track of the characters' names.

Three days later, Sasha stood in Heidi's kitchen, leafing through a *Healing Techniques* book on the counter. On the cover, the ubiquitous Da Vinci man stretched in his circle, except this time he was a woman. Sasha and Heidi were discussing a lesson plan. For a year now, on Saturday mornings, they had been teaching a Painting and Meditation class in Prospect Park. In the summer, it was called Plein Air and Meditation, and in the fall Heidi renamed it Meditation and Foliage.

Heidi was responsible for the meditation part. She arranged the students in a wide circle and made them sit silently and breathe deeply before they began painting.

"*Feel the park!*" she told them. "Let's mimic the landscape with our bodies!"

The women complied. With their arms spread, craning their necks in circular motions, they looked like seagulls at Coney Island, if the seagulls had a prayer meeting. Sasha checked the brushes, prepared the watercolor sets, and taped the sheets of paper to the drawing boards.

After the meditation, it was her turn to do the mimicking. She pretended to be Evgeny Mikhailovich. Ambushing the ladies from behind, she shouted, "What have you *done?*" with such force as to make them jump.

If she was honest with herself, Sasha had to admit that she admired the way art was taught in the U.S. Here, art students followed their interests, picking up the necessary skills along the way. She resented AFTER EATIN for making her into a trained monkey with a collection of tricks. But in her landscape class she felt compelled to put on a show and spread the evil around.

"Use your *eyes!* Is this what you *see?*" she moaned with a disgusted look on her face. She did it in honor of Evgeny Mikhailovich, of Bedbug, of their useless, forgotten socialist realism. She enjoyed playing a bad cop to Heidi's good cop, being the Foliage Ladies' *strict foreign teacher.*

Demographically, the Plein Air and Meditation students were a time progression of the Glow's mothers' group. Once, a woman whose house Sasha cleaned signed up for a class. The woman attended one session and never came again. She also told Sasha that she had found a new housekeeper. *Natural selection,* thought Sasha, but Heidi kept insisting that this wouldn't have happened if Sasha were a little more gentle.

"Sasha, you've got to go easier on them," she said, setting down *Healing Techniques.*

"I thought they wanted to *learn,*" Sasha whined. She knew that no matter what she did, the woman would have left. People didn't want their housekeepers teaching them landscape painting. It was too confusing. Sasha judged Heidi a coward for pretending not to understand this.

"Not necessarily," replied Heidi. "But you do want to get paid. You've got to stop being so *angry*. Anyway, I was thinking next week we should try these breathing exercises," she said, pointing at the book.

"Sounds good." Sasha yawned. "And the week after that, we should make them gather garbage in the Long Meadow. The city will thank us."

Heidi finally laughed.

"And yes, I admit to being angry," conceded Sasha. "I saw Jonathan the other day, and we got into a fight again. I got mad about something so stupid, I can't even remember what it was."

"Jonathan is cute," Heidi said. "But he isn't a good match for you."

"What do you mean?"

"Intellectually, Sasha. I think he's a bit of an airhead. And you're dealing with a lot of complex—"

"*Issues, tissues, excretions,*" Sasha intoned. She liked to watch Heidi deflate. "Give it a rest."

"Which reminds me," sighed Heidi, "some guy called about you."

"Somebody called *here*?"

"Yeah. Asking all about you. I was going to give him your number but he said he didn't want it. He just wanted to know how you were. I thought—"

"Was he Russian?"

"No, I think he was American. He had a weird voice."

Three years ago, newly computer-literate, Sasha Goldberg had found Jake's e-mail address on Heidi's old hard drive. *Are you there?* she'd typed. Her message was returned, recipient unknown. Sasha Googled him, but Jake Tarakan didn't exist online. The only mention of him was on a medical site that reported the effects of orthopedic surgery on children with cerebral palsy. She touched his name on the screen like some digital amulet. It made her feel safe, but guilty at the same time, as if the monitor were a room and she an intruder.

"Heidi, did he leave his number?"

"Not intentionally. The caller ID picked it up. I wrote it down somewhere."

Heidi always wrote things down on receipts, price tags, and flaps of junk mail envelopes.

"Find it."

"Sasha, he called two weeks ago, I have no—"

"Find his number, Heidi!"

Heidi laughed.

"What?" Ben yelled from his room.

"I lost the number of Sasha's secret admirer and she's about to kill me!"

"He was the guy who helped me find you. He e-mailed you, remember?"

"Oh, then I should definitely find his number. I'm going to call him and thank him for destroying my marriage!" Heidi laughed again.

"Heidi, please!"

"If I'm going to find his number for you, I want to hear the whole story!"

"There's no story. I worked for his parents."

"The religious freaks with all the dead animals," Heidi said, digging in the drawer underneath the microwave cart. "You never mentioned him before, and now you're acting like a twelve-year-old with a crush. Were you in love with this guy?"

"He was just a friend," said Sasha. "He has CP or something like that. He's in a wheelchair," she offered as evidence.

"Here, found it." Heidi handed Sasha a crumpled *New Yorker* subscription card. All traces of interest were safely gone from her voice.

Jake had a Manhattan area code. Sasha dialed the number as soon as Heidi closed the door behind her and almost hung up when the machine picked up. It was a recording of a digitized male voice. Sasha had heard this man on so many answering machines, it seemed everyone she knew lived in the same house, and he was the concierge. The machine beeped.

"Jake, this is Sasha. I want to hear *your* voice."

The machine beeped again.

"Hey," Jake said. The speakerphone made him sound as if he were talking from a cathedral or a cave. Sasha could hear the TV in the background.

"I want to see you," Sasha said.

"When?"

Sasha was silent.

"I'm not doing anything for the rest of the week."

"Can I see you now?"

"Sure."

Jake lived on the Upper West Side, on the twelfth floor of an ugly, white-tiled tower. His apartment had low ceilings and gray wall-to-wall carpeting, but one of the living room walls was all glass.

"Wow," said Sasha, squinting into the orange sunset. "This is just like your parents' house."

"I never thought about it that way. I guess you're right. The view is different."

Jake had glasses now, but his face was unchanged, pale and boyish. He wore a button-up shirt and blue jeans, the same plain conservative clothes he'd worn in high school. With his dark eyes behind the frameless lenses and his soft black hair, he resembled the frail young Hasids that Sasha always saw on the train on the way to her father's new apartment in Borough Park, the types that looked like they had been reared underground. Sasha checked her reflection in window glass. She looked years older than Jake now. Maybe she always had.

"I like your glasses," she said, looking for a place to sit down. Except for the TV on a low table, a stack of books in the corner, and a bed in the next room, the apartment was empty. It occurred to Sasha that Jake had no use for furniture. Now that she was standing in front of him, she felt exposed, as if she were about to be tested on her body language, her posture, and her thoughts.

"You look great, too," Jake said flatly. "I was over at my parents' this summer sorting through some old files and found Heidi's number. So I called. I was curious about what happened to you."

"What are you doing in New York?"

"Law school. I just started at Columbia."

"Wow." Sasha thought about Marina, who had finally achieved her dream and was now on scholarship at Yale.

"What about you?" Jake asked.

Sasha considered how to give her life an Ivy League spin.

"I got my GED and started college last year, at Kingsborough. Until then I just worked, though I took some art classes and taught art, too. I also assist this really terrible artist, prepare his canvases and clean his studio. But for the most part I'm still a cleaning lady. 'Feng Shui Maids—Clean Up for the Millennium!'"

Jake laughed. Sasha took off her jacket and sat down cross-legged on the floor. One of her shoelaces was untied.

"See, your mom set me on a career path," she said, looking around. "Do you live alone? Where is José?"

"José left the same year you did. He had some family problems in Mexico. I think his wife was cheating on him."

"José was married?"

"Not just married. Last I knew, he had five kids. Every year he'd go on vacation and the following year his wife would have another baby."

"What a life. How could they stand it?"

"You know. The same way you were able to stand your life. My parents were paying him well. Plus, he and I grew weed in mom's mausoleum. . . ."

"You and José grew weed where?"

"Oh"—Jake laughed—"before I was born, mom set up this enormous playroom. It had a nine foot tall F.A.O. Schwarz bear, a train set, and an easel, and every other imaginable toy. I couldn't play with any of it, for obvious reasons, but Mom kept the setup intact, sort of a temple of shattered hopes. Jason first called it a mausoleum—a clever name, coming from Jason, though rather cruel. He used to grow weed in there before he moved out."

"Where was it? I've never—"

"See, the beautiful thing about the mausoleum was that you could only enter it through my room. So it was entirely in José's domain. Although Mom insisted on preserving it as it was, she never actually set foot in there. It was a perfect place to grow weed. I sold it at school and split the money with José. He was the economic engine of his entire village. He built them a swimming pool. Last I heard, he married his ex-wife's little sister and moved to Minneapolis. A happy ending, I guess. In college I lived with this other guy, who was a total disaster."

Sasha bent down to tie her shoe. She noticed that every time she moved, Jake stopped speaking. She could feel his stare on her neck and arms, and it was making her forget how to tie laces. Cross, tuck under, pull, make two loops, cross, tuck under, pull.

"What happened?" she asked, double-tying her boot like a first-grader.

"Oh, he was a writer. He based a story on me, called"—Jake laughed—
"'The Lesser Deity.' It was brutally realistic. Except he made me mentally retarded. There was this great scene where he takes the Jake character to Ben &
Jerry's, and there is this teenage girl working there. She wants to be nice to the
gimp, so she bends down and asks him what flavor he'd like. To which he
extends his gnarly arm and grabs her left breast. She screams in shock. I think
the point was that the retard was just looking for love because his evil rich
parents put him in a 'home.' The character had my wheelchair, my face, my
diagnosis, and my name. I wish I could move my arms like that, though."

"Jesus," said Sasha, letting go of her shoelace. "He let you read it?"

"It won a campus fiction contest. It was published in the university's
literary magazine and reviewed in the paper. It provoked panel discussions."

"So what did you do?"

"I strangled him with my own hands. What else?"

"There must be something you could—"

"Well, that's why I'm in law school."

"Really?"

"No, I'm just kidding. I just got rid of the guy, what else could I do? He
went to graduate school and last I heard, was teaching a 'Politics of the Body'
class in the anthropology department. So anyway, I've given up on live-in at-
tendants. Now I have these three guys upstairs. I pay their rent, and they take
turns being sort of on call."

"They're getting a good deal." Sasha looked out the window.

"You sound like a real New Yorker."

"What do you mean?"

"You know, the way New Yorkers are about real estate," said Jake.

Sasha felt his eyes on every square inch of her body again, even though he
was just looking at her face. She caught his gaze, and he looked away.

"It's good to see you again, Jake," she said.

"What if I told you I lied?"

"About what?"

"I didn't just stumble on Heidi's number. I've been thinking about you for four years. I had Heidi's number memorized like some numeric prayer. *Barukh atah Adonai,* Seven One Eight Seven Nine Three Zero Five Nine Three. Amen."

"Wow."

"What do you expect? I'm twenty-three years old. You were the only woman to ever touch me who was not an attendant, a nurse, or my mom. Now that you're here, I'm kicking myself for calling Heidi, and my shrink will absolutely kill me. She says I exhibit obsessive thought patterns."

"Fuck your shrink!"

"I don't think she'd let me."

Sasha laughed. "I missed you."

"Meaning, 'I missed Jake. He's such a funny guy, next time my boyfriend and I do something we should take him along, I bet he doesn't get out much.' I can't stand it. What kills me is that even that *one* encounter was a transaction. I felt like shit afterwards, and I acted like shit, and I'm sorry. Not that it matters five years later."

"My entire life was one big transaction, then," Sasha said quietly. "Pretend we just met."

"If we just met, you wouldn't deal with me at all. You'd be my friend, and I'd practice my X-ray vision on you until you'd notice and get disgusted. Then I'd log on to a gimp discussion board and complain. I'd dream that something awful would happen to you, that you'd end up disfigured, so we could be on, uh, equal footing. I guess I'm just trying to warn you up front that I've been in love with you in my own emotionally immature way. Now your job is to smile, ignore what I just said, call me a great guy, go away, and never see me again."

Sasha hugged her knees and watched his face until he glanced up at her and they both started laughing.

"You come on too strong," Sasha said. "*Emotionally immature?* When I'm president, your shrink will be shipped off to assist the workers of agriculture."

Jake smiled. "You're beautiful, and I should've never called Heidi."

"Can you stop feeling sorry for yourself and let me talk for a second? I moved into my building because *the button on the door* reminded me of you. I tried to e-mail you. Every once in a while I go to allmedicine.com, *just to see your name in print.* You had a surgery in 1987 to fix a dislocated hip joint. I missed you. Jake?"

He was looking at her again.

"I want to be out of this chair. I want to be standing next to you. I want to put my arms around you."

"All right," said Sasha, reaching for the restraints. "So do it."

The sound of the peeling Velcro made her realize how quiet it was in the apartment. Except for an occasional ambulance siren, most street noises didn't reach the twelfth floor. The city turned on its lights beyond the window, and the sky turned purple. Sasha felt relief at the absence of music, at the absence of furniture, at the blankness of the white walls. There were no barriers between her and Jake. They were together, protected by silence. Sasha's vision sharpened in the gathering dusk, and Jake's pupils became shelters, twin tunnels of gleaming darkness, waiting for her.

She stood in front of the wheelchair, locked her hands behind his back, and pulled him up. He was heavier than she'd thought, but once he was up, he was able to balance. Sasha leaned against the wall, feeling his weight against her for a minute before his knees gave and they both fell to the floor.

"Are you all right?" gasped Sasha.

"Fine." He looked scared.

"Here." Sasha brushed the hair out of his eyes and put on his glasses. "I'm sorry."

Flat on the carpet, without the support of the wheelchair, Jake's body curled in on itself, obeying its disease. His neck muscles tensed, his head pulled back, and his arms splayed outward like featherless wings. Sasha sat down next to him, folded her jacket, and slid it under his head.

She ran her fingers through his hair and over the rigid muscles of his arms. She felt strangely free from the stomach-turning anxiety of the last four months. She was almost able to forget about the time bomb in her bag, her phone. If it went off now, she might survive intact.

"Keep looking at me, Jake," she whispered, bringing his hands together and slipping them under her sweater, under the wires of her bra.

Feeling her nipples harden against his palms, she kissed him until he turned away.

"What's wrong?"

"Enough," said Jake. There was a change in his voice, a touch of panic.

"Did you come?"

"No, but I think I'm about to."

Quickly, Sasha unbuttoned his Levi's and pulled off her tights and underwear, but he came at her first touch.

"I'm sorry."

"Don't say that."

"After ten years of pretending that sponge baths are hand jobs, I can't deal with the real thing."

"You can practice on me." Sasha smiled, sliding his hand between her legs. "What does it feel like, Jake?"

He closed his eyes. Closer to the edge of ecstasy with every tiny movement of his fingertips, Sasha waited until he was hard again, guided him in, and came. Waiting for Jake to finish, she wondered why fucking him felt like a cure. Was she turned on by his desperation, by the urgency of his desire? As long as he held her with his stare, bound her to himself, she was safely above the gaping hole of Asbestos 2.

"Why are you doing this?" Jake asked after she'd helped him dress.

Sasha gave him an exasperated look.

"Isn't it obvious?" she said slowly, stretching out on the floor next to him. "I want to marry you, throw you in the basement, and buy a convertible with your trust fund!"

Jake laughed. "I suspected as much."

"Now that you know, don't ask me any more questions."

"Can I at least ask you about what happened after you left? About your father?"

"My father turned out to be a human amoeba. Heidi kicked him out. She asked me to thank you for wrecking her marriage."

"That bad?"

"He hid from me until the last minute. He never told Heidi about me, and after I showed up he tried to pretend I wasn't there. After that Heidi sent him to a shrink, who put him on antidepressants. It was the pills that finished him off, I think. Now he barely talks. He mostly smiles and grunts. Apparently he still makes amazing teeth."

"Teeth?"

"Fake teeth. Dentures. He's a dental technician. After the divorce, he moved in above his lab. He has this weird two-room apartment. The rooms are perfect cubes, as tall as they are wide, and the windows are perfectly square. I think somebody built it as an experiment. Live in a cube! Equilibrium through space!"

"Did he achieve his equilibrium?"

"He's working on it. He keeps the place spotless. One time I came over and he was cleaning behind the stove with an old toothbrush, humming to himself. He let me in and went back to cleaning. It was like he was hoping I'd go away if he got the back of the stove clean enough. Heidi won't let Ben near the cube, so Victor comes over to her place. He has so completely obliterated himself, it's a wonder he bothers with the kid. But there he is, every Sunday, tormenting Heidi's couch with his three hundred pounds, smiling and not saying a word. Maybe he comes for the food," Sasha said, turning onto her back.

The evening made the ceiling look like a James Turrell light sculpture: a continuation of the sky. If she could, she would stay here forever, observing the evenly spaced planets of the recessed light sockets like some urban astronomer.

She reached to touch Jake's hand and thought about the increasingly odd gifts Victor gave Ben: a roll of yellow electric tape, a bundle of telephone wires, a photo lens, an abacus, an empty computer case. She had a feeling that she, and not Ben, was the intended recipient of these things. She would have loved each one of them when she was Ben's age. They were surrogate toys, meant for the toyless.

"Sasha, what are you hiding from?"

"What do you mean?"

"You're here with me."

"Don't start," Sasha said, moving closer.

"You're hiding from something. Tell me what it is."

"A kid," Sasha heard herself say. "My daughter. Don't stop looking at me, Jake. You asked."

"You have a baby?"

"Not a baby. She's seven years old. I had her when I was fifteen. My mother raised her."

"Why are you hiding from her?"

"I don't love her."

"Does your mother?"

"My mother is dying. After that, Nadia is coming to live with me, but I don't love her."

"What's her alternative?"

"An orphanage. She has no other family."

"Are you crying?"

"Jake, I think about disconnecting my cell phone. The neighbors won't be able to reach me, and she'll end up in the orphanage."

"Don't disconnect your cell phone."

"I'm not going to. I just think about it."

"You'll be all right. It'll—"

Sasha shook her head. "I used to love her, when she was born. What kind of mother *stops* loving her child?"

"I'm the wrong person to ask," Jake said with growing conviction. "But what choice do you have? To become a human amoeba and live in a cube?"

"I'm afraid."

"I would be, too. Do you need money?"

"Do you think I came here for your money?"

"I just think you could maybe use the money."

"She'll be an American kid, Jake. One day I'll lose her. She'll disappear, and I won't know where to look. I don't love her enough to keep her safe here."

"I imagine kids are the same everywhere. They enjoy movies with singing animals. They eat crap. They suffer through school. Looks like you're stuck with her. I'll help you raise her if you want. I can be her male role model. We'll shoot hoops together on weekends."

Sasha laughed through her tears.

"She'll probably call you a 'lazy uncle,' or a 'robot man.' She's never seen a wheelchair before."

"So buy her one of those disabled Barbies who is also a veterinarian and works at McDonald's. I think Alyssa had one."

"Seriously, Jake. You know, when I left, I think I assumed that everything would remain the same, exactly the way I last saw it, exactly the way it's always been. Then everything changed behind my back."

"In Russia?"

"In Asbestos 2."

Jake laughed. "How could I forget the name of your hometown? It's so over-the-top awful. Cyanide Township. Tumorville. Napalmia. Asbestos 2."

"Shut up! You think it was awful, but to me it was just normal. I had no outside point of reference; *it was my life.* Now my mother is dying, and the town is almost gone. My daughter is probably the last child there. When she leaves, Asbestos 2 will be gone. And who am I without it? When I'm cleaning houses, I do these little compulsive mental exercises, trying to picture things *exactly* as they were. Every time I see less and less. I remember seeing a replica of a Rodin sculpture for the first time, in a basement studio where I took art classes. I remember the door, the radiators, and the mouse traps, but I can't remember which sculpture it was. I remember painting Newton's wig on the wall of my middle school's physics classroom, but I can't remember which floor the classroom was on. Dumb stuff like that scares me. I feel as if I'm forgetting who I am, as if I'm going crazy. What's so funny?"

"Rodin and Newton don't sound especially Siberian."

"So what?"

"I don't know. Maybe you shouldn't try to split your childhood memories from the rest of your life. Maybe people our age have to resign themselves to living in the *world,* not in a town."

"All right, very clever. Like most Americans, you think that where *you* live *is* the World. The rest of the planet is covered with supplemental, curious, yet disposable, numbered little worlds."

"That's unfair."

"Don't you get it? Things get *lost!* Do you even know where your family comes from?"

"Eastern Europe somewhere. I know that Dad's family left right before the war."

"That's what my kid will be saying, '*Eastern Europe somewhere,*'" aped Sasha. "Do you know what your name means in Russian?"

"Yes." Jake laughed. "I had a Russian attendant when I was in college. I heard him laughing about it on the phone. So I looked it up. I bet my forefathers were taunted at school."

"I remember sitting at your parents' fundraiser and pretending that their guests were various insects," sighed Sasha. "I feel like a forefather already, Jake. I feel like I'm a thousand years old. I worry that my kid will fill her head with cartoons that I haven't seen and music that I don't understand. . . ."

"That's just cultural noise, Sasha."

"But if I don't know her now, how am I supposed to get to know her in a country that isn't even mine? There will always be phantoms floating between us. Stories, people, the whole dead half of me, Asbestos 2. How am I supposed to raise a kid if I live split in two, one half at a time? As long as Mama and Nadia live there, Asbestos 2 is still a place I can go return to. Sometimes, when I visit there, it feels like the only *real* place I know. Soon, it will all be contained within me, slowly disappearing. I feel so alone, Jake. You know, your dad's trophy artists spent their lives making fun of the *Homo Sovieticus. Homo Sovieticus* is pretty well extinct, but at least he's documented on your parents' walls. But what am I? *Homo Post-Sovieticus? Homo Nowhere?* My father lives in a perfect cube, making perfect teeth. My mother is dying. And they're giving *me* a child?" Sasha asked angrily, although inside, for the first time in months, she didn't feel angry at all. The longer they spoke, the more she felt *the point* elude her. She was just an immigrant. Nadia was just a kid. She was just afraid.

"Look," Jake said. "You're too caught up in stories. Next thing, you're going to start talking about traditions, and then you risk turning into my mom. Besides, your life isn't terrible enough to be remade as a myth. It has to really suck for that to happen, sort of as compensation. If you're too much into building temples, your daughter might hate you for it. Or she might put your temple to her own use."

"To grow weed for a Mexican village?"

"You never know." Jake smiled. "It's a global economy."

Sasha jumped up. Her phone was ringing in her bag.

"It's Heidi. I'll call her back later."

"I should get Levi. It's almost eleven, and he has school tomorrow. Will you dial for me?"

Sasha found the phone and placed the headset on Jake's head.

"I should go," she said.

"You should meet Levi, you'll like him. He's a painter."

"What's his work like?"

"I don't know, I've only seen one. He said he did it while on acid. It had a razor blade glued to it."

Sasha laughed. "I should go."

There was the sound of a key in the door. At six and a half feet tall, in a tight white T-shirt and cargo pants, Levi was a live Calvin Klein ad. He had biceps the size of Sasha's head, skin the color of dark chocolate, and enviable loose curls.

"How's it going?" he said, glancing at Jake's wheelchair.

"Hi," replied Sasha. For Jake's sake, she liked the indifference in Levi's billboard eyes. He didn't seem the type to write stories.

Levi picked Jake up from the floor and carried him back to the wheelchair.

"You've got to get a couch in here, man. My back is fucked up, I can't do this," he said, refastening the belts.

Sasha put on her jacket.

"Why is your apartment so empty, Jake?" she asked, thinking of Victor again.

"Give me a break, I just moved in here. Mom keeps threatening to come down here and decorate. She's into all things Bali these days. Next time you come over, you won't be able to find me among the carved artifacts."

"All I'm saying is, you gotta get a couch," repeated Levi, opening the fridge. "You want anything to eat?"

"No, I'm tired," Jake said. "Thank you for coming over, Sasha," he added formally.

It was Sasha's turn to get him out of hiding. He turned red when she took his hand. He tried to say something, but she bent down and kissed him on the lips instead.

"I'll call you tomorrow," she said. "Nice to meet you, Levi."

Outside, the rain had stopped, but the cars and sidewalks were still shining wet. Leaping over a puddle at the crosswalk, Sasha Goldberg felt light, dwarfed by the buildings around her, insignificant. She remembered feeling that way at O'Hare five years ago. Did love lift the weight of your unique suffering, dissolve the walls of your cube, release you alone into the world, anonymous and free?

Sasha didn't feel like going underground. She'd never taken a taxi to Brooklyn before, but today it felt like an appropriate extravagance. She hailed a cab, sank into the back seat, and rolled down the window. Feeling the lighted lines of the bridge enter her body like a song, she remembered Moscow, the churches' scattered teeth, and the power lines of Asbestos 2. For a moment, all those things seemed like parts of the same picture.

She would call Heidi in the morning, make nice to the Foliage ladies. She would call Jonathan, too, to apologize and say goodbye. She would need to start paying attention to Heidi's endless musings about the relative merits of different elementary schools. And if the original *Star Wars* should come on TV, she would watch it.

Epilogue

THE FIRST SNOW STARTS FALLING ON THE NIGHT OF HEIDI Goldberg's Christmas party. It's a windless night, and the snow falls slowly, straight down, in loose fist-sized clumps that cling to stoops and awnings, tree limbs and flagpoles, backyard swing sets and fiber-optic horns of the nodding mechanized reindeer. When Sasha passes out on Heidi's couch, Brooklyn is a Snow Queen's kingdom, but by the time the phone rings the snow has melted away.

After a few hours of sleep, Sasha Goldberg is still drunk. Watching the ceiling slowly rotate clockwise, she reaches for the spot of emerald glow on the table.

"*Allo? Allo? . . . Allo?*" says a voice, small and unsure, and Sasha pictures Tetya Vera at once, scrunched up in a grimy corner of a wooden phone booth at the Conversation Point, doing a vocal dance with the squeals and screeches of the terrible connection.

"Tetya Vera?"

"Do you hear me? Sasha *doma*?" Tetya Vera bellows. Scream, is what you do when you cannot hear an answer. Scream and maybe someone will finally hear you across thousands of miles, over fourteen time zones, over the North Pole. The subject of jokes, this telephone etiquette.

"Yes!" yells Sasha, and the connection breaks.

The screen of Sasha's telephone announces that the call lasted twelve seconds.

———

In Asbestos 2, Sasha Goldberg finds that her mother didn't exactly die. That she most likely died. Ninety-nine percent chance that she died. On December 25, while Sasha was drinking coffee in Heidi's kitchen and watching Ben fondle his new GameBoy, Lubov Alexandrovna Goldberg disappeared from her Prostuda hospital bed, never to be seen again.

"We waited a few days, in case she showed up at home," Tetya Vera says quietly. Nadia is in the next room, packing her things into the hot pink Dora the Explorer suitcase that Sasha bought for her at Marshall's on Atlantic.

"Is Mama in the ground?" she asks Sasha later.

Sasha pauses momentarily, about to say no, and then says, "Yes. Do you want to go to America?"

"Yes," says Nadia. "I'm very happy that you're taking me with you."

Since Sasha's arrival, Nadia has been polite and remote. Sasha cannot shake the feeling that it is Mrs. Goldberg speaking, from beyond the grave, through the child's mouth.

She holds Nadia's mittened hand on the way to the bus stop. Tetya Vera walks with them. Squinting against the icy snow, Sasha watches the old woman's mouth move, but doesn't listen to the words. For a while, the landscape resembles an envelope. Four gray triangles: one sky, one road, two walls of trees. Sasha thinks that this is likely her last time here. She can imagine Nadia coming back as an adult, Asbestos 2 a curious footnote to her American life.

Sasha herself is made of it. She will have no reason to return here.

In Prostuda, the airplane turns slowly against the wind, taking its place in the queue. All morning, the wind dragged a film of icy snow along the ground, arranging it in fancy swirls along the tarmac and building white triangles along the terminal walls. Now it's destroying its own work, pelting the snow against the windows of the plane.

Nadia looks up momentarily and goes back to her book, a children's adaptation of H. G. Wells's *The War of the Worlds*. Large Russian print looks bloated to Sasha, like all capitals. She read this book when she was twelve, she remembers, recognizing the dark illustrations. She wants to talk to Nadia about the book, about anything at all, but the child hasn't said a word all morning. She treats Sasha as a fellow traveler who just happened to be alongside her this whole time.

The plane speeds up and takes off, groaning with mechanical reluctance. Gasping, Nadia lets go of the book and grabs Sasha's arm. *That was all it took,* Sasha thinks, savoring the touch of the little cold hand, the fingernails digging into her skin. But it *is* huge—flying, wholly unnatural for a person.

"Don't be scared," Sasha says. "Look."

The plane turns, and for a few seconds the window next to Nadia faces the ground. They watch the matchbox rooftops, black clumps of miniature trees, a toy bus.

"Why don't you talk to me?" Sasha asks.

"You aren't Mama."

"Neither are you," says Sasha, "but I don't make a *morda* at you, do I?"

She demonstrates a sour face, her first stab at parenting. Nadia stiffens and purses her lips, trying not to laugh. Doesn't laugh.

"All right," Sasha says with some newfound confidence, "be nice to me. I don't know what I'm doing."

A stewardess in a sparkly 2001 paper crown walks down the isle offering overpriced vodka. Nadia bends down and retrieves *The War of the Worlds.* The plane breaks through the clouds and flies southwest. Sasha Goldberg turns her thick head toward the window and thinks about the future.

Below, the Ignatiev brothers push a crowbar under the lip of the library's fire exit. Someone has locked the door from the inside, robbing Serezha and Mitya of their spot, their den, their haven, their perfect place to smoke, drink, pee on the wall, a place where shelves upon shelves of flammable material promise many evenings of warmth and baked potatoes.

The brothers consider themselves tenants in the abandoned library. They come here instead of school and after school, and when their father reappears at home between binges, they spend the night here, too. Serezha is the oldest. He discovered the place, he holds the lease. The first girl he ever fucked lay under him on the librarian's desk, her hair invisible against the institutional brown paint, her face a round bluish moon, her eyes black holes of fear. The crowbar slips, Serezha licks his knuckles, shakes his head. What the fuck?

Mitya picks up a lump of concrete. There's some rusty rebar sticking out of it, like a handle. Mitya swings the rock twice, lets go. The brothers crouch by the wall, waiting for the glass music to stop. Someone could be inside, older kids, vagrants. Serezha remembers coming here in first grade, the sleepy comfort of large orderly rooms, the blond librarian's rules. "Be quiet!" and "Don't touch!" There had been a stuffed bunny in the children's section, nailed high to the wall so the children couldn't reach it. First thing Serezha did when he made the library his own was play with that fuckin' bunny.

Nobody comes. The brothers climb through the window, jump down. There is an ice snake on the floor, a frozen stream. Another pipe must've burst. It had happened before, back when the hot water was on. The building filled with steam, and the brothers played Chechens in hazy book-lined canyons.

Mitya walks around the corner to the front desk to get the lighter he left there the time before. He has a bad feeling about it. Whoever locked the door probably has his lighter now.

Serezha takes a piece of chalk out of his pocket and writes a message to the stranger, FUCK OFF OR DIE, when he hears his brother scream. His first thought is that now he will have to live up to the message. It isn't something he is prepared to do. Serezha is small for his sixteen years. He's never made anyone die before.

But Mitya appears alone, eyes wide, lower lip shaking.

"What's the matter?" Serezha asks, relieved. Whatever it was that scared his brother isn't moving.

Mitya opens his mouth, closes it again.

"You swallowed your fuckin' tongue?" Serezha steps around his brother, picks up a crowbar.

"No, don't, Seriy—" Mitya manages, but Serezha is already gone around the corner.

The librarian sits at her desk. Her head is leaning slightly forward, as if she is reading, but her eyes are closed. There is an open book in front of her, and a half-full bottle of cognac, both frozen in mounds of ice. Ropy icicles extend from a dark stain in the ceiling where the pipe has burst.

"She's dead, you dumb pussy!" yells Serezha. "Come, help me get her bottle!"

"Don't!" Mitya encircles his brother's wrist with cold, clammy fingers, pulls him back.

"What's your fuckin' problem? Look, she's got gold earrings and a ring, and nice boots." Serezha tries to sound reasonable, but knows he's lost the argument. Mitya emits a force beyond persuasion, his fear like a bubble, a transporter.

"Fine, you chickenshit," Serezha says through his teeth, and follows his brother outside, back home, where it is no better, where their grandma may or may not be dead, depending on her mood and the weather. Today Grandma is uncharacteristically alive. She floats out of the kitchen, a mass of smelly rags and rotting flesh, wielding a broomstick.

"Where you been, you li'l fuckers? Your father gets home, there won't be a live spot on you!"

"We found a dead woman," blurts Mitya.

"You kill 'er?"

Serezha rolls his eyes.

"Come on, Dmitriy. May as well tell someone, so they clear her outta there."

The policewomen walk to the library, their Niva having run out of gas the previous week. One of them is fat, and by the end of the walk she's annoyed by the chafing on the insides of her thighs. They stand around the librarian, taking notes. The dead woman looks alive, calm, asleep. Her fingers hold open a book of poems.

> At a terrifying height a wandering fire,
> But is this how a star sparkles, flying?
> Transparent star, a wandering fire,
> Your brother, Petropolis, is dying.

The policewomen look at each other and shrug. Until they have their car again, they will have to leave the body here. The fat one takes off her gloves and carefully frees the cognac bottle from the ice, wondering if perhaps the dead librarian could help them drum up some gasoline from the regional government. Back at the police station, she calls her daughter in Prostuda. The next day, her son-in-law, a bank security guard and an amateur photographer, arrives in Asbestos 2 with his camera. He takes the padlock off the library door and blows on his fingers, thinking that the library may as well be made into a morgue. He circles the librarian, focusing his lens on the yellowed edge of the book, on the dead woman's manicured fingers. As an artist, he is aware of the importance of atmospheric details. He shoots a whole roll of film, winning an imaginary photo contest with every click of the shutter.

The following week, the policewoman's son-in-law achieves his long-wished-for fame. His photo of the frozen librarian appears on the front page of *Prostuda Worker* with the caption "Your brother, Asbestos 2, is dying." Soon it's picked up by national press. It makes the pages of *Pravda, Izvestia, Moskovsky Komsomolets*. The captions never bother to identify Mrs. Goldberg, calling her, instead, the Ice Queen, Snow White, the Virgin of Asbestos.

In Moscow, the Duma decries the wretched economic conditions of the northern regions, calling the picture a national shame, a call to action. Putin heeds the call, issues a decree awarding each resident of the Prostuda region a onetime stipend equivalent to $20. The Prostuda regional government delivers a canister of gasoline to the Asbestos 2 police station. The guard of order rubs vaseline into her chafing thighs and toasts the Ice Queen with her cognac.

"Britney Spears!"

"I just got you a backpack."

"They say Dora the Explorer is for babies."

"Who says?"

"They. . . ." Nadia Goldberg raises her head, mouth agape, to all the backpacks that float like clouds under the ceiling of the GIFTS NEWS GIFTS NEWS store.

"Kids in your class say that?" Sasha asks, her mind darting back to her own childhood. "Fine, pick a new bag."

"Really?" says Nadia. "I should get Britney Spears. Or SpongeBob SquarePants?"

Sasha blows on her hands, picks up a pair of gloves, and walks to the register to wait for Nadia. A deliveryman dumps a stack of fresh *Foreign Lands* by her feet. Sasha glances at the photo above the fold, looks again, looks at Nadia. Nadia is talking to the shopkeeper, pointing at her chosen backpack. The sound of her voice restarts Sasha's heart.

"No, shiny. I want buy bag what is shiny!" Nadia explains bravely.

It's only been two months, and she's already speaking English. Sometimes during recess, Sasha spies on her through the school's chain-link fence. Nadia, dressed in all of her new clothes, is hard to find in the sea of pinks and powder blues, and when Sasha finally spots her, she is always in a group of kids.

Momentarily, Sasha forgets about the newspaper, watching Nadia with pride and disbelief. The shopkeeper looks up at her for help.

"She wants the one with all the glitter on the front," Sasha says.

The shopkeeper gets a pole with a hook, hands Nadia the bag.

Sasha flips over *The Foreign Land,* covers it up with *The New York Post* for good measure, and digs in her purse for a wallet.

"Nice bag!" Jake says when they walk outside. "I thought you guys would never come out of that store. It's freezing out here!"

Sasha takes a deep breath and doesn't say anything. She glances at the digital thermometer on a bank's facade across the street—it reads 35F.

"I forgot, it's beach weather by your Eskimo standards. Sorry. I'm cold, all right? What?"

Sasha shakes her head, wishing he'd stop talking. What's on the other side of *cold*? How cold does it have to get before you fall asleep? And then, does it get warm? Nadia puts on her backpack and tightens the straps.

"What happened in there?" Jake asks. "Did you see something?"

"Enough of your clairvoyance, Jake," Sasha says quietly, feeling hot under her scarf. "You're not my psychic."

"I'm your friend."

"I'm your sister!" Nadia yells in English, jumping up and down on the curb.

Sasha unzips the top of SpongeBob's head and drops her apartment keys inside.

"Jake, will you take her home? I'll catch up with you in a second."

Nadia hangs on to the back of the chair, ready for a ride. What an odd couple they make, a confused choo-choo train, Jake's black hair to Nadia's yellow, his paper-white skin to her brown, a wheelchair in between.

You're my lover, Sasha thinks in an in-between language. *You're my daughter.*

When they're gone, she goes back into the store and buys *The Foreign Land.*

Her mother sleeps on the cover, upright, over a book.

On the way home, Sasha Goldberg stares up at the street lamps. The snowflakes dash and scatter in the circles of light. The street is empty. Sasha takes wider and wider steps, waiting to trip, but the sidewalk is strangely uniform, un-Brooklyn-like, and she makes it home without falling.

Acknowledgments

For their guidance and support, I would like to thank my editor at Viking, Molly Barton, and my agent, Anna Stein. I would also like to thank Carmen Scheidel, Eileen Kelly, and Sarah Ferguson for early advice and encouragement. Parts of this book were inspired by the essays and poems of the late Mark O'Brien. I'm grateful to my remarkable parents, Larissa Zhigalova and Sergei Ulinich, for everything. Above all, I would like to thank Ken Collins, without whom this book wouldn't be possible.

This book is in memory of Evgeny Lapin of Moscow Children's Art School Number One. He taught many a bear to unicycle. It is also in memory of Gita Kaganskaya, Roman Ulinich, Dmitri Zhigalov, Alexandra Zhigalova, and Babette Rosen.